24 HOURS IN PARIS

24 HOURS IN PARIS

ROMI MOONDI

w by wattpad books

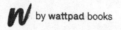 by **wattpad** books

An imprint of Wattpad WEBTOON Book Group

Copyright© 2022 Romi Moondi

Published in Canada by Wattpad WEBTOON Book Group, a division of Wattpad Corp.

36 Wellington Street E., Suite 200, Toronto, ON M5E 1C7 Canada

www.wattpad.com
First W by Wattpad Books edition: May 2022

ISBN 978-1-99025-917-3 (Trade Paper original)
ISBN 978-1-99025-918-0 (eBook edition)

Library and Archives Canada Cataloguing in Publication information is available upon request.

Printed and bound in Canada

1 3 5 7 9 10 8 6 4 2

Cover design by Cassie Gonzales
Author Photo by Rohith Vishal

This book is dedicated to the City of Light.
Being in your glow is magic.

CHAPTER
one

M
The Night Before

Mira had always believed that laughter was infectious. It had the power to spread from one delighted face to the next, but here, in the corner of this chic Paris bistro where the brash American laughter surrounded her in waves, she managed to stay immune.

She pressed her lips together tight, a defensive move to avoid being lumped in with the rowdiness of her tablemates. Mira was simply different from the loud tourist stereotype too often proven right in the train cars, cafés, and cobblestoned streets of Paris. She was different from them, *dammit*, and everyone in this bistro needed to know.

The staff seemed unbothered by the elevated noise, but was it any surprise? Each successive round of laughter meant another round of drinks: more champagne, more pricey vintage reds.

The husband-and-wife owners exchanged a knowing look as they brought out a few more bottles from the cellar. Given that they owned a restaurant off Avenue Montaigne—a notable street in the

8th arrondissement and home to the famous Plaza Athenée—Mira could only assume they were well acquainted with the platinum card–carrying demographic. Early summer was an especially busy period, with swarms of jet-setters descending on Paris, particularly on a night like this, when the glitzy Haute Couture Fashion Week had just gotten underway.

Not that Mira and her crew had anything to do with fashion. They were merely another rowdy group of white-collar Americans who just happened to be in Paris on business. The business of pushing the latest in sparkling beverages, to be exact.

The owners now made a beeline to Frank, Mira's fifty-something boss, who sat at the head of the long wooden table. Even in the soft glow of candlelight, his tailored suit and looming presence made it clear he was the one in charge. In their office back in New York, that meant rejecting an idea with a simple shake of the head. In this bistro, however, that meant being the one in charge of appraising the wine, which he now carefully did by examining the labels.

"Not a bad selection," he acknowledged, his accent a faded tribute to a childhood growing up in Queens. "We'll take both."

The owners shifted their focus to refilling everyone's glasses. They worked their way down the table slowly, starting with the smartly dressed middle-aged executives, and moving on to the younger, more fashion-forward employees.

Mira, at the younger end of the table, could feel her taste buds anticipating a fresh dose of wine, but before her glass could get some attention, it was the thirtysomething man with sandy brown hair and pale blue eyes who received his refill first. He grinned as each ounce cascaded into the glass, a smarmy look that expressed an affection for company-sponsored unlimited refills. The smarm paired well with the hair gel sweeping his shaggy hair into a greasy salesman dome.

Without all that product, he could've been one of those intensely handsome bed-headed men you'd see reading books on the subway, men whom Mira had been known to crush on during her A train trek to the office. Instead, the greasy gel had sealed his fate (and his hair) in her eyes.

Hair aside, he was tall and broad shouldered and had probably been the captain of the rowing team in college (and had likely done a good job of making sure everyone knew it). She noticed him unfasten the top two buttons of his shirt, a sign that he was probably a few glasses in.

"It's hot in here," he said, before holding his fresh glass of wine to the light. "But it's okay; I'm a *glass-half-full* kinda guy." He snickered at his own lame joke, ignoring Mira's immediate groan. After gulping some wine, he elbowed the male colleague to his left. "We men can handle our liquor, amirite?"

"It's not liquor, it's *wine*," Mira muttered, her brown eyes narrowing in disapproval. She tucked a few strands of long black hair behind one ear, frowning at the presence of this irritating dude. She'd always heard that frowning was the dangerous road to deep-set wrinkles, but up until now her South Asian genes had been good to her, and she was often still mistaken for a woman in her twenties, despite being weeks away from turning thirty-five. This ego-boosting clerical error hadn't yet occurred on the business trip, but for the moment she had other pressing problems on her mind. In addition to her latest groan, she'd served up two eye rolls, three smirks, and countless raised eyebrows in the hours since the evening had begun, all of it brought on by the irritating man-child sitting across from her.

She was Mira Attwal.

He was Jake Lewis.

3

And while they worked for the same company, the similarities ended there.

"I *know* liquor isn't wine," Jake finally said. "And so does he." He gestured to his colleague. "And everyone." He gestured to the air. "Which is why when you say it, it's kind of interchangeable." He nodded as if to convince himself that his word salad was legit.

"Thanks for the clarification."

Mira's eyes bore deep into Jake's forehead, as she wondered about the size of the brain knocking around in that oversize skull.

Mira worked in branding.

Jake worked in sales.

And aside from this five-day business trip, they'd never interacted as coworkers even once.

Of course, that didn't mean she'd never noticed him before at the office. It also didn't mean she'd never thought of him, sometimes even for an hour or two, after those rare occasions when they'd shared an elevator and she'd found herself ogling his jawline, or, depending on where he'd been standing, the outline of his ass. But did she have to admit either of those things when he was acting in such a drunken, slovenly fashion? Certainly not.

She studied his face. "Is that oyster juice on your chin?"

Looking slightly embarrassed, Jake grabbed a napkin and wiped it off.

Apart from some time spent studying his physical attributes, Mira only knew Jake from the grandiose persona he'd projected in their meetings during the past few days. She hadn't been impressed by all the showmanship, which made it satisfying to embarrass him during this dinner. Did that make her a bad person? Maybe. Or maybe it was just that his big, greasy dome of hair needed to be brought down a peg (or two).

To Mira's disappointment, his embarrassment was all too brief, his confidence now restored at the sight of the pretty waitress he'd been scoping out all night. By Mira's estimation, the waitress had been doing a very good job; clearing the plates in a timely manner and replacing each carafe before the water got too low—she was a winner. Still, Mira had a feeling that Jake wasn't interested in her customer service.

"You're back," he observed, eyes zeroed in on the kill.

The waitress's only response was a look of coyness.

As Mira wondered which pickup line he'd choose from the greasy-salesman starter pack, she saw him reach into his brown leather workbag and found herself instantly intrigued. She wondered if there was a long-stemmed rose inside that bag. It could've been a napkin and she'd be equally enthralled, as she'd been starved for entertainment since the start of these company dinners.

Night after night, she'd been a bored observer of coworkers gobbling up foie gras *this* and braised rabbit *that*, all while getting drunk at these long wooden tables—and always at restaurants that weren't even on her Paris bucket list. She'd tried to stretch their imaginations, but no one had seemed on board with her idea for a picnic at Luxembourg Gardens, or a stroll along the riverbank with handheld crêpes and the sparkling Eiffel Tower as the backdrop.

So here she was, on their final night, with the saga of Jake and the waitress as her only form of entertainment.

Jake's hand emerged from the bag, his fingers clutching a lavender-colored can of flavored sparkling water called Bloom. Jake was the top salesman at Bloom, but for the moment he was more like Vanna White as he proudly showcased the newest flavor in the company's line of botanical-based, calorie-free fizz. "Now, Chloe . . ." he started.

Mira took immediate note of the waitress's subtle wince, but judging by Jake's come-hither stare he didn't have a clue.

"My name is Colette."

He wasn't the least bit fazed.

"Yes of course, *Colette*. Now tell me: are you ready to be at the forefront of the next big thing in cocktails?" He gestured to the bar. "Let's ask the barman to whip up a little something with this lavender magic."

Colette seemed uncertain.

"I'll make it worth his while."

For some ungodly reason, the waitress started to crack, her neutral expression giving way to a hint of excitement.

At first Mira couldn't believe it, but a moment later she grudgingly realized why Jake was the top salesman at Bloom.

The waitress played with her hair, a clear sign that the mating ritual had begun.

"Perhaps I could speak to the barman."

Jake lowered his voice for the next part: "I'll make it worth *your* while too."

And there it was. The typical line used by basic bros the world over.

Without thinking, Mira reached over and patted Jake's arm. It must've been the wine. "You're coming off a little thirsty."

He turned to her with a look of faux innocence. "I was talking about giving her a *tip*."

Without another word he hopped out of his chair and followed Colette to the bar.

Mira shrugged and sipped her wine, her only entertainment now out of earshot. What remained were the colleagues on her right discussing summer camp options for the kids, a colleague on her left filming a video of herself that was bound to wind up in her Instagram stories, and the guy that Jake had been next to, who was now in the grips of a furious texting session.

Inspired by the way the aggressive texter was ignoring them all, Mira pulled out her phone in the hopes of a decent distraction.

Her eyes brightened at the stream of notifications, but the eager glow dimmed out within seconds, when she realized all the messages were from the Bloom group chat.

The company HQ in New York City had clearly heard about their stellar presentation to the top beverage distributor in Paris, and the overall reaction had been different variations of "Kudos!" and "Congrats!"

Today's big win was the latest high point in Bloom's skyrocketing success, which now included an expansion into international markets.

The brand's popularity had grown in part due to partnerships with Instagram influencers, a strategic move that Mira had suggested—despite being intimidated by the fashionable outfits and makeup filters that were a favorite among the influencing set. The social media superstars had done a great job of showcasing the artsy font and soft, appealing colors of each can in the flavor lineup, sometimes with selfies that garnered endless likes, and other times with curated shots of not-so-casual picnics—where silverware was the norm and not a single hair was ever out of place.

With the influencers locked into multiyear contracts, expansion into Europe had become the next big goal, with countless late nights and strategy decks culminating in this all-important trip. The initial thought had been to nab a bit of shelf space in European grocery stores, but in the presentation to the distributor earlier that day, Jake had mentioned the potential synergy between the speakeasy bar scene and Bloom—which would especially work in Paris, where there were now as many craft cocktail bars as in London.

With a range of flavors like elderflower, honeysuckle, and the recently-introduced lavender, Jake had been right in identifying this untapped market—even though he'd used the word *synergy* in his presentation, a loathed business term in Mira's mind, right up there with *pivot* and *take this offline*.

As Mira scrolled through the company chat, she tried her best to feel a sense of pride, and why not? The brand colors and lettering that the influencers were so obsessed with had all been handpicked by Mira. She was also the one who had convinced the head of marketing to lean in hard on the floral angle, when she'd explained how people seemed to gravitate toward that hippie botanical shit. Despite all of that, she couldn't generate the normal feelings that usually accompanied not only an amazing performance review, but her best year yet as head of branding.

Mira decided that her muted reaction was excusable, given the event that had recently unfolded in her life. Funnily enough, *the event* was also the term for the fated day when an asteroid had slammed into the earth millions of years ago. That one big event had killed off the dinosaurs and brought on a planet-altering ice age, and even though her personal event hadn't caused the death of an entire species, it was, in its own way, equally cataclysmic.

It was the reason why Mira couldn't manage any excitement in the company chat, and the reason why she'd jumped at the chance to accompany the team on the business trip to Paris. On the night before their departure, Mira had spent hours revising her Paris bucket list in obsessive fashion, a list she'd curated on and off for almost two decades. That list had been a life raft during the strict Indian upbringing that had defined her teenage years, and then the awkwardness of marriage pressure in the years that had followed. Recently, with Mira's growing success in the corporate world, there had been plenty of opportunities to visit Paris, but somehow all the buildup had made the thought of actually going seem too daunting.

But then the Bloom business trip to Paris had presented itself: a perfect opportunity to escape the event, daunting buildup or not.

Except, here she was, on her last night in Paris with not a single bucket list item checked off. Ever since she'd gotten here, it had been early team meetings over hurried breakfasts, presentations between work lunches and dinners, and then collapsing onto her bed at the end of it all, too tired to even think about venturing out on her own. Even the hotel, a lovely establishment nestled in a quiet side street of the 1st arrondissement, was closer to sprawling attractions she didn't have time for—like the Louvre—versus anything she could sneak in quickly.

As Mira sipped her wine, she couldn't escape the fact that a business trip was hardly the appropriate scenario for some freewheelin' bucket-list fun. It should've been obvious right from the start, but that was the thing with cataclysmic personal events—they had a way of clouding one's judgment.

Her next sip of wine was more urgent than the last, the liquid laced with the sweet nectar of trying to forget.

She noticed Jake reemerge from the bar, which luckily distracted her from chugging down the entire contents of her glass. She watched as he delivered a complimentary cocktail to the patrons at the nearest table. In his salesman way, he urged each of them to try a sip. Everyone was curious enough to oblige, and then, one by one, every single face lit up.

Jake hurried back to the company table and searched his bag for more cans of Bloom. "Cocktails!" he exclaimed, catching the boss's eye. "Was I right or was I right?"

Frank shook his head and chuckled. "You were *born* to be a salesman."

Mira had no interest in engaging in a Jake-centered love fest, so she turned her attention back to her phone. She noticed the glowing beacon of an email notification, and as she read the contents, every muscle in her forehead tensed into a series of knots.

"You've got to be kidding me."

"What's the matter?" a colleague asked.

"The airline changed my flight." She frowned. "It's later now and they assigned me a middle seat." She glanced around at the others. "Anyone else get a flight change alert?"

Mira's colleagues checked their phones, all except for Jake, who was still preoccupied with his precious cans of Bloom. One by one, they confirmed their flight details were the same.

"Why only me?" she scowled, immediately deciding it was white-collar racism.

"Shirley mentioned something about this earlier today," Frank explained. "She got an alert that the flight was overbooked and said she'd handle it." He smiled. "I guess it's handled."

Even though Mira didn't mind the idea of some bonus hours in Paris, she couldn't help but feel like she'd been cast off to the island of misfit marketers.

Jake noticed Mira still scowling at her phone. "What happened?" He darted his eyes around the table. "Did I miss something?"

Mira wanted to ignore him, but a part of her was sickly curious. "Did you get an email from Shirley?"

He pulled his phone out of his pocket and nodded. "Yup." He opened it and seemed confused. "Why is there another booking number? Didn't I already get this email?" He looked to Mira with desperate eyes. "Can you just summarize what it says? I really need to get back to the bar."

Mira thought about lying and telling him his flight had been delayed by twenty-four hours, but fortunately for him, she wasn't that evil. At least not yet. "You and I got bumped to a different flight; it's three hours later." She glanced at his phone screen. "I mean . . . I'm assuming you're on that flight. You should really check."

He scanned the email and nodded. "Yep, three hours later—awesome!"

Jake sauntered back to the bar, leaving Mira and her colleagues to return to their fun. Or in Mira's case, sipping wine, avoiding nauseating chitchat, and struggling to care about corporate wins.

*

After the last of the plates had been cleared, Mira emerged from the restroom to discover all her coworkers had left. All except for Jake, who was canoodling with the waitress by the bar.

They ditched me, Mira thought to herself.

The woman who co-owned the restaurant noticed Mira standing frozen in place.

"Mademoiselle?" she said softly. Mira turned and acknowledged her with a nod, her face slightly stunned. "Your colleagues mentioned they had to leave for an early flight."

"Oh."

"Everything is paid for, so you may continue to enjoy the evening with your colleague."

The woman gestured to Jake, but from the look on her face, she knew as well as Mira that there wasn't much fun to be had in the land of third-wheel awkwardness.

"Thanks," Mira said, "but I actually need to head out too." She adjusted her blazer. "Big morning ahead."

As Mira made her way to the exit, she inadvertently made eye contact with the hot bartender, he of tousled dark hair and tanned skin. He looked like he belonged on a beach in Saint-Tropez, and as a result she started to imagine him shirtless. Maybe pantless too.

The bartender responded by treating Mira to the sort of smoldering stare she'd previously only read about in books or seen in movies. "Care to join us for last call?" he offered, his voice the auditory version of silky fondue.

Mira looked from the bartender's handsome face to Jake, who was busy putting the moves on the waitress. After making a quick internal calculation, she concluded that the ego-boosting benefit of being hit on by a hot French bartender did not outweigh the cost of being annoyed by the very life force that was Jake.

She politely shook her head and left the restaurant.

Once outside, Mira took a moment to revel in the warm summer air. As the night breeze danced across her face, she realized something equally as important as her cost-versus-benefit math: Was she even in the right emotional state to be flirting with a man right now?

Not even close.

*

Later that night, back in her quaint hotel room, Mira laid out some clothing options for the next morning.

She had already planned to use her extra hours in Paris to wake up early, take an inspirational stroll by the river, and then enjoy a breakfast at one of the places on her bucket list. She felt a nervous twinge at the thought of officially cracking open the list. Each bullet point was laced with high expectations, but it was either that, or wake up late and order room service, which just seemed wrong in a city as beautiful as Paris.

She did her best to calm the nervous feeling by focusing on her outfit; the strolling portion of the morning meant that functionality was key, but the neighborhood of the breakfast spot required something more high-end. She pushed her more practical pieces to the side and zeroed in on anything approaching fashionable.

She ultimately landed on one of her work blazers paired with a T-shirt, a pendant necklace, jeans, and her glossy white-and-rose-gold sneakers. It was hardly on the level of an Instagram influencer, but for Mira, it was more than enough.

Once cozy in bed, she grabbed her phone, set an alarm, and opened the airline app. "You better work this time," she muttered, sounding equal parts threatening and nervous. A few taps and a long pause later, she sighed in frustration.

The convenient online check-in was simply not to be.

Knowing she'd need extra time to check in at the airport, she edited her alarm for some all-important buffer, before placing her phone on the nightstand and switching off the lamp.

In a matter of moments, Mira's nervousness faded into eager anticipation.

Tomorrow is going to be amazing.

CHAPTER
two

M

The Next Morning

The sun burned brightly in the clear blue sky, its powerful rays making the Seine River sparkle.

Mira leaned against the railing of Pont des Arts, the bridge across from the Louvre with spectacular views from all sides. Her current vantage point was the iconic one, with the Eiffel Tower showcased in the distance. She wasn't close enough to admire the famed structure's intricate wrought-iron composition, but it was the only clear look she'd gotten since arriving, and she wanted to make it last.

A long sigh escaped from Mira's lips. It was a moment loaded with the first real semblance of joy she'd felt since the business trip had begun, and with two full hours remaining, she hoped it wouldn't be the last. Her stomach grumbled with anticipation, fixated on the famous French toast that was to come.

Despite her stomach's soundtrack of calorie deprivation, she couldn't leave the bridge without capturing the postcard image. She snapped a photo and immediately examined it. "Why does it look so much smaller?" she groaned. She utilized the zoom feature and gave it a second try, but a frown was her only reward. "Why does it look so blurry?"

It was still quite early in the day for Paris, and Mira's current surroundings showed it, with minimal traffic out on the roads, and only a few locals and early-bird tourists making their way on foot.

Mira crossed the road with brisk steps, passing a café terrace serving coffee to the day's first tourists. Her path led her along the Louvre's outer exterior and then into the smaller side streets, the perfect route for a foreigner wanting to soak in the atmosphere of Paris.

In a matter of minutes, Rue Saint-Honoré became Rue du Faubourg Saint-Honoré, and though the width of the street hadn't changed at all, there was a marked difference in the offerings. Quaint cafés and *pâtisserie* shops gave way to Gucci, Cartier, Hermès, and every other high-end boutique well beyond her financial reach.

Mira's footsteps slowed as she approached an alluring window showcasing all things Chanel. The latest iteration of the Chanel wool suit was prominently displayed behind the glass, an evergreen look, no matter the season. The summer beach collection was the other main draw, with a belted one-piece swimsuit featuring the brand's famous monogram.

But these weren't the pieces that caught Mira's eye. She found herself drawn to an item that could've easily been missed; a full flap leather wallet displayed on a silver table. It was nearly identical to the one Mira's future mother-in-law had given to her at her engagement ceremony.

Mira's understanding of engagement ceremonies held in Sikh temples in upstate New York was minimal at best, but she knew that after an hour of sitting cross-legged on an uncomfortable carpet, you could always count on a series of gifts and several wads of cash. After years of watching cousin after cousin collect their own engagement ceremony cash and prizes, Mira's turn had finally come on that cold November day. Her outfit had been pink with silver accents, dazzling by Western standards, but muted compared to the multiple *lehenga* outfit changes she'd be cycling through on her wedding day. The thing she remembered most about that day was her posed smile, and how strained it became with each additional photo. In the moment, she'd chalked it up to simple fatigue, but looking back, it was an early warning. And she'd missed it.

The past and the present seemed worlds apart, with only the full flap leather wallet tying them together. It was just another thing she would have to return, whereas every single memory stuck to her like glue.

Mira stepped away from the storefront window, eager to escape the somber mood by running from her problems—or in this case, power walking the last few blocks to the restaurant.

Before long, Mira's dark thoughts disappeared into the sights and sounds of a pleasing terrace—and the smell of the best French toast of all time.

Known as *pain perdu* or lost bread, it was a simple dish often made at home with the last stale pieces of baguette. Despite its humble nature, the version of the dish that landed at Mira's table had nothing to do with humility. What sat on Mira's plate was an updated French rendition, something that had gotten food bloggers talking. On the surface, the French toast resembled two fluffy cylinders of goodness. Each toast tower was yellow all around, lightly browned on top, and encircled with maple syrup and fresh blueberries. It was almost too good to eat. *Almost*.

When Mira used her gleaming fork to slice through the first

tower, she could only gasp. Beyond the surface was the sort of light and airy sorcery she never could've conjured, not in her mind nor in her cramped Manhattan kitchen.

If the inaugural fork slice had been good, then the first official bite was an otherworldly joyfest. The delicate eggy flavor and syrupy sweetness surrounded Mira's taste buds in a warm embrace, which immediately validated putting modernized pain perdu on her bucket list.

In a matter of minutes, the only thing left on Mira's plate was a single rogue blueberry she would save for the end of her meal. In the meantime, she sipped her coffee and watched as the occasional chic Parisian woman passed by. Second by second, her *petit dejeuner* faded into her mind, replaced with the playback of Indian dress fittings, cake tastings, exorbitant expenses, the deepening dread with each turn of the calendar . . . it was all coming back to the surface. She wondered what it would take to stop being hit with these emotional waves. Would there be no relief until she faced her problems? If so, that was bullshit—especially because she'd already dealt with her biggest problem of all.

Only weeks ago, she'd helplessly watched as her entire future hurdled toward a marriage with a good-on-paper guy whom she wasn't truly in love with. But then, she'd stopped it, like a driver slamming the brakes mere seconds before a head-on collision.

Most people in Mira's situation would've simply kept on hurdling, opting for a comfortable risk-averse future—before eventually convincing themselves it was everything they'd wanted all along. A part of Mira liked the sound of a risk-averse future, but ultimately, she'd been incapable of taking that path. She wanted something more, even if she didn't quite know what that something was. And now, after having blown up her entire life, she was perfectly free to go find it.

The only flaw in the plan was that so far, freedom felt like shit. She'd risked everything, but inner peace eluded her. She'd shown courage, but there didn't seem to be a reward. It didn't help that courage wasn't a word ever used in conversations with her Indian family. Even as a child while watching *Wizard of Oz* with her parents, they'd never understood what the Cowardly Lion was missing. No heart, no brain, now these were life-altering problems. But no courage? That didn't seem like a problem at all.

So here was Mira, with a pocketful of courage that was not only irrelevant to her family, but worse than that, was viewed as selfishness. She was selfish because her parents had already sent out the invitations, she was selfish for putting them through the nightmare of all this stress, and she was selfish for not letting them marry off their daughter within the prespinster timeline laid out by the Indian community.

Mira popped the last blueberry into her mouth, watching as a mother pushing a bassinet stroller passed by. "Could've been me by next year," she whispered, before glancing at her unadorned ring finger. "Back to square one."

Whether or not Mira's choices were selfish, she'd truly done her best to call off the wedding within a reasonable time frame. In fact, she'd given nearly two months' notice to everyone involved, in a sequence of awkward and hellish conversations she hoped to never live through again. Through it all, she hadn't even missed a single day of work. It should've been a badge of honor, but she was learning the hard way that meeting every deadline and kicking ass in branding wasn't quite the tonic for filling the void.

The one thing Mira could count on, was that she'd officially survived the worst experience of her life. It was a small comfort, but it was something. On a less comforting note, another truth emerged as she sat under the warmth of the summer sun: it would take a lot more than one fabulous meal to feel happy again.

With full awareness of the rough road ahead, Mira opted for a few more minutes of people-watching, which if nothing else was a distracting bit of fun.

After paying for her meal, she strolled back along the designer brick road, armed with some courage and a deep-down hope that time would heal all things.

*

Before long, Mira had returned to the hotel lobby, right on schedule to collect her belongings and make her way to the airport. She wasn't looking forward to going back home and facing the rubble of her blown-up life, but she'd always have Paris—a morning's worth, anyway.

Mira thanked the concierge as he brought out her carry-on.

"*Au revoir, bonne journée,*" he said, gesturing to the revolving doors.

That was strange. "And the car?"

His stare was long and his eyes devoid of emotion. "*Car?*"

"My itinerary says our company hired cars to take us to the airport."

"Ah yes," he said, finally understanding. "There were three cars, and they were occupied by your colleagues for the earlier departure."

She gasped. "They didn't save me a car?" She racked her brain for who could be responsible for this terrible mistake. Frank? Shirley?

Someone will die for this.

Before Mira could plot out her first-ever murder, Jake lumbered out of the elevator and headed her way. She'd almost forgotten he was part of this equation, and truthfully, had kind of hoped she wouldn't see him at all. Especially now, the way he looked so sweaty and worse for wear. He resembled a man who'd spent the night playing the sponge to every drop of booze in the vicinity.

Jake glanced from the concierge to Mira. "Car ready?"

"They only budgeted three cars," she said, "and our *colleagues* already used them."

Not having the time to wait for his reaction, Mira pulled out her phone and opened the ride share app. Her eyes bulged when she took in the details. "A hundred and twenty euros just to go to the airport?" She looked to the concierge for answers. "Doesn't that seem ridiculous?"

The concierge shrugged. "Surge pricing is common on the weekends; you know . . . everyone off to the airport for their little holidays in Lisbon or *Biarritz*." The last part of his sentence was coated in a palpable contempt.

"But it's Friday morning; don't people have to work?"

The concierge chuckled but said nothing.

"Let's just take it and expense it," Jake suggested.

She snorted. "You think *Shirley* will ever let that expense form make it to Frank's desk?" It was well known among Bloom employees that Shirley the overlord/office manager ate power trips for breakfast, up to and including vetoing expenses that would be standard practice in any other company. As VP of Marketing and Sales, Frank always managed to avoid getting involved, which made Mira all but certain there was blackmail in the mix.

Regardless of Frank and Shirley's weird dynamic, surge pricing wasn't the answer to Mira's problems. She turned and made her way to the revolving doors.

"Where are you going?" Jake asked.

She turned back. "I'm taking the R-E-R train."

Jake looked confused.

"It's a train that goes to the airport. Some of them are even express." Her schedule now faced the slight delay of getting to the airport by public transit, but she wasn't going to let it stress her out. She noticed that Jake hadn't moved. "Good luck with the surge pricing."

"I'll come with you!"

"*Why*?"

He headed for the doors. "I don't trust Shirley either."

*

The *métro* station was busy, a fact that instantly stressed Mira out. As she and Jake squeezed their way onto the train, she reminded herself it was only a one-stop subway ride of less than one minute, after which they would arrive at Châtelet, the station that not only connected to multiple métro lines, but to trains that traveled out of Paris. The RER B train passed through the station frequently, and it would get them to Charles de Gaulle Airport in plenty of time. She clutched the nearest metal pole and nodded to herself in affirmation.

"Why are you nodding to yourself?" Jake asked.

"I wasn't."

"You definitely were. That must've been *some* conversation you were having in your head."

"You're not as tall when your hair is messy," she said, while secretly deciding his bedhead looked good.

Mira's comment threw him off, just as she'd intended. He ran his fingers through the mess atop his head. "It's not that bad."

The train braked suddenly, propelling Jake's body toward Mira. The last time she'd been that close to a man was two weeks earlier, when a rollerblader in Riverside Park had stumbled over a rock and crashed into her. In this case, Jake's hovering presence made her heart rate immediately quicken.

"Sorry," he said, backing up, but studying her face like he was looking for an opening to flirt.

Unfortunately for Jake, flirting was not on Mira's agenda. It was getting to the airport that mattered. "I guess you didn't have time to shower this morning, huh?"

He flushed. "I mean . . . you know how it is."

"How *what* is?"

The train resumed its rumbling journey, and in those few seconds, his embarrassment gave way to his usual smarmy vibe. "I didn't make it back to the hotel until morning, *if you know what I mean*."

"Yes, I'm familiar with the construct of time."

He seemed annoyed that she wasn't dishing out high fives for his conquest with the waitress, but was he really surprised? Mira was hardly one of his pals. "It's good that you're wearing cologne," she added. "It pairs well with the vodka sweat seeping out of your pores."

Before he could register the weight of her insult, the train screeched into the station.

As they exited, Mira switched gears to navigation mode, carefully reading every overhead sign so she wouldn't make a wrong turn. Jake followed with a level of commitment on par with a boy who was afraid of losing his mother in the mall. She wondered if he was always like this, or if it was simply a result of being in a foreign city. Either way, she didn't mind, as having control of a situation was something she needed in her life.

After purchasing tickets and following the signs for the escalator, Mira noticed how packed it was. There was no choice but to merge into the crush of bodies, and right away Mira lost her bearings.

Luckily, Jake stepped in and switched from follower to leader, using his stature and long arms to clear a small path for Mira. He even glanced back every few seconds to make sure he hadn't lost track of her. It was a small gesture, but a thoughtful one.

They boarded the escalator without any trouble, but once they got to the platform, everything changed for the worse.

The concierge had mentioned how Friday was busy for holiday goers, but in all the blogs she'd read about planning for a trip to Paris, she'd missed the advice on the best way to handle the hordes of frustrated people in her midst. Sweaty foreheads, aggressive elbows, bad breath . . . they were everywhere, and it felt like there was no escape.

Trying to keep her wits about her, Mira glanced up at the digital information board. The next train would be arriving in four minutes, and the following one eleven minutes after that.

"Okay," she said, her body now sandwiched between two middle-aged women. "That seems normal."

A second later she heard a collective groan.

"Why are they doing that?" Jake asked, standing a few feet away, and somehow unfazed by the elderly man leaning into his body for support.

It took a few seconds for Mira to find the source of everyone's frustration; the next train would now be arriving in seventeen goddamn minutes.

"No!" she cried.

Second by second, the crowd started thinning out.

"Let's take a car," Jake suggested.

"But the *surge* pricing."

"We'll split it." His voice was a sea of calm in the increasingly stressful situation.

The information board soon provided another update; the next train would now be arriving in a mere eight minutes.

"Look," she said, "it'll be here soon. Let's just wait."

"Are you sure?"

The platform filled back up again, the presence of fellow travelers giving Mira comfort. "I'm sure; this many people can't be wrong, right?"

Eight minutes later, there was no train in sight, and the board now offered an entirely different update:

Annulé

The collective groan was even louder than the previous one, and even though Mira wasn't an expert in French, she could translate the word that spelled the kiss of death.

"How could they just *cancel* it?" She inadvertently locked eyes with a balding man in glasses. "Do you know why they would cancel it?"

"It's a strike," he explained, in a nonchalant tone that was deeply disturbing.

She scoffed. "You can't just go on strike without *telling anyone*."

The bespectacled man considered her argument. "There was some discussion on the news last week; we were wondering if it might happen soon."

"*Some? Might?*" Mira crossed her arms. "That's not how it works. You need to officially announce that there *will* be a strike, and then you need to schedule it for one minute after midnight."

"This is France," he said simply, before leaving her there in a stunned silence.

Jake came forward and steered her away from the platform. "My internet isn't good here; we need to get back upstairs to call the car."

Mira glanced at the clock on the train board. With a quick calculation, the panic set in. "Oh my God, we could actually miss this flight."

*

As the traffic crawled to a stop for the fifth time on Jake and Mira's way out of Paris, she felt the cold grip of reality.

If Mira missed her flight, she would need to book another one for later in the day at a price that was sure to be unsettling. She also knew that despite the strike being out of her control, there was every chance Shirley would reject the surge pricing if she felt like being evil, which, she usually did. Whether or not she'd support the over-priced flight cost was a whole other matter.

Normally, Mira wouldn't have been too stressed by unexpected costs, but after losing the deposit amounts on the banquet hall, the decor, and the catering after canceling the wedding, she wasn't exactly in a good financial situation.

"We're going to make it," Jake said, as if he'd somehow managed to read all her worried thoughts.

She gave him a long look. "Time is not a flat circle; you know that, right?"

His smile exuded a level of confidence that was somehow compelling. "We've got this."

*

When Mira and Jake finally arrived at the airport, she headed for the self-serve check-in kiosks, her mind flashing back to the night before when the online process hadn't worked. But the kiosks weren't working either.

"Goddammit."

Somehow, though, that wasn't even the worst of it.

"The check-in counter's closed," Jake said, all that earlier confidence now drained from his voice.

They were up against it, but Mira wasn't ready to give in.

She rushed over to the first uniformed human she could find. She fought. She pleaded. She insulted the entire country of France. But to no avail. Apparently, it wasn't possible to check in new passengers when the flight in question had already begun boarding.

"What do you mean it isn't *possible*? What about all those last-minute losers whose names get announced over the intercom like they're so important and ultraspecial and basically Brad Pitt?" She turned to Jake. "*Right*?"

"Totally . . ." he said, doing his best to support her sudden outburst.

The clerk at the check-in counter remained calm. "As you did not show up on time, your seats were given to passengers on the standby list. Therefore, it is, as I said, *not possible*."

She stumbled away from the counter. "Fuuucckkk."

"It's going to be fine," Jake whispered.

"Let me search for another flight," the clerk offered, still unfazed by Mira's breakdown.

She felt a sudden headache coming on. "Yeah. Sure. Why not."

A minute later, the clerk seemed rather pleased with himself. "All right, mademoiselle, I have found two seats on the next available flight. It will be tomorrow at three p.m."

Mira burst into laughter. Once she'd recovered, she smiled like a woman on the edge. "Are you out of your goddamn mind?"

The clerk was deeply unimpressed. "Do you want the flight or not?"

Her intense vibe switched to utter panic. "How is there nothing for today? There should be tons of flights that go to New York!"

The clerk made no effort to hide his disdain for the fact that Mira continued to exist. "There are not *tons*, there are several. But with so many Americans who are coming back and forth during

Haute Couture Week, and with it being the high season of tourism, this is the flight we have."

"What about *one* seat?" she asked. "Like forget about him," she added in a whisper, "just find one for me."

"Not cool," Jake said, his wounded eyes of little consequence to Mira.

"This is the only flight," the clerk repeated.

"What about a stopover?" she pressed.

The clerk started typing. "Let me see . . . ah yes, you can leave today and have a thirteen-hour overnight stopover in Iceland."

"Fuck that," Jake grumbled. He elbowed Mira. "Let's just go for tomorrow's flight."

She lowered her head in resignation.

Surge pricing . . . the potential cost of another flight . . . a hotel stay—the unexpected expenses were adding up in a major way. "Okay. Book it."

Jake nodded to the clerk. "Two tickets for tomorrow's flight, please." He turned to Mira and grinned. "Ready for another twenty-four hours in Paris?"

CHAPTER
three

M

Twelve p.m.

"Watch out for that pile of garbage," Mira cautioned.

Her words of warning to Jake said it all, as they dragged their luggage up a sketchy street in the 18th arrondissement. Their flight had now been officially booked, and they were freshly back in Paris for another twenty-four hours.

"Is that a used diaper?" Jake wondered aloud as they passed by the trash.

"Why are there half-eaten chicken bones in the street? And why doesn't this feel like Montmartre? I thought the 18th arrondissement and Montmartre were one and the same." She wiped the sweat that was pooling at the edge of her forehead. "This is not what *Amélie* promised me!"

There was indeed no sign of whimsical charm anywhere in the vicinity, in this neighborhood east of the Sacré-Coeur Basilica. Somewhere in the back of Mira's mind, she knew it was silly to base expectations off a film that contained literal elements of fantasy.

When it came to it though, she was a Paris-bucket-list dreamer on a mission, and that was the side of her that would rule the day. She even had an intricate knowledge of the city's map, cultivated over years of imagining being in Paris. The trouble was, it only extended to the places she cared about, and it certainly didn't include this rough-and-tumble area with its train tracks, used electronic stores, rundown laundromat, and shattered dreams.

While sharing an airport taxi on their journey back to Paris—which had thankfully been reasonably priced—Mira had focused her energy on booking a hotel room online. Jake had simply watched without a care in the world, after informing Mira that Colette, his one-night stand, had been more than happy to make it a two-night affair. He'd even offered to ask Colette if Mira could crash on the floor of her studio apartment. As gallant as that was, Mira would've rather jumped into the Seine, and she didn't even know how to swim.

As for available hotel rooms, tourist season plus Haute Couture Fashion Week had made it nearly impossible to find a hotel that Mira could remotely afford. She'd eventually managed to find a place with one last twin room available, and while the reviews were sparse and the photos uninspiring, she was hardly in a position to complain.

"Is this the place?" Jake asked as they rounded the corner.

With squinted eyes, Mira managed to read the lettering on the faded, potentially pigeon shit–stained sign that read HÔTEL.

"This must be it." She stopped a few feet from the entrance and glanced back at Jake. "Thanks. You can go now."

He seemed surprised. "What do you mean?"

"You said you wanted to make sure this wasn't a human-trafficking trap, *and* . . ." she gestured to the sign, ". . . since it's clearly a hotel, and this clearly isn't the plot from the movie *Taken*, you can go."

She cleared her throat. "But seriously, thank you; I appreciate the protective Liam Neeson vibes."

His look of surprise shifted to a salesman swagger. "Are you sure you don't need me? You don't even know what's in there." He approached the wooden door that was rotting at the edges. "Hmm . . ." He peered inside the dirty window and frowned. "It could still be a human-trafficking ring disguised as a hotel." He held open the door for Mira. "Once I know it's safe, I'll leave."

Mira stepped inside, and much to her relief it was a real hotel, despite the sorry state of the check-in desk.

"See?" she said assuredly. "You may go now."

"I'll leave once I know the *room* is safe."

Mira had trouble reconciling his chivalry with the extroverted salesman who only seemed to care about having fun. Except she didn't know him well enough to assess which version was true. "Okay,"—she decided— "you can *quickly* look at the room."

Instead of the clerk simply giving Mira the key, he led them to the room and even opened the door. "*C'est bon*?" he asked.

Mira struggled to restrain her disgust. "It's fine," she said, convincing no one. She turned to the clerk. "*Merci*." He handed her the key and scurried away, not unlike one of the rodents that was probably lurking in the room.

Jake was the first one to step inside, and a few paces later, he was already on the other end of the tiny room. He studied the faded floral blanket that was draped across the small twin bed. "Sixty percent chance of bedbugs."

"Shut up!" She grudgingly made her way in, forcing herself to get used to her temporary home. "And it's just for one night."

"Even so . . ."

"We can't *all* have booty calls to give us shelter, okay?" She dropped her carry-on onto the floor. "Anyway, I'll be fine. You can go."

Jake examined the dusty window, taking in the view of the adjacent building's wall. "Huh." He spun around. "Do you think we could've made the flight if we'd taken the car? Like I'd suggested?"

"I *told* you to take the car," she reminded him. "And you followed me to the métro anyway."

"Really? I think it went a little differently."

"No. Nuh-uh." Mira crossed her arms. "Your revisionist history bullshit won't work here." She gestured to the door. "You can go now." To her surprise, his expression transformed into the faux innocent look of someone who'd been holding back. "What's with the face?"

"The thing is . . ." he started, as he retrieved his luggage and rolled it to an empty corner of the room, "Colette has a couple of appointments this afternoon, and she won't be free for another few hours, so . . ."

She rolled her eyes. "Spare me the life story of your one-night stand."

"*Two*-night stand."

"Sure," she said. "Great. Now what was your point again?"

He folded his hands together like a boy in the Sunday school choir. "I was hoping I could kill some time with you until she's free."

"What do you need *me* for?" she asked. "You're not exactly lacking in the outgoing department."

He glanced back at the window. "True. But meeting people in broad daylight isn't as easy as meeting people in a bar."

She snorted. "Then go to a café and read a book or something."

"I didn't bring any books," he explained. "And sitting in a café for three whole hours might be lonely." He ran his fingers through his hair, a move that was breaking her down. "What do you say?"

Mira bit her lip. She wasn't convinced about Jake's fear of loneliness, nor was spending time with him any part of her Paris bucket list. Still, she liked the idea of having the upper hand and potentially making him beg, an unhealthy urge she would have to examine later. "You need some company, eh? I see, I see."

The innocent boyish expression returned. "And maybe after, you wouldn't mind coming back with me to open up the room so I can get all my stuff?" He gestured to his bags. "If it wouldn't be too inconvenient?"

She frowned. "Why don't you just leave your stuff with the concierge?"

"*That* guy? I'm not trusting him with my laptop."

She considered his plight. "You're right; Shirley would kill you if you lost it."

"Are we good then?" He conjured up a dazzling smile. "I'll make it worth your while."

She sneered. "*Gross.*"

"I meant with my *charm*."

She sighed. "I don't know . . ."

"*Please*?"

Maybe she'd tortured him enough. "Sure, fine."

"Thank you!" He held out his arms. "Hug?"

Her eyes zeroed in on the sweat stains clearly visible through his shirt. "Nah, I'm good." She grabbed her carry-on and dragged it to the bathroom. "Now if you'll excuse me, I need a quick shower."

"Of course, of course," he said beaming. "Whatever the lady wishes."

She studied his face. "I can really see how you bagged that waitress."

His mouth dropped open, just as she'd hoped. Maybe a few hours with Jake wouldn't be so bad.

Mira turned back to face the sliding bathroom door, its composition little more than a plywood-like panel. *Weird.* A small brass ring was the only door handle in sight, and when she gave it a tug, the panel slid back, revealing a tiny, mildew-encrusted setting. Inside, there was no visible barrier between the shower and the toilet, just the fleeting hope that water wouldn't wind up everywhere.

She wheeled her carry-on back out into the room. "Sure as hell not putting this in *there.*"

Jake snuck a peek into the bathroom. "That bad?"

"That bad."

She unzipped the various pockets, pulling out whatever she needed. Finally, with an armful of items, she returned to the bathroom and slid the wooden panel shut. "Remind me to spend as little time in here as possible," she called out.

"Easy on the yelling," he said, in a voice that was perfectly audible from the other side of the panel. "I can hear you like you're standing right beside me."

"*What*?!" she whispered in a sudden panic. She glanced at the toilet and then back at the wooden panel. "You have *got* to be kidding me," she added, forgetting to whisper this time.

"Kidding you about *what*?"

She slapped a hand over her mouth and stood frozen for at least five seconds. When she regained her ability to move, she pulled out her phone and fired off a text to her best friend Sophie in New York:

> Protocol re: going to the bathroom in full earshot of a male coworker?

She added the poop emoji to make things clear.

Sophie answered back within seconds, a clear sign that her newborn was struggling to sleep on a schedule.

I demand full details later, but for now, abort. I repeat ABORT.

"But I *can't* abort!"

Mira couldn't believe this ridiculous dilemma was currently a thing that was happening. But was she really to blame? All her life, people and entertainment and advertising messaging had trained her to believe that the body's miraculous functions were embarrassing and gross. She made a quick mental note to write a strongly worded letter to society when all of this was over.

In the meantime, she gave Sophie a thumbs-up and stared at the cheap wooden panel in silence. After what felt like minutes, it came to her.

"Hey, Jake?"

"Yeah?"

"Remember that convenience store that was down the street from the hotel?" she asked, doing her best to sound as sweet as possible.

"Not really."

She suppressed the urge to punch a hole through the cheap panel. "It had a sign that said *Tabac*. Remember?"

"I dunno, maybe."

"It was definitely there," she said through gritted teeth. "When you exit the hotel it's across the street and to the left."

"If you say so."

"Yeah, *anyway*, could you go down there and grab a couple bottles of water? Because we're probably dehydrated from all that running around."

"I actually feel fine."

She was officially on the verge of ripping her hair out. Or his.

That stupid greasy mop.

"Okay well *I* feel extremely dehydrated," she said. "So could you get me a water?"

"Sure. All you had to do was ask."

Mira silently screamed at the thought of this maddening creature shaped like a man. Once she'd recovered, she slid open the panel and handed him the room key. "Thank youuu," she said sweetly.

Jake took the key and set about his task, with Mira watching his every move as he shuffled out of the room. When the door closed behind him, a flood of relief washed over her, but there wasn't any time to waste.

One small step for embarrassed womankind . . .

*

Not long after, Mira was refreshed, dressed—in jeans and a summery pink tee—and ready for a day of Paris bucket list fun. It was incredible that only a few hours ago, Mira had assumed she would only get to try some famous French toast before heading back to New York. Now though, with a missed flight and another twenty-four hours in Paris left to go, it was time to put her bucket list in the driver's seat. She wouldn't be able to get through it all—since there were multiple categories, pages, and enough items to keep her busy for at least a week—but she had every intention of crossing off some major items.

She brushed her hair in a few quick strokes, smeared on some lip gloss, and added the final touch of a fanny pack.

Feeling satisfied with her look, she slid the paneled door open. "I'm ready!"

Jake sat by the edge of the bed with two water bottles by his side.

When he saw Mira, he laughed. A lot. "Is that a *fanny* pack?"

Mira was not the least bit embarrassed and caressed the fanny pack fondly. "I didn't think I'd get a chance to use it on this trip, but now that I have a whole day of exploring ahead, it's definitely the right way to go."

"*Is it*, though?"

"And they're totally back in fashion," she went on. "Louis Vuitton even makes one."

He stood from the bed. "But *that's* not Louis Vuitton. That's . . ." He bent down and studied the tiny label on the fanny pack. "*Pack 'n' Go?*" He fell to his side and laughed some more.

While Mira still wasn't embarrassed, she started to remember her one visit to India nearly a decade before, when she and her cousin had been led through the bazaar by their bargain-hunting moms. They'd visited one garment shop after another that afternoon, aggressively in search of the perfect outfits for the weddings of the upcoming season. While no one had laughed at Mira that day, she'd been made to feel weird about how she looked, much in the way that Jake was making her feel right now. It may not have been a fanny pack in India, but every glittering lehenga she'd chosen had been met with frowns or tailoring suggestions, whereas everything her cousin slipped onto her frame had seemed perfect. Was it a crime to have prominent shoulders and an actual butt you could see from a distance? Apparently in India, it was. She should have found it funny and pitied the buttless girls, but instead, she'd felt like a stranger in her own skin.

And now, here in Paris, she was starting to feel like a stranger in her own fanny pack.

Not okay.

"Go ahead, laugh it up," she said, "but I'll be the one laughing when I don't get robbed, when I have easy access to all of my essentials, and when my feet don't hurt from walking thirty thousand steps." She thought about it for a second. "I guess that last one's more orthopedic-insole related than fanny-pack related."

"You're wearing *orthopedic* insoles?"

"Guess you've never heard of cobblestone."

He scratched his jaw. "Right; kudos on being so prepared."

"Thanks." She opened her carry-on. "I'm also bringing a cardigan and an umbrella."

"Sorry, can't allow that. The sky is blue and it's *not* going to rain; even the sweater's a bit much."

"It may be sunny, but the rain can come at any time."

"And next up," he said mockingly, "meteorologist Mira with the weather."

"It's actually a tip I discovered in a 'Live like a Local' blog. Here, I'll show you." She pulled out her phone and started scrolling.

"Stop," he said, both hands in the air. "There will be *no more* reviewing of the blogs." She scowled but he didn't seem to notice. "You can have the sweater if you must, but you won't need an umbrella for the next few hours. Trust me."

Mira felt tempted to live-tweet how she was being mansplained about the weather, but she didn't want to lose more time from her day of exploring. She also didn't want to agree with him, which made the whole thing a bit conflicting.

"Carrying an umbrella is not a big deal," she finally said. "And why can't men just say cardigan? It's not that hard."

Jake got up off the floor. "Mira, would you say that I know a few things about life?"

"I don't really know you, but no, I wouldn't say that."

"What I *know*," he continued, "is that ten minutes into holding that umbrella, you'll start whining about how annoying it is, and then you'll ask *me* to hold it for you."

"Wow. Theoretical me sounds horrible."

If this was genuinely Jake's assumption of how Mira would act, it gave her an idea of the high-maintenance women in his orbit.

"I'm just saving you from your worst self. You're welcome."

Mira scanned the room for something to throw at him, but everything seemed too gross to even touch. She glanced at her watch and realized this debate was wasting precious minutes. "You're really passionate about this, aren't you?"

"I am. Keep the sweater, lose the umbrella."

"Fine." She tossed the umbrella back into the carry-on. "But if it rains, you owe me a hundred euros for emotional damages." It wasn't much, but it would help to ease her current financial burden.

"Deal."

She made her way to the door. "Let's go. I've got things to see and no time to waste."

"Gimme ten," he said, reaching for his carry-on. "I need a shower."

Mira bristled at the sudden adjustment to her schedule. "You need to use my shower too?"

He opened the bag and pulled out some clothes. "If you didn't want me to shower, you shouldn't have said I smelled like vodka sweat."

He whistled on his way to the bathroom and slid the panel closed.

Mira spent the next few minutes texting Sophie every detail from her unexpected morning.

> I'll probably have to sell some furniture to make back the money.

She sighed before concluding her harrowing account.

> It's fine, though. I've heard sleeping on the floor is good for your back.

It didn't take long for Sophie to respond.

> When you're back, I'm coming over with wine. Will leave the baby with Tom. Or a random neighbor.

Mira laughed as Sophie continued typing.

> And you should still email Satan—I mean Shirley—and explain the sitch. Who knows, she might throw you a bone.

Sophie's words gave Mira a sense of hope, continuing her streak of giving great advice since they'd met in their freshman year of college.

Mira set to work on writing up the perfect professional and not-too-desperate email. All along, she couldn't help but wince whenever she heard Jake lathering up the soap, or rinsing, or whatever other visceral sound accompanied someone washing their body. She wondered if he'd gotten back from the store in time to hear her viscerally wash herself too. The thought of it made her shudder.

"Ready?" he called from behind the plywood panel.

She felt uncertain. "Ready for what?"

Jake slid open the panel and sauntered out. His outfit was a casual getup of a T-shirt and jeans, but somehow, he made it go the extra mile.

And Mira couldn't help but notice.

He spun around so she didn't miss a single angle. "So?" He ran his fingers through his sandy brown hair, which he mercifully hadn't drowned in too much product. "What do you think of Mr. Vodka Sweat *now*?"

Mira was too busy staring to give him an audible answer.

"Are you really that taken aback by my beauty?" He put a hand on his chest. "I'm flattered."

"What? *No*." She chuckled, smirked, and shrugged, all to restore a feeble sense of nonchalance. "I think I just blacked out for a second," she added, before heading for the door.

"Blacked out from *what*?"

"I dunno; jet lag."

"But we didn't even go on a plane."

Shit.

They stood face to face now. There was no escape. "Actually," she said coolly, "we *were* at an airport, and studies have shown that simply being in an airport can cause varying degrees of jet lag."

"I've never heard that."

"It's true," she insisted, all the while scraping for more pathological lies. "It's like one of those sympathetic pregnancies, when a man gains weight and slowly grows boobs just from watching his partner be pregnant." She shook her head. "Science is strange."

"Right . . . *science* is strange."

The sound of buzzing coming from Jake's phone spared Mira from spewing more random verbal weirdness. She studied his face as he read the message, but his reaction was impossible to discern.

"Everything all right?" she asked.

"Just a text from a buddy."

"At six a.m. New York time?"

Either his buddy—like Sophie— had a baby who wouldn't sleep, or Jake was lying for some unknown reason.

"He's a trader."

"Oh." Mira suddenly remembered that investment banking was very much a thing.

She shifted her attention to the rumbling feeling in her stomach. All the bag-lugging and stress from missing the flight had burned through the calories of the pain perdu, which made her next agenda item more pressing than ever. And, knowing that Jake would be tagging along, she'd specifically chosen a place that could use a little company. "Can I interest you in a bit of a walk for some very important food?"

He smiled. "Consider me interested."

CHAPTER
four

⏐

One p.m.

Mira took the lead in navigating the route through the winding streets of Paris. For Jake, that was a welcome relief, as it spared him from looking at his phone screen and having to see another text from Colette. Yes, Colette, not a text from the imaginary trader he'd described to Mira. His on-the-spot lie was a hell of a lot easier than explaining what was really going on.

Just a casual request for a dick pic, he thought. *Isn't that great, Mira?*

While Jake had experience in taking specific photos at flattering angles, the timing had been horrible. He just couldn't see himself jumping into the bathroom for an X-rated photo shoot, not when Mira had been so generous with her storage space, her shower, and now, her time.

Or maybe she would be cool with it. He began to imagine bro-ing out with Mira over his hookup, but some muddy details from last night's dinner started filtering in. Like how Mira had been disgusted by the moves he was putting on the waitress. Or maybe she'd been disgusted this morning, when he'd stumbled into the hotel lobby and told her about his one-night stand. He struggled to determine which scenario was true.

Maybe he was still a little drunk.

For now, his goal was to avoid spoiling Mira's afternoon, which included steering clear of awkward dick pic conversation.

With that in mind, Jake decided on ignoring Colette, with the plan to apologize later.

Mira sprinted a few yards ahead. "Ready for a little exercise?"

His long strides slowed to a stop, as he fully absorbed the looming set of stairs that stood between them and the next street up.

Jake was glad they'd traded in the sidewalk garbage and cell phone repair shops for quiet streets, corner cafés, and cobblestone—which people always seemed to be obsessed with when dreamily referring to Paris. What he wasn't glad about? The hellish staircase that seemed to go on forever.

"*Well?*" she urged, jogging up the first few steps and staring down at him. "Come on!"

Jake watched as she continued her ascent, making no move of his own. He hadn't slept at all the night before, and now that

he'd seen those stairs, he was even more certain that the alcohol he'd consumed the night before was still swishing around in his bloodstream. "Isn't there a shortcut that's flatter?"

She stopped and looked back at him. "We're in the *real* Montmartre now, Jake. Embrace the hilly charm."

"But I'm tired," he whined. "And it's hot." It really was.

She pulled the hotel key out of her pocket. "You could always go back to the room and take a nap."

"On *that* bed? No, thank you."

"Then hop to it!"

Mira took her own advice and started hopping up the stairs two at a time. Jake tried to guess what sort of drugs she was on, or if her normal state was hyperactive. Based on the handful of times he'd seen her in the elevator, or bored and antisocial during company events (not to mention last night's dinner), he was leaning toward narcotics.

By the time he'd struggled to the halfway point of the staircase, he noticed that Mira had already finished the climb.

"Let's go," she said, clapping her hands in encouragement. "Don't tell me you've been skipping out on leg day at the gym."

"I always do leg day!" he gasped, finally reaching the summit.

She tried not to laugh. "I can see that."

"Tell me," he said, huffing and puffing, "what kind of supergenes are you made of?"

She casually stretched her legs. "My genes are standard issue, but I hired a personal trainer a little while ago, to make sure I'd fit into my . . ." She trailed off and looked away.

"Fit into your what?"

"My jeans," she said quickly. "I bought a bunch of jeans last year, back when they were uhh . . . buy one, get two free."

"Wait a minute," he said, bent over and clutching his knees. "There's a place that was selling jeans for buy one, get two free? Isn't that illegal for women's fashion? Don't the markups make the clothes seem cool?" He had a sudden flashback to a second date in Soho, when a girl he'd met on Bumble had dragged him around shopping for a whole afternoon. He distinctly recalled her picking out a plain gray T-shirt that was somehow priced at seventy freaking dollars. The thought of that T-shirt and the stilted conversation made him shudder.

44

"I didn't buy the jeans at a typical women's clothing store," she explained, shifting her weight from one foot to the other.

He finally caught his breath. "No? Out of the back of a van then?"

"A flea market."

Jake had a sneaking suspicion she was lying, but he didn't know why, and he didn't want to press it. "You've got to hand it to flea markets; they always have the best sales."

"Mmhmm; I love a good flea market deal."

Despite having given Mira an out, a part of him harbored a sick curiosity for seeing where her lies would go. And that was the part that won. "What happened then? You bought the jeans in a size too small, and then you needed a personal trainer so it wouldn't be a wasted purchase?"

"No." She frowned and muttered something under her breath. "What happened was . . . I got hooked on the cronuts they sell at that bakery on Spring Street, and the next thing I knew, I had like this"— she gestured to her hips—"dump-truck ass." She shook her head at the thought of this alleged memory. "I mean, I could've pulled it off, but for the jeans . . . it was *a lot*."

He stifled a laugh. "Right, kudos on the dramatic transformation."

Jake thought back to those times he'd encountered Mira, and he didn't recall her ever having a dump-truck ass. He certainly would've remembered a physical trait like that, which made it clear she was lying but he didn't know why, and he wasn't sure why he was curious.

Jake didn't have the energy to solve the dump-truck puzzle, so he settled for changing the subject. "Now where's this place we just *have* to try?"

She instantly relaxed. "It's just around the corner; c'mon."

✳

Mira and Jake sat across from each other at a worn wooden table in a tiny restaurant, with paintings of waterfront sceneries lining the walls, and sunlight pouring in through the windows. There were only two other people in the dining room, which gave the place a familial and homey quality. He didn't mind it.

"This is probably the only place in Paris that has house-made cider," Mira said. "Which is cool, you know? Because it's not what you'd typically expect."

"And they also have the famous crêpes you were talking about, right?" He rubbed his stomach. "I could definitely use some of those."

"What's even cooler," she went on, "is that the best crêpes in Paris are somehow *here*, at the top of Paris, when the famous street of crêpe restaurants is literally at the bottom of the city."

"Famous street of crêpe restaurants? Is that a thing?"

"You better believe it's a thing."

"How did that even come about? A bunch of people just said 'yup, this is where we're making crêpes?'"

She did a double take. "That's *exactly* what happened. How did you know? Have you read the blog about the origin of crêpes?"

"Can't say I have," he confessed, getting a sense of how Mira spent her time.

"It's kind of amazing how it all unfolded." She leaned in like she was about to share some intriguing culinary secret. Even though it was apparently detailed on a public blog. "The 14th arrondissement is where you'll find the famous street of crêpes, but why that partic-ular location, you ask?"

"Yes, Mira, *why*?" he said, finding himself eager to play along.

"Because the 14th is *also* where you'll find the Montparnasse train station, which is *also* where you'll find the trains coming in from Brittany, which is *also* where this famous style of crêpe was invented." She took a sip of water and shifted her attention to the view outside the restaurant window.

"Don't stop now," he said. "I want to hear more."

"Oh, the rest of it was obvious. Like in conclusion: it was destiny." She finished with a simple shrug.

Jake took a moment to marvel at this strange conversation.

He leaned back. "I have to say, you are *so . . .*"

As much as Jake was used to being the life of the party in every room, he didn't quite know how to finish that sentence. And he certainly didn't have a frame of reference for these kinds of conversations.

"I'm so *what*?"

He ran his fingers through his hair. "I'm not even sure there's a word for it."

"That's fine," she said casually. "I don't feel the need to be described by preexisting words in a dictionary. It's kind of basic."

"That's not a bad way of looking at it." It was getting even harder for Jake to put Mira in a category. Maybe that was a good thing.

"Ooh . . ." she said, her focus suddenly shifting.

Her eyes lit up at the sight of the server carrying a tray with two glasses of cider.

She looked from the glasses to Jake. "Are you sure you're not too hungover for this?"

"Are you kidding? It's just what I need." Maybe it wasn't, but if he was still a little drunk, it was better to keep on drinking.

They raised their glasses in the air.

"Cheers to a really messed-up day," she declared.

"There's nowhere to go but up."

They clinked their glasses before each taking a glug. And he had to admit, it was pretty good.

Jake realized this was his first official time drinking cider that was made on location in a restaurant in Paris. To his surprise, he really liked the idea of having done that. And he really liked how comfortable he felt around Mira. What he couldn't figure out was why they weren't already friends.

He set down his glass and studied her. "What's your deal, then?" She looked at him strangely. "I mean, we've worked at the same place for what, two years now?"

"I've been there for three, but I guess we've shared an office for that time."

"Then how come I'd never even spoken to you until today?"

"Technically it was last night," she said. "When I was repeatedly annoyed with you."

Maybe his memory of the night before had been right after all. "You were very sarcastic, but that's not what I mean. What about before? How come you've never been to the company parties?"

"You mean the parties hosted by the *sales team*? Like the one in March where an ambulance was called?" She shook her head disapprovingly.

"That was a total false alarm!"

The raw and unfiltered story was that Jake's coworker Pete had ended up getting his stomach pumped, but it wasn't exactly a detail he felt he needed to share. Still, as he thought about the shit show that had led to calling 911, he was starting to see it from her point of view.

Mira rotated her glass of cider on the table's surface, clearly done with the party talk.

"Last August," he blurted out, as the memory took shape. "The company barbecue at that hotel rooftop in Brooklyn. You were there that time."

"Oh, was I?"

"I distinctly remember chatting in a circle with Frank, a couple of sales guys, that dipshit from finance, and you." He frowned. "You ignored me the whole time."

She scoffed. "I don't remember that at all."

Maybe she didn't remember it, but he was certain that was what had happened. Everyone had laughed at whatever he had said that afternoon. Everyone but her. He'd even tried to include her in the conversation, but she'd only looked away, her long strands of dark hair getting caught in her face whenever the wind kicked up.

As he watched Mira now, he could see that she was avoiding his stare yet again. He wanted her to admit it, but he wanted to get back to the pleasant conversation even more. "What do you do for fun? And who do you do it with?"

She stared at him like he'd asked her something incredibly awkward. Had he? Maybe it had sounded like he was asking her if she was single. "I may have worded that wrong."

He wasn't even sure why he'd asked her a question like that. He didn't care if she was single. Especially not when he was hours away from a second hookup with a French hottie.

"What do I like?" she finally said, throwing him a bone. "I guess I like reading, and—"

Before things could really get back to normal, the server arrived with two big plates of savory heaven.

She gasped. "Oh . . . my . . . God."

Jake silently stared at his plate, not wanting to interrupt her special moment. Finally, he spoke: "Looks pretty solid."

"You know what I love most about the savory buckwheat *Crêpe bretonne*?" she said, eyes never leaving her plate.

"The runny egg?" He shook his head. "No, the cheese."

"The shape!" She outlined the shape of a square around her food. "Look how it's folded up on every side; it reminds me of an envelope, but instead of having a phone bill or a threatening notice from the IRS inside, it's a gooey love letter to your stomach." She folded her hands against her chest, clearly infatuated.

"I take it you're a foodie."

"Ever since age three, when I tried my first vegetable pakora."

"Those are so good," he said, feeling glad they had something in common.

"Right? And living in the city only made my love of food a full-blown obsession. I now think about food during most of my awake hours."

"You and me both. I mean, when I was a kid . . ." He trailed off before sharing the memory.

Those shows. Every day after school.

He could barely grasp that he'd almost shared a heartfelt, intensely personal childhood memory with someone he barely knew. Which could only mean he was absolutely a little drunk.

"You were saying?" she asked with an expectant look.

"Let's put that on pause and eat this before it gets cold."

She shrugged. "Don't have to ask me twice."

Their conversation dissolved into the comfortable silence of chowing down. Jake tried to remember the last time he'd eaten something this delicious. He almost wished he'd taken a picture of it before he'd started eating, so he could post it on Instagram and describe how amazing it was. But then he remembered that he never posted food on Instagram. What the hell was going on with him today?

In between bites, he snuck in glances at Mira.

In less than two hours, she'd made him obsessed with crêpes, and had almost gotten him to talk about his childhood. It was weird.

"Why are you looking at me?" she mumbled as she covered her mouth with a napkin. "Do I have food on my face? Or in my hair?"

He set down his knife and fork. "In your *hair*?"

She finished chewing and moved the napkin away from her face. "I don't *always* get food in my hair, but sometimes when I'm *all up in it*, foodwise, it winds up getting here, there, and everywhere." She gestured to various body parts to complete the imagery. "I mean, who among us hasn't found a pile of Dorito crumbs in their cleavage on a Friday night in?"

He smirked. "So *that's* what you were doing instead of coming to our parties."

"Not always," she said defensively. "Like for most of the last two years I've been really, really busy. I'm talking social calendar *jam-packed full.*"

"And now, not so much?"

She avoided his gaze—a move that was becoming standard practice—but before he could change the topic to something lighter, his phone buzzed in his pocket.

It was another text from Colette, only this time she was telling him her second appointment had been canceled. In other words, he could come on over whenever he was free. She added an eggplant emoji, which made the implication crystal clear.

It was settled then. He and Mira would finish their meal, walk back to the hotel to get his stuff, and then he'd call a car to drive him to Colette's. It really couldn't be simpler.

"Everything all right?" Mira asked. "Was that Colette messaging you? Did she say you can meet her now instead of later?"

He stared at her in a stunned silence, wondering if she'd somehow read the texts in the reflection of his eyeballs. Or maybe it was a woman thing, the way they could creepily read minds sometimes, or know what you were thinking before you even realized you were thinking it. She waved her hand in front of his face. "Hello? Earth to Jake?"

All he had to do was tell her she was right. Then pay for the meal, go back to the hotel, call a car, and wish Mira well.

"It wasn't her," he said casually. "Let's order some more cider."

CHAPTER
five

M
Two p.m.

What goes up, must come down.

At least that was the rule in Montmartre.

After climbing endless stairs to get to her beloved crêpes, Mira now found herself navigating a downward slope with no end in sight. She and Jake were walking along Rue Lepic, a historic street lined with charming shops and restaurants. She wasn't just there for the scenery, though; it was also where she'd find the next item on her Paris bucket list.

Mira had planned the navigation well, but what she hadn't planned for was the man who was tagging along on her solo day. She glanced over her shoulder, and like the last time she'd checked, he was right behind her on the narrow sidewalk that necessitated being single file.

She still couldn't believe she'd lied about having a dump-truck ass, when simply admitting she'd hired a personal trainer to fit into her wedding day lehenga would've been far less awkward. Except, that would've meant admitting that her wedding was no longer happening, an update she hadn't yet shared with anyone at the office.

And then there was the rooftop barbecue. She of course remembered it in vivid detail, along with Jake's effervescent charm, and how he was able to make each person in the circle laugh, no matter the demographic. She'd kept her own laughter under lock and key, and while she hadn't been able to grapple with the reason why at the time, it was now plainly obvious: he reminded her of the joy she was missing in her own relationship. If she kept avoiding him, she wouldn't have to face it, except eventually, it all caught up to her anyway.

Despite her random—and likely unconvincing—set of lies, Jake hadn't seemed disturbed enough to ditch her after lunch. Instead, here he was, perfectly eager to spend every spare minute following along with whatever she had in mind. And, if she was being honest with herself, she was perfectly fine with that. More than fine. She just wasn't ready to admit it out loud.

"Is it a museum?" he guessed, keeping up with her pace. "Or booze? Or a store? Or cheese?"

She glanced back at him. "You'll see."

They turned left onto a street that was somehow also called Rue Lepic. It was strange, but not exactly unexpected for Paris, a city that was fine with being aloof whenever it felt like it.

With the time spent studying Paris's map, Mira had accounted for this geographic anomaly, so without any navigational delays, they arrived at Café des Deux Moulins a few minutes later.

"Here we are."

Jake seemed uncertain. "A café?"

"Not just any café. It's the one from *Amélie*."

"Is that a movie?"

She ignored him and made her way inside.

"This is definitely it," she said, studying her surroundings.

From the vintage overhead lighting to the patterned floor tiles, it was just as Mira had imagined. She gestured to an oval-framed poster of the film. "See?"

"I definitely see it."

"You should really watch the movie if you haven't," she said, before getting distracted by the floor tiles. "I think this is the spot where she melted into a puddle."

"Huh?"

Without a word she nabbed the last empty table. As he took a seat across from her, she wasted no time in ordering a round of *café crème*. Bucket list efficiency, and all.

Mira spent a few more minutes blathering on about the movie, her rambling description petering out when two cups of espresso topped with foamy milk arrived at their table.

"Okay," she said, giving herself a moment to take it all in. "Here goes." She held the cup in both hands and slowly brought it to her lips.

Jake seemed unimpressed. "Would you just drink it already?"

Blocking out his cynicism, she closed her eyes and officially took the first monumental sip. She let the hot espresso and frothy milk mingle on her tongue, hoping her taste buds would carry her away. A second later she opened her eyes. "Huh."

Jake's cup was raised to his lips but now he seemed uncertain. "Is the milk rotten or something?"

"No, nothing like that." She set the cup back down. "It's just . . . I guess . . ." She was struggling to articulate the feeling. "It basically tastes like your average run-of-the-mill café crème, like the one we had in the crowded square by La Comédie Française." She looked to him for confirmation. "Remember?"

"Not even one percent."

Mira should've known he wouldn't remember. He'd taken no less than three work calls while they'd been at that café, on what was supposed to have been a nice break between meetings. It seemed that when he wasn't busy being the star of every conversation, he was busy being an actual salesman. Frank had been thrilled by his dedication, but Mira had found it annoying. It was one thing to be on a business trip, but to be so oblivious to the beauty of Paris? It was criminal. There was the architecture, the charming little shops, the food—which incidentally made up half her bucket list—and he hadn't cared about any of it, until the crêpes, that is.

Mira stared into her café crème. "I just thought it would be better." She sighed. "Like *this* is the place where they filmed a cinematic classic." She gestured around to the bar top and the lighting and the patterned tiles. "Why doesn't the coffee reflect that?"

"Is that what happened in the scene?"

Mira barely heard his question; she was too distracted, willing her coffee to somehow taste better with the second sip. It didn't work. She finally noticed him staring. "What?"

"The scenes from the movie that were filmed here," he said. "Did the main character come here and have a cup of coffee that blew her mind? Is that why she melted into a puddle on the floor? Was she just so *turned* on by the espresso beans?"

As Mira watched him mime a person getting horny from coffee, she realized her problem was bordering on ridiculous. "Actually, the quality of the café crème never came up in the movie."

"Then everything's fine, don't you think?"

"It's true," she admitted. "Nothing's wrong at all. I guess I just thought that after hitting a home run with that amazing crêpe place, the hits would keep on coming." She studied his reaction. "You can laugh at me now."

"I'm not going to laugh at you. I save my laughter for things like Pack 'n' Go fanny packs." He started laughing. "Ah man, still so good."

She let him have his mockery; he'd made a good point after all. "Are you done?"

He switched gears to a solemn demeanor, joining his hands in a prayer pose. "First, let me give you my philosophical advice."

She couldn't help but feel a little intrigued. "Okay . . ."

"Even the best baseball player doesn't always hit home runs." His voice sounded weighty and significant. "Or even get hits at all, for that matter."

She scrunched her nose. "A baseball analogy? *Really*?"

"You were the one who started the baseball analogy."

"I guess I did." She quickly decided she hated when he was right.

"For your next lesson: Do you know that a really good batting average is only around three hundred?" She stared at him blankly. "That's like thirty percent."

"I know what that means. I used to go to Yankee games all the time with . . ." She stopped herself in the nick of time. "And yes, okay; I get what you're saying."

She could finally see how a curated bucket list made during the times when she'd been seeking out a fantasy, probably had no chance of living up to reality.

"Real life isn't just one home run after the next," he continued. "If that's what you're hoping for, you're setting yourself up for disappointment."

Jake's last words hit harder than she'd expected. It wasn't just about a bucket list anymore; what if she'd blown up her entire future all because it hadn't been a big home run?

He must have noticed her changing mood because he suddenly

clapped his hands. "Now hurry up and finish that coffee. We've got a whole day planned of potential home runs and possible strikeouts."

"*We've* got a whole day planned?"

He frowned. "Huh?"

"You said *we've* got a whole day planned." The possibility of more time with Jake immediately lifted her spirits.

As for Jake, he seemed a bit embarrassed like the night before, when she'd pointed out the oyster juice on his chin. "You know what I meant," he said dismissively. "You've got a whole day planned of things on your list you'll be doing on your solo adventure." He patted her on the shoulder in an almost patronizing way. "And you're going to do *great*."

It was obvious he was protecting himself, a feeling Mira knew all too well. So she let it slide. "Thanks."

He finished his coffee with an aggressive glug, and when he set down the cup he was left with a foamy moustache.

"You have some . . ." She gestured to her upper lip.

Jake caught his reflection in the mirrored panel behind her. "Oops." He leaned forward, his foamy face now suddenly flirty. "Care to help me out?"

Instead of lapping it up (quite literally), Mira quite wisely took a beat. In Jake's world, he was being that normal hot-blooded guy who'd never miss a chance to flirt. But in Mira's world, she'd only recently broken off an engagement, a move that had disappointed family members all around the world. And then there was Dev, her former fiancé, who was probably still recovering, or at least that was what she assumed. They hadn't spoken since that horrible conversation.

Dev had no way of knowing what she was doing in Paris, but the thought of crossing any lines with Jake triggered a guilty feeling.

Mira gestured to the paper napkin that was resting underneath her saucer. "Take mine. I didn't use it."

✳

When Mira and Jake left the café, they found that the street had grown quiet. It was that peaceful time between lunch and the start of *apéro* drinks; the time for lazy strolls, summer sun, and maybe a little romance (at least for someone else who wasn't Mira).

"I'm hungry again," he announced, the grumpiness apparent in his voice.

At first, Mira was surprised by his admission, but as she took in the full scope of him, she noticed how tall and broad he really was. Maybe it wasn't strange for him to need the extra calories. He was also undeniably hot, but that was the sort of observation she didn't need on her mind. "You should've ordered something else," she said quickly.

"It was kind of hard to focus with all your drama about the *café*."

Mira now realized that rebuffing Jake's flirty advances may have hurt his feelings a little. Perhaps she could've been more sensitive, given that he had no idea she was fresh from a massive breakup.

She had no intention of divulging her secret, but that didn't mean she couldn't make it up to him. She peered down the hilly street, her eyes laser focused and in search of something. She spotted it within seconds. "I have an idea."

✳

Mira and Jake waited in line at the *boulangerie*, their turn up next after the elderly woman on a choosy expedition for the perfect baguette.

Mira closed her eyes and inhaled deeply. "*Mmm* . . . do you smell that? It's the aroma of the gods." Mere minutes ago, she hadn't been hungry at all, but now everything was different. Bakeries in France had that power.

He studied her intense reaction. "Haven't you already been to a bakery since we got here?"

"Yes. Five times." His eyes widened. "It's Paris," she added defensively. "Baguettes and croissant and *pain au chocolat* are each their own food groups here."

"You lost me after croissant."

She pointed to the stack of fresh pain au chocolat in the display case. "Those ones." She regarded them fondly. "Buttery, chocolatey, flaky goodness."

"Are you sure that's the one we should get?" He scanned the display case. "They've got a lot of different options."

"You can't leave Paris without having pain au chocolat. It's the law."

A few minutes later, they emerged from the bakery with afternoon treats in hand. Mira led them to a shady corner, perfect for some street-side devouring.

"I still can't get over it," she said, her face brimming with glee. "It's the middle of the day and it's *still warm*."

"I'll admit it, I'm impressed." Jake pulled the golden square-shaped delight out of its paper bag.

Mira couldn't remember having ever had a fresh croissant in the middle of the day in New York, especially when most of her breakfasts consisted of chugged smoothies on the way to branding meetings. Weekends were different, with opportunities to treat herself to enormous cookies from Levain, but the last time she'd had one had been with Sophie, when she'd made the trek from New Jersey to get a much-needed break from the baby. Mira had always hoped her food hobby would rub off on Dev, but as much as he'd tried, to him food and hobbies were like two opposing forces. She'd never been sure if *he* was the one who was normal, and *she* was the one too obsessed with food, but since he wasn't here now, she decided it was fine to dig in.

"Ready?" she asked.

"Ready."

They each took a bite. And it was everything. Eyes rolling back in heads, fireworks exploding in brains. The fact that it was warm only made it a bigger home run.

Mira's eyes eventually rolled back to the front of her head, and as she wiped the flaky bits from the corners of her mouth, she froze when her gaze absorbed the sight of him. "Um, Jake?"

He stopped eating and instinctively wiped his mouth. "Is there something on my face?"

"No. But there's something on your shirt."

He glanced down at the big blob of melted chocolate on his otherwise gleaming white tee. "Shit." Using the empty paper bag, he made a sad attempt to wipe the chocolate off his shirt. He assessed the result of his handiwork. "Hmm." He looked to Mira. "Better now?"

Mira remained frozen in place. The more she stared at him, the more he reminded her of the before part of a laundry detergent ad, only the current state of his shirt seemed worse than the grass, mud—and sometimes blood—the powerful liquid formula would magically scrub away. "I think you made it worse," she whispered.

"How bad is it? Be honest."

She cringed. "It resembles the inner contents of a diaper."

He paced back and forth. "Dammit." Within seconds, his exasperation shifted to a look of anger. "Seriously?" He stopped and faced

Mira with an accusing stare. "I shouldn't have gotten the chocolate one. There were so many options in there; why did you make me get *that* one?"

She narrowed her eyes. "Why are you saying I *made* you get it?"

Her tone seemed to spook him a little. "I don't know, you're kind of bossy."

"Maybe I am, but I still didn't make you pull the whole thing out of the bag before taking the first bite." She crossed her arms. "You knew it was warm—you knew the risks."

He glanced at her fanny pack. "Got one of those laundry detergent pens in there?"

"I'd need, like, ten of those for whatever you've got happening on that shirt. And no."

He attempted to stretch out the fabric, as if somehow that would make it better. And then he sniffed it. "Smells better than it looks." He looked back at the hilly street. "I've got to go change. Do you mind?"

Mira realized that if Jake was headed back to the hotel to change, this would probably be the moment when they parted ways. The thought of it gave her a strange feeling.

"I don't mind," she said, opening her fanny pack and pulling out the old-school hotel key. "You can pick up your stuff while you're there, but you'll have to find me later to give back the key." She held out the key, but he didn't make a move to take it. "Just message my work email whenever you'd like to meet up." She waved the key around to make sure he hadn't tuned out. "Sound good?"

A cloud of concern swept across his face. "You're not coming with me?"

Jake's neediness stopped her in her tracks. For a moment she considered upending her entire schedule to accommodate his needs. But only for a moment.

"It doesn't make logistical sense," she explained. "It's a half an hour walk to get back to the hotel, which is the opposite direction from Galeries Lafayette."

"Say that again?"

"It's Paris's most famous department store. And now's the perfect lull before it gets too busy." She stuffed the key into his hand. "The hotel's address is on the back of the key. You can map it." She smiled. "Thanks for keeping me company. It was fun!"

Before Jake could respond, Mira turned away from him and headed down the street. It was easier this way, because she knew any sort of long good-bye would bring back the strange feeling, something bordering on liking someone she'd barely spent any time with. It was illogical, and more than that, it felt like a betrayal to the relationship she was no longer in. Like a phantom limb, or in this case, a phantom engagement. Completely illogical.

"Wait!" he cried.

Mira didn't have to turn around because she heard him jogging toward her. Despite her concerns, she felt a nervous anticipation for what was next.

"That store," he said, his steps now in line with hers. "Does that store sell shirts?"

Was this really happening?

She gave him a sideways glance. "Yes, it's a department store."

"Then let's find me a shirt."

With a simple nod she led him down the sloping street. Had there been words, she would have risked admitting just how pleased she felt to not have to say good-bye.

My little secret.

CHAPTER
Six

<u>M</u>

Three p.m.

It was easy to get to Galeries Lafayette via métro, but with the blue-sky day showing no signs of letting up, a fifteen-minute walk seemed the better option.

Logistics aside, Mira relished the chance to spend more time soaking in the streets of Paris. The 18th arrondissement had now given way to the 9th, a relaxed stretch of streets containing everything a local could want.

As they made their way down Rue Blanche (a straight shot to Galeries Lafayette), Mira found herself peeking into the side streets, tempted to stop at one of the charming little terrace bars for a drink. She reminded herself there would be plenty of time for that later. In fact, she'd have all the time in the world to keep herself busy once Jake went off to see the waitress.

Despite having scored some extra time with Jake, Mira wondered when that moment of parting would be. She still hadn't gotten an answer out of him about his schedule; all she knew was that the closer they got to central Paris, the farther away they'd be from that grimy hotel and his personal belongings. A fact that made things logistically tricky.

"People are staring," he said suddenly.

She glanced in both directions. "Staring at what? A corpse?"

"At the *stain*."

She struggled to keep a straight face. "I'm sure people can figure out it's probably chocolate."

He jogged ahead and turned so they were face to face. "What is *probably chocolate* supposed to mean?"

"They don't actually know you," she said calmly, "which means they don't really know what kind of weirdo shit you get up to—no pun intended."

As Jake stood there looking like an outcast, he reminded Mira of the colorful characters—or more accurately, problematic customers—she would often encounter while working in discount retail as a teenager. From the ones who hoarded canned beans whenever they went on sale, to the lady with ketchup stains splattered across her shirt (or maybe it was blood?), Jake would've fit right in.

He crossed his arms, doing his best to hide the stain, but now looking even weirder.

"Just tell me we're almost there," he grumbled.

"We're almost there."

And they were.

Mira knew it without even looking at the street signs, because the shift in the atmosphere was palpable. The low hum of noise had slowly been building, and as they turned the corner, the sounds took the form of voices, music, and honking horns, all forming a crescendo at the primary entrance to Galeries Lafayette. The closest Manhattan equivalent was probably the Bloomingdale's on Lexington Ave, but with Galeries Lafayette's famous Haussmann-style exterior—six stories worth of elegant stone and wrought-iron details—not to mention how the side streets converged onto the retail nucleus, there really wasn't any comparison.

Officially, Galeries Lafayette had three different stores: women and children (the main one), home, and men. Mira should've led Jake to the entrance of all things men, but that would've delayed her personal reason for making the trek at all.

Me before you.

Even in the off-peak hours, the main street bordering the store was crowded. Mira couldn't imagine how bad it would get in a couple of hours, which made her happy that she hadn't messed up the timing by accompanying Jake to the hotel.

They crossed the street and joined the slowly moving cluster of humans making their way into Paris's retail landmark. Upon entry, Mira was hit with the designer labels first. They were categorized row by row, with some even occupying a boutique within a boutique. A large portion of the ground floor was arranged this way, resulting in a dizzying display of designer goods, enough to suit the taste of any woman with money to burn.

Jake got turned around when two aggressive shoppers hustled their way into the Lancel display of leather bags. He now stood facing a pyramid of medium-size satchels, looking incredibly lost. "Um, Mira?"

Mira noticed him from the Longchamp section of leather goods, but she found herself too distracted to acknowledge him. She was captivated by the high-end merchandise in her midst, and as she stood there frozen, it occurred to her that there wasn't enough Longchamp being paraded around by women in the streets of New York. She imagined how cool she'd look with a Longchamp crossbody satchel draped across her front, but her daydream stopped short when she remembered the lost deposits from her canceled wedding.

Grudgingly accepting reality, she made her way over to Jake.

"What's up?" she said.

"You tell me." He gestured to their immediate surroundings. "Did you just take me to the most expensive store in Paris? Because I only need a T-shirt."

"Most expensive?" she scoffed, her mind recalling the storefronts of Chanel, Hermès, and the flagship LV on the Champs-Élysées. "Hardly."

"Then where are the men's T-shirts?"

"We will get you your basic men's tee, I promise. But first we have to pass through these showcase items designed to entice the rich tourists."

The enticement must have been working, as the area was abuzz with shopaholic activity. The only section that wasn't shoulder to shoulder was the one that was affordable, or in other words, the private-label branded bags, scarves, and sunglasses. Apparently being the most famous department store in Paris wasn't enough to help Galeries Lafayette escape the private label stigma. Not that Mira supported this elitist mindset. She was, after all, the unofficial ambassador for Pack 'n' Go nylon goods.

"Now follow me," she instructed. "It's important." She led Jake to the inner maze of the cosmetics counter and glittering jewelry display cases. Without missing a beat, she spritzed her wrist with the nearest fragrance tester, which happened to be made by Dior. Jake watched as she rubbed the inside of each wrist against the other. "What?"

"Nothing."

"I won't be going back to that shitty hotel until I absolutely have to," she explained. "Which means I have to stay fresh." She rubbed her left wrist onto the sides of her neck.

"Smells good," he admitted, never taking his eyes off her. She noticed that his usual easygoing smile had been replaced with an intense stare. As the seconds passed, she felt the full weight of it and didn't know how to react. So she relied on what she knew: awkwardness.

"It's the bergamot!" she blurted. "That's why it smells so good. And the sandalwood too." She nodded. "Powerful combination."

Jake grabbed a box of perfume from the counter and examined the ingredients. "Weird; I don't see bergamot listed here . . ."

"That's because it's unlisted," she lied. "Only the most nasally advanced would detect it." He looked at her strangely, but she didn't let it deter her. "If you know, *you know.*"

"Dior's got nothing on you. Now where's the men's section?" He sniffed himself. "I need a refresher too."

"The men's stuff . . . *right*." She glanced around. "If we go to the left, it'll just be in a separate building, or whatever."

His eyes widened. "What?"

"It's literally right over there," she added, vaguely pointing to the left. "We'll arrive in a mere moment."

Jake quickly folded his arms across his chest, like he'd suddenly remembered the ugly stain on his shirt. He narrowed his eyes at Mira. "Every added minute I'm still wearing this shirt is a further moment of humiliation."

Mira wanted to tell him she knew that, and that she reveled in his mortification, but the truth was, she just needed to see the thing she'd been waiting to see. She could technically see it now if she really wanted to, but she wasn't positioned in the perfect spot to admire this important thing.

"The *last* thing I want is to humiliate you," she finally said, in a tone that was almost convincing. "But if you follow me just a few more steps, I can show you something that's worth the extra moments of shame. I promise."

Since he didn't seem convinced, she had no other option but to lead him by the arm—the toned, rock-hard arm—through a few more turns in the cosmetics counter maze. When she felt she'd arrived at the perfect vantage point, she stopped. "Now look up," she instructed, while doing the same.

There, in its round magnificence, was the gorgeous domed ceiling of Galeries Lafayette. Each floor of the department store had a circular railing where shoppers could gather to admire the view, but the vantage point from the ground floor was known to trump them all—at least according to her research. Judging by her current view, the book on Parisian architecture had been right. Intricately designed in a neo-Byzantine style and bathed in a warm yellow light, the iconic dome could almost make you forget you were standing in the middle of a department store.

The first time Mira had seen a photo of this ceiling was in high school, on the day she'd bumped into her parents at the mall back in Ithaca—while on a date with a guy who most certainly didn't share her Indian background. Her parents had spared her from an all-out humiliating scene right there in front of the pretzel bites shop, but even as they'd walked away, she could sense there would be a shit-storm waiting for her at home. Before leaving the mall, she'd stopped by the bookstore and picked out the most beautiful book she could find—a glossy hardcover all about Parisian architecture. An entire chapter had been dedicated to this famous domed ceiling, which had proved to be a balm after an evening of berating and tears. And now she was seeing it right up close.

Mira lowered her gaze to observe Jake's reaction. "What do you think?"

She watched as he studied the details of the dome. Or stare at it blankly. She wasn't sure. "It's impressive," he acknowledged. "You definitely don't get that at Bloomingdale's."

"You shop at Bloomingdale's?" she said teasingly.

He turned his focus from the ceiling to Mira. "My mom used to take me," he said, looking a little embarrassed. "When I was a kid."

"Ah, I see. No grown-up Mommy and Me trips to *Bloomies*, then?"

"Definitely not." He looked even more uncomfortable now. "Where's the men's section?" he asked, obviously changing the subject. "You said it was in another building?"

"Sure is!" Mira didn't know what had caused the sudden shift in Jake's mood, but whatever it was, she wanted to switch things back. "We'll just exit over there and cross the side street."

"Sounds good."

She took the lead and guided them to the exit, not stopping for any detours this time. All the while, her mind tried to sort through what had happened. She guessed that she'd hit a nerve of some sort, and so far, he didn't seem keen on getting back to his lighthearted self. It must've been the fact that she'd brought up his mom, she decided. Had Jake and his mom had a falling out over money? Had she hated one of his girlfriends? Mira quickly realized that despite being born in the USA, her knowledge of All-American family dynamics began and ended with the predominantly all-white-cast TV shows and films she'd seen growing up. As she started to wonder if it was better to leave Jake alone, she felt him elbow her side.

"Thanks for helping me out, by the way," he said. "I'd be lost without you."

"No sweat."

She led him across the street and into Galeries Lafayette Homme, feeling instantly relieved his good mood had returned, and maybe even a little happy.

*

The men's fragrances and accessories section was a much more subdued affair than the women's one next door.

Belts in brown and sometimes black? Square leather wallets that look exactly the same? We've got you covered!

"This is why I wanted to hit up the main store first," Mira said. "Here, it stays calm, whereas the women's section gets more and more feral by the hour." She turned to Jake. "Like did you see those women fighting over the last of the diptyque lotion tester?"

"*Those* women?"

"Not that I blame them," she added, blatantly ignoring him. "That shit is pricey."

"Those women?" he repeated. "You were spritzing yourself with free Dior."

She should've been annoyed that he wouldn't let it go, but instead found herself enjoying it. "Spritzing is different than fighting."

"Righttt . . . *you're* different." He turned his attention to the men's cologne. "Now what about me? Should I go with my usual?"

"What's your usual?" She studied the photos of sexy men representing the various brands. "Do you think there's a correlation between having a severe jawline and being a model for men's cologne?"

"I'm not going to comment on men's jawlines. But my usual is Hugo Boss."

She studied the Hugo Boss display, where the model was all buttoned up in a three-piece suit. "No," she said firmly. "Not Hugo Boss."

Her eyes continued to scan the displays, stopping at the one for Tom Ford. The male model featuring the brand's latest scent was not only shirtless, but also dripping wet. "Tom Ford," she said, reaching for the tester in a zombielike state. "It needs to be Tom Ford."

"You don't even know how it smells. You literally just chose it for the guy in the photo."

She brought the tester over to Jake. "What can I say, advertising works." Before handing him the bottle, she spritzed some into the air and took a sniff. "Whoa; is it possible for a cologne to smell *hot*?" She inhaled more deeply. "Damn."

He studied her reaction. "You really think it's hot?"

She closed her eyes and inhaled again. "*So* hot."

He snatched the tester out of her hands. "I guess I could maybe try it."

She watched as he drenched himself in Tom Ford cologne. "Need it to last all night," he explained, spraying it here, there, and everywhere. "Now let's get that shirt."

*

Officially speaking, Galeries Lafayette did indeed carry items of affordable clothing, but to find said items, you really, really had to look. In between all the searching, Mira had somehow convinced Jake to model clothing that was totally impractical. While she sat outside the fitting room waiting for Jake's latest runway show, her phone screen lit up with a text from Sophie.

> How was lunch? Is he gone now?

Mira glanced at the fitting room door before replying.

> Would you believe he's modeling clothes for me right now?

"I'm expecting to see the leather pants," Mira called, as she waited for Sophie's next text.

WHAT? Keep me updated #betterthanthebachelor

Mira heard Jake's groan from behind the fitting room door. "Can we please skip the leather pants?" he said.

"Don't you dare disappoint me like that. I've had a really rough morning."

"So have I!"

The saleswoman who'd been helping Mira find options for Jake pressed her lips in a tight frown, her patience wearing thin. It was almost like she'd figured out they had no intention of buying this impractical attire. As a retail alum herself—even though it had been discount goods—Mira could certainly sympathize. Just not enough to stop playing this delightful game.

"I'll make you a deal," Mira said. "If you pair the leather pants with the feathered vest, we can officially end Haute Couture Fashion Week."

Jake didn't answer, but a minute later he emerged like a modern-day Derek Zoolander.

"Yes!" she squealed.

He didn't seem happy in his leather and feathered getup, but he did a quick twirl for her anyway. "Satisfied?"

"It's everything I ever dreamed it would be. And more."

"All right," he said, making his way back to the fitting room. "Party's over."

"Wait!"

He spun around. "I'm not trying on the kilt, if that's what you're thinking."

"Nothing like that, I promise. I just need to take a picture of you to remember this outfit forever."

"A photo you could use for blackmail?" Jake shook his head. "No way."

"It's not blackmail," she insisted. "And even if you think it is, I'll give you some collateral in return."

He seemed intrigued. "Oh yeah?"

"I'll take a picture of myself from the worst selfie angle known to man." Mira reclined on the small leather cube she'd been sitting on, going all the way back until her body was nearly horizontal. She then positioned her phone so it was practically underneath her chin. Finally, with one quick tap, she took the ugliest photo on earth. She examined the result and nodded. "Yup, the selfie from hell. See?"

She showed him the photo and he burst into laughter. When he'd recovered, he studied the photo in greater detail. "I was expecting the collateral to be very different; but you definitely have a deal."

Jake held up his end of the bargain by striking a dramatic pose in his ridiculous getup. Mira gleefully snapped the pic, and unlike her disappointing photos of the Eiffel Tower, this one was perfect. "Incredible," she sighed.

"Now send me your horrible selfie."

"Okay. I'll email it to you now."

"Over *work* email? No way." He gestured to her phone. "Give it here."

"Why?" She was instantly suspicious.

"Just trust me."

She quickly deleted the text thread from Sophie and handed him the phone, but not before hovering close to see what he was doing. She watched him add his name and number into her contacts, a move that gave her an immediate twinge of excitement. He then sent himself her hideous selfie.

"Done," he said, handing back the phone. "Time for me to change."

Jake returned to the fitting room, leaving Mira fixated on her phone screen, specifically the name *Jake* in her list of messages. As her excitement grew, it reminded her of that whole other world, the one where something as simple as a new saved contact could awaken every cell in your body. It was the world of beginnings full of promise, rare but extremely potent. Mira was surprised to find herself in such a state, and while it gave her a rush, it also meant the guilt wasn't far behind.

Luckily, Jake snapped her out of it when he sent her an inaugural text.

> Added you to my contacts. Guess what your profile pic is?

The fact that he'd messaged her was thrilling, but the thought of that photo being used as a profile picture gave her the urge to scream.

You just HAD to be sassy.

Mira deleted the horrendous selfie, focusing instead on the positive aspect of having a new friend.

Just a friend.

Her positive focus gave way to an immediate question: Now that her friend was Tom Ford fresh with a clean shirt and all, would he immediately ditch her for his hot French date with the waitress from the night before? Perhaps the more pressing issue was how she would handle things if Jake chose to stay. On the surface, it sounded simple and hassle-free, but if Mira had learned anything in the last few hours, it was how easily you could find yourself wrapped up in someone new.

She probably wasn't ready, but she was certainly curious.

CHAPTER
Seven

Four p.m.

After paying for his T-shirt, Jake—now happily stain-free—followed Mira down the escalator and back out onto the street.

On their way outside, Jake waited for Mira to explain what was next. If she wanted to go her own way while he grabbed his stuff from the hotel, he wouldn't have known it, as she hadn't given him the hotel key or mentioned anything at all about leaving. The only thing she'd said was "exit's that way."

They stood on the corner in silence now, and while the cars whizzed by and the seconds passed, he realized it would have to be him to give an update on his plans.

After letting Colette's messages go unanswered for almost two hours, Jake had finally replied to her in the dressing room. In his reply he'd said he was exhausted from the night before, and that he wasn't yet up for round two. Since it was also in Colette's best interest to get him at his fullest energy—she wasn't exactly into him for his brains, after all—she'd suggested meeting up at ten p.m., which she'd explained wasn't all that late for a Friday night in Paris. He'd imme-diately agreed, as he would've had to be on his deathbed to pass up a second night with someone as sexy as Colette—not to mention that his buddies would destroy him if he broke the most sacred bro code rule of *never say no to no-strings sex*.

What he hadn't figured out, was where that left things with Mira. She'd kept him company for the last few hours, just like he'd asked, but requesting more time seemed needy and lame. He also didn't want to message Colette and ask her to meet up earlier, as they'd already confirmed their plans.

He clearly hadn't thought things through, but luckily something popped into his mind: maybe he was wrong in assuming that Mira wouldn't want to keep hanging out. He could tell she'd been enjoying his company so far, and if he truly had a way with people like every-one said, why wouldn't the same be true with Mira? All he had to do was make use of his salesman skills.

"Which do you want to hear first?" he asked. "The good news? Or the *good* news?"

"It sounds like you're about to tell me something I don't want to hear, but you're trying to dress it up, so it seems better than it is."

Maybe he wasn't as good of a salesman as he thought. Or maybe she just knew how to see through his bullshit.

Dropping the bravado, he stuffed his hands deep in his pockets and drew a long breath. "My date's been delayed until ten."

"Oh."

"And since you've already been so generous with your time, I can get out of your hair now. If you want."

"Huh. And after you *get out of my hair*, how will you keep your-self busy for the next six hours? Planning on having some solo fun?"

The thought of solo fun in Paris horrified him, much as it would for anyone who'd worked so hard at being an extrovert. Jake had been that way for as long as he could remember, but that didn't mean he'd been that way forever. He just wasn't willing to talk about the time when his entire world had come crashing down.

"I could have solo fun if I wanted," he lied, not wanting to seem pathetic. "I could walk around, have a drink, maybe even go to a museum."

She snorted. "You are so *not* going to a museum by yourself in a city you don't even know."

"I might," he insisted.

"Okay, museum-lover, whatever you say."

Jake tried his best to see through the jabs. If Mira was making fun of him, maybe that meant she wanted to keep spending time with him. If his guess was right, he would need her to say it. If he was wrong, he would need to convince Colette he'd had a sudden burst of energy, or maybe meet another waitress.

Jake stepped aside as a cluster of tourists passed by. "Do you have any museum recommendations, then?" Even as he said it, he was crossing his fingers that she'd stay with him. "You've got that list and all."

"I have a better question." She shifted her eyes to the street before saying anything else. "If you don't mind my bucket list, do you want to keep hanging out?"

Jake momentarily thought about playing it cool, but his immediate relief was overwhelming. It wasn't just relief though; he was feeling kind of happy too. "I'd love to."

She skipped past him. "All right, let's go!"

"Wait," he said, suddenly remembering an awkward logistical item.

She trotted back. "What is it?"

"My stuff's still in your hotel room." His happiness was losing out to the feeling of being a burden. "Would it be *totally* annoying if I grabbed it from you in the morning?"

She sighed dramatically. And then looked at her phone. And then shook her head like he was really the worst. "I *suppose* I could let you do that; but promise me one thing."

"Anything," he said, the happiness returning.

"Just shower before you get there, okay? I don't need to see you in all your vodka-sweat glory for a second morning in a row."

"You got it."

"Now before we get on the métro, I need to see something."

He nodded. "Lead the way."

Jake followed Mira down a street bordering the side of a large structure. Was it a museum? He wasn't sure, but the large columns and statues carved in stone gave him the feeling it was something important. This had to be the next thing on her list. They rounded the corner, coming face to face with the front of the building. As he took a moment to study the details, he saw a domed roof in a greenish hue, framed by two gleaming golden statues on either end. This was definitely the thing.

Mira stood back to admire the full scope of it. "You did *not* disappoint me," she said, speaking directly to the building, it seemed. A moment later, she seemed to remember Jake was standing there too. "Sorry . . . was just having a moment with Palais Garnier, Paris's two-hundred-and-something-year-old opera house." She shrugged. "I'm a little fuzzy on the exact date."

"You could lie, and I'd still have no idea."

"I guess that's true." She sighed. "Stunning, isn't it? The gold! The majesty! And the dome that used to be copper but turned green due to oxidation!"

It was a first for Jake, to be charmed by someone's dorky passion, but it was undeniable. "I see you've done some research on the build-ing, then."

"I have, and I can finally see why some people say it's the most famous opera house in the world."

He hadn't caught her mention of an opera house earlier, but this time the words reverberated in his ears. "Is seeing a live opera on your bucket list?"

"Oh, they mostly only perform ballet here now."

"*Ballet*?"

"Calm down, there is no ballet on my bucket list." She snapped a few photos of the opera house before turning away. "Come on—it's time for a little surprise."

*

Ten minutes later, Mira and Jake jogged up the steps of the métro, finding themselves in a starkly different neighborhood. Jake had no idea where they were, only that the fancy department store and opera house had been replaced with quieter streets, humble shops, and locals going about their business.

As they walked along with Mira in the lead, Jake noticed her check her phone periodically, but her pace never really slowed. She was a navigational pro, but with her focus preoccupied, she didn't seem to notice how the blue skies had given way to a patch of dark clouds. He remembered that moment back at the hotel when he'd refused to let her take an umbrella.

Shit.

He only hoped that whatever she had planned, it was something they'd be doing indoors.

Their journey continued for a few more minutes, leading them to a wider street that was parallel to a canal.

"Here we are."

He glanced up at the darkening skies and felt a building sense of dread. "Is it a restaurant?" he asked, clinging to the fleeting hope of doing something indoors.

"It's Canal Saint-Martin! I say we stroll for a bit, grab a bottle of wine and drink it by the canal, just like the locals and expats do."

The growing cluster of storm clouds was getting harder to ignore. Did she really not see it? Not wanting to burst her bubble, he quietly followed along, hoping the weather gods would somehow spare them.

As Jake tried his best to focus on the sights of the canal, he noticed how narrow it was, and how he could see the faces of the people sitting on the other side. They seemed to be rushing to finish up their wine and snacks, almost like they were trying to get ahead of a downpour.

"It's not that hot out anymore," Mira said. "Feels refreshing."

Jake had a feeling it was about to get a lot more refreshing. Sure enough, he heard the loud rumble of thunder, followed by a fat drop of rain that landed on his forearm. "Mira . . ." he started. More rain-drops followed in quick succession, leaving no time to take cover.

"Shit!" She made a sad attempt to cover her head with her hands, the rain relentlessly falling in sheets. "Where should we go?"

Jake tried his best to see through the sudden downpour. People were already packed tight under the awnings of the nearby terraces, but farther down, he saw a big blue door with a bit of an overhead cover. "Blue door!"

He instinctively grabbed Mira's soaking wet hand, and despite Mother Nature's chaos, he couldn't ignore this was the first time they'd really touched. He liked how it felt and found himself wanting more. By the time they reached the doorway they were breathless.

From afar, the doorway had seemed like it would offer a lot of space, but now that they were here it was a tight squeeze, the cold surface of the door on one side, the pouring rain on the other.

"Don't look at me yet!" she cried.

This downpour had turned into a wet T-shirt contest, and Jake had inadvertently snuck a peek when she'd yelled out her sudden warning. He averted his eyes as instructed, but the feeling in his body was already taking over.

"Okay," she said. "You can look."

He faced her now, and the cardigan she'd had tied around her waist was now worn over her T-shirt for some modesty. Both the sweater and the shirt were soaking wet, a combination that seemed anything but comfortable. Her hair was also dripping wet, and some of her mascara had smeared onto her cheeks. Despite all of that, he couldn't take his eyes off her.

"Feeling comfortable?" he said, trying to sound normal.

She frowned. "This is all your fault. You didn't let me bring my umbrella."

He put his hand over his heart as earnestly as possible. "I admit it, okay? I was wrong."

"Your hair is what's wrong," she muttered.

"You look like a soaking wet rat that crawled out of a sewer."

"Wasn't it enough to say I looked like a rat? You had to add the sewer element too?"

"It was easier than saying what I really think." His mind suddenly shifted to the autopilot thoughts brought on by his body.

She looked into his eyes. "And what do you *really* think?"

He noticed that a strand of tangled wet hair had fallen along the side of her face. "I think . . ." He could hear the rain pouring down, a steady beat that drove him to take a step closer. He took the fallen strand of hair between his fingers. Slowly, he tucked it behind her ear, his gaze never breaking from hers.

"Jake . . ." she said softly.

He interpreted the sudden change in her voice as the opening he'd been waiting for.

This is happening.

He leaned forward, closed his eyes . . .

"Jake, there's a spider on your shoulder!"

He immediately jumped back. "What? *Where?*" He bounced around and grabbed at his back like a madman.

"Hold on," she said, before flicking something off his shoulder. "Okay, it's gone."

His frantic movements came to a standstill, and with it the realization that he'd almost kissed her. It was significant, except, maybe she'd invented the spider because she didn't want to kiss him at all.

Mira wiped her eyes and looked out at the canal. "The rain's letting up; but now it's too wet to sit outside and drink wine."

"Yeah," he said vaguely. Had she truly not wanted to kiss him? He started to wonder if it was weird to feel so shocked; maybe all the years (and years) of dates had inflated his ego a little.

"I have an idea," she said suddenly.

"Cool." He could barely hear her. Maybe she had a boyfriend. She hadn't exactly been clear on that front, when he'd asked her about her personal life in a roundabout way over lunch. Perhaps he'd been too impulsive by going for the kiss, but at least she didn't have a ring on her finger. That would've been a whole other messy situation.

Mira stepped away from their makeshift shelter. "Looks like people are heading back out." She turned. "How about we try my backup plan?"

Whatever idea Mira had in store, it had to be better than getting soaked and potentially rejected.

"I hope you're not opposed to some afternoon booze," she added.

Yes, it would definitely be better.

*

A few minutes later, Jake and Mira found themselves at the bar of a cramped café, where a bearded man resembling Colin Farrell poured two glasses of wine.

The place reminded Jake more of Brooklyn than Paris, with faded posters of French musicians plastered on the walls, and alternative nineties music playing in the background. The clientele was split between older locals who could've been regulars—with French conversation boomeranging back and forth between tables—and twentysomethings with picnic bags who'd been sheltering from the rain.

"*Voilà*," the man said gruffly as he handed them the glasses of wine.

"Merci," Mira chirped.

Jake and Mira clinked their glasses and immediately got down to the business of drinking.

"Do you like the wine?" he asked.

"I do, but that's kind of been the theme of every glass of wine I've had in Paris." She pulled out her phone and scrolled through her bucket list. "Take a wine-tasting course at a cellar in the first arrondissement," she said, reading off the screen. "It was supposed to be my intro course before doing it for real in Bordeaux." She shrugged. "I guess I could do it next time."

"If it's any consolation, I know nothing about wine." He took another gulp of the grown-up Kool-Aid. "Was this café on your bucket list too?"

"Actually yes, but it wasn't really meant for today. It was more for a longer trip, when after a few days of cobblestoned charm, you're in the mood for something different." She took a big sip. "But it's a pretty good rainy-day backup, don't you think?"

"Sure is."

Jake stepped away for a bathroom break, and when he made his return to the bar, he noticed Mira scrolling her phone and looking troubled. "Everything all right?"

She immediately switched her screen off. "Everything's great."

The fakeness in her voice clashed with her words, making him wonder what was wrong. He sat back down and soaked in the awkward silence. Something she'd seen on that phone had disturbed her, and while he didn't feel right to ask, he was struggling to find a way to break the tension. He felt closer to her now, that much was certain, but a fashion show and a failed kiss were hardly the basis for sticking his nose in her business.

As he wondered how long the silence would last, he heard Mira let out a gasp.

"Oh my God."

He searched the bar for the catastrophe. "What happened?"

"French Colin Farrell is pouring himself a shot of Jack Daniels!"

Feeling relieved by the change in subject, Jake looked on with anticipation as the bartender downed the shot. "Epic."

"You've got to respect that," she said, before downing her own dose of wine.

With the awkwardness fading away, Jake finally processed her choice of words. "Wait; you think he looks like Colin Farrell too?"

"Does a pig have wings?"

"Uhh . . . no?"

"Oh shit, wrong analogy."

He elbowed her playfully.

"Honestly, I think I'm buzzed."

He started counting the calories in his head. "Really? Didn't you eat enough today?"

She gestured to her nearly empty wineglass. "I've been drinking this kind of fast."

"I see," he said with an appraising nod. "You're a heavy drinker, then."

"Not normally," she insisted. "But I ended up chugging most of the wine after seeing Colin Farrell take the shot. It was a very suggestive act."

It was a shame Mira wasn't influenced by other suggestive acts, like how he'd tucked that strand of hair behind her ear. It's not that he thought he was so attractive that any woman should immediately succumb, but it was clear there was something between them. Didn't she feel it too?

He reminded himself not to be too greedy; he had a hookup on deck, after all, so maybe it was best to just enjoy the conversation.

"Either way, you're an alcohol trouper," he said. "Which means you *really* should've come to those sales parties; you would've had a good time."

"Don't worry, I'm having a good time now."

Their eyes met. "Me too," he said, two small words he meant wholeheartedly.

"Me too."

"You literally already said that."

"Buzzed, remember?"

Mira finished the rest of her wine and placed her glass on the bar. "Should we continue the cycle then?"

He was intrigued. "The *cycle*?"

"Food, alcohol—sometimes coffee—food, alcohol . . ." She checked her watch. "Would you look at that? It's time for food again!"

He finished his wine and felt the beginnings of a pleasing buzz. Limitless food and booze, great conversation with someone as cool as Mira, and guaranteed hot sex at the end of the night?

I love Paris.

CHAPTER
eight

<u>M</u>

Five p.m.

The return of sunshine perfectly aligned with Mira and Jake's exit from the bar. It was enough to believe the universe was rooting for Mira.

Except for having seen that Instagram story twenty minutes too late.

After a trek on foot toward the historic Marais quarter in the 4th arrondissement, Mira's T-shirt was finally dry enough to conceal the explicit details of her boobs. She tied the cardigan back around her waist, her fanny pack once again positioned overtop of it for easy access.

The streets had grown narrower and the shops more unique, making this neighborhood a popular spot for wide-eyed window-shoppers.

"Ooh, a honey shop," Mira cooed, pointing at a storefront that was dedicated to all things honey- and beeswax-related.

"Seems overpriced," Jake said.

"Fair point." She slowed to examine the handwritten price tags. "One-percenter price points without a doubt. But it's still fun to look."

She wasn't lying, not entirely, anyway. She was indeed one of the wide-eyed window-shopping pedestrians, ogling the offerings from local designers, chocolate shops, and stationery stores; it was everything a big department store wasn't, which offered a nice contrast to the Galeries Lafayette browsing from earlier.

And yet, that wasn't the whole of it. This was merely another step in the process of distraction, which she desperately needed after seeing something so unexpected on her phone.

It had all started when Jake had gone to the bathroom. She'd immediately texted Sophie that she'd almost kissed Jake, and while she'd expected to be applauded for holding back, Sophie's response had been surprising:

Shoulda kissed him

Mira had demanded an explanation, but she never could've guessed what was next:

Look at Dev's insta story from last night

The same day of their broken engagement, Dev had unfollowed Mira on social media, and she'd responded by doing the same. It was standard practice in the world of modern breakups, and, given that Mira had been the one to break it off, she'd refrained from creeping his account. Until the moment she read Sophie's text.

It was fifteen seconds of a bottle blond with her paws all over Dev at a loud West Village bar, and Dev with that ear-to-ear grin she knew all too well. He was loving every minute of it.

Mira knew it was normal for Dev to get back out there, but for someone who had taken six whole months to go Instagram official with her, his brash display had bruised her ego in a way she hadn't expected. Maybe she'd wanted him to mourn their relationship for longer, though she knew she wasn't entitled to his pain.

At least one thing was clear: if he was out there having the time of his life, she was just as entitled to get back out there too.

If only she'd been able to have that realization in the doorway, in that breathless moment when Jake had almost kissed her. Jake; the fun, easygoing, and handsome guy she'd been having an absolute blast with.

Fuck.

The moment with Jake had well and truly passed, so they continued strolling, and the neighborhood continued to offer the needed distractions. "Three wick for *days* . . ." she murmured, as they passed by a darling little candle shop.

It was all going great on the distraction front, but then, in a flash, the protective bubble burst, when a tongue-locked couple stumbled out of an ice cream shop with double-scoop cones in hand. Mira and Jake barely averted their sugar-laced horny energy, and by the time the couple was safely in the rearview, it was already too late.

Pouring rain. Slick skin. Deep stares.

Mira's mind ran wild, playing back every microsecond and wishing she could turn back time. She'd only known Jake for hours, but this wasn't about deep-rooted connections, it was about being hot-blooded mammals—aided by the fact that Jake was extremely attractive. That kiss would have undoubtedly been steaming hot, a fact she knew from her seven educational viewings of *The Notebook*. Pouring rain was nature's way of releasing the dam of pent-up human urges. And she'd missed it. All because she'd been busy serving a sentence of self-imposed guilt.

Instead of kissing Jake, she'd freaked out and invented a spider, a lie that not only disrespected the generosity of the weather, but also would've annoyed the population of spiders, who surely would've preferred to be excluded from her narrative.

"Are we almost there?" he asked, his voice breaking through her cloud of regret.

Mira checked her phone and realized they'd missed their left turn into an inner side street.

"Almost there," she confirmed, a little too cheerfully. "We just need to turn back toward the street we just passed."

Jake gasped in a mocking tone. "Did you just *miss* a direction? And here I was, thinking navigation was your thing."

"It is," she insisted. "But now we're in the Marais, which is full of confusing streets," she lied. "What's a girl to do?"

He leaned in close, a move that made her turn to meet his stare. "You got distracted by the make-out, didn't you?" His low voice peeled away her protective veneer.

"We didn't make out," she blurted. "We didn't even kiss—we were just staying dry!"

"Um . . . I was talking about that couple getting ice cream."
Fuck.

"I know," she said, struggling to recover. "That's what I meant." She rubbed her forehead. "Whew . . . I think I'm getting heatstroke. Let's head to the shop and get out of the sun."

To her massive relief, Jake simply gestured for her to walk ahead, a move that spared her any additional humiliation.

Mira now led them down an even more quintessentially Marais side street, so narrow it could barely fit the width of one car. To top it all off, the microstreet was bordered by thin strips of sidewalks that had you constantly on the lookout for invading pedestrians. Mira hoped a stroller-wielding mom would crash into her; anything to wash away the heavy embarrassment that lingered in the air.

Meanwhile, Jake was little help in relieving the tension that had built up between them since her accidental acknowledgment of the almost-kiss. His chitchatty ways had dissolved into silence, with his footsteps taking on a brisk, colder quality.

She was hopeful that their next destination would restore his mood, but one thing was for certain: the next time a man she was attracted to offered up a no-strings kiss—Jake, some other rando, a Tom Ford model—she would remember she had the green light, and she definitely wouldn't flinch.

*

Mira stood facing the counter of delicacies at the tiny Marais location of Pierre Hermé, ready to emotionally eat her thoughts into oblivion. The male employee in the all-black uniform stood at full attention, waiting to take instructions from Jake and Mira, the only customers in the shop.

As soon as they'd arrived, Mira had been relieved to see a change in Jake's mood. Maybe it was the large selection of colorful macarons that had lifted his spirits, or maybe it was a break from the simmering sun. Whatever it was, she was glad to see the return of the guy who was always game for some fun.

"What do we do?" Jake whispered.

"Ignore the array of chocolates," she whispered back. "Wait, why am I whispering? What I mean is, people come here for the macarons, not the chocolates." She turned to the man behind the counter. "They're the best in Paris, right?"

The employee's thin-lipped mouth registered a hint of upward movement that Mira gladly accepted.

"They look different than the ones I've eaten before," Jake observed. "Like how come there isn't any shredded coconut on top?"

She gasped. "Easy on the ignorance! They'll kick you out of France for that. And those coconut things are *macaroons*. *These,* are *macarons.*"

He scratched his head. "How many should we get?"

"Four. Crème brulée, matcha and rose, coconut and coriander, and pistachio and raspberry. Unless you want something else."

"The flavors are fine, but four?" His face twisted in confusion. "As in four in *total*?"

"Four."

He struggled to compute the math. "But they're so small . . ."

She cupped her hands over his ear, the scent of Tom Ford cologne momentarily overwhelming her. "They're three euros *each*," she whispered.

As she stepped away from the closeness of Jake's neck, she found herself feeling embarrassed for having to be so frugal, especially when Jake clearly wasn't as concerned. But such was her current reality. It reminded her of growing up around kids who were given an allowance every week for doing little more than existing. That sort of frivolity had never even entered the realm of possibility in the Attwal household, reducing Mira to the twelve-year-old girl who'd join her friends at the food court but never order anything, always under the guise of not being hungry.

Mira felt the vibration of her phone and pulled it out of her fanny pack. She'd just received a new email, and the sender caught her by surprise. "Holy shit, she actually replied."

"Who did?"

"Shirley."

He sneered. "What the hell does *she* want?"

In the email she'd crafted while Jake had been in the shower, she'd asked Shirley to approve their additional expenses, given the extenuating circumstances. In any other company that would've been the norm, but with a stickler like Shirley you basically had to beg.

Mira feverishly read through the contents, summarizing the email for Jake: "First paragraph laced with shaming . . . *typical* . . . need to be more responsible . . . flight costs this high would normally never be covered . . . blah blah blah, I mean of course they were high, it was totally last minute!"

"That's it?" He shook his head in disgust. "Typical Shirley."

"Wait!" she exclaimed. "Due to extenuating circumstances . . . for this *one* time only . . . oh my God, she's going to submit the expense form to Frank!"

Once the expenses made it through the gatekeeper known as Shirley, there was never any question of getting it approved. It didn't solve all of Mira's financial problems—given the money she would never get back on the deposits from her canceled wedding—but it was something.

She noticed Jake grinning. "I take back everything I said. Shirley is a goddess."

"Let's not get carried away . . ."

"Whatever, go team!" He raised his hand, positioning it in front of Mira. She stared at it for a second before realizing he was expecting a high five. She held up her hand to mirror his. Was it her job to do the smack? Would it be mutual? She'd never played team sports, so this was all a bit confusing.

Luckily, Jake took the lead by hitting her hand, but instead of breaking away after the smack, his hand lingered over hers. She didn't make a move to retreat, and simply watched as his fingers curled over, slowly interlocked with hers.

Mira looked into Jake's eyes, wondering what to do next. But he seemed to be equally clueless. This left them with a limp sort of hand clasp thing, a clasp that was so incredibly awkward, it managed to stop time and pause the rotation of the earth.

The employee—who'd been watching all of this—made a light coughing sound, which mercifully put an end to Mira and Jake's special joining of the hands.

She acknowledged the worker with an embarrassed nod, and when she noticed the four measly macarons he'd put into a clear plastic bag—Pierre Hermé's cheapest packaging—she had a idea.

She nudged Jake. "How do you feel about a celebratory splurge?" It may not have been the wisest financial move, but with the cost of the flight now covered, Mira couldn't help but think about her younger, cash-strapped self. She owed this treat to the girl in the food court who'd never had the option to supersize those fries.

Jake's eyes sparkled. "A splurge sounds great."

Mira waved dismissively at the cheap plastic bag. "Cancel that. We'll take the deluxe gold box collection."

The employee nodded and got to work on the new request.

"Huh," she said, watching his measured movements. "Interesting."

Jake followed her gaze. "What is it?"

"I thought there'd be balloons or confetti for ordering the premium package, but it's almost like he doesn't even care about his VIP customers." She frowned. "*Big* mistake. Huge."

The employee wasn't sure what had happened. "Is there a problem?"

"Please ignore her, she's just paraphrasing *Pretty Woman*." Jake pulled her away from the counter. "We'll just quietly wait over here, *won't we?*"

Mira crossed her arms in defiance. "It was a pertinent reference."

"You're not a sex worker and he didn't refuse to serve you."

She struggled to keep her defiance intact. "Whatever," she muttered, nearly breaking into a laugh.

Though she managed to stay silent as the rest of the transaction proceeded, she found herself increasingly intrigued by Jake. In a few short hours, he'd changed so much from the guy in the restaurant serving up cocktails powered by Bloom and drunkenly hitting on waitresses. He knew *Pretty Woman* as well as she did. He didn't mind embarrassing himself by trying on leather pants. He'd almost kissed her.

Maybe it wasn't much, but it made her eager to learn even more about this guy who'd stumbled into her day.

And she hoped she would.

*

Armed with ten different flavors for a total of twenty macarons—and bottled water to use as a palette cleanser between tastings—Mira led Jake even farther into the narrow streets of the Marais.

"Can we find somewhere to sit?" he said. "I'm getting tired."

"Somewhere to sit is exactly what I have in mind."

Mira crossed the street and stopped at one of the neighborhood's few large facades. "We're here," she announced.

He approached the sign welcoming visitors. "I don't know a lot of French, but I *know* that word means museum." He looked like he was about to cry. "Please don't make me; I'm too tired to look at artifacts."

He was right, they were standing outside Musée Carnavalet, the museum dedicated to the history of Paris.

And yet, he was also wrong.

"You will *not* have to look at artifacts," she said.

"Then . . . *why*?"

"Do you trust me?"

"No."

"I see," she said. "I won't say I'm not disturbed by your lack of hesitation in providing that response, but I *am* the one holding the macarons, so it's really up to you."

Without waiting for him to respond, she strolled through the empty queue and made her way inside.

The museum was more reminiscent of a massive historical mansion than a grand collection of artifacts, and the best part in Mira's eyes was the free admission.

She glanced back to see that Jake had followed her inside. "We're in!"

She studied his befuddled look with a hint of amusement; he clearly had no idea that they wouldn't need to pay.

Jake gestured to a man at the far wall, arms crossed and seated in a small chair. He appeared to be one of those power-hungry volunteers, the ones assigned to making sure no one ever touched any artifacts.

"I wonder if we can scam one of those chairs," Jake said.

"We don't need those chairs. Just follow me."

Following the signs, Mira eventually made her way back outdoors, stopping at the edge of a well-manicured courtyard. It was a gorgeous little hideaway, enclosed on all sides by the impressive architecture, and with two geometrically identical gardens forming the central focus. The best part of all was the lack of other humans and the number of empty benches.

It was the perfect place for Mira's quest to get to know Jake a little better.

She looked over at him. "Is this a good enough place for a rest?"

She could see him eyeing the nearest bench. "I will never not trust you again."

After they settled onto the bench, Jake made a play for the Pierre Hermé bag.

"Not yet." Mira squinted into the windows surrounding them, which was difficult to do from her vantage point. "They were pretty chill about me bringing in the bag, but if they notice us eating, they'll probably kick us out." She narrowed her eyes. "Do you see anyone?"

"Do I see anyone with their face plastered against the window creepily staring at us?" he said sarcastically. "No, we're all clear."

She ignored his tone and tucked the bag between her feet, opening the box from the ground-level position. She discreetly pulled out two macarons and placed them into his hand.

"*Really*?" he said. "This is what we're doing?"

She studied the courtyard with shifty eyes. "I have traumatic memories of being yelled at for sneaking cookies into the living room. So, yes, this is what we're doing."

She took a couple of macarons for herself, before giving the go-ahead nod to Jake.

As they ate, her eyeballs seemed to expand at the sheer deliciousness of it all. "Holy shit."

"Mmhmm," he mumbled.

"Olive oil and lavender; whoever thought of that is a genius." It was an experience tailor-made for the live-to-eat crowd, and it only further validated her food-forward bucket list.

Jake put out his hand. "More."

They continued like this for two more rounds before finally taking a break.

"I'm loving the lack of tourists," he said.

"An American in Paris Instagram account wrote a soliloquy's worth of a caption about this courtyard. Clearly, it was valid."

Jake leaned back and took it all in. "It's really peaceful."

"Sure is."

"Should we keep eating?"

"Definitely." She handed him another macaron.

"Can I have another orange one instead? I've already had one but it's amazing."

"No," she said firmly. "We only get one of each flavor; them's the rules."

He seemed taken aback. "I . . . did not expect that response."

"You also aren't expecting the *crème brulée* flavor in your hand to be delicious; but it will be."

He took a bite. "Okay, maybe it's good to expand my horizons."

"Is that what you were doing the first time you watched *Pretty Woman*?" she said teasingly. "Expanding your horizons? And how did you even remember that reference?" she probed. "Have you seen it more than once?"

The silence that followed left her stunned. She couldn't figure out what she'd said or done wrong, when it was Jake who had mentioned the movie in the first place. Maybe this was the trouble with getting too comfortable with people you hardly knew: the unexpected landmines.

"Back when I was in college," he finally said, "my mom got really sick. I took a semester off to spend time with her." Mira held her breath, willing herself into silence. This was the most Jake had ever shared with her, and she didn't want to say anything to ruin it. "She spent a lot of time in the hospital for treatments, so when I visited, I would bring her favorite DVDs and we'd watch them together. I think I've seen everything from the eighties and early nineties." He smiled. "Including *Pretty Woman*."

Mira was grateful that Jake was finally opening up to her, but she wasn't sure if now was the right time to be asking about his mom. Deciding to stick with the familiar, she veered in the other direction. "Was it weird watching a movie about a sex worker with a heart of gold with your mom?"

To her relief, his expression brightened. "You would think so, but mostly it was nice to just spend time together."

"That makes a lot of sense."

"Did you and your family watch movies together when you were growing up?"

Mira immediately laughed, a sound that contained the sharp edges of bitterness. "Definitely not." She felt an awkward memory bubble up to the surface, something she'd never shared with anyone. "Except for that one time, when the popularity of *Titanic* was just too much for the family to ignore."

"And how did it go?"

"It was fine until the nude scene."

Jake laughed.

"I was probably too young to be watching it anyway, but the awkwardness . . . fuck, I can't even describe it." She shuddered. "It was the first and *last* family movie night, and by the time I started making visits home during college, streaming services had luckily been invented. Just me, my laptop, and my room; *thank God.*"

"That's kinda sad," he said. "But kinda funny too."

It was strange for Mira to see her childhood memories reflected in the eyes of someone else. There had certainly been some happy moments in her childhood, but for the most part, all she'd known growing up had been lack of eye contact, lack of hugs, and never talking about anything.

School hadn't exactly been a picnic, either, being one of only a handful of kids who weren't white, right up until the end of high school. Once she'd figured out how to bottle up her culture, things had gotten better, which, when she thought about it, actually *was* kind of sad.

She consoled herself with how things had gotten better. It hadn't happened overnight, but after years and years of bottling everything up, she'd finally spoken her truth before marrying the wrong guy.

Better late than never?

Mira made a move to mainline another macaron, but before she could resort to eating her feelings, she remembered that Jake had been sharing something quite profound.

"Hey, Jake," she said softly. "Is your mom doing better now?"

The silence that followed said it all. "She's not."

"I'm really sorry."

"She made it to my college graduation though, and I don't think I'd ever seen her happier." She could sense that he was playing back the memory in his mind. "It was only six months later that she died."

Mira could feel her eyes welling up with tears, but luckily Jake didn't notice. She felt relieved, as the last thing she wanted was to make him even sadder. Without thinking, she squeezed his hand. "She must've been so proud of you on graduation day. I bet she still is now."

His eyes became a little glassy. "Thanks. It's been thirteen years and I've barely even talked about it." He chuckled. "Except for now, I guess."

"I don't mind listening," she said. "Just so you know."

He studied his surroundings. "My mom would've thought it was cool that I was here being a tourist."

"Oh yeah?"

"She'd always planned on traveling once we were older, and we'd even watch all these travel shows together when I was a kid."

Mira found herself marveling at his childhood memories, ones that were starkly different from her own. "That sounds like a lot of fun."

"It was. She always wrote down the places she wanted to visit in a notebook, along with all the food she would try."

She gave him a playful nudge. "Kind of like a bucket list?"

"Ha, exactly like that."

"Maybe in some way you're honoring her by seeing Paris."

They locked eyes. "I think you might be right."

She suddenly had a thought. "Wait a minute; if you watched all those travel shows, then how come you didn't know—"

"What a macaron is?"

"Well, yeah!"

"I must've missed the episode on Paris," he confessed. "The French one we saw was an episode on Provence, where in this little town of Aix there are these shops that sell different kinds of chocolate bark. There's dark chocolate, milk chocolate, ones with nuts, ones with nuts and nougat; they literally hack off pieces of it and sell it to you by weight."

"Chocolate shops that sell *giant pieces of bark*?" It was a revelation. "How did I live my entire life not knowing this?"

He squeezed her shoulder and nodded sympathetically. "It's okay, Mira, you can add it to your bucket list."

CHAPTER
nine

M
Six p.m.

After a bit more chatting in the museum courtyard, Mira and Jake wisely opted to save some macarons for later. She'd explained to him how important it was to vacillate between sweet and savory food items, so that as soon as you got sick of one category, you could quickly move on to the next. This strategy lined up well with her food-heavy bucket list, and so far, Jake had been game for every part of it.

Despite her lighthearted tutorial on being a glutton, Mira couldn't help but notice how much quieter Jake had grown. His playful laughter and conversation starters had all but come to a halt. Not that she could blame him. He'd shared something intensely personal, after all. She only hoped he didn't regret telling her.

What mattered to Mira now was the time that remained, these precious few hours before he'd finally leave for his date. She could already see herself getting wrapped up in his presence, and a part of her had even started hoping he would cancel so they wouldn't have to say good-bye. If she told him, maybe it would even make a difference. Only, she knew herself, and she hadn't fully overcome her tendency to bottle up her feelings.

But that was a problem for another day. For now, she simply needed the next few hours with Jake to stretch the very fabric of space and time, so it wound up feeling endless.

Since leaving the museum, Mira and Jake had been heading south and were now just a block away from the noisy traffic of Rue de Rivoli.

She stopped and pointed at a bakery. "You get the baguette; I'll get the cheese."

It was a surprisingly firm command given the prolonged silence, but she hoped it would pull Jake out of his somber mood.

"Shouldn't we get this stuff later? We just ate."

The fact that Jake was questioning her instructions was a positive sign. Even so, hadn't she already schooled him on the food consumption strategy earlier? Maybe he hadn't been paying attention.

"Jake," she said, grabbing him by the shoulders. "It's sweet, savory, repeat. And even if we're not going to eat it right away, we need to forward-plan so we can keep on drinking wine and maybe have a picnic too."

"More wine?" His expression brightened. "And a picnic? You didn't mention that before."

"We're in France, so it's kind of implied," she said. "Now the bakery and cheese shops close in less than an hour." She clapped her hands. "Chop-chop!" She made a start for the cute *fromagerie* across the street, but seconds later, turned back. "Wait."

"What is it?"

"Make sure you ask for the *tradition*," she instructed, wanting to ensure he selected the most classic and famous version of a French baguette.

"I'm not saying it in that weird French accent you just did."

"Just get it done."

A few minutes later, they reconvened on the street with the required items.

"That lady thought I sounded like an idiot," he moaned.

"We're in France and we're American; it happens."

Jake looked from the baguette he was holding in one hand, to the leftover macarons in the other. He struggled to stuff the baguette into the Pierre Hermé bag. "Now give me the cheese," he said. "Maybe I can fit it in here too."

"Don't bother." She casually opened her fanny pack and pulled out a thin tote folded into a square. She opened it up and dropped the packages of cheese inside, along with the baguette and the remaining macarons. She slung the tote over her shoulder and smiled. "Shall we?"

He shook his head in disbelief. "I will *never* make fun of that fanny pack again."

"Told ya," she said as she strutted past him.

Jake followed her to a busy intersection on Rue de Rivoli, where honking horns and early evening traffic were in full effect.

"Any guesses on what we're doing next?" she asked.

"Hmm . . . some sort of park?"

"I will neither confirm nor deny."

They crossed the street and made their way to the expansive square of Hôtel de Ville, one side bordered by a striking structure resembling a royal estate.

"Ooh," she gushed, craning her neck to capture the full view.

"Is this another museum?"

"Hardly. More like City Hall."

He turned sharply. "Are you kidding me?"

"No."

He turned back for another look. "But it's so . . . majestic."

She was charmed by his newfound admiration for buildings. "It *is* kind of majestic."

"When we get back to New York I'm writing an angry letter to City Hall," he grumbled.

"About the ugliness of their building?"

"Yeah, and I'll include some pictures of this one."

Once he'd snapped a series of photos, she steered him away from the building. "You have your evidence; now let's go or we'll be late." She power walked ahead.

"Late for what?"

Mira didn't answer and she didn't slow down, forcing Jake to pick up the pace to match her hurried steps. Up until now they'd been making good time, but she didn't want to take any chances on their next adventure.

They emerged onto Quai de l'Hôtel de Ville, the Seine River sparkling on the other side of the road.

"Come on," she called.

She scurried down the stone staircase that led to the riverbank, anticipation building with every second.

And then, she saw it.

It was far from majestic and close to horrifying—a lineup at least a hundred people deep, queued behind a Seine River tour boat.

"Shit."

"A boat ride!" Jake said, full of cheer, and apparently blind to the lineup of sweaty bodies waiting to embark.

She checked the time. "These boats don't leave until forty-five minutes past the hour every hour." She frowned at all the people in line. "So why are all these losers almost half an hour early?"

"Let's just get in line and see what happens."

Mira admired Jake's optimism, but the harshness of reality was already casting a shadow. Despite her pessimism, she didn't want to dismiss his hopeful approach, so she followed him toward the back of the line.

As they made their way closer, she did her best to avert her eyes from all the people. If she didn't, she knew she would wind up counting them up, and then applying that amount to the estimated number of spots on the boat. It was the sort of mental math she'd excelled in during grade school, but if she did it here, it would only destroy her thin shred of hope.

While she ultimately succeeded in avoiding the exact headcount, with frequent glances she was able to eyeball the number of humans in batches of ten. It wasn't looking good.

As Jake and Mira took their spot in the back, a man in a fluorescent orange vest made his way over. "How many?" he asked, in a voice that made it clear he'd been doing this all day.

It took Mira a moment to process the miracle of not getting immediately kicked out of the line, but she managed to conceal her dorky glee and calmly gestured to Jake. "There's two of us."

The man consulted the electronic tablet in his hands. "It will be fifty euros for the twenty forty-five departure time."

She nodded happily until the military math added up. "You mean . . . eight forty-five p.m.?" The fluorescent-clad man simply shrugged. "But that's in over two hours."

"It is Friday evening in the summer," he explained. "High season."

She looked off into the distance, hapless and hopeless. "Right . . ."

"We can wait," Jake said. "I don't mind."

She barely heard him. Instead, she felt herself wandering out of the queue, and before long, she heard Jake jogging up behind her. "Are you sure you wouldn't rather wait it out?"

"It's not worth it," she said sadly. "Our time is so limited, and I don't want to waste two hours of it standing in line."

"*Our* time?"

She quickly realized what that one-word variation truly meant, like earlier in the day when Jake had inadvertently *we'd* them. Had she used that word on purpose or was it simply a slip of the tongue? Either way, she wasn't about to engage in some sort of riverbank confessional. "Yeah *our*," she said coolly. "We only had an extra twenty-four hours to spend in Paris, remember? Which means *our* official time—until the flight tomorrow—is really ticking down."

"Oh," he said, his placid expression refusing to reveal his true thoughts. "I guess that makes sense."

Jake's ambiguous words were good enough to shift from the awkward topic, which in this case, meant staring at the river with longing. "I was *so* looking forward to it, though," she said. "Dammit."

"Just think; this morning you were about to leave Paris with a whole list of things you hadn't done."

She looked back at him, starting to see the beginnings of his wisdom. "That's true."

"But look at you now," he added, throwing in some jazz hands to emphasize the positive angle. "Just living it up in Paris!"

The jazz hands combined with his sunny attitude instantly made things better. "You're totally right."

"I am. Now how about you check that list of yours to see what's next, hmm?"

Despite his pep talk, she could feel renewed frustration brewing from within. "I guess it's just . . . I mean, the sun's really hot so I'm feeling kinda off, and I think I'm hungover too." She frowned. "And I really wanted to float across the river with the magical views!" She felt herself pouting. "It's just a lot, you know?"

"Day hangovers are rough," he agreed. "But you know what the best cure is?" She shook her head. "More wine."

Jake had a point; wine solved everything, or at least that was what she'd read on a novelty wineglass one time. "Okay," she said. "Let's hit up the Left Bank."

The Left Bank—or everything south of the Seine River—had so far been a mystery to Mira and Jake, as their Bloom business meetings and dinners had been happening in offices and upscale restaurants in the city's livelier Right Bank.

As they made their way back up the stairs, her curiosity about the Left Bank managed to lift her mood. Maybe it would even be a fun adventure.

They crossed the bridge to Île de la Cité, home of the Notre-Dame Cathedral. She'd completely forgotten they'd pass by the cathedral, despite her intricate knowledge of the Paris map. She'd also forgotten it was still under restoration, since that fated day when it had nearly burned down, to the collective horror of the history-and-architecture-loving world. But there it was, partially obscured by a construction barrier.

The partition had blocked off the expansive square that would normally be filled with tourists, leaving today's dozen or so onlookers to admire Notre-Dame's gothic exterior from the road behind the barrier.

Mira's footsteps slowed as she approached. She felt herself entering a trancelike state, her memory taking her back to the bright orange flames that had dominated every viral news clip from that day. "Yup," she murmured. "*That* happened."

Jake came up behind her. "Thinking about the fire?"

"I knew the cathedral wasn't ready for my bucket-list eyes, so I hadn't even thought about it for this trip." She sighed. "It's just so strange to see it like this, in the midst of all this architectural surgery." She shook her head sadly. "No boat ride, depressing cathedral . . . quite the Friday evening in Paris."

"You really *are* in the middle of a daytime hangover," he said, trying not to laugh.

"Affirmative."

"But look at the bright side," he urged. "Isn't the front of the cathedral still intact?"

"Yeah."

"And can't you still see most of it?" He pointed to the top. "Like the special uhh . . . architectural carvings with all those uhh . . . gremlins?"

She immediately laughed. "Gargoyles!"

"Yeah, *those* things! Pretty awesome, right?"

Mira wasn't sure if he was joking about the gremlin thing, but he sure had a way of looking at the bright side, and she couldn't help but admire it.

"Let's keep going," she said. "I'll save the photo for my next visit."

Jake and Mira now made their way down Petit Pont or Little Bridge, for a short walk that would take them directly to the Left Bank.

The Left Bank was vast, spanning from the Eiffel Tower and the 15th arrondissement below it in the west, all the way past Jardin des Plantes and the 13th arrondissement in the east. While the atmosphere vacillated between quiet residential pockets and historical hot spots teeming with tourists, overall, the area had a quality that bordered on sleepy, with minimal nightlife compared to its northern counterpart.

Mira and Jake finished crossing the bridge and took their first official Left Bank steps, landing them in the 5th arrondissement, famously known as the Latin Quarter. This neighborhood was home to the Sorbonne, which Mira had once fantasized attending as an American on an adventure-filled semester abroad. Before long, she'd figured out how jaw-droppingly pricey that would be. Given the disadvantage of not having been born into the Rockefeller family, she abandoned any dreams of exchange-student exploits then and there.

Today, though, she could take it all in, along with the overall historical significance of the area. From the Panthéon, which entombed the remains of famous French icons like Voltaire and Victor Hugo, to the Cluny Museum of medieval artifacts, the past was very much alive in the 5th, between the bustling Rue Mouffetard market and a range of cafés and bistros.

Here, in the section of the Latin Quarter nearest to the river, the educational vibe lost out to a selection of overpriced tourist trap cafés and restaurants. The literary ghosts of Hemingway and Fitzgerald were just a few streets away at Café de Flore and Les Deux Magots, but even those famous spots drew a line by sharing a zip code with the posher and more refined 6th arrondissement.

Since these immediate surroundings in no way represented the best and brightest of Paris, Mira decided it was best to pass through quickly. Her plan was upended a few seconds later, when they stumbled upon the Shakespeare and Company bookshop.

"Whoa," she whispered. "I totally forgot that was here."

The original and most historically famous Shakespeare and Company was no more, but this current iteration facing the river was very much alive. It had opened its doors in 1951 under the original name of Le Mistral but was later renamed in honor of Sylvia Beach's famous bookshop (and with her blessing).

"Still pretty old," Mira said to herself, grasping for historical significance.

"What?"

She ignored Jake and continued to have herself a moment. "Pretty important too."

This may not have been the place where Sylvia Beach had famously published James Joyce's *Ulysses*, but it had still played host to live readings from Allen Ginsberg and Anaïs Nin, while carving out its own rich history of housing starving artists over the years. For those reasons, it remained a worthy literary beacon in Mira's eyes, despite having a home in the heart of the tacky tourist trap.

Jake edged closer to the bookshop. "You know, this place looks familiar."

"You would've seen it in *Before Sunset*," she explained. He seemed unsure. "Part two of the Richard Linklater trilogy." It wasn't registering with Jake. "The series of films where the characters spend the entire time having amazing conversations?"

He looked like he was searching through the various filing cabinets of his brain. "Still drawing a blank." And coming up empty.

She made a last attempt. "*Ethan Hawke* is in it?"

"Ethan Hawke! Yes. I've definitely seen it."

Mira had guessed right that the famous American actor would resonate with Jake, as opposed to the French actress, writer, sometimes musician, and overall tour de force Julie Delpy.

As Mira tentatively approached the shop, she couldn't help but wonder what the clearly underrated Julie Delpy really thought of the modern-day version of the bookshop. Since Mira couldn't ask her, she would simply have to experience it for herself, but before she could even make it to the entrance, she was inadvertently pushed aside by a throng of teenage girls.

Seconds later, the teens huddled together for a group selfie.

"You didn't get the whole *name* in," one of them whined, gesturing to the green sign hanging over the shop.

Mira found herself backing away. "Nah; we can skip it."

Jake gave her a gentle push. "Come on, it's famous; Ethan Hawke was here."

"It's actually a lot more famous for much more historical reasons," she mumbled.

"What?"

"I said we'll do a quick pop in!"

Shakespeare and Company was on Mira's bucket list, but it wasn't displayed in bold, nor featured in the largest font. It was one of those places that had such an interesting history and so much charm in photos, that you'd think it was almost too good to measure up to reality. And, if she'd learned anything from the *Amélie* café experience earlier in the day, it was best to avoid having unrealistic expectations.

The bookshop also reminded her of a childhood spent squirreled away in her bedroom writing anything and everything. That secret time had been the perfect escape from the awkward nightly dinners where her parents were only interested in hearing about her grades, or in judging her complexion under the harsh dining room lighting of money-saving LED bulbs.

Could she have made something of her writing if she hadn't given up? It was impossible to know the answer. All she knew was that she'd opted for the salary-plus-benefits world of marketing, a life of comfort, nice restaurants, and occasional fancy things. Which, if she was being honest, wasn't so bad.

The door chime jingled softly as Mira stepped into the shop. To her right, she noticed two cashiers in their early twenties, busy with a lineup of customers. Up ahead, she spotted several displays of books.

She passed by the section of books on all things Paris.

That's cute.

Beyond that, she saw a section of curated picks featuring middle grade and young adult titles.

Harry Potter. The Hunger Games. That best-selling love story where one of the teens is dying.

Without warning, Mira felt the first sharp pangs of a headache. She squeezed her eyes shut, trying to will away the pain.

"Are you okay?" Jake asked.

"Huh?" She opened her eyes.

"You look stressed, and now your left eye is twitching."

She instantly became aware of the rhythmic pulsation and covered her left eye. "Must be the air in here."

"They just made a movie about that," he said, pointing to one of those books about women who witness murders but aren't really believed because they drink too much wine. Mira loved those addictive novels, but what about the fact that Anaïs Nin had spent time here? Or that starving artists had worked here for room and board? That classic literary atmosphere was nowhere in sight, which made for an extremely conflicting experience.

"You don't like it here," he said. "I can tell."

She felt a rush of embarrassment. "God, am I doing it again?"

"Doing what?"

She blew a strand of hair from her face. "Looking on the bad side instead of the bright side."

"Well . . . *are you*?"

She did another scan of her surroundings. There had to be something she was missing.

And then, she saw it. A small, tattered sign that said LIBRARY, with an arrow pointing to the stairs.

Mira climbed up the narrow staircase. The first thing she spotted was a vintage typewriter on display. She wasn't sure if the typewriter had actually been used by one of the writers who used to live here, but it gave her a good feeling. She then saw a sign that prohibited flash photography. That had to mean this room held historical significance.

She noticed the bookshelves next. Each shelf was filled with dusty old titles predating modern publishing; there wasn't a single glossy cover in sight. She carefully pulled out one of the books, bringing it over to a velvet-upholstered bench that was bolted into the wall.

Jake sat down next to her, his presence coming as a bit of a surprise, given how deeply immersed she'd been in her literary exploration.

"What's the book about?" he asked.

"Not sure." She flipped through the yellowed pages and inhaled deeply. "I'm just here for that musty old book smell."

"Was it everything you dreamed it would be?"

She wasn't sure if Jake was asking about the smell or the bookstore, but if the question referred to both of those things, her answer would likely be mixed.

That was the thing about daydreams, though; they only offered up a hopeful glimpse, and after that, you had to make the discoveries for yourself.

CHAPTER
ten

⌐

Seven p.m.

Jake followed Mira out of the bookshop. He could tell she'd had mixed feelings about it, but he was hoping to see a seismic shift in her mood within the next few hours. It all hinged on his special surprise, and whether it would actually work out.

Colette still hadn't confirmed if she'd be able to help Jake with his idea, and he was getting the sense she was questioning his motives. He couldn't really blame her, when the night before at the restaurant, he'd spent the evening treating Mira like a pest he'd been forced to interact with, due to their flimsy coworker connection. Since then, everything had changed. Hour by hour, Jake had been having a wonderful time with Mira. It was a great feeling, but admitting that to Colette was not the way to get in her good books.

When Jake had been brainstorming ways to convince Colette to help him out, he'd almost explained the idea as a Make-A-Wish type thing, only, the fear of bad karma had stopped him. He'd ultimately landed on a sob story of a coworker in debt, one who had already spent two thousand dollars on a last-minute flight. He'd concluded with an inspirational flourish, by playing up how this one little thing might cheer her up after a truly terrible day. The money thing wasn't even a lie, really, as Mira had clearly been worried about the additional costs of an extra day in Paris. The fact that the company had ultimately covered the flight cost? Just a small detail he didn't feel the need to mention to Colette.

With the fate of the evening now firmly in the hands of Colette and her connections, Jake quietly followed Mira down the street. With each step, he convinced himself that if Colette wanted to see him badly enough, she would find a way to bring this surprise to life.

He paused midstride, wondering if he was slowly becoming the Julia Roberts character in a gender reversal of *Pretty Woman*. Was he *Pretty Man*? Given his current tactic of dangling his eggplant emoji on a highly conditional string, maybe he was. Or maybe this was all just an innocent favor for the benefit of a hopeless colleague.

"I need to sit down," Mira suddenly announced.

As he studied her face, he wondered if the blazing sun had gotten to be too much. "Are you dehydrated? Dizzy?"

She reached for the baguette in her tote bag and ripped off the crusty end, wasting no time in popping it into her mouth. "I need to eat again," she mumbled, "so I need to sit down."

It didn't seem like the right moment to question Mira's urge for additional food, so he turned the corner and followed. A few seconds later, he found himself standing in front of a charming little park. It was one of those spaces that barely left a footprint on the map, a green space so small, you could walk the entire perimeter in under a minute.

Mira headed for the only bench and sat down. He settled in beside her, watching as she furiously unwrapped the various packages of cheese. Her eyes were so focused, she didn't even notice what was right there in front of her. He finally gave her a nudge. "Look."

She followed his gaze across the river, to the unobstructed side view of the Notre-Dame cathedral. The cheese she'd been holding fell into her lap. "Wow."

"I know it's still missing some parts because of the fire," he acknowledged, "but it's better than when you tried to see it up close; right?"

"Definitely better."

Jake watched her closely, waiting to see if she'd switch gears to a pessimistic follow-up. He wouldn't have been surprised, given the recent misses in her quest for a perfect day in Paris. He may not have fully understood why she needed these moments so intensely, but if discovering that magic made her happy, he wanted to help her find it.

"I'm so happy I got to see this," she said.

He was glad to see that look of wonder in her eyes, but it faded out sooner than expected. With renewed fervor, she dug into the packages of cheese.

"Hungry, huh?" He cringed at his lame attempt to keep the conversation going.

Why don't you just talk about the weather, shit-bird?

"Yes and no," Mira said, not explaining anything at all.

"If you're not hungry, wouldn't you rather save this stuff for the picnic?"

Her expression was a patronizing one. "Ohhh, Jake . . ."

"What?"

"Haven't you ever eaten in response to a need for emotional comfort, stemming from a series of unexpected moments that covered both spectrums of the emotional roller coaster called life?"

She looked at him like it was the most obvious statement in the world, but he was too overwhelmed by the scope of her words to formulate a quick response. The way she spoke reminded him of his philosophy professor in college. The professor taught an elective course that Jake had only taken to get an easy credit, or at least that was how he'd explained it to his frat buddies. In reality, he'd taken the class as a way to gain some deeper meaning about existence, something he felt he needed while he watched his mother struggle through her illness. In the end, the professor's sweeping statements had all been a bit too much, so he'd dropped the course and instead, wound up listening to his favorite Radiohead album more often than any normal human should.

When it came to Mira's confusing question, he could easily nod and wait for a change in topic, but unlike that class in college, he felt the desire to understand her meaning.

"You mean *emotional* eating?" he asked, taking a stab in the dark.

"Yeah, sort of. Except people always associate emotional eating with a bad breakup or that Emma Stone GIF where she's sobbing into a tub of ice cream."

"That's kind of what I was picturing, to be honest."

"But it's *more* than that," she insisted. "Emotional eating can cover as many emotions as there are, and it's not always a bad thing."

"I've always liked birthday cake," he said fondly.

She looked at him strangely. "Okay . . ."

He instantly became uncomfortable, much like those times in that philosophy class when he felt like he'd given the wrong answer. And just like then, it was time to turn it back on the prof. "So, what you're saying is—"

"That sometimes when it's been *a day*," she said, mercifully taking the bait, "eating all the things is a major comfort. Like stressfully cramming for an exam and then writing it and then tossing it at the professor and then getting the hell out of there?" She shuddered. "Talk about *a day*. And missing a flight to Paris plus whatever the last eight hours have been? *A day*."

Maybe she wasn't being so confusing after all.

"It's definitely been a day," he said. "I'll have some of that bread and cheese now."

Mira handed him a package of cheese, but he didn't quite know what to do with the soft gooey substance. "Got a knife?"

She pulled out a small wooden implement. "Saw these on the counter at the cheese shop and snagged a few. Could come in handy tomorrow morning, if I find myself in a spreading-butter-in-the-streets situation."

And just like that, he was back to being baffled. "Excuse me?"

"Obviously I'm going to treat myself to a morning baguette slathered in butter." She cut into the block of hard cheese that was balanced on her leg. "I'd take it on the plane if I could, but baguettes don't travel well."

"Sounds sensible." An alarming thought creeped into his mind. "If we eat all this now, is the picnic canceled?"

Jake imagined how nice it would be to sip wine and talk and lounge on the grass. A moment later he returned to reality, all too aware of what a cheese-bag daydream that really was.

"It doesn't mean it's canceled at all," Mira said, sounding surprisingly worry-free. "We'll do the picnic after we take a little stroll to get some wine, and after I grab my dinner."

"Dinner?" he sputtered, almost choking on a piece of baguette. "You'll be hungry again that soon?"

"It's less about hunger and more about a final chance to carb-load. Otherwise, with more wine plus the cocktails later," she shook her head, "it'll be a scene, man."

"And where will you be having these cocktails?"

"Well, after you leave for your *hot* date"—she paused to get a smirk in—"I plan on checking out a cocktail bar that's been getting a lot of attention."

If Jake's special surprise for Mira panned out, they wouldn't be parting ways as quickly as she assumed. But the point of the surprise was to keep her in the dark. "Cool; and what's on tap after the cocktail bar?"

"Just the shitty hotel room, I guess."

The thought of Mira spending a night alone in that dreadful hotel room seemed horrible. He could save the day by ditching Colette and spending the rest of his time with Mira, but after the downpour and the kiss that didn't happen, he still wasn't sure if she saw him as more than a friend. He might have been more open if it were eight or ten years ago, but ever since his only serious girlfriend had left him for a job in Australia, the casual encounters had always been the easier option.

There was also the other reason, the one preventing him from getting close to anyone at all on this trip. But he had no intention of bringing that up to Mira.

He ripped off a piece of the crusty baguette, stuffing it into his mouth along with a glob of cheese.

He was now a full-blown emotional eater.

It's been a day.

*

While Jake had enjoyed their pit stop in the tiny park, he was excited to get to the main event of a grassy picnic and a bottle of wine.

Mira zoomed in on her digital map. "Can we take the longer way to the wine shop?"

Her detour would mean delaying the anticipated main event, but he wasn't about to interfere with her quest for Parisian magic.

"I literally don't know the difference between the shorter way and the longer way."

"Longer way it is."

They turned into a pedestrian cobblestoned street packed with tourists. The aromas of fries and savory dishes wafted out of restaurants on either side of them, and Jake couldn't help but inhale it all in. "Damn; maybe eating semiconstantly isn't a bad idea after all."

"No," she said, a one-word statement that threw him off his game.

"*No*? I'm going to need you to elaborate."

"We're in the tourist trap," she whispered. "Beware of waiters who are waving, smiling, and beckoning for your business."

Ten seconds later that exact thing happened. Jake shook his head in amazement. "You're good."

"You also don't want these souvenirs," she explained, gesturing to a display of Paris-themed aprons and placemats. "The better stuff is in Montmartre. And it's cheaper."

"Weren't we already there?"

"Yup. And I'll be back there in the morning after I leave that crap-ass hotel."

"Makes sense," he said, before almost getting trampled by a family of tourists shouting at each other in German. "But you know what doesn't make sense?"

"What?"

"It doesn't make sense why you're taking the *longer* way, if it means going through a tourist trap."

"I needed to see something. And actually, it should be *right* here."

They swung a left and the crowd thinned out, giving way to a wider pedestrian street. At its edge was a cathedral that looked like it had been there for almost a thousand years.

"Looks old," he remarked.

"Old as fuck." She stopped to take it all in. "Incredible."

"Want to go inside?"

She scoffed. "I don't have time for that. I just figured if I couldn't see the gothic stylings of Notre-Dame *close up*, this might work as a quick little sideshow."

"Smart," he said. "And hey look: one of those gremlin things!"

Mira immediately laughed and it gave him a warm feeling, like he'd be perfectly happy to hear that laugh every day. It was the sort of feeling he couldn't help, which only deepened the inner battle between backing off and living in the moment. "Should we keep going? I don't want to miss that picnic."

"We won't," she said, before finally peeling her eyes away from the gargoyles. She took a quick look at the map. "We'll go right, then left, then Boulevard Saint-Germain and then the wine shop."

Jake didn't quite catch the French-sounding part, so he focused on what he did best and followed.

After making the first turn, they were hit with a strange sight: a large Canadian flag hanging from a weathered facade.

"Books . . ." she murmured.

Mira was right, there were two small tables on either side stacked with books.

As they drew nearer, he could feel her excitement building. "And no young adult titles," she said. She peeked inside the open doorway and gasped. "Do you see that? It actually looks like you're *in* a Harry Potter book."

Jake understood what she meant. There were books stacked tall, books stacked diagonally, and books bursting out of the packed shelves. As for the two aisles, they were incredibly narrow and running in a crooked line.

"Look how everything's bathed in a warm yellow light," she sighed.

The shop was empty aside from a man who looked to be in his fifties. When they saw him headed for the doorway they stepped aside, watching as he grabbed a stack of books from the table.

"*Bonsoir*," she exclaimed.

"Bonsoir," the man said in a kindly voice. "Where are you from?" he added, in a North American accent. He glanced back for an answer as he brought the books inside.

"New York," she answered.

Jake could see how intently Mira was staring at the man, and he knew exactly what she wanted.

"Are you closed?" she asked, as the man came back and grabbed the next stack.

"About forty minutes ago," he said sheepishly, making his way back inside. "I lost track of time," he called out.

Mira nudged Jake. "He lost track of time," she whispered. "Like a clumsy Harry Potter professor."

Jake was enjoying her enthusiasm, but that didn't mean he wasn't going to mock her. "Don't the clumsy, innocent-seeming ones turn into Voldemort?"

"Shush," she hissed, as the man reemerged from inside.

The man must've sensed her desperate thirst to browse around the shop, because he gestured to the doorway and smiled. "I already fell behind on the closing time once, so why not twice? Go ahead."

Jake looked over at Mira and could see that she was holding back a squeal. He turned to the owner and smiled. "Thank you," he said, giving Mira a moment to gather herself. "It's an amazing shop and we'd love to check it out."

"Do you like coffee?" the man said as he followed them inside. "I just made a fresh batch."

Jake and Mira exchanged an excited glance. "I mean, it *has* been a day," he whispered.

She nodded. "Yes please."

In between the narrow bookshelves, the man had somehow made room for a pot of coffee and paper cups.

She elbowed Jake. "Look, a secret coffee section."

"Maple syrup?" the man asked. Jake and Mira stared at him blankly. "Well, I *am* Canadian."

The man, they learned, was the owner of The Abbey Bookshop, and so far, he was proving the nice Canadian stereotype true.

"Let's go with maple syrup," Jake said. "Because you know, when in Paris, do as the Canadians do."

The man laughed gently. "I like him."

Jake's eyeballs boomeranged back to Mira. He was dying to know how she'd react to that statement. Would she agree and make her feelings known? The rational side of his brain was telling him he shouldn't care, but that didn't stop him from wondering.

She simply shrugged. "He's all right."

Jake may not have gotten an emotional soliloquy, but the gentle teasing made him happy, and the coffee laced with maple syrup proved to be a winner too.

The cave-like basement of the bookshop was another highlight, with a low, carved-out ceiling, and a wealth of books on history and philosophy.

As they browsed every corner of the charming shop, Jake made sure to give Mira the space to get high off all the bookish ecstasy. It may have meant taking a break from their enjoyable conversation—while he pretended to browse the teachings of Aristotle from a distance—but it had given him the chance to truly see her in her element. And he enjoyed that too.

At the end of it all, she even made a few selections, and after paying for the books they waved good-bye, before continuing down the quiet cobblestoned street.

"Which one do you think you'll read first?" Jake asked.

"*Shakespeare's Monologues for Women*," she said firmly. She peered into the paper bag and examined her purchases. "Or maybe the one about the visual history of the changing map of Paris." She frowned. "Actually, I've been looking at maps all day. So, Voltaire." She nodded. "Definitely the philosophical musings of Voltaire."

"Sounds like you've got yourself a plan."

Jake found Mira's enthusiasm for books as cute as her love of envelope-shaped crêpes, domed ceilings, crème brûlée macarons, and a half dozen other things he'd found to be endearing about this woman so unlike his usual hookups and one-night stands.

He just didn't know how to take the leap from silent admiration to something that could stretch beyond the next few hours. Especially now, when Colette had texted back, confirming that his surprise for Mira was a go—but only if he held up his end of the deal to spend the night with Colette.

The time really was ticking down then. He just hoped the look on Mira's face would be worth it.

"Oh shit," she said suddenly.

"What's wrong?"

"The wine shop closes in two minutes, and . . . unlike the book-shop, I don't think they'll have a lenient closing time."

"Dammit," he said, thinking that his chance for a cozy picnic was over.

"How about grocery store wine?" she suggested. "They still have good options, and it's not like our basic asses could tell the difference anyway."

He let out a small sigh of relief. "Sure," he said. "I don't care."

The trouble was, Jake was starting to care a lot about his time that remained with Mira. This picnic would be their last one-on-one opportunity, and preserving that experience meant everything to him. Even if none of it would matter once they made it back to New York.

That was tomorrow's problem.

CHAPTER
eleven

M

Eight p.m.

Things with Jake were feeling date-y.

Mira understood that "date-y" wasn't anything approaching an actual word, but no one could argue that it wasn't a vibe. This palpable feeling was the best description for the energy flowing between herself and Jake, and she couldn't help but embrace it.

There was, however, one little thing that conflicted with Mira's assessment. The last two hours had been heavily focused on bookstores, a fact that made her date-y label crumble under the scrutiny of Tinder law. Then again, there were several precedents in landmark romantic comedies to support her claim. The unplanned date . . . the strolling-around date . . . the browsing-around-a-bookstore date . . . the lamenting-the-destruction-of-a-historic-cathedral date . . . or maybe that last one was a stretch.

The more date-like things became, the easier it was to stop obsessing over Dev's Instagram story, fifteen seconds that had cycled through her brain at least a dozen times. Her former fiancé was moving on, even if it was just a temporary fling to get over things. So why not her?

Why not indeed, as Mira found herself increasingly drawn to Jake, even if it was only temporary too. It wasn't just the way he made her smile when she was feeling glum, it was his sharp sense of humor and his openness to having new experiences. From macarons and big staircases to dousing himself in new cologne, he always seemed willing to give things a chance, whereas Dev had always seemed to shy away from stepping outside of his comfort zone. There was nothing technically wrong with sticking to what worked, but it no longer fit with someone like Mira, who was still figuring out what made her happy.

What made her happy for the moment, was being around Jake, someone who felt like a wonderful breath of fresh air. In the context of time, however, he was more of a passing breeze, and just as soon as you started to bask in the feeling, he'd move on to the contentment of the next sun-soaked face in his path.

The next face he'd see would belong to the waitress, but until that time, Mira would revel in every second that remained.

They emerged from the Franprix grocery store, armed with rosé and paper cups. They had one stop left before the picnic, but as Mira glanced to her right, taking in the bustling Boulevard Saint-Germain, she couldn't help but think of something else. "Maybe another time . . ." she said, sighing.

"Come on," he said teasingly, "don't hold back if there's something you need to see."

"There isn't," she insisted. "I was merely taking note of the fact that just down the way, you'll find two iconic cafés that were once the literary hotspots for writers of the Lost Generation." She pointed to the green awning. "See that sign? Les Deux Magots. And right next to it you have . . ." she squinted her eyes, "I mean, you can't really see it, but beside it is Café de Flore."

"That's major," he said, though it was clear he didn't know how major it was at all.

"Maybe we can just pass by it."

"Are you sure that'll be enough?"

With only twenty-four hours to roam Paris, limited discretionary income, and a mere two hours remaining with Jake, Mira was getting used to bite-size experiences being enough.

"It's fine," she said. "I mean it has to be; because it's either a brief walk-by, or we hang out in the café and miss the picnic."

Jake was suddenly at full attention. "Brief walk-by."

To her surprise, he took her hand and led her down the boulevard at a hurried pace. He weaved through groups of tourists and the elderly in a deft manner, as she marveled at the feeling of his strong hand gripping hers tight. The last time he'd held her hand like that, they'd been getting soaked by the rain, a memory that made her aware of each nerve ending in her body.

They slowed to a stop in front of Les Deux Magots, the first iconic café.

She felt a wave of disappointment when he dropped her hand, but to fill the ensuing void, she focused on the famous café.

Unfortunately, it didn't quite do the trick.

It wasn't like she'd been expecting the terrace patrons to be decked out in the latest 1920s fashions, but the modern folks with their smartphones and trendy clothes and complicated shoes were a little too removed from Hemingway's musings in his memoir *A Moveable Feast*. She was again reminded of that moment from earlier in the day, when she had sipped the average coffee in the famed café from *Amélie*. Maybe it *was* the smarter choice not to scratch beneath the daydream surface, especially when the reality of the day had turned out so much better than she ever could've planned.

After passing Café de Flore, which had a similar energy—plus a smattering of tourists taking photos of the famous terrace—Jake paused midstride.

"I don't know where we are anymore," he confessed.

She remained charmed by his navigational effort, short-lived as it was. "We're actually on the way to get that dinner of mine."

"Oh yeah," he said, checking his watch. "I forgot about that."

"It'll be fast, I promise."

Within minutes, Mira and Jake were standing in line at a sandwich shop. This was not your average place to pick up a ham-and-cheese baguette, or a caprese-style baguette, or the many other kinds of baguette sandwiches you could find in almost any corner shop. This was the kind of place with made-to-order options and fresh-baked bread, a place with so many tantalizing sandwich ingredients, that deciding what to order was the hardest part.

"I'm hungry," he said, clearly entranced by the sights and smells.

"You don't want to spoil your appetite before your big date," she said, making every effort to sound casual and not at all jealous.

"Won't ten o'clock be too late for dinner?" He looked to her for answers, like she somehow had a role to play in planning his hookup agenda.

"Not if you don't have kids to put to bed." She tried her best to sound encouraging, even though she wanted him to cancel. "Besides, the sun won't even set until, like, ten." She smiled. "The night is young."

"Sure, but I doubt there will be any food on the . . ." He caught himself like he'd almost revealed a season finale spoiler.

"Don't worry, Jake," she said, with a wise and worldly air, "it's none of my business if you're having *dessert* for dinner."

He lowered his head, their eyes meeting straight on. "Are you jealous or something?"

It was clear that her attempt to sound wise and worldly had failed. The resulting possibility of Jake catching on that she was jealous felt embarrassing. She was loving being in the moment with him, of course she was, but she didn't love the thought of him knowing how she truly felt. Especially not when it was looking more and more like he wasn't going to cancel the date.

Perhaps things would've been different if she'd kissed him in the doorway.

Dammit.

She may not have been able to change the past, but she could certainly change the subject. "The only thing I'm jealous of is whatever's on his tray." She gestured to a tall man headed to the seating area.

"That does look good," Jake admitted, appraising the sandwich stuffed with fresh ingredients.

Mira stepped forward, her turn up next, and with a bit of effort, she managed to request all her chosen ingredients in French—with only two brief looks of impatience from the young cashier.

"Can you ask her to make two?" Jake whispered in her ear.

Mira could feel his warm breath right against her neck. It gave her a rush that made it difficult to focus. "But . . . you don't even know which ingredients I picked."

"It's okay," he said, his lips so close she could almost feel his touch. "I trust you."

*

Armed with fresh sandwiches, Mira and Jake made the short walk to Jardin du Luxembourg. A part of her was still buzzing from the way Jake had made her feel, but it slowly faded into a different sort of excitement; she'd been waiting to see these sprawling gardens all day.

As she and Jake passed through the open wrought-iron gate, they nearly collided with a pair of joggers getting their evening cardio in.

"Whoa!" she gasped, jumping back just in time. It could've been enough to throw her off her garden-loving game, but this wasn't like earlier in the day, when micromoments not explained in the blogs had nearly sent her on a disenchantment tailspin. Whenever that had happened before, Jake had always been there to pick her back up. This time though, she wouldn't need his intervention. This was Luxembourg-fucking-Gardens, and she wouldn't allow the most grand and exquisite park in Paris to disappoint her.

"Which way?" he asked.

The gravelly path they were on formed the circular perimeter of the gardens, a popular route for joggers, but not so much for meanderers who weren't quite sure where to go.

The fastest way to the picnicking area was to the left, but on the right-hand side, the path sloped downward. From Mira's research, she knew exactly where that slope would lead.

"To the right," she said.

It wasn't long before they rounded the corner, finding themselves in an otherworldly nook. This tucked-away area was home to the Medici Fountain, a broad structure with carved columns situated at the end of a long, rectangular pool. It featured a statue in greenish blue, a shade that paired nicely with the surface of the pool—which captured the reflection of leafy tree branches swaying overhead. The lingering evening sun had lost its way in the maze of branches, giving Mira the sense that she'd passed through a moody portal.

She approached the pool with shuffled steps, completely taken in by the atmosphere.

"Is this where we're having the picnic?" Jake asked, gesturing to the chairs surrounding the pool, but sounding a little disappointed.

Mira didn't blame him, as this wasn't exactly the sort of place where you'd gulp down rosé and smash carbs into your face and play cards and hold hands and make out. This was the place where you'd stare off into the distance, or better yet, stare into the depths of the reflecting pool, as you nostalgically played back the good, the bad, and the ugly moments of the dance called life.

Officially speaking, Mira's dramatic scenario wasn't the fountain's official use, but from the first time she'd laid eyes on a photo of the Medici Fountain, its broody vibe had enraptured her.

As Mira studied the faces of the people surrounding the fountain and its pool, she noticed that not a single face belonged to a child. The elderly man taking a drag from his cigarette stood out the most, his wrinkled face full of melancholy. Was he reflecting on the one that got away?

Mira leaned on the railing and stared into the pool, her own reflective moment now upon her. Compared to the old man whose narrative she'd just invented, Mira hadn't lost someone, she'd simply said no to the man who didn't fit inside her reality for happiness. But if she'd played her cards so differently than the sad old man, she had to wonder why she found herself feeling as broody as he looked. Maybe it was how her past decisions were completely reshaping her future. A future of starting over at almost thirty-five. Terrifying, to say the least.

Mira took a break from the melancholy pool and noticed Jake staring, not at the pool but at her. Somehow, his eyes were full of brightness.

"Not the place for the picnic, then?"

She didn't know how Jake had managed to stay impervious to the gloomy surroundings, but his can-do attitude was just as endearing as always. Maybe more. "No, definitely not the place." She stepped back from the railing. "I just needed to see the fountain for . . . historical purposes."

He gave the fountain a quick scan. "Cool."

As they turned back onto the gravel path, Jake unexpectedly stopped. "Want to throw a coin in the fountain?"

She stared at him blankly.

"To make a wish?" he added.

"No thanks," she said abruptly, her mind traveling back to that time Dev had asked her to close her eyes and throw a coin into the Central Park fountain. They hadn't been seeing each other long back then, so she'd been instantly charmed by his coin-tossing move—and had of course made a wish that centered on a future with Dev. Maybe one day she would laugh about it all, but for now it was a little too soon.

"Are you sure?" Jake said, the sound of his voice reminding her she wasn't in Manhattan. "You can wish for anything."

She almost gave in, wanting to wish that Jake would ditch the waitress and spend the rest of the evening with her. She wouldn't be gambling her whole future on the coin, just one night; was that so bad?

"Nah," she said, managing to quell the urge. "I'm good."

He took a step closer, confronting her head-on. "Don't you believe in wishes or magic?"

"I do."

He seemed confused. "You do?"

"Yes," she confirmed. "I'm actually very superstitious. But only for the bad stuff."

He scoffed and spun around. "One of these days," he said, shaking his head, "I'm going to figure out what that dark little corner of your mind is all about."

She managed a chuckle, letting him assume she'd enjoyed his little joke. What was really on her mind was how difficult it was to compute his wording of "one of these days." The only thing she could process was how unlikely it was for this intense, hour-by-hour interaction to extend past the next two hours, let alone beyond the borders of France. Would they start hanging out nonstop in New York? She could hardly imagine being first in line at one of his next sales parties. It was all just a silly daydream.

The gravel pathway gave way to a needed distraction, in the form of the impressive Luxembourg Palace. It was a landmark with a seventeenth-century royal past, and a present-day function of holding meetings for the senate. But Mira wasn't concerned with what went on inside the building. She was too busy admiring the beautifully manicured flowerbeds surrounding it.

She looked away and was hit with another distraction; a fountain, only this time it wasn't a fountain of murky regrets tailor-made for your inner masochist. This one was cheery and circular in form, filled with little boats being steered by little children, each of them standing at the fountain's edge and wielding not-so-little wooden sticks. The fountain was encircled by parents sitting in the park's green chairs, comfortably watching their children play while soaking up some after-dinner sun.

Mira tentatively approached the fountain. She made sure to stay a few feet back, a move that allowed her to watch the children without seeming like a predator. Jake stood beside her and pointed at the girl in the striped dress. "She's the best with the boats," he declared.

Mira turned her attention to the girl, and within seconds, it was clear that he'd been right. The little girl was the confident captain of her little toy ship, and it was a lovely thing to see. Mira sighed, and second by second, the broody energy from earlier floated out of her body.

She nudged Jake. "You hungry?"

"I was already hungry at the sandwich shop."

"See that lawn over there?" She pointed to the area at the opposite end of the palace. "That's where we're going."

He seemed excited by this prospect, so excited in fact, that she got the sense he was forcing himself not to power walk. It was cute.

Mira maintained a slower pace, which managed to keep Jake somewhat tethered; it also gave her time to admire their surroundings in more detail. A set of stone steps gave way to a second level, complete with an outdoor café, bandstand, and more clusters of revelers lounging in chairs.

"The next time I'm in Paris, I'm coming here every day," she said.

"Then I'll see you there."

Right.

Mira felt the sudden buzz of her phone. It was another text from Sophie:

Sha-la-la-la-la-la KISS THE BOY

Sophie had added the crab emoji, making it clear she'd been paying homage to Sebastian from *The Little Mermaid*, or more specifically, his river serenade when he tries to convince Eric to kiss Ariel.

As Mira put her phone away, she barely managed to keep a straight face. She wasn't sure if Sophie was already watching Disney movies with her six-month-old, or if she'd gone a bit loopy from lack of sleep. Whichever it was, time was moving fast, and despite her best friend's encouragement, Mira was running out of courage to make a move.

They approached the grassy section of the gardens next, an area made up of three rectangular lawns positioned side by side. The one in the middle was crowded with picnickers.

Food, drinks, and merriment. These were the things that encompassed the prevailing energy, a stark contrast to the Luxembourg Gardens that Hemingway had described in so much detail, with hard snow crunching underneath his feet and bare trees surrounding him at every turn. But that was fine. These summer joys would've probably been lost on the legendary author, unlike Mira, who had so much range she could stare into the bleakness of reflecting pools while also enjoying the laughter of children. Or perhaps she was being borderline unhinged to declare superiority over Hemingway. It had been a long day.

"What's in the sandwich?" Jake suddenly asked. "I know it was roasted turkey and I saw some tomato, too, but then I lost track of what was happening."

Her thoughts on Hemingway flew out of her head, replaced by her favorite topic. "For your information, the tomato was marinated in extra virgin olive oil and *Herbes de Provence*."

"Fancy."

"And I'll explain the rest when it's feeding time."

Jake jogged up to the edge of the lawn. "It's feeding time!" He didn't seem to care that everyone was looking at him strangely. Yet another thing she found appealing.

As Mira glanced at her watch, it was clear that her list of great things about Jake would soon transform from real-time observations to a memory. He would either leave for that date in an hour, or he would change his mind and stay.

But only if he had a good reason.

The surefire way to make him stay was to match the seductive skills of the waitress. Mira glanced down at her fanny pack, followed by the sneakers with the orthopedic insoles. And then she remembered how attractive the waitress had looked.

With Mira's harsh assessment complete, the plan for her final hour with Jake was settled.

Crush carbs into face. Drink feelings away.

CHAPTER
twelve

M

Nine p.m.

From the mind-blowing sandwich to the leftover macarons, Mira's carb-slamming plan was progressing nicely, and the wine wasn't half bad either. It was a fine thing; the way food and drink could fog the mind, effectively shielding it from matters of the heart.

As long as there was always enough.

She peered into her empty wine cup and shook her head.

"I need a top-up," she announced. "And remember," she added in a low voice, "be cool."

"You keep saying that, but I have yet to see one of these intimidating park security *special agents*."

"Because they're *that* good." Mira kept her eyes zeroed in on Jake. She watched his every move, making sure he didn't stray from the *ultradiscreet* wine-pouring tutorial she'd demonstrated earlier.

Exactly as instructed, Jake kept the base of the bottle hidden in the tote bag, before tipping it and making wine-to-cup contact without anyone being the wiser.

He handed her the cup. "Was that *secretive* enough for you?"

"You were supposed to casually whistle while you poured, but it's fine."

Mira wouldn't have normally been so uptight, but she'd read too many articles detailing how it was fine to chug booze on the riverbanks of Paris—or at the Eiffel Tower lawn, or at the other parks in Paris—but that Luxembourg Gardens was not okay with any of it. Which of course meant that everyone did it anyway, but in a very low-key manner. The last thing she wanted was to wind up getting tossed from the park during her final hour with Jake. It was this looming fear that made her deeply committed to breaking the rules without getting caught.

All they needed to do now was blend in, but as much as Jake tried, he wasn't making it easy.

He let out a belch, his second of the evening. "Sorry," he said sheepishly. "It's those pickled onions."

Mira didn't mind Jake's reaction to the onions, but before she could let him know, she found herself distracted by a couple passing by. They had a South Asian background just like her, along with the telltale sign of being recently married. "Look at those newlyweds," she said, trying to ignore the glaring irony. "They're so cute."

"How do you know they're newlyweds? I don't see a 'Just Married' sign attached to either of their asses. Or like that trail of cans and streamers . . ."

"Their asses aren't the back of a car," she said, smirking.

He shrugged and took a sip of wine. "But seriously, how can you tell?"

The man and wife dragged two chairs along the gravel, stopping when they found a quiet spot to sit down. "They're newlyweds because she's wearing the Punjabi *chura*," Mira said. "And by that, I mean the bangles." He nodded. "You typically keep them on for two weeks after getting married." The glaring irony was getting harder to ignore. "She's also got the hardcore *mehndi* going on, and when it's right up to the elbows like that, it can only be the look that's tailor-made for a bride." She had a sudden memory. "Except for that one time, when my cousin got the mehndi artist to give her a pattern as extravagant as the bride's; that was a shit show."

"I thought it was called henna," Jake said. "Like I distinctly recall the henna shop at Six Flags."

"*Six Flags*?"

"Yeah. It was where I took my girlfriend back in high school." He took a sip of wine. "It was actually more of a kiosk, between the cotton candy and hot dog stalls."

"Oh yeah?" Mira said, struggling to keep a straight face.

"I got her the biggest flowery design they had." He finally noticed Mira's expression. "What?"

"Oh, don't mind me; that was a charming little anecdote of cultural appropriation."

He lowered his head. "Sorry; I sounded dumb, didn't I?"

"I'm actually just messing with you."

"Promise?"

"Yup. It was a simple theme park world, and we were all just living in it." She leaned in. "But for future reference, henna is more of a co-opted Westernized term, whereas mehndi is how we say it in the South Asian world." He seemed embarrassed. "Don't feel bad though; it was a gripping tale, and don't let anyone tell you different."

"You literally just told me different!"

"I'm kinda buzzed," Mira admitted, as he gave her a playful shove. "By the way; was it a lower-back tattoo?"

Jake's lingering embarrassment transformed into indignation.

"What are you implying? That white girls can only get *lower-back* tattoos?"

"You're right, my bad." She coughed. "So, it *wasn't* a lower-back tattoo?"

"It was . . . it fucking was."

Mira immediately cackled, a release that was partially brought on by the rosé. By the time she'd calmed down, she noticed the newly-weds again. Their wedded bliss was unmistakable, making for a scene that was hard to watch without thinking of her own almost-wedding.

"Damn," she said.

"What is it?"

Judging by the look on Jake's face, she could see that he'd moved on from their playful exchange to showing genuine concern.

Mira felt the pull of her old habit, the one where she would bottle up her truest self. She'd been holding back the details of her personal life all day, and while it would've been easy to continue the pattern, she could feel the truth bubbling up to the surface. "I was engaged. Like, as of three weeks ago."

She watched Jake's expression change as he absorbed her sudden confession. When he didn't say anything, she gulped some wine and kept right on talking. "I was the one to break it off, and let's just say it did *not* go over well." She frowned. "Anyway . . . still feeling those aftershocks."

He took his time before responding. "If it's none of my business, you can ignore what I'm about to ask."

"It's okay; you can say whatever you're thinking."

Of course he could. This was twenty-four hours suspended from reality, or at least that was how she felt being in his presence.

"I guess I'm just wondering why you broke it off. Did he cheat on you or something?"

"Not at all. Officially speaking, he was kind of perfect." She reflected on Dev's standout qualities; the ones most women would've loved. "He was caring, generous, had a great career . . . my family and friends really loved him too."

"But what did *you* think?"

"For a while I thought he was great, even if we didn't quite share the same hobbies." She pulled at the blades of grass on either side of her. "Which is fine, right? There's no rule that says you need to have everything in common." He nodded. "When he asked me to marry him, I thought that was pretty great too." She flicked away the grass and hugged her knees against her chest. "But then I started getting this gnawing feeling."

"Like heartburn?"

She managed a laugh. "At one point that *was* one of the symptoms. I guess I just started wondering . . . is this really the whole love thing everyone talks about? Or is this more of a *mild amount of affection* thing?" She shook her head. "And then I thought: What's the love thing even supposed to be? Aside from what you read about and see in movies, I mean."

"You've never been in love?"

Mira twisted a strand of hair around her finger, distracting herself from his question.

"Don't be embarrassed," he added. "I'm not sure I have either."

"Seriously?" Even if Jake had an air of being the typical guy on the endless pursuit of fun, she'd assumed he'd still had plenty of time for girlfriends and falling in love.

"Maybe I fell in love once," he admitted, "but it didn't last long enough to know if it was something *really* real, or just that initial high."

"You think it takes a long time, then?" she asked, tentatively meeting his eyes. "To fall in love?"

He held her gaze. "I think that the older I get, the more I'm learning that every situation is different."

His words simultaneously landed in her brain and heart. Her heart felt full, not giving a damn that she'd only really known him for eight or nine hours. As for her brain, it was busy logging every word so she could text it to Sophie later.

"I think you might be right," she managed to say.

He ran his fingers through his tousled hair, reshaping the bedhead that was looking more attractive than ever. "How did you finally make the decision? The one that told you 'a mild amount of affection' wasn't enough?"

Had he really been listening to her words that closely? She wasn't used to that.

"You don't have to answer," he added, when she didn't immediately respond.

"I'll answer. But first I need a little more refreshing rosé." She noticed it was getting hotter out here, and it wasn't because of the weather. She brought her cup to her lips and gulped the remaining contents. "How did I decide . . . hmm . . . it wasn't a snap decision, that's for sure. More like this sickening feeling, and it seemed to get stronger the closer we got to the wedding." She felt a shiver. "I guess the thought of my entire future being based on *mild affection* made me ill."

"Sounds scary," he said, with genuine fear in his eyes.

"And at a certain point I realized it was scarier to keep on hurdling down that one-way tunnel to the future, than to risk being alone and never finding anyone." She shrugged. "So, I ended it."

Jake handed her his cup of wine. "Here, you need this more than I do."

She chugged it down. "Thanks."

"I take it your family still hasn't gotten used to all of this?"

"You are correct. But I assume they'll have to talk to me eventually?" She laughed, but the despair was obvious. It was painful not having her parents address her in the family group chat, because even though she'd grown up in an emotionally repressed household, there had also been some nice moments too. Like that time her dad had gotten her a pair of ice skates, so she wouldn't miss out on all the winter fun. Or when her mom had attempted to cook a turkey one Thanksgiving, a failed experiment resulting in laughs and take-out pizza instead.

She knew they cared, but they didn't seem to understand that not getting married had nothing to do with turning her back on family traditions, and everything to do with Dev not being the one.

"I think you're brave," Jake said, cutting through the fog of complicated family dynamics.

No one had ever told her that before. Without thinking, she leaned over and hugged him. He immediately hugged her back, and while the intoxicating smell of Tom Ford cologne was sexy as hell, it was the toned muscles of his broad shoulders that made her want him intensely.

As she slowly remembered that their conversation had been bordering on something deep, she managed to pull away. "Thanks for listening."

"Don't sweat it. I like talking to you."

"And now you officially know I'm a Louis Vuitton three-piece set of emotional baggage."

"Louis Vuitton? More like the Pack 'n' Go nylon collection."

"I walked right into that one, didn't I . . ."

"Too easy." He checked his phone and his expression turned serious. "It's time to go."

Her heart sank. "I guess that makes sense," she said, but when she looked at her watch, it didn't make sense at all. "It's only twenty minutes to ten; do you have to leave already?"

"I'm not leaving you yet, but there's something we need to do."

Before she could ask for more details, she noticed the park security guy making his way through the maze of picnickers. "Shit."

As he moved closer, Mira crushed the disposable wine cups with her mighty fists.

And then she sat on them.

"What the hell was that?" Jake said, oblivious to the security sweep that was happening right behind him.

In response she started whistling, a sad attempt that went on until the threat was over.

"You crushed our cups, Mira." He pulled out the bottle of rosé. "And the wine wasn't even finished."

"Guess we'll have to drink from the bottle then." She did a quick scan of the area. "Coast is clear."

He took a long sip before handing her the bottle. "The rest is all you."

She downed the remaining rosé like a champ, her buzz now firing on all cylinders. And that's when Jake's comment from earlier finally sunk in.

She smiled. "So, where are you taking me?"

*

For once it was Jake in charge of navigation, and not because she'd shared the directions in advance, like on that quick stroll along Boulevard Saint-Germain.

With quick strides they left Luxembourg Gardens behind, crossing back into the side streets of the 6th arrondissement.

"You didn't answer me before," she said, doing her best to power walk with a buzz on. "Where are we going?"

"You'll see."

The small street gave way to a cobblestoned square. "Stop," she said.

"This isn't the place."

"I know, but look." She pointed at the columned structure on the other side of the square. It had gold lettering that read Odéon Théâtre De L'Europe. "This theatre burned down twice, and it was also the place where *The Marriage of Figaro* first premiered." She gave him a pleading look. "And it's on my list."

He sighed. "Thirty seconds."

Jake waited while Mira took a moment to admire the scene in front of her. The quiet square, the banners featuring the latest plays, hints of sunshine reflecting off the golden lettering. It was magical.

She spun around. "Okay, I'm done."

"Finally. Now hurry up so we don't miss it."

"Miss what?"

He didn't answer, but her Spidey-senses told her they were headed toward the river.

Sure enough, they emerged out onto the quay a few minutes later, with the last of the fiery summer sun glowing in the Seine's reflection.

"Let's cross the street," Jake said, his steady instructions forming a shell around whatever he was really thinking.

Mira followed him to the other side, and up the wood plank steps of Pont des Arts. This bridge had been the spot of her early morning Eiffel Tower view, and while there hadn't been anyone around at the time, there were now several couples holding hands, admiring the oncoming sunset.

Was that really why he'd brought her here?

He glanced at the horizon and checked his watch. "Just two minutes to spare." He laughed nervously. "That was cutting it close."

Mira found herself staring at Jake, marveling at this unabashed romantic move. As the seconds passed, all the emotional baggage she'd been carrying seemed to float away. "Jake . . ."

His smile radiated warmth. "You're not the only one who can research things about Paris."

"Apparently not."

"By the way, the sun doesn't set at ten like you said. It happens at nine fifty-six."

She snorted. "Dork."

"Just watch, okay?"

He was right, she didn't want to miss it.

They leaned against the railing, watching as the blazing sun sank beneath the horizon, leaving streaks of pinkish sky in its place. It was a sunset you could easily get lost in, which was the reason why Mira was barely aware when she leaned her head on Jake's shoulder.

She was definitely aware of the next thing, the moment where his hand brushed hers. This was different than the times he'd grabbed her hand in the rain or on Boulevard Saint-Germain; this touch made her nervous and euphoric all at once.

"Was this on your list?" he asked, his fingers interlacing with hers.

"Definitely," she whispered.

He turned to face her, and unlike the rainy moment in the doorway at Canal Saint-Martin, she didn't pull away.

He took her other hand and drew her closer. As he leaned forward, she closed her eyes, feeling the warmth of his breath against her lips.

What she should've felt next was his mouth on hers, but instead it was an auditory sensation, brought on by the unrelenting ringtone of a phone call.

She hoped and prayed he would ignore it and kiss her.

But he didn't.

She felt him pull away from her, and when she opened her eyes, she could see that he resembled a man who'd awakened from a dream.

In a matter of seconds, reality crept its way across his face.

"I—" he started.

A moment later, Mira heard the distinctive sound of wedge sandals clomping along the planks of the bridge.

The next sound she heard came directly from the depths of hell.

"*Jake!*"

The waitress had arrived, and her time with Jake was over.

CHAPTER
thirteen

Ten p.m.

Jake spun around at the sound of his name.

There she was, in a sexy flowered dress with her blond hair blowing in the breeze.

Colette.

She was every guy's dream for a two-night stand in Paris, and yet Jake now found himself wishing he'd never met her. If he hadn't, he'd be kissing Mira on the bridge right now, with an entire night of possibilities ahead. He didn't care that she'd been recently engaged, and that she wasn't in the headspace to date someone new. If anything, her circumstances made him feel relieved, given his own set of personal complications.

But one perfect day in Paris with Mira? That he could handle. And yet here was Colette, throwing a wrench in the whole damn thing.

Colette sauntered over to him; arms outstretched for a reunion hug.

"Hey . . ." he said, trying to sound excited.

Only, it wasn't just a hug.

She wrapped her arms around his neck and kissed him immediately.

He couldn't bring himself to turn around and see Mira's reaction, but if he had to guess, she probably thought he was a total pig. The only way he could salvage things was by giving her a surprise she would hopefully love.

He finally managed to pull himself away from Colette. "Are we good?" he asked.

"It was difficult . . . but yes, we are good." She pushed past him and extended a hand to Mira. "Hello, I am Colette. We met at the restaurant last night."

Finally, Jake snuck a peek at Mira. She shook hands with Colette and didn't seem enraged; it instantly lowered his stress levels.

"Nice to meet you," Mira said, her voice sounding calm and not at all pissed.

"I was sorry to hear about all of your financial troubles," Colette said gently.

Mira immediately frowned. "Excuse me?"

Jake stepped between them and laughed, his best attempt to deflect from the awkwardness.

"Her English is really bad," he whispered to Mira.

"Okay . . ." Mira said, her eyes shifting to the small set of steps leading back to the street. "I should probably get going." She looked over at Colette. "It was really nice meeting you and seeing you when you're not, um, refilling glasses of water." She looked like she might die of awkwardness. "Bye."

Jake stood frozen for a second, knowing that if Mira left, the surprise would've been for nothing.

"Wait," he called out, stopping her before she managed to scurry away. "If you leave, you'll miss the special surprise."

She turned back. "Surprise? I thought the sunset was the surprise."

Colette scowled. "You came here to watch the sunset together?"

Jake was losing track of the order of importance of who not to piss off; Mira had to stay, but Colette had the power to ruin the surprise.

"I was just trying to be nice," he whispered to Colette. "She's *poor*, remember?" Colette simply shrugged. "So where is it?" he urged, wanting to access the surprise before Colette snatched it away.

Colette extended a pointed finger at an intimate-looking party boat docked by the edge of the river. "It's there."

The boat had dark wood paneling with a glassed-in interior and a three-hundred-and-sixty-degree viewing deck. It was there that thirty-odd guests were currently mingling and sipping drinks.

"It's perfect," he said, squeezing Colette's hand.

"Then you will show me your appreciation?" she said coyly. "That was the deal."

"Of course," he said, reaffirming his role as *Pretty Man*, the kind of guy who'd put out for some boat-shaped compensation.

Now that Colette was appeased, he turned his attention back to Mira. From the look on her face, she was running out of patience fast. He approached her with his best salesman confidence. "Remember when the wait for the boat was two hours long? That really sucked, huh?"

"Yup; it was a total drag." She sighed. "Jake, I should really go. Have a good night." She sounded tired or maybe a little sad. He wasn't sure.

"Just wait a second." He nodded toward the river. "Look over there before you leave."

She made her way back to the bridge's guardrail, side-eyeing Jake the whole time. "What am I supposed to be looking for?" When he didn't say anything, she peered down at the water. "Is it something in the river? A corpse? Oh, wait; is it that big white tour boat floating by?" She turned back to him looking hurt. "Why must you open old wounds?"

"Okay, I'll put you out of your misery." He came over and pointed at the special boat. "It's down there."

She took in the sight of the guests on the party boat; drinks in hand, having themselves a time.

"*No way*," she whispered.

"What if you could get on that boat right now? No lineups. No cost."

She broke into a grin. "You *didn't*."

He really had, and by the look on her face, it had definitely been worth it.

*

Jake, Colette, and Mira made their way down the steps to the riverbank, en route to the nighttime cocktail cruise.

Jake glanced from Mira who was in front of him, to Colette who was behind him; an awkward throuple if there ever was one.

A man on the boat came down to the embarkment area, and as he pulled back the rope barrier which separated the revelers from the peasants, Jake realized he recognized him. It was the bartender from the restaurant.

Colette flashed a smile and gave the bartender a double-kiss greeting. "Bonsoir, *mon chéri*," she exclaimed. She gestured to Mira. "I am sure you recognize this girl from last night, although . . . slightly different fashion choices."

Jake watched as Mira slid a protective hand over her fanny pack. The man stepped forward and pecked Mira on both cheeks.

"Bonsoir," she said.

Jake stood back, watching in silence, a feeling of dread taking over.

"I am Alexandre," the bartender said. "And I believe we spoke last night."

"A little bit," Mira said. "It's nice to officially meet you."

Colette squeezed Jake's arm. "I am *so* glad he was free tonight," she whispered.

"Why?" he muttered, studying Alexandre's tall stature and tanned, muscled arms.

"Because now we do not have to babysit your sad little friend." She kissed him on the cheek. "It is perfect, right?"

"Sure."

Fucking perfect.

*

The boat hadn't been out on the water for long, but already Jake was struggling to have a good time. He should've been standing next to Mira, taking in her every reaction. Instead, he found himself a few feet away, drinking beer and watching the bartender say things in that thick French accent women seemed to love. Was it karmic punishment for convincing Colette to help him under false pretenses? Probably.

"Your eyes may be searching for la Tour Eiffel," Alexandre said, "but for now we are heading east, toward the *douzième*. We will eventually turn back and head toward the major landmarks." He made a dumb, sweeping gesture. "Like a grand finale."

"I know," Mira said, clearing her throat. "I've spent some time studying the map."

Jake shook his head, disgusted at how this loser guy didn't even know she was a walking map of Paris. As Jake's resentment grew, he felt Colette's warm hand snake around his neck.

"Babe?" she cooed.

"What's up?" he said, drinking his beer a little too fast.

"Shall we go to the other side where it is easier to talk?"

Even though Jake had no claim to Mira, and even though she was a three-piece set of emotional baggage, he didn't like the idea of leaving her alone with that strange guy. He knew his feelings didn't make any sense, but the day itself hadn't made a lot of sense. Meanwhile, Colette was right in front of him, the one who'd made this boat ride possible. He stroked her arm. "Sure; let's go to the other side."

He glanced in Mira's direction before turning the corner, and while their eyes met for a brief moment, that was all.

Jake followed Colette through the chatty crowd. They didn't make it far before she ran into a woman who was clearly a friend. He dutifully waited on the sidelines, as the two women gasped, hugged, squealed, and chatted away in French words he didn't understand.

Colette turned back. "Alexandre! *Viens ici!*"

Jake's ears immediately perked up. He recognized that name as belonging to the French blowhard, but what did the other part mean? Maybe she was calling him over.

"*J'arrive,*" Alexandre called from around the corner.

Jake was no linguistic genius, but that last word sounded a lot like *arrive*.

Sure enough, Alexandre appeared from around the corner a few seconds later, and Jake couldn't help but notice that Mira wasn't by his side.

As Colette, the friend, and Alexandre got swept up in an animated conversation, Jake made his way back to the other side of the boat. And there she was. Sipping water and gazing out at the river, her long, dark hair blowing in the breeze.

He set down his empty beer bottle on a nearby ledge, before making a quick attempt to fix his windswept hair. When he was done, he sidled up next to Mira and said a quiet hey.

She continued staring out at the water. "Hey."

"I never got a chance to ask you before; what do you think of all this?"

She turned to face him. "It's a hell of a surprise, that's for sure."

Jake wasn't sure if that was a good thing, since many people hated surprises. "But do you like it?" His entire self-esteem was hinging on the answer.

"Do I *like* it? It's fucking amazing."

He felt immediate relief. "Good."

"When did you have time to plan all of this? And how?" Her gaze deepened. "And *why*?"

Jake needed a moment to organize his answers. "Well, as you know, I had a French connection."

She plastered on a smile that seemed a little fake. "You sure did."

"So, I got the idea, asked for a favor, and a few messages later—"

"Here we are."

"Yup." He ran his fingers through his hair again, relieved the line of questioning had passed.

"But why?" She elbowed his side. "You didn't answer that part."

He glanced over his shoulder before responding, paranoid that Colette might pop out at any second. "I guess I had a feeling it would make you happy." He stared into her eyes. "And I wanted to see that."

He studied her face for any hint of emotion. It was there, despite her best efforts to hold it back.

"I can't believe you did that for me," she whispered. "Thank you." She reached for his hand but caught herself before he could feel her touch. "It was really nice of Colette to help you out like this."

Was she really bringing up Colette right now?

"Yeah," he said. "It was nice of her."

"She didn't mind delaying your date for all of this?"

"Technically we're on the date *now*."

She laughed. "Yeah, it really seems like it."

He leaned on the railing and buried his face in his hands. "*Fuck*; what a day."

"I take it you're not the type to ditch someone who does you a favor?"

He uncovered his face when he heard the hint of hopefulness in her voice. He knew what he wanted to say, and he wanted to say it immediately. Unfortunately, he couldn't. "To be honest, no, I'm really not that type."

Jake didn't have the heart to tell her it was more than just a little favor; it was a promise. If he ditched Colette on this boat ride and deleted her number and never spoke to her again, he would always know how much he'd used her, which would make him feel like the biggest asshole on earth. Still, it was hard to see that look of disappointment on Mira's face.

"Besides," he added, "we're on a boat. If I leave her, she'll throw me overboard."

"You're very pragmatic."

"That's how people usually describe me."

"Oh, I bet." She took a sip of water. "Well, I'm sure you two will have an awesome time!"

The sound of Mira's voice was a little too cheery for his liking. If she thought he was looking forward to the date, she was dead wrong.

158

"I'm just holding up my end of the bargain," he said, leaving out the part where it was a deal etched in stone with the promise of sex. "At least for a few hours." He shrugged. "If I'm a good date, it won't seem like extortion."

"Okay . . ."

She seemed confused, but it was better than sharing the explicit details of the contract he'd signed with the devil.

Want to do something to make Mira happy? Then pay the price with Colette.

And also: watch a French guy hit on Mira.

As reality sunk in, he felt Mira's gentle touch against his arm. It was a pleasant feeling that brought him back into the moment. "It's okay, Jake. I had a really nice time today."

He leaned closer. "Don't say it like it's over."

Now Mira was the one glancing over her shoulder. "Technically, it kind of is."

He slumped his shoulders in resignation. "I know."

"Look at it this way, though," she added brightly, "before today, we'd never even had a real conversation. But now we know each other, right? Which means we'll never be strangers again."

Of course she would think that; she didn't know the truth.

"Was that too cheesy?" she added, scrunching up her nose. "I knew it was cheesy as soon as I said it."

"It wasn't," he said, though he struggled to sound convincing.

As the boat began its slow turn back in the westerly direction, Mira started applauding. "Ooh, we're turning." Jake suspected she was looking for a distraction, and that she wasn't truly excited about a boat being capable of turning.

"Don't you get it?" she went on. "Turning the boat means we'll see the important landmarks."

"Oh yeah?"

"Not that I mind the current setting," she said.

Jake took note of the six-story buildings on either side, lit from within and bordered by the warm glow of streetlamps. "I don't mind it either."

"It'll only get better," she said. "After this, we'll see the illuminated facade of Musée d'Orsay, the glowing fountain of Trocadéro Gardens, the golden statues of Pont Alexandre the Third—which is a bridge, by the way—and last but not least, a close-up look at the beaming and *iconic* Eiffel Tower."

Maybe she'd been excited by the turning of the boat after all. While he was enjoying the return of her passion for Paris, he'd noticed the mention of the bartender's name in her description.

Named after a bridge? Idiot.

"I'm glad you'll get to see all that," he managed to say.

Mira reached for his hand for a second time, only now she squeezed it tight. "None of this would've happened without you."

He had the sudden urge to kiss her, and he didn't care who saw it, promises be damned.

"Jake?" Colette called.

Or maybe he did.

Mira dropped his hand and switched her focus back to the view, acting like the whole thing had never happened.

Meanwhile, Colette and Alexandre reappeared from around the corner. She had a beer in one hand and an Aperol Spritz in the other. "Here you go, babe."

Jake liked where her head was at: more alcohol, less thinking.

Alexandre held two drinks, as well, and he offered one of them to Mira. "Are you ready to switch from water to this special cocktail? It has gin and citrus notes."

Mira peered into her empty glass. "Hydration complete." She then looked at Alexandre warmly. "And I love gin and citrus notes."

Jake just stood there, watching the revolting scene in silence. He didn't like the sound of this special cocktail, and he didn't think Mira should be trusting a guy who may have just slipped her a roofie.

As Jake considered the possibility of Alexandre having criminal tendencies, he noticed Colette staring at him. "You look beautiful," he said, hoping it was enough to hide his true thoughts. Not that it was a lie; she really did look good. Unfortunately, it didn't matter to him in the slightest.

The only person who mattered was busy getting wooed by a sleazy Frenchman.

And all he could do was watch.

CHAPTER
fourteen

M

Eleven p.m.

Twilight had now given way to darkness, the sky a perfect contrast to the glittering lights of Paris.

Mira took in the stellar view from her own little corner of the boat deck, but all the while, the wheels in her brain kept spinning in a steady rotation.

It had only been twelve hours since Mira had received the stressful news that she'd missed her flight back home. That unexpected event had been associated with everything negative—inconvenience, anxiety, and even a dreadful feeling of financial doom.

Since then, her day had taken on a different set of qualities—laughter, delight, human connection, flirting, even a fluttering stomach butterfly or two. That last one was the most surprising, as Mira had assumed that any lingering butterflies had long since moved on to more hopeful settings.

And then there was the sunset. Jake had almost kissed her, and she'd finally been ready. But Colette had come along and ruined it all.

Mira had given Sophie a quick rundown of the debacle, and the theme of her replies had been clear: to buckle up and have some fun with the hot bartender.

Maybe Sophie was right, but it was hard to focus on the hot guy at hand when he was off getting another drink. His absence left Mira searching for meaning in this unexpected day with Jake.

Maybe the day had happened to remind her of what was out there, a way to prepare her for that future moment when she'd be ready to take the plunge. But did a helpful reminder have to include watching Jake get pawed at by a sexy Frenchwoman?

Or maybe today's purpose had been to form a bond with Jake, so that later, on some rainy afternoon in Manhattan, they could passionately reunite.

Or, more simply, maybe the universe was absolute chaos, with human-shaped collections of buzzing atoms routinely colliding for no reason at all.

She immediately decided it was the colliding atoms thing, since the logical explanation was usually the right one.

And so, Mira did her best to get used to the idea of chaos, like the absolute lawlessness of grabbing Jake's hand and hoping they would kiss while he was literally on a date with someone else.

Dare to dream.

"Are you a friend of Colette's?" said the voice of a Frenchwoman.

Mira absorbed the ridiculous question and spun around, now face to face with a young woman, whose short brown hair ended sharply at her chin. The woman wore black-framed glasses, and one of those outfits that would've looked unflattering on anyone who wasn't stick thin: a cropped T-shirt, mom jeans, and shiny black loafers.

"I don't know her," Mira said, channeling the famous Mariah Carey

GIF, and hoping her definitive words would make Colette disappear into the ether.

"Oh. I was confused because . . ." The woman gestured to the starboard side of the vessel, where Jake and Colette were busy drinking and laughing. "You are with the American, no?"

"What?" Mira scoffed. "I'm not with him; we're completely independent organisms. Or whatever."

"Maybe my English is not right," the woman said. "What I mean is, you two know each other, yes? You are on the same trip?"

"Oh, that." Mira nodded. "Yeah."

"Colette had mentioned something about the arrival of two Americans tonight."

It sounded like this woman was on team Colette, which made Mira put her guard up immediately.

"Is this your boat?" Mira asked, her voice central-air-conditioner cool.

The woman laughed; a delicate lilting sound that Mira instantly found annoying. "*My* boat? Of course not."

"It was a legitimate question," Mira said defensively.

"I work in the tourism industry, and I have some connections in Paris." The woman gestured to the boat. "Including cocktail cruises."

"Uh-huh." Mira was slightly intrigued now, though still reluctant to fraternize with the enemy.

"When Colette asked me if I could secure a spot on the boat for herself and a few friends," she went on, babbling in a way that was very unlike the stereotypical Frenchwoman, "I thought it would be fun to join in as well." She extended her hand. "I am Eloise, by the way."

"I thought French people do the double-kiss thing," Mira said, though Colette hadn't done it—which of course made her glad, as she probably would've thrown Colette over the bridge for replacing Jake's kiss with her own double peck from hell.

"That is often the case," Eloise confirmed. "But the *bisous* are more for initial greetings, and er . . . not to use a nautical reference, but I believe that ship has sailed."

Though Mira found the dorky analogy to be somewhat endearing, she promised herself to remain suspicious of Eloise's out-of-the-blue kindness. For the moment, she was simply glad to be chatting with this woman instead of Alexandre, whose casual mansplaining of Parisian landmarks was growing a little tiresome.

Mira shifted a few feet to her left. "The breeze is better here," she explained, gesturing for Eloise to follow. Mira's quick move had nothing to do with the breeze; she simply wanted Colette and Jake to disappear from her line of vision.

"So how do you and Colette know each other?"

"We actually grew up together in a *banlieue* outside of Paris. Alexandre too." She noticed the look of confusion on Mira's face. "Sorry, I cannot remember the English word for this. It is like a smaller city outside of Paris, more homes, everyone has a car . . ."

"Oh, a suburb!"

"Yes, that must be the word."

Mira grinned. There was nothing better than getting the right answer in quizzes, something she'd learned at weekly pub quiz nights with Sophie back in college. Despite the high of always being right, Mira frowned when she played back Eloise's words. She wondered if a childhood growing up with Colette meant the two of them were BFFs. And then she wondered if this whole conversation was a recon mission to find out something embarrassing about Mira.

"Are the two of you like sisters or something?" Once again, Mira's voice was icy cool.

"Definitely not. We attended different universities before moving to Paris at separate times. We keep in touch a little, but not very often." She shrugged. "When I heard from her, I just thought it would be fun to see her and Alexandre before I head to a party later."

"So, *is it* fun?" she probed.

Eloise adjusted her glasses. "I suppose it is fun. But I was not fully aware that I would be joining a double date."

Mira snorted. "It is *not* a double date."

As if to contradict Eloise's assertion, Alexandre reappeared with a cocktail in one hand, a glass of sparkling water in the other, and finally, a smoldering look in both eyes.

"Voilà," he said, as he handed the water to Mira.

Mira noticed Alexandre exchange a look with his old pal Eloise; it was a look that said he wanted her to make herself scarce. Only, Mira was finding that she didn't want that at all.

"Eloise, you need more wine," she blurted, before leaning into Alexandre's chest and staring up at him like a doe-eyed girl. "Would you mind?"

"It would be my pleasure," he said, his neutral expression masking any possible annoyance.

Mira sighed as he disappeared into the glass-walled interior of the boat. "Thank God."

Eloise smirked. "What was that about?"

"I just felt bad that you were running out of wine," she lied.

"That is very kind, but be honest: Do you not like Alexandre?"

Mira thought about how Alexandre and Eloise were childhood friends. This would've been the time to talk him up in case the conversation ever got back to him. It was also what Sophie would've told her to do. Still, something stopped her. "He's definitely cute," she acknowledged, a fact that could not be denied. "But I'm leaving in the morning, so what's the point?"

Deep down, Mira knew her explanation was a weak one. It also wasn't the fact that she'd been recently engaged. The real reason she couldn't get close to Alexandre was too embarrassing to admit.

"I can understand this thinking," Eloise said. "But can I ask you another question?"

Mira took a sip of water, wanting to stay alert if this turned into a dirt-digging mission after all. "Ask away."

"How long have you had feelings for Jake?"

Nice try.

"Jake is cute, but I don't have feelings."

Mira didn't care if Eloise believed her, she didn't owe an explanation to this woman she'd only just met. She spun around and focused her attention on Pont Alexandre III, which was now clearly visible in the distance. Just behind the bridge, the Eiffel Tower glowed in golden hues. It was a closer vantage point compared to when she'd seen it during her solo morning, and the view would just get better from here.

Eloise joined her in taking in the sights. "The only thing I wanted to tell you is, you do not have to worry about Colette staying in touch with him; once he is back in America, I mean."

What is with this woman?

Mira gave her a long look. "I thought you said you and Colette only occasionally stay in touch. So how would you know what she'd do?"

"I suppose sometimes, when you know people, you really do know them." Mira struggled to decode Eloise's cryptic message. "Also, she hinted at this outcome earlier when we spoke."

Ah, much less cryptic.

"I have another question," Mira said, wanting to get to the bottom of whatever this was.

"Of course. It is only fair."

"Why do you care what happens to me? Or who I might have feelings for?"

She broke into a smile. "Recently, I fell in love, but it was a complicated journey with some obstacles." She shook her head, seemingly playing back said obstacles. "I am so relieved that we never gave up, and I suppose when I see those beginning sparks in others, along with the apparent challenges, I just hope they will not give up either." She was grinning now. "I am simply in love with love."

Mira took another sip of water. "I don't know if I find you endearing, or vomit-inducing."

"I am not sure what this last part means; something involving vomit?"

"It means, I'm not sure if you make me want to puke."

"Ah, I had a feeling it was something like that. Well, I hope it is the first conclusion."

Mira considered both options, and ultimately landed on endearing. She also remembered to be wary of stereotypes, because all French women couldn't possibly be cold when Eloise was so warm. She certainly wasn't perfect, though, being so clouded by the love bug and all.

"There's something you should know," Mira said. "About the American, Jake."

"Yes?"

"I've only known him for a day, like literally only a day. We work together, but we never even really spoke before today."

Eloise frowned. "I see."

"Which means the *feelings* you're seeing? It's just a mirage. Like a vacation haze that'll clear right up, as soon as we're back at terminal 2A."

"Then I suppose my instincts were wrong."

Mira was glad the case was closed, even if what she felt inside was starting to contradict the verdict.

"Then again . . ." Eloise added, "if the Before trilogy taught us anything . . ."

Mira's eyes lit up. "You love that trilogy too?"

"Of course. Julie Delpy is a national treasure."

Mira couldn't argue with that, but she could always keep on arguing in general.

"Those are just movies, though. None of that's applicable to real life."

"If you say so."

As Mira switched gears from finding Eloise endearing to finding her annoying, Alexandre returned with Eloise's wine.

"Et voilà," he said.

The regular doses of water had balanced out Mira's buzz, but not so much that she couldn't take in the pleasing aspects of Alexandre's being. Like the cologne she smelled when he sidled up next to her. It certainly wasn't as good as the Tom Ford cologne Jake was wearing, but it was nice.

Not surprisingly, her mind soon drifted to everything Jake; his broad shoulders, his big, blue eyes, that bedhead hair, she could have kept on going, but it was pointless. He was off with Colette, and it was out of her hands.

The only thing for Mira to do was focus on what was in front of her, just like Sophie had said.

She leaned into Alexandre, needing to stay where she could see him, smell him, and feel him.

"We are getting close now," Eloise exclaimed, pointing to the glowing Eiffel Tower that was now looming large.

"I thought Parisians hated the Eiffel Tower," Mira wondered aloud.

Alexandre pulled away from Mira, facing her now with a teasing look. "Where did you hear this?"

"I don't know . . . from that episode of *Sex and the City* when Carrie goes to Paris?"

As soon as she said it, she felt idiotic and shifted her gaze to the water. When she finally snuck a peek at their reactions, they seemed upset, but only mockingly.

"We hope your new reality will replace the ideas from television," Eloise said.

She felt immediate relief. "Done and done."

Mira was beginning to like this little crew she'd formed, and as much as she enjoyed the majestic Eiffel Tower drawing ever nearer, she was sad to think it might spell the end of the evening with her newfound friends.

Before she could enjoy the last of the boat ride, more and more passengers made their way up front for a better view. The onset of the crowd blocked the breeze she'd been enjoying this entire time, making things a little sweaty.

To top it all off, the famous duo was back.

Mira struggled to remain nonchalant as they sauntered over. She noticed Colette's fingers busily working their way through Jake's hair—the audacity—and to make things worse, he seemed perfectly fine with being fondled in this way.

As they got closer, Colette squeezed her way between Mira and Eloise, with Jake forced to stand behind her. Despite the close quarters, Colette didn't waste any time in taking Jake's arms and wrapping them around her waist. Mira only noticed this arm-wrapping move because she and Colette were squeezed in so tight, that she felt Jake's hand brush against her side. From that one excruciating moment, Mira knew she'd been right: things didn't happen for some higher reason, the universe was simply chaos.

"Let's take a selfie!" Colette squealed.

A chaos that was hellbent on getting even worse.

"We're facing the wrong way for a selfie," Jake reasoned. "We wouldn't get the Eiffel Tower view in the background."

Yeah, idiot.

"Then turn around," she demanded.

"Okay," he said, struggling to shift his body. "It's just a bit crowded over here."

Colette gave Mira a pleading look. "Could you move to the other side?"

Mira conjured up a smile so fake it held the subtext of imminent murder. "Sure." As she moved away, she backed right into Alexandre's body, making sure to lock eyes with Jake as she did. His big blue eyes seemed dimmer than she'd remembered them; like the real him was trapped somewhere deep within his body, with the outer him persisting in going through the motions.

Mira reminded herself this wasn't her problem, not in the least. If Jake felt too guilty to ditch the woman who'd done him a simple favor, then he would have to live with the consequences, obnoxious selfies and all.

The boat passed underneath one last bridge before making its final approach, with the Eiffel Tower on the left, and Trocadéro Gardens on the right, its glowing fountains serving as the jewel of the 16th arrondissement.

As Mira tried her best to focus on the sights, she sensed the feverish energy of Colette trying to execute the perfect dumbass selfie. Based on Colette's shriek of delight a moment later, it was clear that she'd succeeded.

With no feverish energy at all, Mira snapped some photos of the tower and the famous fountain. She studied the result and frowned. "Looks blurry at night."

The boat slowed as it made its approach to the dock, and while Mira was relieved to get the hell away from Colette and Jake, she wasn't quite ready to disembark. And who could blame her? While the boat ride had come with its share of cringe-worthy moments, she'd been treated to a magical journey with all the best river views. And all because of Jake.

Slowly, Mira peeled away from Alexandre's body. After telling him she needed to get away from the crowd, she turned to Jake, trapping his deadened eyes in her intense gaze.

"Best surprise in the world," she whispered.

He didn't say anything, but there, just for a moment, his blue eyes came back to life.

CHAPTER
fifteen

M
Midnight

Even though the boat hadn't been full, a bottleneck formed at the narrow exit when Mira tried to disembark.

She found herself getting swept into the crowd, and before she knew it, she was off the boat and standing on the dock on the Right Bank side of the river. She had no idea what to do next, but the Eiffel Tower filled in the blanks, when its top-of-the-hour glittering light show began.

"Wow…" she murmured, to no one at all. It didn't matter if she was alone; this magical moment was strictly between herself and the wrought-iron landmark. Nothing in books about Parisian architecture or on throw pillows or coffee mugs or postcards or movies could've prepared her for the feeling of being up close to the Eiffel Tower. As she looked on in amazement, she finally understood why bucket lists were built on the "do it before you die" philosophy; it was beyond worth it, and something she'd never forget.

She craned her neck to get the best view, and without ever peeling her eyes from the scene, she pulled out her phone and started filming it. She doubted that taking videos for social media was included in the bucket-list philosophy, but it seemed wrong not to capture some evidence of this dazzling moment. To keep things pure, she made sure to stare at the sparkling light show with her eyeballs and not through the phone screen.

One for me, one for the 'gram.

Halfway through the five-minute display, she heard the footsteps of someone approaching from behind. Whoever they were, they were wise enough to keep their distance, allowing Mira to enjoy the rest of the light show.

A few minutes later, when the Eiffel Tower returned to its static golden glow, Mira remembered there was someone standing behind her.

She turned around, secretly hoping to end up face to face with Jake.

Instead, it was Eloise.

"It was great meeting you," she said.

"You too." It seemed strange to Mira that she'd probably never speak to her again, and sad even, given how hard it was to make new friends as a grown-ass adult. "Are you on Instagram?"

As soon as Mira said it, she worried Eloise was much younger than her, and would therefore respond by telling her to join TikTok or go to hell. Luckily, her expression remained warm.

"I am on Instagram, and we should definitely add each other. But what are your plans for the rest of the night?"

It was a very good question; one Mira couldn't answer. Her original plan had been to go to the cocktail bar she'd mentioned to Jake, and then promptly head back to the hotel—it was already midnight, after all—but now that Alexandre had entered the picture, she was wondering if things would be different. If this was really a double date, was Alexandre expecting an all-night bangfest? If so, maybe an all-night bangfest wouldn't be such a horrible thing. It certainly didn't require being emotionally available. The only possible downside was that Mira was rusty in the hookup department, after spending the last five years of her life completely committed to Dev.

"So . . . your plans?"

Mira's inner voice quieted down when she remembered there was a real live human standing in front of her. "No big plans," she finally said. "Maybe just a cocktail, then bed?" Given the double date uncertainty, Mira refused to assume that a hookup was inevitable. But if Eloise wanted to be a wingman and encourage that option? That was her prerogative.

"Have you ever been to a picnic at the Eiffel Tower?"

Or maybe Eloise wasn't planning to be a wingman after all.

"I haven't," Mira said, shifting her gaze to the sky. "But it's night-time now. As in *midnight*."

"Is that a problem?"

"Isn't the park area closed?"

Mira's mind wandered to Luxembourg Gardens, and how even though it stayed open later in the summer, there was still a rule to kick everyone out by ten p.m.

"Champ de Mars is not your typical kind of park," Eloise explained, referencing the massive lawn at the foot of the Eiffel Tower. "And after midnight, means *after* tourists. No arguing families, no problem."

"No arguing families?"

Family disagreements over which landmark to see or which food to eat were part of the reason Mira had tried so hard to avoid the tourist traps. That, and the fact that it reminded her of her own bristly family, who couldn't be trusted to go anywhere without making a scene. Like that time in Manhattan, when she'd arranged for her parents to come down from Ithaca for the weekend. Her dad had complained incessantly about the hotel pillows, the busy intersections, and the floppy New York–style pizza. She'd tried smoothing things over by taking them to an Indian restaurant, but somehow that had been worse, with her mother complaining about the greasiness levels of the naan, the spice quotient, and how inferior all of it was to her own flawless cooking.

Mira hadn't taken her parents anywhere since then, and now that they weren't even speaking to her, she wouldn't have to worry about an awkward family outing for a while. At least that was something.

Eloise waved her hands when she saw Alexandre approaching. Jake and Colette trailed behind, looking as close as ever. "You should *all* come!"

"Where?" Colette asked.

Eloise approached her and switched to French, a language change that led to a rapid-fire back and forth between herself, Alexandre, and Colette.

While all of this was going on, Jake stole a glance at Mira. With neither of them able to translate the French conversation, they helplessly stood there, the rest of their night in the hands of three people they barely knew.

The possibility of another picnic made Mira think of the one she'd just had with Jake. It wouldn't be the same location or time of day, but if she agreed to go, she wondered if she'd end up spending the whole time comparing two sides of a grassy coin. Or worse, would she end up spending the whole time watching Jake and Colette make out?

Once the chatter died down, Colette sauntered back to Jake. Eloise meanwhile made her way to Mira. "It is all confirmed. We will join my boyfriend and some friends for a picnic, and there is already plenty of wine for us to share."

"That's a very nice offer . . ." Mira said, her voice trailing off as she attempted to study Jake's reaction.

While Colette explained the details to Jake, he rubbed the back of his neck like he wasn't sold on the idea. Mira hoped Jake would reject the plan and take Colette somewhere else; that way, she wouldn't have to witness the two of them getting any closer.

"You'll come, then?" Eloise pressed. "Or are you ready for bed?"

Mira imagined what was waiting for her at the grimy, crap-bag hotel.

"I'm in," she said, in a voice loud enough for Jake's ears. She hoped he would get the message and stay away.

Before they made their way back to the street, Mira remembered something Eloise had said. "I thought you had to go to a party."

"I do," she confirmed. "It's in the 7th so I will head there afterward."

Mira gasped. "Afterward? As in like *one a.m.*?"

"Yes."

Mira marveled at the stamina of these wild Europeans, who allegedly had jobs and other grown-up responsibilities. How did they do it? In Mira's world, she'd either be sleeping by now, or reading a crime thriller in bed. There were also those rare date nights with Dev, but even then, staying out past eleven was considered rebellious.

But that was before.

With the old normal behind her, Mira figured it was time to try a new one.

"We should get going, then," Mira said. "We've got a midnight picnic to get to."

As Eloise made her way toward the staircase that led to street level, Alexandre wandered over to Mira.

He was the other piece of the puzzle that would form the rest of her night, and despite Mira's recent fixation on Jake and Colette, she found herself feeling some nervous anticipation.

"Would you still like to have my company?" he asked.

He may have been wearing average-smelling cologne, but he certainly had an above-average face.

"I'd like that very much."

Alexandre put his arm around Mira's shoulders. It gave her a good feeling, one that almost made her forget the selfie attempts she'd been forced to endure on the boat.

She didn't even bother glancing behind her to see what Jake was getting up to; he'd either be following Mira to the park with Colette still clinging to his body, or he'd be walking away with Colette still clinging to his body.

And she *definitely* didn't need to see that.

*

"Champ de Mars is *this* way, Mira."

Mira could hear Eloise's voice, but she was too busy taking photos from underneath the Eiffel Tower to respond. The glowing structure stretched into the sky from the bottom up, and Mira was nothing short of captivated. "Incredible," she said, pointing her phone at different angles. "Who knew you could get such interesting pictures of the bowels?"

She immediately heard a snicker coming from behind her. A Frenchwoman's snicker. It wasn't Eloise, as she was already several feet ahead. Which only left one culprit, aka one half of the hottest new power couple, the duo now known as "Jaklette" (in Mira's mind, anyway). They had decided to join the picnic after all, much to Mira's dismay.

"I liked you better when you were a waitress," she muttered.

"What did you say?" Colette asked.

Mira took one last photo and spun around. "Oh, nothing." She noticed Colette's arms wrapped tightly around Jake's waist. Which was fine. Completely fine.

Mira sashayed ahead without a care in the world. "Shall we?"

There was a massive lawn at the foot of the Eiffel Tower, divided into three partitions cascading in a vertical direction. The one in the center was abuzz with late-night energy, and Mira couldn't help but find it captivating.

Clusters of nocturnal picnickers were sprawled out on blankets, enjoying wine, beer, and makeshift platters of charcuterie. She heard laughter, boisterous debates brought on by the booze, and even music, though she couldn't locate the source. It reminded her of those hazy summer nights in Brooklyn, back when the roommates were many, the wine was cheap, the pizza was the best, and everything was funny. While Mira couldn't turn back the clock to the days of boundless possibilities, she could certainly embrace the magic of a summer night in Paris.

"Do you see them?" Mira asked.

Eloise stepped onto the weathered grass and peered into the crowd. "He said they were in the middle." After scanning a few more faces her expression brightened. "I see them!"

Eloise led the way, carefully stepping between the clusters of lounging revelers.

Mira followed along at a slow pace, which gave her time to take in the voices in her midst; from what she could hear, the crowd was a mixture of French-speaking locals, expats, and savvy tourists.

Eloise stopped when she reached a checkered blanket, where two men and a woman were lounging and drinking wine. "Bonsoir." She lowered herself onto the blanket and hugged a man wearing a yellow golf shirt and jeans. She then greeted the other couple, people she also clearly knew. Finally, she turned to Mira and her fellow tag-alongs, who now stood awkwardly at the edge of the blanket.

Eloise introduced Mira and the others to her checkered-blanket crew, spending most of her time gushing about Dembe, the man in the golf shirt who was clearly her boyfriend, based on her gooey-eyed expression. She gestured for them to sit. "There is plenty of room—and wine—for everyone."

Mira tried her best to keep her distance from Jake and Colette, but Eloise's definition of plenty of room was warped to say the least. She wound up with Alexandre on one side, Dembe across from her, and Jake's right foot inadvertently touching her leg. She wished it had been his hand instead. She also wished that everyone else would leave. It was torturous in a way, to have him so close without having him at all.

Dembe offered a disposable cup of wine to Mira. "Do you like rosé?"

But then there was rosé at midnight, which would hopefully solve all her problems.

"I love rosé," she confirmed, feeling sufficiently hydrated and poised to reenter the world of wine. "Thank you." Everyone was already drinking so she dove right in, as the night seemed long past the usual formalities of toasts and clinking glasses.

"You're from England, then," she said, having noted Dembe's strong accent.

"I am," he said, in a tone that was shockingly cold.

She felt her face going flush. "Sorry . . . did I say something wrong?"

"Just waiting for the typical follow-up." He sounded deeply annoyed for some reason. "Go ahead, it's *fine*."

She still couldn't figure it out. "A follow-up like . . . *where* in England are you from?"

His expression instantly relaxed. "My mistake. I just assumed you were going to ask me where I'm really from. As in, where in *Africa*."

She finally understood. "You think I would do to *you*, an innocent stranger, the annoying thing that always happens to *me*? Like I was literally born in Ithaca, bitch, don't let the brown skin fool you."

Dembe laughed. "Right then; so you're not one of the typical ones."

"She's definitely not," Jake piped in.

The surrounding conversation slowed to a halt, brought on by Jake's unexpected declaration.

Mira wasn't sure whether to be flattered or annoyed. On one hand, Mira already knew she was an authentic genuine article, so she didn't really need the validation of some rando man. On the other hand, Jake was not some rando man; he was himself an authentic genuine article, one she'd had the pleasure of getting to know all day. Which, she concluded, made his sudden declaration rather touching. On the *other* other hand, Colette was currently snuggled up against his body, a move he didn't seem to mind in the slightest. Maybe he was a rando after all.

What Jake really meant to her was turning into a maddening puzzle. At least she had rosé.

"Who else needs wine?" Eloise asked, a crafty move to steer attention away from the awkwardness.

The wine continued to flow, and the atmosphere mellowed out. As for Mira, the return to wine had broken through her wall of carbs and hydration. She needed reinforcements fast, an urge that made the picnic platter more crucial in her eyes than any of the hot, nice, or genuine guys in her vicinity. While she approached the platter with the outward appearance of a fromage enthusiast, in her mind it was all a blur; just various pieces of emergency cheese, assigned with the task of keeping her buzz from getting out of control.

There was a secondary effect of the heightened buzz, and it was every bit as unattractive as gobbling up chunks of cheese. It was her lowered standards of humor, which had now descended to the level of jokes Alexandre could understand without needing a dictionary. In a sober state, Mira would've skipped the humor altogether, opting instead to play it straight to overcome the language barrier. But in this current state of being buzzed, the sound of his laughter appealed to her narcissistic tendencies. And anyone who appealed to her narcissistic tendencies while drunk? An instant hottie. It wasn't exactly dignified, but it had been years since she'd gotten to chase her animal instincts. She needed this. Then there was the crisp rosé, which further convinced her she needed and was entitled to the hot French bartender.

To attain her prize, Mira would follow the cue of the basic animals sitting next to her, the ones formerly known as Jake and Colette.

Because, after all, if Jaklette could have some no-strings fun in Paris, she sure as hell could too.

*

Mira's hookup plan was progressing like molasses, as the conversation with Alexandre was now dragging at every turn.

"Oh wow," she exclaimed, pretending to be dazzled by Alexandre's boring story of that time he'd seen the Euro Cup final in person.

He pulled up a picture on his phone. "See how many people? Maybe a hundred thousand."

"Sooo many people," she said, her voice reminiscent of a brain-dead zombie.

Despite the excruciating conversation, Mira's belly was once again full, and Alexandre's chest was a good place to lean on. Her only stress was worrying if all the cheese she'd eaten would later result in a physically uncomfortable one-night stand. As Mira considered the fallout of a bloaty romp, she could hear Eloise and Dembe having a serious conversation, their voices low and their words indistinguishable.

When they emerged from their secret deliberation, Eloise clapped her hands. "We have to be leaving soon for the party," she said. "Which means there are two choices: go your own way, or come along for my cousin's birthday at his gorgeous apartment in the 7th!"

"Your cousin Gabriel?" Alexandre asked.

"*Exactement!*"

Colette gasped. "I have not seen him in so long."

"Which is why it would be a lovely surprise if you came."

Mira worried about this sudden development. Pursuing a hookup was one thing, but crashing the birthday of someone she'd never met? Another thing entirely.

She peeled away from Alexandre's chest. "You guys should definitely go, but I'm going to head back."

"Me too," Jake said. "But you guys have fun."

Jake's simple words stopped Mira in her tracks. If Alexandre went to the party and Colette went to the party, the coupling of Jaklette would finally dissolve, leaving Mira alone with Jake. The last time Mira had been alone with Jake was on the boat, during that brief encounter when Colette and Alexandre were MIA. They'd almost had a moment back then, and the thought of what might happen if they reunited sent a shiver down her spine.

"It was great meeting you all," Mira said, wanting to wrap this up ASAP.

Eloise sat up a little straighter. "I must insist that both of you join us."

"*Oui*," Alexandre added. "*C'est normale.*"

Mira found herself feeling a little cornered. "C'est normale?"

"Of course," Eloise said. "There must be one party a month that I attend, where I have never even met the host. Many nights in Paris are this way."

"*What* way?" Mira asked, intrigued by these strange customs.

"Not very planned," Eloise explained. "The evening comes, and the plans take shape."

Mira was amazed by this strange city, where people didn't plan out their coveted weekends a month in advance in their trusty digital calendar. How on earth did they know which friends would be free on which nights? It was absolute chaos, and despite how much she wanted to run off with Jake, she was intrigued by this rare opportunity.

Alexandre took Mira's hand. "What do you say? Will you join us?"

Mira didn't answer at first, because deep down, she wanted to hear what Jake would say first. It was annoying how much she cared, when this attractive Frenchman was waiting to show her a good time—and when she didn't even know if Jake wanted to be with her, now that he'd spent so much time cozying up to Colette.

Mira watched as Colette leaned into Jake, whispering something in his ear. She saw a hint of playfulness creep into his eyes, a brief moment that made her decision clear.

Mira squeezed Alexandre's hand. "I'd love to join you."

CHAPTER
sixteen

⌄

One a.m.

As the picnic wrapped up, Jake volunteered to gather up the trash and toss it in the nearby bin. A couple of the others offered to help, but he managed to scoop everything into his arms in one go.

"See?" he said. "I got it."

Jake's sudden passion for picnic waste had nothing to do with living out a childhood dream of becoming a garbageman. The trash-collecting task was merely an escape from the awkward situation that was causing so much inner frustration.

Twice now, he'd been on the brink of some alone time with Mira, and both times, she hadn't seemed interested at all. Maybe if he'd sent her the text he'd started typing once they'd gotten off the boat, she would've reconsidered her plans. He'd wound up deleting it after seeing the French guy put his arm around her. He'd felt the second glimmer of hope when Eloise had mentioned the party. It would've been the perfect time for Jake to slink away with Mira, given that they'd never even met the party's host. Colette would've been angry and maybe even made a scene, but at least it would've been a legitimate excuse to bail—both on the party and his promise to give her a night of passion.

And yet, Mira had happily gone for it.

He'd had too much to drink to analyze why this even bothered him, when nothing after tonight would matter anyway.

Jake dumped the trash in the bin and glanced back; without Mira and her key to the hotel room—his only alternative shelter, shitty as it was—he finally accepted he was bound to Colette until morning. That meant spending time at the party—which also meant seeing Mira hanging out with that jerk. If she really wanted to like someone as basic as a sleazy French bartender, he couldn't stop her. All he could hope was that the party would be much too crowded to notice.

Jake wandered back to the lawn, resigned to his fate.

Only six of them remained, as Dembe and Eloise's other friends had opted out, running off to catch the last métro of the night.

"You guys ready?" Jake said. Colette and Eloise responded by running away in a giggling frenzy, with Alexandre trailing behind.

Jake watched them hurry off. "Is that a *yes*?"

Dembe patted Jake on the shoulder. "They said they can't make it to the party without stopping for a wee; the restaurant around the corner will let you go if you pay two euros." He walked ahead. "We can wait out front."

As Jake glanced over his shoulder, he noticed Mira looking very still. Her eyes never shifted from the Eiffel Tower, which was once again doing its light-flashing thing.

"Are you coming?" Jake asked, his first words to Mira in what seemed like forever.

"You guys go," she said. "I want to catch the last two minutes of the light show."

Dembe looked back. "C'mon, Jake."

Jake followed, assuring himself that Mira wouldn't have any trouble finding the restaurant. It was just around the corner, after all. But what if she somehow got lost late at night all alone in Paris?

He knew he was being overprotective, but that didn't stop his footsteps from dragging more and more with every second.

"Fuck it," he muttered.

He spun around and made his way back to Mira.

She seemed to sense his presence but never took her eyes off the light show. When it ended a few seconds later, she finally turned, regarding his presence with a strange look.

"You came back."

He shrugged. "It's late and if anything happened to you, I'd never hear the end of it from corporate."

She smirked. "If anything happened to me, I'm pretty sure you'd be talking to the cops and explaining your whereabouts and making up an alibi and pretending you didn't kill me."

"Good point; you could drive a man to murder."

Mira gasped.

"Sorry," he quickly added, "I've been drinking; head's a little foggy."

"Same here. We're probably on the edge of our third hangover of the day."

"It *has* been a really long day."

"Sure has."

"But a good day," he added, carefully making his way across the vulnerability tightrope.

She caught his gaze. "One of the best days, really."

Jake wanted Mira to say more, but she didn't offer anything beyond a nostalgic smile.

"Day's not over," he said, trying his best to pull her into the moment.

"Let's go, you two!"

The loud reverberation of Dembe's words flung Mira and Jake into reality.

"You're right," she said, her eyes scanning the street. "Day's not over. We've still got a party to go to."

She skipped ahead as Jake looked on.

The day itself may not have been over, but *their* day seemed like it was already behind them.

*

The streets grew quiet as Jake and the gang drew nearer to a residential neighborhood, and a fancy one at that. His assessment wasn't based on being an expert in architecture—because he certainly wasn't—but rather on what he felt when he studied the width of the doors and the fullness of the trees. Or, maybe it was simply that Mira's fun facts had found their way into his memory. He recalled how she'd described the Left Bank as being the sleepy side, and how the richest of the rich lived somewhere in these streets.

"Nearly there!" Eloise called out, several feet ahead at the front of the pack.

Jake felt Colette squeeze his forearm, a sudden reminder she was still in his life. "I want an apartment in this neighborhood someday," she cooed.

"Uh-huh," he replied, his conversation skills having mostly gone dormant since his marathon day with Mira.

"Would you ever want to move to France someday?"

His eyes bulged.

Stage-five clinger.

"Not sure," he said. "I'm an All-American kinda guy."

"I have never been to New York."

"Are we there yet?" he called out desperately.

Dembe glanced back. "Eloise *just said* we're almost there." He studied Jake's desperate expression. "Why? Do you need a wee?"

"That's right," he said, hoping they could pop into another restaurant so he could take a quick break from Colette. "Totally need a wee."

"Just go behind that car," Dembe said, pointing to a Fiat parked on the street. "Be careful though, it's posh in these parts; not like the rest of Paris where blokes are just pissing everywhere."

"And women," Eloise chimed in. She noticed everyone staring at her. "Just a couple of times . . . after the bar . . . behind a bush." She thought about it. "Once in the street as well." She threw her hands up. "I was young!"

Everyone shifted their attention to Jake, waiting for him to wee behind the Fiat.

He shuffled over to his very own open-air urinal, each step making it clearer that he should've just let Colette ramble on. Did he even have to piss?

Ever so slowly, he opened his fly. The street was so incredibly quiet he could hear his zipper echoing in the night air. He zipped it back up and spun around. "You know what?" he said laughing. "It's the damndest thing, but it passed."

The strange looks kept shooting Jake's way, but he no longer cared; he was willing to do a lot to make it through this night, but that didn't include pissing in front of an audience.

"Let's get to that party."

*

The crew stepped inside a shiny lobby, where a smartly dressed doorman waited to greet them. Eloise announced their presence, and after making a quick call, the doorman led them to one of the elevators. He pressed the button and waited, monitoring the progress on the analog indicator, the kind with an arrow that slowly moved backward from five to zero.

As the elevator door creaked open and Jake peered inside, he could see that it wasn't big enough to fit all six of them.

Eloise pulled Colette and Alexandre inside. "He thinks it is only me and some friends he has never met," she explained. "He will never expect to see you two; what a birthday surprise it will be!"

Their laughter faded as the elevator doors closed shut, leaving Jake, Dembe, and Mira staring at each other in silence.

As they stood there, Jake imagined taking Mira by the hand and bolting. They'd rush out into the street holding hands, make out in various doorways, and then, when they finally got too tired, they'd lie on the grass in front of the Eiffel Tower, stuck to each other like glue. It all seemed perfect, until he remembered that at no point in the last two hours had she given him a sign she would want that.

Jake turned his attention to the doorman. "Can we take one of the other elevators?" It was all he could think of to end this awkward standstill.

"We are waiting for the *private* elevator," he said, speaking in a hushed voice.

Jake could already see the excitement in Mira's eyes. "I guess her cousin lives in the penthouse," she said. "Fancy."

The talk of a penthouse and a private elevator had Jake feeling nervous. He'd been hoping for the sort of balls-out party where the lights would be low, the music would blare, and his alcoholic stupor could peacefully progress, all without catching a single glimpse of Mira and the bartender. Now he was imagining a cocktail party with fancy hors d'oeuvres, white-gloved waiters, and Mira's every move right in front of his face. It was almost as bad as pissing for an audience.

Almost.

If it turned out to be a cocktail party after all, Jake didn't understand why Eloise hadn't dressed up. He chalked it up to one of the mysteries of France, since without Mira's guidance, he was lost in the dark about anything concerning French culture.

As the elevator doors opened and they stepped inside, he reminded himself that no matter the country or the foreign customs, he could still hide out in the bathroom and pretend he had diarrhea.

It's all about having options.

*

The party turned out to be nothing like the fancy affair that Jake had been imagining, but it wasn't exactly a balls-out bash either. Casually dressed guests mingled in the grand foyer with drinks in hand, while the latest hip-hop music played in the background.

Dembe turned the corner and disappeared, leaving Mira and Jake to marvel at this strange new environment.

She caressed the marble table in the center of the foyer. "I've never been in an apartment this fancy," she whispered.

"You think I have?" he whispered back.

"Who knows, you're a privileged white male."

He smirked. "Touché."

Mira moved toward the gilded mirror. When she caught her reflection, she gasped. "How could you not tell me?"

"Tell you what?"

"The mascara runoff, the oily forehead . . ." She shook her head in dismay. "Sixteen hours of foundation coverage *my ass.*"

"Did you forget we got soaked in the rain this afternoon?"

"But I fixed that in the bathroom ages ago."

The way she'd glossed over their moment in the rain disappointed him, but he managed to keep it to himself.

Mira grabbed the nearest napkin and used it to blot her forehead. "I guess things got a little sweaty on the boat." She turned. "You still could've been a pal and told me."

Pal? She might as well have called him her brother.

Jake did his best to keep it together. "Not sure when I would've told you; we've barely talked in the last two hours."

Her annoyance dissolved, replaced with an expression that was almost profound. "I guess that's true."

"And you don't look bad at all," he added, meaning every word.

"Thanks."

"Except your hair," he said, shaking his head. "Don't you own a hairbrush?"

She playfully pushed him. "Don't be a dick."

"I'm just trying to help!" He stepped forward and ran his fingers through her hair like a human comb. "You need to get rid of this rat's-nest vibe; this is Paris, for fuck's sake."

They laughed, but as he continued running his fingers through her hair, the laughter gave way to the weight of the moment. It reminded him of that almost perfect sunset.

His fingers traveled from the strands of her hair to the edges of her shoulders, slowly making their way to her neck.

"Where are you two?" Eloise called out. "I need to introduce you."

Eloise appeared from around the corner, trapping them all in an awkward silence.

Jake pulled his hand away from Mira and jammed it into his pocket. As the blood rushed to his face, he felt more and more like a thief who'd been caught stealing the silverware.

"Sorry," he said. "We must seem rude hanging out by ourselves." He smiled sheepishly. "We'd love for you to introduce us to your cousin."

"It's okay," Eloise said. "We can definitely do it later." She almost seemed guilty for interrupting them, which he couldn't help but appreciate.

Unfortunately, Mira was having none of it.

She bounced toward Eloise. "Let's meet that cousin of yours." She glanced back at Jake. "Are you coming?"

*

The grand foyer had been an accurate preview of the rest of the apartment. Jake now found himself in the formal sitting room, though the atmosphere wasn't formal at all. While some of the furniture was modern, it still had a regal (and expensive) feel. That was the formal part. But the room itself was packed with casual people, the atmosphere abuzz with noise. Everyone was either drinking, having snacks, or finding little corners to cozy up to their dates. There was even a balcony, but it was currently too crowded to properly see the view.

A few minutes earlier, Eloise had introduced Jake and Mira to her cousin Gabriel, whose father owned an internationally renowned interior design firm. His affluent background explained the fancy apartment, as well as Gabriel's path in joining the family business.

From Gabriel's fierce hugs, it had been obvious he was already several drinks deep, and he'd even invited Jake and Mira to play King's Cup in the dining room.

Before Jake could respond to Gabriel's invitation, Colette had appeared and answered for both of them, promising him they'd join in on the drinking game later.

For the moment, Jake was trapped in a fancy armchair, wedged between the carved wooden armrest and Colette's body. She'd at least gotten him some wine before proceeding to run her hands all over his body.

Pretty Man, starring Jake Lewis.

Technically speaking, Jake didn't mind the way Colette was using her hands, or how she was kissing his neck, but he couldn't stop thinking about Mira and where she may have disappeared to. When Gabriel had invited them all to play the game, Mira hadn't explicitly given an answer, only saying how fun it sounded. Right after that, the greasy bartender had grabbed her by the hand and led her away.

"Do you like this?" Colette whispered as she nibbled his ear.

"Mmhmm," he confirmed, his body in tune with Colette's every move, but his mind still somewhere else. He drank more wine to shut out his thoughts, but it was going to take some time to reach the alcohol-fueled tipping point.

Meanwhile, his thoughts sank deeper into a jealousy-fueled mania. How many bedrooms did this place even have? Given that it was a penthouse, he wouldn't have been surprised if the answer was four or five. He wondered if the rooms were occupied with people hooking up. Maybe this was a sex party, which explained why Gabriel had welcomed Eloise's tagalongs. Was he beefing up the numbers for the group orgy scheduled for later?

"Where did you go, Jake?"

Jake looked into Colette's searching eyes for the first real time since they'd arrived at the party.

"I'm right here," he insisted, but all along he wondered what the hell he was doing. Here was Colette, literally on his lap and ready to have a good time; what was the problem, then? It was obvious he and Colette hadn't connected on a deeper level, but given that he'd be back at the airport in less than twelve hours, deeper-level connections weren't exactly relevant.

Of course, it wasn't just the fact that he would soon leave Paris. Even after that, once he returned to New York, he wouldn't have room for deeper-level connections.

Jake finished his wine as he came to the unwelcome conclusion. Maybe it had been real, or maybe it had been a daydream, but whatever had started in Paris with Mira, would end in Paris too.

He checked his watch to find that it was nearly two a.m.

The countdown to leaving Paris was officially underway.

CHAPTER
seventeen

M
Two a.m.

When Alexandre had taken Mira by the hand, she thought he would whisk her away to one of the penthouse bedrooms. Instead, they found themselves in the spacious kitchen, along with a handful of party guests who were searching for something to nosh on. One of those people was Dembe, who danced his way through the kitchen as he filled up a paper plate with snacks.

"A little sweet, a little salty," he sang, "a little veggie, a little pastry—" He noticed Mira laughing but wasn't embarrassed at all. "I'm passionate about food," he said, before dancing right out of the kitchen.

"You're not the only one!" she called out after him.

He turned back, giving her an air high five before dancing away.

Mira turned her attention back to Alexandre, maintaining a bit of distance so he could peruse the snacking options. As he made his selections, she took a moment to admire the overall aesthetic of the kitchen. She studied the marble island with amazement; the sheer notion of a Parisian apartment having enough room for a kitchen island was wild, almost like an urban legend.

As she moved on to studying the pendant lighting, Alexandre came over and squeezed her shoulders. "You should eat something," he said.

Mira had already packed a good portion of cheese into the various crevices of her stomach, so she took his suggestion as a sign of flirting. "Because I'll need some *energy* for later?"

He wrinkled his brow, clearly confused by her lame-ass line. Before she could make a second attempt, he recognized someone in the hallway and wandered over.

Feeling embarrassed, Mira did her best to focus her attention on appraising the rest of the kitchen. The extralarge double-basin sink was another rarity in Paris, but it was also a trigger.

Years ago, Mira had offered to help her parents pay for their kitchen renovation, but her mother had immediately rebuffed the offer, reminding her to save for her wedding—a wedding which at that point, wasn't even scheduled and didn't even have a groom. But it was always about the wedding, wasn't it: the saving for it, the spectacle of it, and more recently—the scandal of not going through with it.

Mira tried to concentrate on the happier memories; the ice skates . . . the burned turkey and ensuing hilarity . . . that time her mother had taught her how to make vegetable pakoras . . . the disappointment on their faces when she told them she had canceled the wedding . . .

It was no use.

Mira turned her attention to the party's playlist, the heavy bass thumping into the kitchen through the built-in sound system. The song was about a recent breakup because of course it was. Not that a song about falling for someone would have been any better, given that she was standing in a stranger's kitchen all alone.

She tried to distract herself further with some late-night grazing, but the sight of the various platters wound up putting her into a trance. The charcuterie, fresh fruit, fancy crackers, and bite-size pâtisserie certainly had their merits, but it was Jake who was on her mind.

Their foodie adventures. The wine. The long look in the foyer. That moment when his fingers wandered over to her neck. That last one gave her a rush of excitement, until she remembered that Jake was likely still in that armchair with Colette, playing tonsil hockey and who knows what else.

Not that Mira had actually seen them making out. She had, however, caught a glimpse of Colette getting comfortable on his lap.

Without thinking, Mira grabbed a strawberry tartlet and stuffed it in her mouth, reminding herself that she shouldn't feel bothered, not when she'd already seen them canoodling all night. Still, the feeling gnawed at her, the thought of what might've been if Eloise hadn't interrupted them. Maybe they would've bolted, running breathlessly into the street before falling into one another's arms.

But here they were, at a stranger's party and hopelessly apart. Each minute more at the party, was a minute more she wasn't spending with Jake. And it was too late to get him back. All that was left was to salvage the night by sleeping with a hot Frenchman.

Even when she said it in her head, it came out sounding awkward and unnatural.

Convincing herself it was nothing more than prehookup jitters, she sashayed over to Alexandre, waiting for him to notice her. Someone like Colette would've surely been more aggressive, whispering in his ear or squeezing his arm. But that wasn't Mira.

Especially not tonight, during her first random hookup attempt in more than five years.

Baby steps.

Alexandre turned and noticed her standing there. "Are you ready?"

Mira was relieved they were on the same page. It spared her from asking him to take her home. All she had to do now was say yes.

The liquid courage sloshed around in her veins. "I'm definitely ready." She pulled out her phone to get things rolling. "Should we check if there's surge pricing?" She may have been trying to seduce him, but that didn't mean she couldn't be sensible.

Alexandre looked at her strangely. "We are not leaving the party. We are going to play King's Cup." He gestured to the food platters. "I hope you have eaten enough. It can get intense."

Oh.

How arrogant she'd been, assuming that a night of passion was a done deal. It was humiliating.

She quickly excused herself, citing the need for a bathroom break before joining the drinking game.

She wound up in the powder room nearest to the kitchen. It was resplendent, with embroidered wallpaper and an antique golden faucet. There was also an embellished monogrammed towel, made of plush Egyptian cotton that dried Mira's hands in expert fashion.

She folded the towel back into place and thought about what was waiting outside of the bathroom. The embarrassment, the intimidating drinking game; it made her reluctant to leave this elegant refuge. And so, she lowered the toilet lid and sat down, firing off some texts to Sophie with the latest developments. She wasn't expecting a reply this time, as it was more to vent than anything else. She was shocked then, when her phone screen illuminated less than a minute later.

It was a FaceTime request from Sophie.

Mira accepted the call to find the outline of Sophie in a dark and blurry room.

"Hello?"

The camera seemed to be swaying, and right away Mira understood; Sophie's baby boy was nestled against her chest, her body rocking back and forth to keep him from waking up.

"Are you chickening out?" Sophie whispered.

"Not sure what you mean," Mira whispered back, doing her best to play dumb.

"You said you got embarrassed and now you're hiding in the bathroom!"

"I'll go back when I'm ready to go back," she said defensively. "And shouldn't you be putting Charlie to bed instead of FaceTiming?"

"I can multitask," she said. "Just do me one favor, okay?"

Mira could sense where this was going. "And what's that?"

"Go fuck the French bartender!"

"Sophie . . ."

"Do it for the moms stuck in nurseries around the world. *Please.*"

Mira groaned. "You don't think I'm trying? He thinks I'm awkward and I'm not even wearing sexy clothes."

"You really think men give a damn about clothes? All that matters is what's underneath."

She frowned. "Are you my best friend or my pimp?"

Even from the dark nursery, Mira could see Sophie smiling. "Why not both?"

Mira laughed. "I feel like we're in Cancún."

"Oh my Goddd, take me back." She sighed. "But for now, just live in the moment, okay?"

"Okay." Mira had been trying to live in the moment all day, only now she had to do it with someone who wasn't Jake.

"And stop thinking about him."

"I wasn't," Mira insisted.

"I'm serious; there's no rule that says living in the moment has to happen with one specific person."

"I guess that's true."

Charlie made a whiny sound that threatened the onset of screams. "I better go. Good luck."

"Thanks—kiss Charlie for me."

"Kiss the bartender for me! And fuck him. The fucking part is critical."

"*Bye.*"

Mira made her way back to the kitchen and found Alexandre waiting for her.

"You will play, then?" he asked.

"Sure, why not?"

He led her down the corridor to a pair of lacquered double doors.

Those doors were the time-traveling portal to the wild and reckless nights of college drinking games.

And who doesn't love a good throwback?

*

Ten minutes into the game, Mira was certain of one thing: her college days were far in the past for a reason. Maybe it was the fact that she was on her way to her fourth hangover of the day, or maybe it was simply that her brain and her stomach were too old to bear the weight of a late-night drinking game.

"It's your turn," Alexandre whispered.

Mira barely heard him over the laughter and heckling that bounced between the players surrounding the massive dining table. In the center of the table the King's Cup awaited, encircled by a chain of playing cards. The cup in this case was an oversize golden goblet, and, depending on which card turned up, the cup would progressively get fuller with different kinds of booze—forming a cocktail so deadly it belonged in the fires of Mount Doom.

Mira set down her glass of white wine. She'd only taken two sips so far, a protective move since she knew she was reaching the edge. She prayed she wouldn't have to drink more.

She stared at the card she'd been assigned to flip, knowing that if she turned up a king, she would have to take a drink from the cocktail of death. She took a deep breath and readied herself to flip it, just as Jake and Colette slipped into the dining room to watch.

Gabriel gestured to them aggressively. "No spectators allowed; you must play!"

The others made room for them to squeeze into a spot at the table, but Mira didn't pay much attention. She had a game to play. She flipped over the card and grinned. "Six!"

Since six meant dicks according to the outdated rules, the men including Jake had to follow the rules and drink. He didn't seem fazed at all, which wasn't surprising given his history of sales parties.

Mira sat back in relief, glad to be out of the spotlight, and ready to switch to water for the rest of the night. Unfortunately, she'd forgotten that if someone pulled a queen, all the women would have to drink. Which was exactly what happened next. Now faced with the challenge of drinking from the glass of wine she'd barely touched, the truth became crystal clear: she had reached her alcohol limit.

Mira shook her head demurely. "Sorry, I'm cutting myself off."

"NO," Gabriel boomed, spittle flying out of his mouth. "We must follow the sacred rules."

"Relax with your *Game of Thrones* sacred *rules*." She slid her wine glass over to Alexandre. "Do you mind filling in?"

"NO," Gabriel repeated. "There is no . . . *transference* of turns."

Mira made no motion to grab the glass of wine. Instead, she crossed her arms.

"That is really your decision?" Gabriel went on. "To flout these special rules?"

Within thirty seconds the rules had gone from being sacred to special, which made Mira feel even better about her decision. The whole situation reminded her of junior high. She hadn't backed down then—when she'd declined the offer to smoke a cigarette behind the bleachers—and she wasn't going to back down now.

What she wasn't sure of, was the consequence she'd face for playing it safe.

In junior high, she was shunned from the cafeteria and told to spend every lunch hour in the library. Little did they know, she loved it. *Idiots.*

Here though, the punishment seemed unclear. If she was turned out onto the street in the middle of the night, hopefully Alexandre would join her.

Mira waited for Gabriel to drunkenly blather on, but before he could resume his scattered tirade, Alexandre rose from the table. "We need a break," he announced. "And you have *two* extra players right here," he added, gesturing to Jake and Colette.

A few of the players booed and hissed but Mira didn't care, and why should she? The college throwback was over, and she'd probably never see these people again anyway.

More importantly, there was now still a chance for a one-night fling.

✶

"There is a balcony here," Alexandre said, leading her to an undiscovered area of the penthouse.

Mira grabbed a bottle of water on the way out, sipping as she stepped outside. A moment later the water dribbled down her chin. She blamed it on the view. "Damn," she whispered.

While the Eiffel Tower had shut off its lights and gone to bed, the view of the river and the Right Bank beyond it was stunning, with shimmering drops of gold dotted across the horizon.

"Do you like it?" Alexandre whispered.

She turned to him, aware of the seduction that was now under-way. "I like a *lot* of things."

She wanted to vomit as soon as she said it.

As her horrible pickup line hung in the air, she felt like she had floated out of her body, leaving her to observe this strange brown woman laying it on thick.

"Mira, it's okay. I know this is not our outcome for this night."

Though his sentence was oddly structured, she had a feeling she knew what he meant. "No hookup then?" she said, wanting to make sure.

"That is how it seems."

Mira didn't know if this was happening because of her lingering fixation on Jake, or because of her garbage seduction skills. Either way, she had failed.

"Okay," she said, deciding it was the latter. "Can I ask you something?"

"Sure."

"Did you not, at any point, think we'd hook up?" She was reach-ing for some scraps to salvage her self-esteem, and she didn't care who knew it.

He laughed. "I definitely thought we would." With those simple words, she could almost feel the shattered pieces of her ego coming back together. "I was even playing my suave game," he added.

Mira's crisis in confidence had nearly blinded her from the facts of the night; the cocktails, the smoldering stares . . . of course he'd been putting on the moves. "That's good to know," she said.

"And that was also the reason she invited me."

Colette. Of course.

"What changed?" she asked, needing to hear the words.

"I am not a madman."

"Huh?"

Was the prospect of sleeping with a woman who owned a fanny pack so ridiculous?

"I had a talk with Eloise," he explained. "And we could both see your big distraction."

Even though Mira needed to hear it, she was tempted to deny it. Then again, it was nearly three a.m., and her energy for posturing had run out. "I'm not good at compartmentalizing," she admitted. He seemed confused. "Like one dating option in *one* box, another option in *another* box. And then what, just go to whichever one you reach the fastest?" She shook her head. "That doesn't work for me. Everything for me gets mixed up and messy in one big pile."

"This seems complicated."

Mira liked his earnest way of absorbing things. Maybe there was more to him than being suave. "It is indeed very complicated," she confirmed. "And it pretty much sums up this day."

"I enjoy having many boxes," he declared.

She laughed. "Good for you."

He glanced back at the balcony doors. "Are you finished with the game?"

Her eyes widened. "*Definitely* finished."

"What will you do now? It is very late."

"I guess I'll try to sleep in that horrible hotel bed."

"I do not like this idea."

"Do you have a better one?" she asked, a part of her wondering if the one-night stand was back on.

"Yes. The Laboratory."

She gasped. "No. Way."

"You know this bar?"

"It's on my list! I was going to go there tonight, but then the boat happened, and then the picnic happened, and then this party happened—"

His eyes twinkled. "Then we must go there now."

Mira's building excitement immediately dimmed. "But I really can't drink anymore. Like my body will *not* allow it."

"They have a wide selection of nonalcoholic cocktails. I would recommend the one with ginger beer."

A hot French guy concerned for her digestion? She wanted to squeeze him in a hug. Instead, she got a different idea. She stepped forward, putting both hands on his chest. "Can I kiss you?" She could feel his heart beating underneath her palm, steady and strong. "I just figured I should ask, in case you wanted to say no."

"I told you, I enjoy many boxes."

It was a good joke, but Mira had a serious mission. She pulled his face toward hers and kissed him, slow at first, and then deeper. His lips felt warm, and he tasted of wine.

Definitely worth it.

When she pulled away, his hazel eyes met hers. "Better than the American?" he asked.

She frowned.

Oh, Jake.

"I actually don't know."

He seemed shocked. "How could this be?"

4 Hours in Paris

"We *almost* kissed," she said defensively. "Twice."

He rubbed his forehead. "This is Paris! You must kiss him before sunrise."

"What are you, my French fairy godmother?"

"Why not?" He gestured to the balcony doors. "Come. We will go to the Laboratory now."

"What about the *sunrise deadline*?" she said, her voice dripping with sarcasm.

"That can be arranged."

She followed Alexandre inside, wondering all the while what alternate reality he would conjure up to arrange a kiss with Jake. In her current reality, Jake would finish the game and kiss someone else, the gateway to his two-night stand. And even if she somehow found a way to kiss Jake, sloppy seconds were not on her bucket list.

Not without a toothbrush and fluoride, anyway.

Once they made it back inside, the first thing she noticed was Jake slumped in an armchair, just a few feet away from the balcony doors. He was alone and sulking. She glanced back at the balcony, wondering if he'd seen her kiss with Alexandre.

"Eloise," Alexandre called out. "We are going to the Laboratory!"

Even if Jake had seen it, there wasn't any time to find out.

07

CHAPTER
eighteen

M

Three a.m.

A car had been the quickest way to get to the bar, and the view from the bridge had been incredible.

Officially speaking, Mira had seen a superior view from the boat only hours earlier. Still, throughout her day of exploring Paris she'd realized something: it was all about perspective. Just from turning your head at a different angle, you could see the same thing in a whole new light. From riverbank views to people, the logic seemed to apply.

For the moment, Mira didn't care about people, or, more accurately, one person. She'd opted for something much less confusing—sticking her head out the open car window to catch the night breeze and the city lights.

I am a golden retriever now.

The speed of the car and the strength of the breeze made her eyes water. She ducked her head back into the car, trading in her canine-like enthusiasm for regular human behavior.

She glanced over at Eloise and Dembe, needy for some in-car attention. They were squeezed in beside her in the leather-upholstered backseat, but their eyes were drawn downward, faces aglow in the bluish light emanating from their phones. Mira decided she didn't have the energy to creep what was happening on their screens. She looked to Alexandre instead, who was sitting up front with the driver. Sadly, he too was busy on his phone, no doubt texting one of the woman-shaped options he stored in the organized boxes inside his head.

As for Jake and Colette? She didn't know, and she didn't ask. She'd last seen Jake still sulking in the armchair, right before Alexandre had whisked her away to the elevator. Even after five whole minutes of waiting for the car, she hadn't seen either one of them emerge. She could only assume they had stayed at the party, which meant Alexandre's plan for Jake to kiss her could now be labeled a bust.

Not that Mira had believed it would ever happen.

Two false starts were as close as she would get to kissing Jake, but she wasn't going to feel disappointed. Especially not after kissing a hot Frenchman. She closed her eyes and thought of Alexandre's warm lips, along with the light taste of wine and something salty she couldn't place. She squeezed her eyes tighter to feel it more, but she couldn't get beyond the surface-level hit to her senses.

And she knew why.

Alexandre may have been fun and sexy, but he wasn't the one who had made her laugh, or shared his secrets, or held her hand, or shown her a sunset, or made her feel okay about blowing up her life. There was no one else she wanted to kiss more than Jake, but time had gotten away from her, and now it was too late.

She opened her eyes and pulled out her phone, resigning herself to the touch-screen hypnosis that had taken hold of the other passengers

ROMI MOONDI

in the car. With no compartments of men to send late-night messages to, she thought about texting Sophie. But then she did the time-zone math. Sophie had probably put Charlie down to sleep, which meant her sacred alone time had begun; that blissful period of drinking wine and watching whatever season of Housewives she was on.

Mira didn't want to interfere with her routine, especially when Sophie had been such a good friend, despite the demands of being a new mom. Now it was Mira's turn to be a good friend.

Without any dudes or friends left to message, Mira scrolled her photos from earlier in the day instead. She smiled as she traveled back in JPEG time, reliving the Eiffel Tower, the river views, Luxembourg Gardens, the bookstore(s), the macarons, and that photo of Jake in a feathered vest.

She immediately snort-laughed, a sound that broke through the 5G slumber of the other passengers.

"What happened?" Eloise asked, as Dembe tried to sneak a peek at Mira's phone.

Remembering her promise to never share the photo of Jake in the feathered vest, she clutched her phone protectively against her chest. "Oh, nothing; just one of those viral videos where someone falls down a stairwell and face-plants onto the pavement." She lowered her head in shame. "I really shouldn't have laughed."

As soon as the coast was clear, she zoomed in on Jake. His expression was full of pride, a stark contrast to his comical attire. It was one of the many secret little moments that had wound up meaning so much, something she only realized now, after a day spent trying to diminish it.

Before she could truly revel in the feeling, she remembered an important fact: after this little stop at the bar, her next destination was the horrid hotel, and the end of her amazing day in Paris.

She immediately stuck her head back out the window.

210

*

When the car was just a few streets away from the bar, Mira asked the driver to take a spin around Place Vendôme in exchange for a higher tip. A few minutes later, after seeing the classic cobblestoned square illuminated by the lights of the Ritz hotel and surrounding designer shops, she knew she'd made the right decision.

A little bougie vibe before the bedbugs.

The driver dropped them off on a side street tucked into the 2nd arrondissement, just around the corner from the bar.

Mira, Dembe, Eloise, and Alexandre spilled out of the four-door sedan, their surroundings relatively quiet at this late-night hour.

With confident strides, Alexandre led them around the corner, where twentysomethings were having a smoke near a nondescript black door. A football player–size bouncer stood guarding the door, dressed all in black and sporting a thin-lipped frown. As Mira got closer to the entrance, a young couple rushed past her. They immediately launched into an impassioned plea to the bouncer.

Alexandre stopped midstride and gestured to Mira. "Let's stay back here for a moment."

Mira was more than happy to stop for a minute and soak in the drama of the desperate couple. *It's just the two of us*, they reasoned. *One last nightcap*, they insisted. The bouncer simply shook his head, and it might as well have been the defining slice of the guillotine. They were destroyed.

As the couple wandered away, heads intact but nonetheless lifeless, Alexandre approached the bouncer with a grin. His gesture was returned with a smile and a hearty chuckle, which instantly made Mira feel superior to the rejected couple. After a few quick pleasantries, the bouncer opened the door for her crew.

And we're in.

After spending time on an open-air boat ride, at a picnic, and in a sprawling penthouse, the small, crowded bar was like sensory overload. The trippy music, the faint smell of incense, the red velvet curtains blocking out the windows—or maybe they were purple? In the candlelit setting it was hard to tell. A few armchairs and ottomans were scattered around the bar, but none of them were being used at this late-night hour. The real ticket in town was the long bar, the black marble surface crowded with the elbows of sweaty humans jostling for prime position.

Alexandre led Mira to the hotbed of action, and with another one of his grins the whole world opened up; each of the bartenders recognized him immediately.

"Do you all hang out together?" Mira shouted over the music. She and Alexandre squeezed into their own little spot at the bar, with enough room for elbows plus some VIP buffer. "Or do you all meet up at bartender conventions?"

He shrugged. "Everyone knows everyone."

Mira was fully on board with this incestuous bartender community if it meant getting special privileges. Alexandre whispered something to the nearest bartender, a platinum blond–haired woman with intense eyes and a bold red lip. With a quick smile, the woman set to work, making two fresh cocktails in a dizzying haze.

"Mine's alcohol-free, right?" The strawberry tartlets from earlier were the only thing keeping the tenuous state of her stomach from falling apart, which made the no-booze clause nonnegotiable.

"Alcohol-free," he confirmed.

Despite his reassurance, Mira kept an eagle eye on the bartender's supersonic process, making sure not a drop of booze found its way into her glass. She didn't really have a reason to be suspicious—as

212

Alexandre had shown her a lot of kindness—but she also didn't have a reason to trust him, given that they'd only just met a few hours ago.

Tonight's sensible switch to alcohol-free was nothing like Mira's roaring twenties, a time when she'd always been game for a round of shots, no matter how heinous the taste. Sometimes the shots had been bright blue like windshield-washer fluid, while other times they'd been the cheapest, grossest tequila. Without fail, she'd always said yes.

It was a wonder she wasn't dead, she decided, and as she took a moment to give thanks for her continued existence, the bartender unscrewed a bottle of nonalcoholic ginger beer. She poured it into the glass and topped it with grated lemon and a sprig of mint, before sliding it over to Alexandre.

He handed it to Mira. "Fresh and not too sweet."

"Thank you." It was the perfect tonic for Mira's stomach, and it tasted delicious too.

Alexandre took a slow sip of his bourbon-forward cocktail, eyeing her all the time.

"What's with the face?" she said.

"I was just thinking how different this moment would be. If you were not here with the American, I mean."

Mira edged closer to Alexandre, her mind now racing with the renewed possibility of sex. "He's not here with me *now*," she teased, surprised at how quickly she'd conjured up a pickup line.

"That may change."

Of all the responses to a pickup line she'd been hoping for, his remark was near the bottom of the list. "Cool. I guess we'll see."

The return to Alexandre's fairy godmother–like assuredness annoyed her, especially because there wasn't any basis for it. He must've been drunker than he looked.

Mira searched the crowd for Eloise and Dembe. She couldn't

see them anywhere, so she focused her attention on the lanky DJ spinning beats from just a few feet away. She wanted to ask him how much DJing had changed since the use of laptops, but before she could ask her obnoxious question, she noticed someone else making his way through the bar.

He was nearly a head taller than the people around him, which made his tousled hair and serious expression impossible to miss. As he made his approach, Mira noticed that he wasn't alone. It was a shame, really, as she'd been hoping to never lay eyes on Jaklette again.

Jake made a move to capture Mira's attention, craftily approaching when Colette got distracted by a bartender.

"You shouldn't be hanging out with that guy," he said, his voice surprisingly cold.

So that's how it's going to be.

"Don't I even get a hello?"

"I'm serious," he went on. "When Eloise mentioned you were going to a bar, I had to come check it out." He surveyed the scene like a demented cop. "You shouldn't be alone with him."

"Okay, *Dad.*"

"I'm not kidding. This is the classic case of taking advantage of a tourist who's been drinking too much." He gestured to her mocktail. "Do you even know what's in there? He could've slipped you something."

She shook her head sadly. "This side of you is so unattractive."

"I'm not trying to be attractive; I'm trying to protect you."

Mira was certain every grown-ass adult had their limit when it came to being treated like a child, and she'd officially just reached hers. The feeling of anger rushing through her body reminded her of all those times her parents had insisted on telling her how to live—as if she were somehow a moron. For her parents, it had always seemed like they were grasping at the scraps of staying relevant, a form of denial that was easier to swallow than accepting that their children were all grown up.

As for Jake's motivation? It was nothing but jealousy, through and through.

"I'm a grown-ass woman," she said through gritted teeth. "And if you put your evolutionary instincts on pause for *one second*, maybe you could get some yourself some actual facts." She stopped to take a breath, but the rant wasn't anywhere near its end. "Because if you'd *gotten* those facts, you'd know I stopped drinking an hour ago, since I forgot to bring my Advil and Pepto-Bismol chewables in my Pack 'n' Go."

"Okay . . ." he said, looking a little afraid.

"You would also know that this drink is a *mocktail*, which my good friend Alexandre kindly arranged for me." She turned to Alexandre, who was busy on his phone. "Again, thank you." He glanced up from his phone screen and nodded.

"Do you always kiss your good friends like that?"

Jake's blunt question nearly threw Mira off her rant, but she wasn't about to take the loss on her impassioned tirade on behalf of all women. "I can kiss whoever the fuck I want. Good friends, fast friends, boyfriends, randos off the street . . . I've done it all and I would do it again." That statement wasn't entirely true, but that was neither here nor there. "I can also get as drunk as I want whenever I want, and I if *had* been packin' that Pepto, believe me, we would've had a wild situation on our hands." That last part also wasn't true, but she needed to bring this rant to a dramatic conclusion. "Now why don't you get back to *your* special friend and leave me the hell alone?" She added a sarcastic wave. "See you at the airport!"

She stomped off and bumped into Eloise.

"That was intense!" Eloise exclaimed.

She shrugged it off. "I was just clearing the air."

The music changed from trippy vibes to something a lot more upbeat, matching Mira's mood of no longer needing to worry about Jake.

Eloise pulled Mira onto the dance floor, or, more accurately, a ten-foot-wide patch of random floor where people had started to congregate. "Let's dance!"

Mira liked the music, but that didn't mean she had any rhythm. "I can't dance when I'm sober, too much hyperawareness."

"You told me you have been drinking since this afternoon."

It was a solid point. There was no way her bloodstream would pass through a three a.m. breathalyzer.

Mira leaned into the blood-alcohol levels that remained, freeing her mind and body from the endless overanalysis. The freedom flowed for two whole songs, ending abruptly when Mira felt a tap on her shoulder.

She spun around to find Jake standing in front of her. His stare was intense, but not like before, when he'd tried to act like her dad. This was something else.

"Can we talk?" he shouted over the music.

"You killed my vibe," she said flatly.

"It'll be worth it, I promise."

The overanalytical part of Mira's brain returned to the main control panel. She was dying to know what exactly would be worth it.

Jake led her to a less crowded corner of the bar. It wasn't that much quieter, but at least there was less interaction with other people's sweat.

"What's going on?" she asked, her voice holding back just how much she cared to know the answer.

"I'm sorry about before." He ran his fingers through his hair, now damp with sweat but still looking good. "I think I'm kind of drunk or maybe I've been drunk for two days? I dunno."

She felt a hint of sympathy. "I can understand that."

"Or maybe I'm not that drunk at all. I think we ate twenty thousand calories today." He rubbed his temple. "And sleep. I don't think I've slept for two days. Anyway, I guess I was making some assumptions tonight. I don't know. It was pretty dumb." She didn't respond, wanting him to get to his point before he passed out from lack of sleep. "But I talked to that guy. Your friend. And he explained things in a way that made sense."

She'd underestimated Alexandre; a French fairy godmother after all.

"What did he say?" she asked, scraping together the last bits of nonchalance that remained in her body.

"He said the kiss didn't mean anything, because . . . your box is already all mixed up with me." He frowned. "It made more sense when he explained it."

The compartments! Alexandre, you magnificent bastard.

Mira was getting close to the tipping point of zero chill, but there were still a few things she needed to know. She did a quick scan of the bar, but the results were inconclusive. "Where's your date?"

He inched closer. "She left."

"On her own?" She shook her head. "No way."

"Definitely not on her own," he acknowledged. "I told her it was really fun hanging out, but that I realized there was someone else I wanted to spend my time with."

Mira could feel her heart bursting open, or fireworks exploding in her chest, or whatever it was that made a person acutely aware of being alive. In five years, she'd never felt that way with Dev. She wanted to live inside this feeling forever, but what kept her going was the sheer anticipation of what might happen next.

"How did she take it?"

"Not well. I got slapped."

"*What?*"

"Probably deserved it too."

Without thinking, Mira placed a hand on the side of his face. "I'm sorry you had to go through all that."

"It was actually the other side."

Mira knew he was trying to be funny, but for once she wasn't going to let him.

She rested her other hand on his bare cheek, which left her cradling his face and staring deep into his eyes. Her sense of smell told her he'd even taken a breath mint for this special occasion. It wasn't the extra fluoride she thought she would need when she'd imagined this moment earlier, but it was enough minty freshness to make her forget about the risk of sloppy seconds. That, and the fact that it was nearly four a.m., she was really exhausted, and probably still a little drunk.

Mira felt Jake slip his arms around her waist, and she knew it was now or never. She pulled him toward her, not stopping until her lips met his. The time for analyzing the aspects of kissing was over. All she would remember in the days that followed, would be the sense of falling, and a deep-down feeling in her soul she'd been missing for too long.

CHAPTER
nineteen

⌐

Four a.m.

The lights went up while they kissed. It should've lasted longer, but the lights . . . those goddamn lights.

Mira was the one to pull away first. They stood in silence now, staring at each other under the harsh yellow spotlight. Jake knew it was a kiss that would need to be processed—and soon—but for the moment he didn't care; he was happy to bask in the afterglow.

The basking turned out to be all too brief, as Dembe noticed them and wandered over, one arm slung over Eloise's shoulders. "Come on then," he said, gesturing to the door. "It's time for the next stop."

Jake had been hoping to spend some time alone with Mira, especially given everything that had happened. They'd officially crossed the threshold into no longer pretending, and even though it had only been a day, it felt more real than anything he'd ever experienced. All he wanted was more of her words and laughter and touch, but when he really thought about it, where would they go? He couldn't think of any place besides the hotel, and he wanted to avoid that shithole as much as possible.

Mira nudged Jake. "They're going to throw us out if we don't leave soon."

"Right," he said, his brain struggling to think up a plan. "Outside is good; I could really use some air." He noticed the change in her expression. "Not from you, though," he added quickly. "I don't need air to like, *get away* from you, just general air."

He could see she was trying not to laugh. "Okay then, general air it is."

They followed the crowd back out to the street, where the energy was a mixture of superamped and barely conscious.

As Jake observed his surroundings, one thing was clear: he was standing in the presence of a lot of couples, all of them doing couple-y things. There was kissing, ear nuzzling, and bodies leaning into bodies. It was the sort of four a.m. affectionate displays that were hard not to notice.

Jake wasn't sure if the people making these moves were in long-term relationships or had only just met, but it didn't matter. What mattered was the gnawing feeling in his gut: Should he be doing these things with Mira?

He had literally just made out with her, but now, as she stood beside him scrolling her phone, she already seemed far away. He was confident their moment had been real, and not manufactured by the right music, low lights, and slight impairment of the senses, but he didn't know how to recapture it in this starkly different setting.

He made a slight move to reach for her hand but stopped himself; he was nervous. As he backed away, he noticed Dembe kiss Eloise and shuffle over.

"Ready?" Dembe said.

The more Jake thought about it, the more another stop seemed like an easy way to keep the good times rolling. "I'm in," Jake said. "What did you have in mind?"

Mira stepped forward with a worried look. "Guys, my body can literally not handle another bar. And I don't just mean the alcohol; like all the people, the dancing, the noise . . ." She shook her head. "I'm spent."

"It's been a long day," Jake acknowledged, bracing himself for a sudden end to the night.

Dembe took a few more steps toward Mira. "It's not a bar, darling," he explained. "We're going to the only crêpe stand that's still open at this ungodly hour."

Maybe Jake should've seen it coming, but he was nonetheless stunned when Mira's eyes lit up like a pair of LED bulbs. "Handheld crêpes? That's on my list!"

Annnd she's back.

"C'mon," Dembe said, leading the way with Eloise at his side. "It's not far; just in the 1st down on *Rue Saint-Denis*."

A crêpe stand may not have been what Jake had envisioned, but her excitement was enough to make it seem worthwhile. That, and the fact that after sixteen hours of a food-and-drink marathon, he somehow still had room to eat.

Dembe and Eloise were several feet ahead, far enough to have their own private conversation. This only made Jake hyperaware that he and Mira weren't talking at all. Just when he thought he'd be able to break the silence, they made the turn onto Rue Saint-Denis, which brought them face to face with the bright red lights of a sex shop.

"I wonder if they actually sell DVDs," Mira mused. He didn't understand. "The sex shop," she explained, gesturing to the brightly lit sign for DVDs in the window.

Apparently, they'd be chatting about sex shops after all.

"Maybe it's an old sign," he said.

"Even so, isn't it a bit too prominent? Like who needs DVDs when every video to satisfy every fetish is available online?"

"How do you know? Have you seen them all?"

He could see she was carefully considering her response. "You know how they say the Louvre is so big, it would take like, *three years* to see every artifact?"

"That's the first time I've heard that," he said. "Sounds accurate, though."

"That's the same amount of time I've spent scouring the internet for porn; and trust me when I tell you that everything you've ever or *never* imagined is there."

He knew she was lying but he loved playing along. "After spending all this time *scouring*, are you done? Have you reached the end of internet porn?"

"Not yet; there are still a few streaming sites I need to review."

"That's fair; you're a busy gal."

"I mean it, though," she went on, "everything is there. Foot stuff, earlobe stuff, kneecap stuff . . ."

"Kneecap?" Jake shook his head in disbelief. "Come on."

"Seriously," she insisted. "I'm unclear on if the fetish is strictly kneecap-specific, or more like the general knee *region*, but it's a thing." She used her index finger to trace an outline around her left knee. "It's something about the grooves, I guess." She scratched her brow. "And it's catching the world by storm; it may even make the transition from fetish to mainstream."

"*Mainstream*?" He scoffed. "No way."

"*Yes* way," she countered. "We're on the precipice; like there's even a Twitter account that's dedicated to pictures of kneecaps."

"I need a moment to process that."

"Take your time."

As they strolled along, their hands lightly brushed every now and then. It wasn't a kiss, but it gave him a warm feeling.

Before long, the seedy shops gave way to casual restaurants that had shuttered for the night. Maybe it was a sign that it was time to transition to a normal conversation. And yet, every time Jake had stopped to reflect on their special day, it was the absence of normal that had made it so memorable and fun.

"Tell me something," he said, eager for the feeling to last. "How can someone who's basically memorized the entire map of Paris, have extra room in her brain for things like kneecap Twitter accounts? Unless—was it *you*?" He gasped and placed his hands over his denim-clad knees. "Have you been checking out my kneecaps this entire time?"

She leaned into his shoulder and looked down at his knees. "Nah. From the outline I'm seeing, they're too bony and asymmetrical."

He lowered his gaze, his attention now focused on the close-up scrutinization of this previously neglected body part. "*Asymmetrical*?"

"Has my obvious bullshit made you insecure?" She squeezed his shoulder. "Because you should be," she added mockingly.

He shifted his eyes back out to the street. "Nope," he lied, "knee confidence intact."

"And to answer your question, my cerebral cortex has an endless capacity for useless info. So that's how I know about kneecaps."

He found himself recalling her various fun facts from the day. "I don't doubt your endless capacity at all."

"You don't?" she said. "I mean, we only just met today—or technically now it's *yesterday*—so I doubt you know me well enough to know anything for certain."

Initially, Jake felt deflated by her comment. But then he realized that using defensiveness to shield one's heart was a game he knew all too well. He also knew how to counteract the game.

"Logically, you're right. "He put an arm around her shoulder and gave it a squeeze. "But does it *feel like* we only met today?" He looked into her eyes. "It doesn't feel that way to me."

Instead of returning his stare, she lowered her gaze to her shoes. "No," she said, "it doesn't feel that way."

"Hey."

She turned toward him, and while he thought about kissing her in this seedy street full of sexual temptation, he pulled her into a warm embrace instead.

As they continued strolling, hand in hand, Jake started to wonder if he could trust what he was feeling—given all the walking, drinking, and none of the sleeping. Would everything change after a good night's sleep? He wanted it to feel as significant tomorrow as it did right now, walking alongside her on this strangely special night in Paris. But without a frame of reference from his own not-so-serious dating past, he didn't feel sure about anything.

With clarity eluding him, Jake felt relieved when Dembe jogged up to them.

"Do you smell that?" Dembe said, grinning wide. "Do. You. Smell. That."

Mira closed her eyes and inhaled the night air. "Flour mixture rapidly cooking on an ultrahot surface—a buttery essence . . ." She opened her eyes and grinned at Dembe. "It must be the handheld night crêpes!"

Without warning, Mira and Dembe started chanting *night crêpes!* repeatedly, and dancing like they'd choreographed it all the night before.

Eloise watched from a few feet away, exhausted but smiling. "It is like you two have known each other your whole lives."

It took Jake a second to realize she wasn't talking about him and Mira. He laughed along like any normal person would, all the while wondering, predicting, and maybe even wishing. The wishing part was the nicest because it allowed him to disassociate from reality, a reality he couldn't face.

And so, he followed his crew to the crêpe stand, extending a night that should've ended hours ago—a night that shouldn't have happened in the first place.

✳

The crêpe batter sizzled when it hit the round griddle.

Jake had insisted on everyone getting theirs first, and at last his turn had come. He looked over at Mira, who was cradling her folded Nutella crêpe in both hands.

"You should eat yours," he said.

She shook her head. "Not until you have yours."

"Thanks. Shouldn't be long, then."

"I was thinking we could eat by the fountain after."

He peered down the street. "I don't see any fountain."

"It's there," she said with confidence.

The man working the griddle sprinkled sugar onto Jake's crêpe. It was the only ingredient he added before folding it into triangular sections. Jake frowned. "How come he's not putting Nutella in mine?"

"I didn't order you that one," she said. "You're getting the *crêpe sucré*. The one with sugar."

"Are you kidding me?" he whined. "I want the Nutella."

"Have you forgotten what happened the last time you tried to eat something brown?"

He immediately laughed. The shirt stain. The department store. The fashion show. Another collection of wonderful memories.

"Well?" she went on. "Do you really trust yourself with creamy brown ingredients?"

He cringed. "Maybe I'll stick with the sugar one."

"It's for the best."

With crêpes in hand, they crossed the street and made their way to a square called Place du Châtelet, where, as promised, there was a fountain complete with water shooting out of the mouths of stone sphinxes.

Mira and Jake sat together on the edge of the fountain, knees touching and ready to chow down. Without a word they dug in, immersing themselves in a simple pleasure requiring zero thought. Which was exactly what he needed.

"How is it?" she asked.

He nodded and gave the thumbs-up.

"I told you."

Jake caught sight of a blob of Nutella oozing out of Mira's crêpe. She noticed his look of longing and shoved the crêpe in front of his face. "*One* bite. And be careful."

Jake took a bite and forgot everything else; it was delicious, and once again proved that his appetite had no limits. He was so busy enjoying it, that he didn't even notice Mira take a photo until it was already too late.

"Hey!"

She seemed incredibly satisfied with the outcome. "You're a mess; and now I can always remember it."

"Let me see." He struggled to pry the phone out of her hand, and as she yanked it away, he found himself hovering over. For a moment they didn't say anything, the chemistry between them palpable.

"You'll delete it," she said breathlessly.

"I won't. I swear."

"Fine." He backed off to give her some space, but she kept the phone at arm's length. "You can look, but you can't touch," she said playfully, having seemingly recovered from their intense moment. She flipped the phone around and there he was, brown smears on his lips and chin.

"That's disgusting," he said.

"Really? I think it's quite fetching."

"I still have that photo of *you*," he said, in a tone that was somewhat threatening.

"What photo?"

"That selfie you took from your finest angle."

She tried to push him off the fountain's edge, but he barely moved. He could see how much it annoyed her, which he found to be incredibly cute.

"You should really delete that photo," she muttered.

"Only if you delete the one you took right now." He took a strand of her hair and tucked it behind her ear. "And that other one where I'm wearing the weird vest."

She leaned close. "The vest one is nonnegotiable."

"Fine," he conceded, resting his hand on top of hers. "But the Nutella one has to go."

"Okay," she said, her stare intense. "But we have to delete them at the exact same time."

He stroked her arm. "Okay."

"Like in those Western movie duels where they spin around and shoot."

"You know in those duels they're trying to kill each other, right?"

"Exactly," she said. "This is like that; but the opposite."

"Right . . ."

He pulled away to get into position, a little disappointed that she hadn't picked up on his physical cues. Still, he was enjoying the ridiculous tangents in their conversation. "Okay. I'm ready."

She turned away from him with phone in hand. "Do you have your phone cued up to that photo?"

He pulled up the horrid but amazing selfie. "Got it," he said, trying not to laugh.

"On the count of three, we turn back, point the phone at each other, and tap the trash button simultaneously."

"Sounds good."

"One, two, three!"

They turned toward each other and tapped the button in sync.

"Wait," he said. "It's asking me if I want to delete the photo."

"Oh yeah, you have to confirm if you really want to delete it." She shook her head. "Wow; that did *not* work out how I'd imagined it."

"It was pretty bad."

She sighed. "I am *so* tired."

He hugged her tight, burying his face in her hair that faintly smelled of perfume. "Me too."

"It's almost five a.m. now."

"Almost morning, huh? Wow." He breathed her in even deeper now, losing grip of his escape from reality.

"But almost is only *almost*, right?"

He pulled back and saw the hopeful look in her eyes. Maybe the downward spiral could wait. "You're right," he said.

"And you know what the best part about *almost* is?"

He stroked her hair. "Tell me."

"We still have time."

He nodded. "Plenty of time."

CHAPTER
twenty

M

Five a.m.

Eloise stood from the fountain and stretched her arms to the sky. "Are you absolutely certain you do not need a place to stay?"

Mira smiled. "I appreciate the offer," she said, "but since *you're* in the 14th and *we're* in the 18th . . ."

Mira's choice of words had been entirely deliberate. It was her subtle way of letting Jake know that as far as she was concerned, the kiss wasn't just a fluke. She only hoped he wasn't too exhausted to notice that she'd "we'd" them.

"I suppose you are a little far," Eloise admitted. "What will you do now?"

Eloise's question was the one thing Mira had been wondering about since they'd left the bar. The crêpes had killed some time—and given her a late-night tour of the 1st arrondissement's east end—but now the big question was back.

"There's only another hour until daylight," Mira noted. "It'll fly by." She hoped she sounded more unbothered than she felt, given her lack of a plan and the dread of not wanting the hours with Jake to slip away.

"Quite right," Dembe said, "It'll be morning before you know it." She sensed he was tired, as well as eager to get rid of them.

Mira knew that when Eloise and Dembe left, each minute would carry the weight of what had happened with Jake. She'd made the first move, and while Jake had kissed her back, she hoped he didn't regret it. The physical gestures he'd made since then were a good sign, but people were funny about late-night kisses in bars, all hot in the moment and awkward in the aftermath.

"Is it safe by the river at this hour?" Mira asked, remembering the soothing sound of the water lapping against the riverbank. It had only been five hours since they'd disembarked from the boat, but it felt so long ago, given everything that had happened.

"It is often safe," Eloise said. "It depends."

"On what?"

"On the area, the time of night, the sorts of characters."

"But it's nearly morning," Dembe said. "Joggers will be out any minute."

Dembe's thirst to get rid of Jake and Mira was palpable, and she didn't blame him. Back at the party, she'd noticed his fixation on Eloise when she'd seen them in the corridor; eyes glued to her, hanging on her every word. It was the first time she'd seen them without anyone else around, and it was obvious how much he adored her.

Eloise placed both hands on her hips, sort of like a drunken security guard. "If it is truly safe, I will need to see it for myself."

Mira looked over at Jake, hands stuffed into his pockets like he was waiting for what came next. "Are you cool with going to the riverbank?"

"You're the boss."

Mira was glad that Jake hadn't forgotten her bossy ways from their long day of touring Paris; that fun dynamic was how all of this had started, with each new discovery and playful argument bringing them ever closer. It was something she would keep as a fallback, should things become awkward once Dembe and Eloise departed.

But she hoped she wouldn't need it.

Mira and Jake followed Dembe and Eloise across Pont Louis-Phillippe, but instead of making their way into the charming streets of Île Saint-Louis, they opted for the stone steps that led to the river-bank. Mira was tempted to plot out a morning on Île Saint-Louis—it was so close, after all—but first she needed to see what the following hour had in store.

As soon as they finished their descent down the stairs, Mira was struck by how different this version of the riverbank was, compared to the area where they'd disembarked from the boat. It wasn't just the absence of the Eiffel Tower, it was the fact that it wasn't even really a riverbank, but more of a raised stone walkway that rounded the corner of Île Saint-Louis. She noticed how if a person sat with their knees hanging over the edge, their feet wouldn't even come close to touching the water. She also noticed how easy it would be to fall in.

"I don't think anyone's here," Jake observed.

The lack of seedy late-night types was a serious plus, as was the series of benches made from concrete slabs. She also didn't have to strain her ears to hear the gentle ripple of the water.

Dembe clapped his hands. "Well then, friends, it seems you've got yourselves a safe spot for a rest."

"Wait!" Eloise cried. She ambled over to Mira and wrapped her in a hug. "Do you really have to leave Paris so soon?"

Mira grimaced at Eloise's surprising strength. "As much as I'd love to stay, I don't think I can miss another flight."

She released Mira from the hug, but not before gripping onto her shoulders. "I may be moving to New York for a while."

Mira looked over at Dembe. "Is that the alcohol talking?" she whispered.

"She speaks the truth," he confirmed.

"Our domestic travel company is opening an office in New York next year," she explained. "And who could be more perfect to work there *than me*?"

"No one," Mira whispered, slightly afraid of her crazed eyes and the tightening grip on her shoulders. She wondered how much alcohol Eloise had consumed, and it was clear in that moment that Dembe was trying to take her home so she could sleep it off.

"Did you know you can fly from Paris to Biarritz for as little as nineteen euros?" Eloise quizzed.

"Uhh, no."

"Neither do any of the other Americans!"

"Yeah, we're really dumb." Mira would've said almost anything to escape Eloise's drunken second wind.

"You can also rent these entire beautiful homes through our company, instead of having to use those stupid apps, BUT YOU NEED SOMEONE TO TELL YOU THESE THINGS."

"Like you?" Mira said meekly. "In the brand-new office in New York?"

"EXACTEMENT," she boomed.

"Cool. I guess I'll see you next year then?"

"No. We will trade homes. Like in that film *The Holiday*. But for longer than two weeks."

Mira tried to back away, but the shoulder grip was as tight as ever.

She looked to Jake for help, but he just stood there looking amused. The only way out of this was to play along some more. "You want me to move to Paris? But what about my job?"

Eloise snorted. "You love *nothing* about that job."

"I don't think I even told you where I work."

"Irrelevant. Your soul is sleeping."

"Ah; thank you for your input." It was all Mira could say without spiraling into late-night introspection.

"Do something creative," Eloise instructed. "This, I could see for you."

Mira thought back to growing up with all those books, and how much she'd loved writing about anything and everything—before it all became about branding materials for Bloom. For the last few years, she'd thought that was fine, but hearing Eloise describe this other option—alcohol-fueled as it was—gave her pause. Unfortunately, there wasn't a moment of contemplation to spare, not with Eloise's face inches from hers.

"Okay," Mira said. "I will live in your Paris apartment next year."

Eloise frowned. "Not Paris. Italy."

Mira didn't even know how to respond to that. She guessed that Eloise was in a blackout state, just saying random things on autopilot. Mira had experienced her share of blackouts too (not that she could remember them), so she found herself feeling a twinge of sympathy. She gestured to Dembe, hoping he would come and collect his woman.

But Eloise wasn't done.

"My Paris apartment would suffocate you," she said. "But my family's villa in Italy? That you would love."

Mira liked the sound of Eloise's magical blackout world, but she didn't want to lose more precious one-on-one time with Jake. "Sounds good," Mira said. "You'll stay in my Manhattan apartment, and I'll stay in the Italian villa."

"*Géniale*," she sighed, before finally releasing Mira's shoulders and wandering over to Dembe. "*Au revoir!*"

Mira waved. "Au revoir! And say good-bye to Alexandre for me; it was so nice meeting him." The last time Mira had seen Alexandre was not long after he'd thoughtfully gotten her that nonalcoholic cocktail. Wherever he was, with his mental compartments to organize his various women, she hoped he was happy.

Dembe led Eloise directly up the stairs, only allowing her a moment for a quick farewell wave.

When they finally disappeared from view, Mira let out a long breath. "Damn."

"Seriously," Jake said.

She spun around to face him. "You were kind of useless back there."

"I was just so curious about where it would go."

She couldn't blame him. "It was pretty wild; I mean I like her, but that was intense."

He came over and rubbed her shoulders. "Seemed kind of painful too."

Mira felt herself getting lost in his touch. But something kept tugging at her mind.

"How did she know my job bums me out? Is she a witch or something?"

"Bloom bums you out?" Jake stepped away and sat down on the nearest bench, gesturing for her to join him. She didn't hesitate.

"God, it feels good to sit down," she said. "Even if it's on concrete."

"Bloom bums you out?" he repeated.

It was clear he wouldn't let her avoid his question. "I didn't think it did, but ever since she made that comment, it's been gnawing at me. Like the way people's eyes light up when they talk about work?" She looked to him for clarity. "What's *that* about?"

"I think those people are just passionate about their jobs."

"Even in the corporate world?" She crossed her arms. "I always thought it was normal not to love your work." She could feel the influence of her parents seeping in, as a good education, job title, and salary were all they had ever seemed to care about.

"You thought it was *normal* not to love your work?" Jake said. "That surprises me."

"Why?"

"Didn't you just break off an engagement because you weren't in love?"

She gasped. "That's different! Like you're *supposed* to be in love with the person you spend your life with—work is different."

"I guess you're right," he said, though it was clear from his tone he didn't mean that.

She wanted to fight about it, but it was well past the hour for feistiness. She slumped her shoulders instead. "Can we please change the subject? I haven't had time to explore this dilemma, and I can't have my personal and professional crises overlap."

"Fair enough," he said, before leaning forward so she couldn't avoid his stare. "Should we talk about the fact that we kissed?"

She felt herself blushing. "It's not usually the guy who brings up a topic like that."

"I watched rom-coms with my mom, remember?"

He was truly the most endearing person on earth. She just didn't know how to tell him. "And your thoughts on the kiss?" she said, sticking to the safer topic. "Any regrets?"

"Nope. You?"

"Nope."

Uncertainty flashed across his face. "Were you drunk when it happened? Are you still drunk now?"

Jake's bluntness stunned her into silence. But it was valid. "Hmm . . ." she finally said, tapping her fingers on her chin. "I don't think I was, and I don't think I am right now. Like there's a lingering buzz layered on top of a hangover, but I think it's been that way for the last fourteen hours. This is who I am now."

He chuckled. "Me too."

A long silence followed, and in that time, she realized that despite having talked about the kiss, they also hadn't. Not the *why* of it, anyway.

"I like you," he said suddenly.

She let out a tiny gasp. With those three simple words she was a girl of seventeen again, or maybe nineteen, since she'd never had a date in high school. She steadied her breathing and met his gaze. "I like you too."

To her surprise, he frowned. "Wait; did we already cover the liking part?"

"You mean at Luxembourg Gardens?"

"Yeah."

She leaned in. "That was more of a *friendly* liking, and I think by now, the liking has escalated."

He took a strand of her hair between his fingers and studied it, seemingly fascinated by the powers of keratin. "It didn't count, though."

"What do you mean?"

"The kiss. Kisses don't count when they're at four a.m. in a bar; unless you never plan on seeing the person again." He inched closer. "And here we are, still technically seeing each other. So, that kiss didn't happen."

"Are you saying there might be another kiss?" The thought of another kiss with Jake filled every atom in her body with pulsing anticipation.

Jake let the strand of hair slip through his fingers and stroked her arm. "Yes. But you're not going to know when."

She bit her lip. "I'm not?"

"No. It's not something you can plan by using a map, like one of your bucket-list things."

She rested her head on his shoulder. "Why must you speak ill of my bucket list? Did the bucket list not show you a wonderful time?"

He struggled to maintain a serious expression. "It was serviceable."

She pushed him away. "*Serviceable*? Go jump in the river. Our business is concluded."

"All I'm saying is . . . it's time for *me* to plan a thing or two."

Mira's aggression melted away. "Okay; I guess that's fair." She loved the idea of Jake surprising her with a kiss, even if it meant spending every moment from now until then obsessing over when it would happen.

He leaned back on the bench. "First order of business: we need a power nap."

Worry creeped into Mira's mind. "I could definitely use a nap," she said, "but if we close our eyes, I'm afraid we'll pass out and miss the sunrise. And wouldn't it be wrong to have only seen the sunset, when we could've seen the sunrise too?"

He didn't seem the least bit concerned. "Already checked the sunrise time. Already set an alarm with a five-minute warning. Already chose the most annoying ringtone so we don't sleep through it."

Her jaw dropped. "How and *when* did you do all that?"

"Are you forgetting I'm the man who planned the perfect sunset on the bridge?"

She squeezed his hand, remembering the feeling of his breath against her lips on Pont des Arts. "That's not something I'd forget."

"Consider it part one," he said. "And I hope you'll like the sequel even more."

She wanted to kiss him right then, but she'd already been the initiator once, and she didn't want to ruin his plan of choosing the perfect moment.

"Can't wait for part two." She leaned back and shifted in her seat, trying to find the best position. "But first, a quick nap."

He looked at her strangely. "What are you doing?"

"Trying to make this concrete slab feel comfortable."

"You won't get comfortable all the way over there." He put his arm around her and pulled her into his chest. She gave in immediately, wrapping both arms around him tight, and finding a spot in the warmest nook of his neck. "Now isn't that better?" he said.

"Mm-hmm," she mumbled. "Screw the sunrise, let's stay here awhile."

"No way. Back up on the bridge in thirty minutes. I'm not letting you miss a thing."

She nuzzled deeper into his neck. "You still smell like the Tom Ford cologne."

"I may have sprayed on a lot of it when you told me you liked how it smells."

"I know, I saw you do it," she murmured. "So hot and thoughtful of you; mmm . . . hot . . ."

He pulled away from her. "Wait; are you still talking about me? Or the photo of the male model in the ad?"

She lifted her head. "Sixty-forty split."

He pushed her away. "Get outta here; go find your own bench."

"Nooo, I need the cozy nook." She wormed her way back into her new favorite spot, passing out almost immediately.

*

Mira wasn't sure how long she'd been asleep, but she jolted to attention when she heard a wolf-like howl.

"What the fuck was that?" she whispered.

It was followed by a second and third howl, each one louder than the last.

"Shit," Jake said, rubbing his eyes. He gestured to the rowdy trio of teenage boys bounding down the stone steps.

Mira's heart rate immediately quickened, and she could feel the tension building in her spine. "Are they going to kill us?" Her annoyance for teenagers had shifted to a primal fear somewhere around the time she'd turned thirty. They were wild and unpredictable and full of dangerous exuberance. Anyone would be afraid.

"They're *not* going to kill us," he said. "They're just enjoying the last part of a typical teenage night."

She held her breath as the teens ran toward them. And released it when they ran right past. "Thank God."

"We're still six minutes from sunrise," Jake noted, "but it's getting kind of noisy down here. Want to head up to the bridge?"

"Immediately, if not sooner." She snuck a quick glance at the frightening teens, before stretching out her legs as best she could, her body now feeling the beginnings of soreness.

It's been a day.

As Mira and Jake made their way up the staircase and back onto Pont Louis-Philippe, she took in the view of the eastern sky. From the shifting colors it was clear the night was ending, the darkness giving way to orange hues spilling out of the horizon.

The dawn of a new day brought uncomfortable things to mind: the airport, a transatlantic flight, and the ruins of the life she'd eventually have to face.

Jake came up from behind her, wrapping his strong arms around her waist. He rested his chin on her shoulder and sighed. "A new day, huh?"

"Yeah," she said, without even a trace of excitement.

"Don't do it."

"Do what?"

"Think about the *after*. If you do, you'll miss it." He pointed to the first real glimpses of the morning sun.

He was right. She didn't say a word and she didn't even think. She just watched.

CHAPTER
twenty-one

M

Six a.m.

The fiery sun was back in its full morning glory, for what promised to be another perfect summer day in Paris. Mira only wished she'd be around to enjoy it.

Not that she'd be dead, so why was she making it sound that way?

She shifted her mind away from her theatrics and promised herself to follow Jake's advice.

Don't miss it.

"We don't have to leave for the airport until noon," Mira noted, still enjoying the feeling of being wrapped in Jake's arms.

"Oh yeah? That's a long way away."

"Literal ages from now."

"And is there, by any chance, an item or two you're still wanting to cross off your bucket list?"

"I'd have to check," she said, taking out her phone for a noncommittal scroll. "I suppose we could cross something off."

"Are we in for a lot of walking?" he asked, releasing her from his arms.

She turned and saw that he was looking worried. "Strolling, yes. But nothing too intense. Think of it as bucket-list *lite*."

"I'm definitely down with something light after yesterday." He stretched out his legs. "We must've walked like fifteen thousand steps."

She checked her watch. "More like twenty-eight thousand."

His eyes bulged. "No wonder we were always so hungry."

"Right? All those calories were just for survival."

He looked in both directions. "Where to next?"

As much as Mira tried to keep following Jake's advice of embracing the present moment, she wasn't immune to dwelling on things.

To dwell is human.

Her current focus was dwelling on the thing that hadn't happened. "How come you didn't kiss me?"

"Kiss you?" He took a pause to run a hand through his hair—now greasy and matted after another all-nighter, yet still incredibly sexy. "Not sure what you mean."

"Sunrise. It was the obvious moment for a kiss."

He shoved his hands into his pockets and strolled past her. "Which is exactly why I didn't." He stopped in his tracks and glanced back. "Wait . . . am I going the right way?"

"You're not." She gestured in the other direction. "Île Saint-Louis begins *there*."

"And what's there?"

She couldn't believe he hadn't kissed her.

"It's charming and it's good for strolling and it makes people happy."

"Are you pouting?"

"No."

"Are you pouting because you didn't get a visit from the candyman?" He started making mocking kissy sounds.

She scrunched up her nose. "Why did you have to make it weird?" She turned and headed toward Île Saint-Louis. "So, so weird."

She could hear Jake laughing and when he finally caught up to her, he took her hand and didn't let go. It was a simple thing, but the way it radiated warmth was a lovely feeling.

"Didn't see that coming, did you?" he whispered into her ear. His satisfied salesman energy from the day before had disappeared, giving way to something sweeter. She squeezed his hand. "I think I like this *surprises* thing."

*

Île Saint-Louis was a pocketful of charm. It was also nearly pocket-size. With one main street running through the middle and a few microstreets in between, it was tailor-made for anyone in search of an adorable jaunt with café pit stops and a scoop of famous ice cream or two. The only problem when jaunting in the early morning hours, was that nothing was open for business; not a shop to browse in, not a single café wicker chair to sit on.

"I feel like my footsteps are happening in surround sound," Mira said, as she and Jake strolled through one of the idyllic tree-lined streets.

"It's the quietest Paris has been, which is nice, in a way."

"But hostile, in a way."

He looked at her strangely. "How do you mean?"

"Like if one needed to . . . I don't know, burp or *whatever else*, you'd want honking horns to drown it out. Or at least the ambient chatter of nearby pedestrians."

He studied her with concern. "Are you currently experiencing this problem?"

"Nope. Just making conversation."

And what a shitty conversation it was. She really needed sleep.

"Glad you're okay, then," he said. "But if the need should arise, let me know and I'll start cawing like a flock of pigeons to drown it out."

"Pigeons don't caw, they coo."

"I thought that's what doves do."

"How do you even know that?"

"I don't know!" he cried. "I'm really tired right now and the facts are just pouring out!"

"I'm really tired too!"

They both sighed dramatically.

"How are we supposed to stay alive until the coffee?" she whined.

"It shouldn't be long; cafés open at seven, right?"

"I dunno," she said, sounding even whinier. "That's what Google says, but who even knows? French people are wild; they don't follow the rules. They don't even give you a night-before warning before going on strike."

He placed his hands on her shoulders and turned her toward him. "If that train hadn't gone on strike, we wouldn't be here right now."

"You're right," she muttered. "We'd be sleeping in our nice comfy beds in New York."

"Do you really mean that?" He searched her eyes.

"No," she admitted, feeling the weight of his stare. "I just get a little whiny when I reach the tiredness point of no return."

"A *little* whiny?"

"I would punch you in the arm, but I don't have the strength." She made her arms go limp and dramatically swayed her body. "See? You have to catch me before I fall." She may have been tired, but she wasn't above having a big strong man scoop her up into his arms.

Except, he didn't. Worse than that, in all her swaying she lost her balance and wound up falling on the ground.

Jake burst into laughter as Mira took stock of the gravelly dirt now coating her hands. "Shit." She looked up at him with contempt. "What the fuck, dude?"

"It was the only way you'd learn!"

"What's the point of a body like that if you don't even use it to catch grown women in distress?" She struggled to pick herself up off the ground. "*Broad-shouldered tease.*"

His expression turned serious, just as she'd hoped.

"A tease, huh?" He bent down and grabbed Mira by the thighs, hoisting her over his shoulder in one fell swoop. "Is that *broad-shouldered* enough for you? Huh?"

She giggled happily. "Yes."

"What now?"

She clapped him on the back. "Go forth!"

He started walking. "Where?"

"Anywhere; just keep me off my feet."

"Aren't those orthopedic insoles supposed to help you walk all day?"

"It's the next day, genius. And would you please stop remembering everything?"

"I'll try. How's the view back there?"

She couldn't see much of Île Saint-Louis from her vantage point, just the cobblestones below. She *could* see a new side of Jake, though. "I'm looking at your ass, so the view's pretty good. How about you?"

"Can't see anything; your ass is blocking my entire view."

She slapped him on the back. "Hey!"

"You're the one who said you have a dump-truck ass."

She'd almost forgotten about her pathological lying streak, all to keep him from knowing she was freshly off a broken engagement. It felt great not to have to do that anymore.

She wanted to hug him, but with her arms dangling down his back it was impossible. "I think my energy is restored now; you can put me down."

"Is it because of the ass thing? Because your ass is pretty nice."

She felt herself immediately blush. "We're good on the ass front, I promise; but you need your rest too!"

He put her down as gently as possible. And then, there they were, standing face to face on a tiny island, madly attracted to each other. Or at least she was. The trees swayed in the morning silence, no one around and no one to see them.

She made an executive decision.

"Jake?"

"Yeah?"

"I don't want to be surprised anymore," she whispered, every cell in her body aching for the second kiss.

"Are you sure?"

She nodded, and almost immediately, Jake's hands found their way behind her neck, his fingers quickly entwined in her hair as he pulled her face to his. He pressed his lips against hers for a deep, urgent kiss, like the way she knew he would've kissed her in that doorway in the rain. Slowly, his fingers moved down the front of her neck and then farther, his teasing touch making her want him even more. As their kiss deepened, his hands made their way down her sides and then around to the lowest part of her back. He pulled her in, pressing her body tight against his.

Her fingers clawed all the way up his neck, landing in that mess of hair she'd been dying to get her hands on.

It was the best kiss of her goddamn life.

And then, she heard it. A trickle. Followed by a steady stream. And a grunt of relief. Mira didn't want the kiss to end, but on this silent island where every sound was amplified, the distraction was just too much. She pulled her lips away from Jake's, turning to face the sound head-on.

And there he was.

A middle-aged man just a few yards away, taking a piss in broad daylight. After zipping up, the man strolled past them, his eyebrows wiggling in encouragement. "*Bonjour,*" he said in a gruff voice.

"Bonjour," she said meekly, Jake's hair still between her fingers.

Once the man turned the corner, Mira and Jake burst into laughter.

"Guess it's just as well," Jake said, his hands now stroking her back. "Not really sure what the endgame would've been out here on the street."

She slid her hands back down his neck, resting them on his chest. "Yeah; it's a hostile environment."

He shook his head sadly. "Not even any grass."

"Uh-huh."

"At least we'll always have Paris."

Did she dare say it? Did she dare even hint at the possibility of what came next? Mira was aware of all the post-engagement emotional baggage she still had to purge, but that didn't mean post-Paris kissing wasn't allowed. Or other things.

She could feel her stomach tightening in knots as she edged closer to putting her feelings into words. As nerve-racking as it was, she didn't want to wait to say it later, when the intensity of the kiss faded into a memory.

"Thank God this isn't one of those movies where two people meet and they live in a different city," she said, doing her best to sound casual and calm.

"Huh?"

His face was suddenly hard to read. Was he tired? She decided to be more direct. "At least we'll still be able to see each other again; once these twenty-four hours are over, I mean."

By the time Mira got to the end of her little speech, she was already starting to feel a little stupid. And when she noticed the flicker of darkness in his eyes? She felt like a total moron.

"Good point," he said, in the most unconvincing fashion.

Mira stepped back, giving herself the space to decipher his sudden change in tone. She started to wonder if he thought she was clingy and obsessed. Had this entire day for Jake been nothing more than killing time with the nearest rando?

She let out a tiny gasp. Or maybe he had a girlfriend back home in New York.

She shifted her weight from one foot to the other, avoiding his eyes and feeling worse with every added second. If that middle-aged man hadn't peed in their vicinity, who knows what would've happened. Maybe she and Jake would've found a patch of grass after all.

Jake glanced at his watch. "I think we can get that coffee now." His voice was as dispassionate as an automated phone line for local information.

"Great," she exclaimed, trying to balance out his robo-tone with a glossy sheen of excitement.

They turned back in the direction of a café they'd passed by earlier. To Mira's relief, the wicker chairs and round wooden tables were now neatly arranged on the terrace, ready to welcome the first patrons of the day.

"That worked out well," he said.

He was right, but what Mira *couldn't* figure out was why everything else was unraveling. She'd always had this vision of sipping coffee on a terrace on Île Saint-Louis, overlooking the bridge and the glittering water of the Seine. She settled into a chair with this exact daydream view now in front of her, but somehow it all felt wrong. She was mad at herself for letting the mood of a guy she'd only known for a day interfere with all the things that usually made her happy. But she also didn't know how to stop being human.

The only thing Mira knew for certain, was that her eyes were burning from intense fatigue, and she needed an immediate fix.

She ordered a triple espresso and a café crème.

One problem at a time.

CHAPTER
twenty – two

⌄

Seven a.m.

Jake and Mira waited for their coffee in silence.

He glanced at his watch for the second time in as many minutes. They weren't due to leave Paris for another five hours, and while the time had been flying by before, each second now was an exercise in torture. Out of the corner of his eye, he noticed Mira browsing her phone. When he saw that she was scrolling through the weather app, he realized he wasn't the only one doing the avoiding. He hadn't wanted it to be this way, but the funny thing was, it wouldn't have been like this at all if it hadn't been for her. If she hadn't made that casual mention of hanging out in New York. Without those words, he would've succeeded in denying reality, replacing the facts with the blinding enjoyment of five more hours in this made-up world of their making.

But she'd said it.

And now he found himself with no other option but to finally tell the truth.

He let out a long sigh.

"Stop," she said.

He was completely thrown. "Stop what?"

"You don't have to say it." She crossed her arms defensively.

"You have no idea what I'm going to say."

"I don't? I make one casual mention about the silver lining of living in the same city, thus *maybe implying* the vague possibility of a future hangout, and in less than two seconds you go from being a Casanova to a cardboard cutout of a human man."

He nodded. "Fair."

"But you don't have to worry."

"Mira—"

"I'm not expecting anything because of a mind-blowing kiss."

He couldn't stop himself from smiling. "Mind-blowing?"

"Shut up."

"For the record," he said, "I wasn't thinking you were expecting anything."

She unfolded her arms and they fell to her sides, her defenses falling along with them. "You weren't?"

"Why would I think you were expecting anything, when you told me you just broke off an engagement and still have a lot to figure out? I *do* listen."

"Okay," she said, looking curious. "Then what's the problem?" The first signs of cynicism creeped across her face. "Oh wait; it's the other thing."

He wrinkled his brow. "The other thing?"

"*Girlfriend*, am I right?" She tossed out the words like they were yesterday's trash. "Or maybe you're one of those guys who's married with three kids, but you don't want it dragging down your *cool Manhattan life*, so you keep them tucked away in a six-bedroom house upstate. Is it weird having a secret family?" She cringed. "Oh my God, do you have a minivan?"

He stared at her for several seconds before responding. "Do you really, genuinely, think that's the kind of guy I am?"

She shrugged. "I've only known you for a day."

Jake wasn't sure if she was being nonchalant to protect herself, or if, with the return of reality, she truly didn't feel like she knew him. Either way, the words stung. He lowered his eyes, not ready or willing to respond.

The next thing he heard was a heavy sigh. "Not that it's been a *normal* day," she admitted.

He raised his eyes a little. "Yeah?"

"I'm not made of stone, you know."

"You're really not. You're someone who would definitely have some thoughts about a day like this."

"Oh, I will *give you* thoughts." She straightened her posture, now suddenly alert. "I think it's strange that after only a day, I feel like I know someone really well, even though I'm missing all the major details."

"It's unorthodox," he agreed.

"And it's strange to not tire of talking, when there's already been so much talking."

"That's a first for me too."

Her expression softened. "And it's strange how many moments from the last twenty-four hours, have risen through my rankings of all-time greatest memories."

He felt a burst of warmth. "Incredibly, fucking, strange."

Mira frowned. "Wait—does that mean my standards for happiness are low? Are my rankings lame?"

"Did you just put low standards and me in the same category?"

She cringed. "Oops."

"Don't insult me like that again," he said playfully. "And if you really had low standards for happiness, you'd still be engaged."

"I guess that's true."

"And to answer your question," he went on, "no girlfriend, and no secret family living upstate. I am totally single."

A part of him was hoping she would toss the table out of the way, jump into his lap, and kiss him hard. Which he realized was a stupid thought when she slumped her shoulders instead.

"Then I'm still not sure what's wrong," she said, staring at her hands. "Is it me?"

"*No*. Don't even think that for a second." He wanted to blurt it out fast like ripping off a Band-Aid, but the waiter arrived before any of his pent-up words could pour out.

He shifted his focus to the triple espressos now resting on the table. "I've never had a triple espresso before," he said. "Will my heart stop?"

"If you're scared, why did you order it?"

He studied the cup. "Because you did."

"I see."

"I guess I couldn't decide what I wanted for myself." The irony of his words wasn't lost on him. "Not when things were so awkward."

"An awkwardness of your own making."

"Right." He shifted his gaze from the cup to Mira. "About that . . ."

She held her hand up. "Wait. Not before my espresso." She opened a pack of raw sugar and poured it into her cup. Once that was done, she grabbed a second packet and looked in his direction. "Yes? No?"

"Yes."

She poured it into his drink, and then, taking one tiny spoon in each hand, stirred the contents of both cups—while staring at him the whole time. "Scared?"

His eyes grew wide. "Terrified."

She set down the spoons and handed him one of the espressos. "It's *go time.*"

They clinked their cups and downed each drink in one shot.

She blinked hard. "Wow."

"Yeah."

"How do you feel?" she asked.

"The opposite of dead."

"Exactly. It'll be even better in ten minutes."

He noticed her look toward the bridge, the same bridge where they'd watched the sunrise.

"You were saying . . ." she said.

"I'm leaving New York," he announced, deciding to throw down the hammer all at once. She didn't say anything for what felt like a long time. "Mira?"

"I'm here." She didn't elaborate any further.

"Do you want to know more?"

"Sure." She finally faced him. "Are you moving somewhere far away? Different time zone?"

"Different time zone."

"Chicago?" she asked, with what sounded like a hint of hope.

"LA."

Mira's face seemed to calculate the distance immediately. She turned away from him and lowered her gaze to her lap. "You'll love the weather." He could hear the emotion seeping through her voice.

"Mira . . ."

She took a long breath. "Does this mean you're leaving Bloom?"

"Actually, no. I'll be going to the west coast sales office we opened a few months ago."

"Oh. Has this been in the works for a while?"

"There was always a plan to build up the west coast sales team." He scratched his head. "They were hesitant at first; all those fancy California brands having such a stronghold and all. But now that we've gone international, they're ready to go big out west."

"Sounds awesome."

Jake knew she didn't mean it and he couldn't blame her. "They want me to lead the west coast team," he said, continuing to say things just to fill up the silence. "And they'll probably announce it on Monday." He sighed. "And that's the news."

She managed a weak smile. "I know you'll do an amazing job; really."

From those few encouraging words, he could already feel the distance between them growing. It was enough to create a sickening feeling in his stomach. "Thank you."

"I guess that means you'll be moving soon?"

"I have to fly to LA tomorrow to set myself up."

Her bulging eyes broke through her calm inquisition. "You're moving to LA *tomorrow*?"

Mira's dramatic knee-jerk reaction felt more like the person he'd been getting to know since yesterday; it was comforting. "*Not* tomorrow. I'm just spending a week in LA to get acquainted with the office. And to look at a few more apartments before signing a lease."

"Got any neighborhoods in mind?"

"Do you really want to know all this?"

She nodded encouragingly. "Of course."

"Maybe WeHo . . ."

She stuck out her tongue in disgust. "Did you just call West Hollywood *WeHo*? Gawd, you're already one of them."

He could feel himself blushing. "That's what the real estate agent called it!"

"Maybe you should move to Los Feliz," she said, sarcasm dripping from her voice. "I heard the guy who played Don Draper lives there. It's a happening 'hood."

"Don't act like you don't know that his name is Jon Hamm. Women love him."

"Just because I know he hails from St. Louis and used to be a teacher, that doesn't mean I love him."

He shook his head in amazement. "This is *not* how I thought this conversation would go."

"This is how I process unexpected news." Her expression became more serious. "After you're done with your week in LA, what comes next?"

"I'll be back in New York."

"For how long?"

"I'll be spending one more week in the office, to say good-bye to um, Shirley, I guess, and tie up any other loose ends."

"Shirley's going to miss you," Mira said, doing a good job of concealing her emotion.

"She'll only miss telling me I'm doing my expenses wrong."

As much as Shirley annoyed him, right now she was the only bridge between Mira and Jake, the only thing that made any of this news seem normal.

Thanks, Shirl.

"In two weeks' time, you'll be living in LA."

And just like that, the bridge called Shirley crumbled away.

"That's right," he said. "Two more weeks."

The waiter returned, this time with two large cups filled with café crème.

Mira and Jake immediately grabbed their drinks, and before long, their slow sips filled the inevitable silence. Everything was out in the open now, and there wasn't a damn thing to be done.

Mira set down her empty cup. "Can I ask you something?"

"You can ask me anything," he said, all pretenses gone.

"Would you have told me all this before leaving Paris, if I hadn't suggested hanging out in New York?"

He rubbed his chin, taking his time to consider his response. "Actually, I'm not sure I would have."

"I don't blame you," she said.

"Because even though these hours added up to a lot, at the end of the day, we've still only known each other for a day."

"That *is* a fact."

"I guess I would've worried about sounding too intense; like wouldn't it have been a bit much to warn you I was moving away in two weeks?"

"Yes. A hundred times too intense."

"Exactly."

"Wait a minute," she said. "If you thought *that* would've been too much, didn't you think it was way too excessive when I told you I broke off my engagement?"

Jake was struggling to keep a straight face. "*So* excessive. I wanted to bail as soon as you said it."

Mira slugged him hard, making him wince and laugh all at once. "I like you the least when you're impressed with yourself."

"But you *still* like me," he said. "Even then."

"I also like those gross-looking hairless cats, so don't read too much into it."

He grimaced. "Point taken."

She turned toward him. "Now that you're no longer self-obsessed— for the time being—I have one last question."

He rested his arm against the back of her chair. "Shoot."

"Why did you plan a romantic sunrise and a second-kiss surprise if you knew this was going nowhere?"

He stared into her warm brown eyes. "We're not nowhere. We're here."

"We are. But you know what I mean."

"I don't like wasting time."

"But that's my point. Knowing what you knew from the very beginning . . . don't you find this all to be a waste of time?"

"No."

She raised an eyebrow. "Care to elaborate?"

He gave himself a moment to think, trying to find the perfect words to explain how he'd felt with each passing hour of their time in Paris. If only there were a Hallmark greeting card for that.

"It's okay," she said suddenly. "Maybe certain things don't have a clear-cut explanation."

While Jake appreciated the easy out, he wasn't quite ready to take it. "You're right, I *don't* have a clear-cut explanation. But what I do know is . . ." he searched for the words, "there wasn't any choice but to watch the sunrise or to hold your hand or to think about that second kiss." He moved closer, his face inches from hers. "Or to *have* that second kiss."

"But why?"

"Because if I *didn't* do any of those things, I'd be wasting the fact that one missed flight gave me all this time with someone who turned out to be, a pretty fucking memorable someone."

Mira lifted her chin and inched closer, not stopping until her full lips pressed against his. It wasn't anything like the kiss in the street, but in some other way he couldn't quite explain, it was better. She traced her fingers along his jaw and kissed him deeper, before pulling away and resting her head on his chest. "You're pretty fucking memorable too."

He reveled in the quiet closeness, not wanting it to end.

"What now?" she said, after a few minutes of silence.

It was an important question, and one that he couldn't ignore. He glanced at his watch as he stroked her hair. "We've got four more hours until we have to leave for the airport."

"Don't say *airport* to me," she murmured. "Airport *bad*. Airport like Voldemort."

"Couldn't help bringing out the nerd vibe, could you?"

"Old habits." She stared up at him, looking a little concerned. "Seriously, though, since *you're* the one who's ruining everything by leaving, you have to find a way to fix it for the next four hours."

"Okay. Let me think for a minute."

He let the memories he'd made with Mira filter through his mind. In the end, he could only find a single solution to salvage the rest of the morning. And he wasn't even sure if it would work.

"Before I told you my news, we were still pretty bummed about leaving Paris, but decided to enjoy whatever time was left. Remember?"

"I remember."

"Why don't we do that anyway?"

He knew it wasn't the best plan, but their current situation wasn't exactly bursting with positive options. In fact, their whole situation was supremely fucked.

She stroked the back of his neck. "I think that's a great idea."

He wasn't sure if she truly meant it, or if she was simply trying to distract herself from their supremely fucked situation.

Either way, there was nothing they could do but make the best of it.

CHAPTER
twenty-three

M

Eight a.m.

The emotional roller coaster of Île Saint-Louis was over.

It would now live on like a postcard in Mira's mind, detailed and incredibly nostalgic.

They weaved their way back through the streets of the Marais, no pit stops for macarons this time, but also no friend-zone boundaries. Jake held her hand firmly in his grasp, and it gave her the feeling that everything would be okay. For the length of one block, anyway. After that, she'd find herself aching for what was already slipping away. And so it went, back and forth, the paradoxical two-sided coin of being human.

Before they'd left the café, she'd weighed the various options of how to spend their final hours in Paris. She had seriously considered heading back to their picnic spot of Luxembourg Gardens, where they could lie on a patch of comfortable grass and hold each other close until the inevitable moment arrived. The problem with the marathon snuggling session—and maybe something more if no one noticed—was that Mira hadn't slept for twenty-four hours, and Jake hadn't slept for two days. There was a 100 percent chance they would both fall asleep, a sleep that would likely be impervious to whichever annoying alarm sound he chose. It wasn't even just the flight she was worried about; it was this special time with Jake, and she didn't want to miss a single minute.

She also didn't want to keep torturing herself about the fact that he was moving far away, and so soon. Her only hope of avoiding both the torture and the sleep was to stick with what the two of them did best: following her bucket list and embracing whatever randomness ensued.

She studied his face as they crossed the little side street of Rue des Francs-Bourgeois, leading them into the 3rd arrondissement.

He's moving to fucking LA.

They still had a bit of walking to do before they reached their next destination, so the bucket-list distraction wasn't yet having its intended effect.

He's moving in two weeks.

She shifted her focus to the shops, all of them shuttered at this early-morning hour. It was strange to think that soon, the city of Paris would fully awaken to the endless possibilities of a new day, whereas for Mira and Jake, the day was quickly winding down, progressively unraveling until it met its unfortunate end.

Shut up, you're not dying.

"So, what's new?" she asked. It was a dumb question, but she needed him to say something, anything at all, so his words could give her mind another job, something different from its current nonstop commitment to freaking out.

Jake looked down at her, his big blue eyes shining in the sun. They seemed warmer now, his eyes, like a swimming pool on a hot afternoon in July. "Are you okay?" He gave her hand a quick squeeze.

"I'm good," she lied, not wanting her freak-out to spread like a virus. A silence followed, one in which she realized that close-ended statements weren't particularly helpful in sparking conversation.

"I like this area," he said, his words offering Mira a life raft from the choppy waters of her mind. "Weren't we here yesterday?"

"A few streets over."

"Which means we're seeing something new right now."

"We are."

How did he do that? How did he know when it was time to make everything okay? It was a highly skilled trait that she'd noticed several times the day before, and he hadn't lost his touch even a little.

Even though Jake seemed to be fine, she didn't let that make her insecure. His different response was simply a result of being a different person, not from an absence of feeling anything.

You're a really fucking memorable someone.

Mira smiled to herself as she remembered his words, a feeling that made her squeeze his hand a little tighter.

"What's behind here?" he wondered aloud, gesturing to a small area enclosed by wrought-iron fencing. "I see trees."

Mira searched for the little blue sign that would hold the answer. "It's the Square du Temple. A mini square-park type thing, if you will."

"I think I will."

Jake veered off, searching for the gate. It turned out to be a waist-length enclosure you could easily swing open. He gave it a little push and glanced back. "Guess it's open."

They wandered in, following the gravelly path that curved in both directions. Each side was lined with benches sparsely occupied by early risers, a mix of people reading the news or simply reveling in the morning sun. One side of the park had a children's playground, and the other was marked by a cluster of trees and a botanical garden, complete with a quaint little pond at its center.

Without discussing it, Jake and Mira headed for the foliage-rich pond. They sat on the bench across from it, and as Mira nestled into Jake's arms, she felt peace in the morning stillness.

"I like Paris," Jake said, the first words between them after several minutes of silence.

She looked up at him with a smirk. "You only like Paris *now*? Were the last twenty hours just garbage to you?"

"Not at all, that stuff was great too. I just like how in Paris, you can wander your way into unassuming places, and find different things that are nice."

"*Nice* is the word people usually use for something they secretly hate."

He sighed in exasperation. "Okay, beautiful; it's beautiful! Are you satisfied?"

She snorted. "Why do beautiful things make you so upset?"

"Just look at it, okay?" He adjusted the angle of her head so it pointed at the view. "See? It's so green. And look at the flowers. And the pond. And is that a lily pad? Like fuck. That's some beautiful shit."

She muffled her laughter in her hands. "Mmhmm."

When she'd finished mocking him, she really did focus on admiring the view.

And he really did have a way of making everything all right.

✻

After their little detour, Jake and Mira walked a few blocks and wound up in Place de la République, a large square made memorable for the statue at its center. It was a monument of Marianne, the famous French symbol of liberty, equality, fraternity, and reason. If Mira hadn't read about it, she would've recognized it anyway, as she'd seen it online in videos of protests in Paris.

At the current morning hour, the square was largely empty, but given that it was a hub for five different métro lines, it wouldn't stay quiet for long.

She squinted ahead at the street that led north.

"Where to next?" Jake asked, breaking through her stream of geographic thoughts.

"We have two options."

He stretched his arms over his head. "Let's hear it."

Mira pointed north. "That street up there passes through Belleville, a neighborhood known for being a bit hilly."

"I choose the other option," he said immediately.

"How come?" she asked, though not at all surprised.

"After the stairs we did yesterday? And the twenty million steps?" He pouted. "Please don't make me."

"I was hoping you'd say that."

His face lit up. "Really?"

"I'm exhausted, man; this dump-truck ass can only do so much."

He immediately howled, unable to control his laughter. "You have to stop saying that about your ass! Please, I might die."

Mira couldn't help laughing along; everything was funnier when delirious from lack of sleep.

When they'd both recovered, she pointed to the red and green métro sign. "Four stops. Let's do this."

*

The métro car was empty aside from a young woman and an elderly couple, which mercifully allowed for Mira and Jake to sit down.

They sat diagonal from each other, stretching out their legs in exhaustion but smiling.

He kicked her foot. "Remember the first time we were on the subway?"

She smirked. "I remember it like it was yesterday."

"Ha-ha."

"I remember you smelled like vodka."

"I remember the paranoid look in your eyes when the subway car slowed for no reason."

She scowled. "It was supposed to be a one-minute ride!"

"I remember how, even then, I *knew* you would end up liking me."

"You knew nothing of the sort."

"It's true, I didn't. I just thought I'd have someone to talk to—and maybe flirt with—on a train ride to the airport. Then get on a plane, probably sit next to some smelly guy, and eight hours later wind up back in New York."

She found herself hanging on his every word. "Little did you know . . ."

"You can never really know what'll happen from one day to the next."

"That's true." She narrowed her eyes. "Wait—you thought we would flirt?"

"I mean, yeah, I was still kind of drunk."

"God. Of course you were."

"Not drunk now."

She flipped her hair. "Still wanna flirt?"

"No."

Mira hadn't expected the outright rejection. She felt embarrassed. "Whatever. It was just a suggestion."

Without warning, he leaned forward, grabbed her hands, and pulled her onto his lap. He swept her long hair over to one side, exposing her bare neck. Within seconds her heart was racing, and when she felt his warm breath against her ear, she couldn't stop herself from gripping on to his chest.

"Who needs flirting?" he whispered in her ear.

Before her brain cells could organize and form a response, she felt his lips work their way down her neck, and then, she felt his tongue work its way back up. She gasped.

Who needs words?

*

Fucking on the Paris métro had never been on Mira's bucket list.

Nor had fucking in an airplane bathroom, or in any other vestibules related to public transportation.

With the germ risk alone, she typically avoided these scenarios at all costs.

As Mira and Jake emerged from the métro stairwell and back out onto the street, none of this had changed.

Because they hadn't.

The intense necking had somehow transitioned into intense staring, like the kind of staring where you dive into the eyeballs of someone else's soul and take a little swim before reality rudely yanks you back out. Mira had never found herself in a situation quite like this, knee-deep in the melancholy twist of meetings and partings converging into one. She'd never watched her brave hero go off to war, and she'd never met an amazing guy at an all-inclusive who happened to live a world away. All she'd ever had were meaningless encounters in college, and then her twenties in Manhattan, when her heart had been aflutter with romantic possibilities after too many late-night sessions of watching *Sex and the City*. Trying to be a cross between a brown Charlotte and a brown Miranda hadn't led to more than boring dates, unmemorable sex, and periodically getting ghosted.

But all of that had ended with Dev.

Things had of course turned out messier still, so here she was, with a new possibility for romance, one more intense and incredible than anything she'd ever experienced. The circumstances between Mira and Jake were beyond complicated, but even if their time was running out, Jake was too special to hook up with in a place like the métro, where people were known to pee, vomit, and sometimes poop.

With sex firmly on the back burner, Mira was forced to grapple with the fact that Jake's tutorial on necking had left her with a case of the morning hornies. She didn't have a bucket of cold water on hand, but she hoped their next destination would calm her down.

Jake pointed to the church across the street, its facade a broad triangular shape converging into a narrow steeple. "Is that where we're going?"

"Nope." While religion wasn't on the menu, she thought about how a church might be useful in shaming away the horny urges.

"It must be something around here." He glanced around at the quiet intersection, looking for clues. The area was dotted with shops, but not in the way where you would take out your phone and document the endless charm. This area of the 20th was more of a low-key place for the basics of Parisian life. "Wait a second." He spotted the bakery across from the church and looked back at her. "You're kidding, right?"

"Nope," she repeated.

"When we had the croissant yesterday, the place you picked was random."

"It was."

"And you kind of made it sound like *every* bakery is good."

"I did."

"But now you had to take the subway to specifically come to this one?"

"Yes."

"That's all you have to say?"

"Oh wait, there *is* one more thing—yesterday we had pain au chocolat, not croissant."

He seemed exasperated. "Fine. *Pain au chocolat*. Happy?" He noticed the change in her expression. "Why are you smiling like that?"

She was smiling because his reaction was giving her a sneak peek into how they would be as a couple; traveling to new places, holding hands, being annoyed with each other, eating amazing food . . . the works. But she certainly wasn't going to admit that.

"You're right," she said. "Bakeries in Paris do dole out delicious-ness pretty much across the board."

"If I'm right, then why did we come here?'

"Because *sometimes* there will be a blog that will spend six para-graphs describing how the *croissant au beurre* at an unassuming bakery in the 20th arrondissement will change you. How the layers of flakiness combined with the folds of the chewy center will make you want to build a shrine to it." She wiped away the sweat that was pooling on the sides of her forehead, her croissant description having the opposite effect of killing her horny vibes.

She noticed Jake licking his lips. "That does sound pretty good."

"Then are you ready to change your life for the low, low price of a euro and ten cents?"

He squeezed her hand. "I'm ready."

*

Mira and Jake sat on the church steps, the sun shining down on their epic croissant experience. She'd been adamant that they take the first bite simultaneously, and not long after they'd breached the crispy golden exterior, the moaning sounds had ensued.

"Oh my God," he mumbled.

"Mmhmm."

Once they'd made it to the chewy, buttery, artery-clogging center, their audible reactions could not be contained. It was louder than their reaction to the pain au chocolat, and it included random eff-bombs too; it was everything a church would find offensive on a Saturday morning (or at any other time, for that matter).

As soon as Mira had finished, she let out a loud sigh. "God . . ." she gushed, wiping her forehead of its latest sheen of sweat. She propped her elbows on the stone steps behind her and leaned back. "That was incredible."

"I take it all back," Jake said, leaning back alongside her. "You always know what to do."

His acknowledgment of her dominance reminded her of their first few hours together, back when he'd been the follower and she'd made all the rules. It was strange to feel nostalgic for things that had only happened a day ago, but such was the hand that destiny had dealt. Mira forced her mind to shift back to *viennoiserie* pleasures. In a way, the croissant had satisfied her animal instincts, and it was probably even better than a lot of the sex she'd had.

But could a mind-blowing croissant replace the experience of being with Jake? She looked over at him, her eyes scanning his body from top to bottom.

Definitely not.

"Are you eye-fucking me?"

She immediately blushed, the glaring sun having made her unaware that his eyes had been open when she'd been busy devouring him with her own. She wondered if she should deny it, and what that would even do.

She sat up. "What if I was?"

"Then I'd be relieved."

Her mouth twisted in confusion. "Why?"

"Because I already eye-fucked you yesterday when your T-shirt got wet in the rain."

She gasped and instinctively covered her chest. "You did?"

"And a couple times after too."

She dropped her hands, reveling in the idea of being wanted. "I guess we're even, then."

"No, we're not; do it some more!"

He sexily posed on the church steps, and it was hilarious.

Even as she found herself enjoying the lighthearted moment, she realized there were a lot of things she would miss about Jake when he was gone. And him being sexy?

Not even the half of it.

CHAPTER
twenty–four

M

Nine a.m.

Paris's reputation as a strolling city continued to prove itself in spades. Mira felt satisfied with the ground she'd covered since that bonus morning in Paris and the twenty-four hours since. The fancy French toast in the 8th, the crêpes and homemade cider in the 18th, the famous retail of the 9th, the offbeat bar in the 10th, the macarons in the 4th, the bookstores in the 5th, the picnic in the 6th, the city tour via the Seine—thanks to Jake—the cocktail bar in the 2nd, the handheld crêpes in the 1st—wildly different from the savory crêpe experience—Île Saint-Louis, that mini park in the 3rd . . . and now here. There may have been a few métro journeys and car rides in between all the strolling, but Mira and Jake were humans, after all, not those robots from Boston Dynamics that were known for their ability to jump-squat onto a table.

"What are you smiling about?" Jake asked, as they sauntered down a side street hand in hand.

"Just loving Paris in the morning," Mira explained, not wanting to give him the rundown of her Paris strolling report card. She didn't doubt he would've done his best to seem interested, and maybe he would've even cared, but that wasn't really the point. She'd been wanting to explore Paris this way for years, long before Jake, and even before Dev. It was something between herself and herself, and it felt nice to have this special thing that was only meant for her.

Mira continued her mental rundown, not bothered that she'd missed the 14th arrondissement (*already had better crêpes somewhere else*), or the residential-minded 15th, 16th, and 17th (*why*), or that she'd also skipped the 12th and 13th (*literally the lowest priorities*). It would've been nice to meander around Bastille in the 11th and make a pilgrimage to the café featured in *Before Sunset*, but this whole experience with Jake had been enough of an homage to the film.

After making the trek for the delicious croissant, she could now partially cross off the 20th from her list (*but definitely Belleville next time*), along with the adjacent 19th arrondissement, now only a few steps away.

"It's quaint here," Jake observed.

"That's . . . very astute."

"I can feel you making fun of me, but I'm right." He pointed at the schoolyard on their left. "Look; what a lovely neighborhood for raising a family."

"Idyllic."

He pointed up ahead. "Is that a post office? Like not a UPS, but an actual, regular post office?"

"It is."

"See? *Quaint*."

"I believe you!"

He scanned the area. "I also love the uhh . . . abundance of trees . . ."

Mira snorted.

"And what appears to be primarily residential buildings," he went on. "Low-key, yet charming."

She stared at him with admiration.

"What?"

"I love when you do that."

"Then I'll just have to keep doing it." Jake slowed down when he noticed the street forking off in two directions. "Does it matter which way?"

"It does," she confirmed. "Go left, please, and just across the street you'll find our next destination."

They rounded the corner and on the other side of the street, a massive park awaited.

"That is *not* a mini square-park type thing," he said.

"No, it isn't."

"Another picnic, then?" He frowned. "Oh, wait—we don't have any stuff."

"And it's nine a.m.!" She gave him a playful shove.

"I have zero concept of time right now."

Mira and Jake had that in common. This had felt like the longest and shortest day of all time.

Mostly way too short.

"What I'm thinking of is very different from a picnic," she explained. "You'll see."

They crossed the street and passed through the open gate, stepping into a scene that was a stark contrast to their picnic spot from the day before. While Luxembourg Gardens was everything regal and perfectly manicured, Parc des Buttes-Chaumont was everything chill.

The first difference between the two locations was the perimeter surrounding the park. The path here was spacious, leaving plenty of room for serious joggers and dog walkers alike. And, judging by the scene around them, Parisians loved their dogs.

"I see, like, ten different breeds," Mira whispered.

"I don't think they know what you're saying."

"I'm partial to the ones with short legs!" she yelled, hoping he would be embarrassed.

"That's discrimination!" Jake yelled back, before getting so close that she could feel his breath in her ear. "And you can't embarrass me, but nice try."

It sounded like a challenge, but her sleepless mind wasn't ready to take it on, so she focused her sights on the rolling hillside that emerged on their left, a glittering lake just beyond it.

"This doesn't look like Paris at all," she observed.

"You don't like it?" His forehead crinkled with worry. "We can leave if you want."

"I love it. Different is good." She breathed it in. "It kind of gives the city some depth, like there's more to it than the cobblestoned postcard esthetic."

"It sounds like you're describing *me*," he said. "Like how there's more to me than my rock-hard chiseled exterior."

She stopped midstep, her eyes growing wide.

"What?" He failed to hide his self-satisfaction.

"I just . . . where do you come up with this shit?"

"The mirror?"

She burst into laughter. "Stop!"

He put his arm around her and led her down the path. "It's okay; you'll get used to it."

As Mira's laughter petered out, his innocuous remark kept ringing in her ears. She liked the sound of getting used to Jake, but she couldn't wrap her head around a logical way to exist in that reality.

The sloping, downward path went on, and her eyes brightened when she noticed a café terrace at its edge. "We're here."

"Are you thinking of getting more coffee? Won't that kill us?"

"Not coffee. Something else we need more desperately."

He slid his hand down her back. "I don't think you'll find anything like *that* in a café."

She snuck a peek at the hillside, wondering if a horny tumble through the grass might be better than the thing she was planning.

After a brief internal debate, she decided they needed the other thing more.

She leaned into his shoulder. "Just wait—you'll see."

The Saturday morning crowd was sparse, so Jake and Mira chose a table closest to the edge of the path, giving them the perfect people-watching view.

When the waitress arrived, Mira rhymed off an order in French, feeling a bit more confident in her skills, after a night spent hearing all those French conversations. The waitress nodded before slipping back inside the café.

Mira looked over at him. "Aren't you wondering what I ordered?"

Jake angled his face toward the sun. "Nope; I trust you."

While it was nice to hear he felt that way, she wasn't sure if his trust would withstand her latest choice.

A few minutes later, the waitress returned with two tall glasses, each of them containing a murky greenish liquid. It wasn't sexy, but Mira was no longer a spritely gal of twenty-five, one who could toss back gallons of booze between mountains of carbs without feeling like a pile of shit.

She noticed Jake tense up when the waitress set the glasses on the table. "Oh wow," he said, clearly more horrified than amazed. "I didn't know they had this sort of stuff in Paris."

"The detox movement is growing," she explained. "Which makes sense in a place like this, what with the jogging demographic and all."

"True."

She stroked his arm, reminded of the rock-hard exterior he'd mentioned earlier.

Damn.

"It's not gross," she quickly said. "And the banana and mango will mask all the parts that would normally taste like dirt."

He cringed. "*Dirt?*"

"You know, like the spinach, the beets . . ."

"Beets, huh . . ." His voice trailed off as he examined the contents of the glass.

"You said you trust me, right?"

Jake nodded.

"Then do the math; we've been living off a diet of booze and cheese and bread and fat and sugar for twenty-four hours. If we don't stop and have some vitamins soon, we might die."

"You're right. And this is right." He kept nodding to himself like it would somehow make it better.

It won't, darling.

She took his glass and clinked it with hers before handing it back to him. "You can do this."

While Mira had reassured Jake that the fruity flavors would mask anything unpleasant, she really had no idea if it was true.

There was only one way to find out.

She took a long sip and set down the glass. It wasn't bad, but it certainly wasn't delightful. "What do you think?" she said.

He wiped the sludgy residue from the corners of his lips. "At least it'll make us strong and indestructible."

She patted him on the shoulder. "You've definitely got the right attitude."

"Guess I'll be drinking a lot of these in LA."

Right. LA. That place you'll call home in two short weeks.

"That's true."

Jake must've noticed the change in her voice because a moment later, he took her hand and held it tight.

"Sorry. I shouldn't have said that."

She swallowed the pain and did her best to hide the sadness. "You can talk about LA if you want to," she said. "LA isn't Voldemort."

"Oh right. The Voldemort thing is the air—"

Mira pressed a finger to his lips. "Shh. We don't say that word in these parts."

He moved her finger out of the way. "If I can't talk . . ."

He caressed her cheek and kissed her, but as she started to kiss him back, he pulled away.

"You taste like dirt."

Her expression was defiant. "So do you."

"Let's just take our vitamins, then."

Mira followed his cue, downing the rest of the detox sludge in a few more gulps.

Once they were done, they instinctively shifted their focus to the joggers passing by.

"Are you judging them?" he asked.

"Judging them hard."

"Like it's Saturday morning, you fucks. What are you running from?"

"Emptiness. A boring personality." She thought about it for a second. "Or maybe their girlfriends or boyfriends who they secretly despise?"

"It's disgusting," Jake concluded.

"Seriously; like eat a baguette and call it a day." Mira shifted uncomfortably in her seat. "God, these jeans are getting tight."

"Mine too."

"Fuck it." She unhooked the brass button that was digging into her belly. "Much better." He stared at her in amazement. "What? Like you've never given yourself some breathing room?"

"I'm just admiring your bravery. You're opening doors for others. Or buttons." She watched him fumble with his pants. "Ah . . . that's the stuff."

Mira frowned when she heard the sound of unzipping. "Don't unzip. People will think you're a flasher."

"Oh, right," he said, looking slightly embarrassed. He zipped up and leaned back. "I guess the button's plenty."

They continued watching the joggers in a comfortable silence.

Until Mira finally spoke: "We're disgusting."

"I know."

＊

Mira was acutely aware of the time, and with each passing minute the feeling became worse. The awareness was so strong, that it even made it difficult to enjoy the cheery sunshine, its golden rays clouded by the truth.

You're running out of time.

This looming inevitability was the reason she needed to make sure they didn't linger on the terrace for long. She still had something important she desperately wanted to do, and while it technically fell within her bucket list, the atmosphere would be poignant, which was exactly what she needed to close out her time with Jake.

He followed Mira back to the path. "It keeps going downhill, right?"

Oh, sweet summer child.

"Actually . . ."

Parc des Buttes-Chaumont had by far the hilliest circuit of any park in Paris, which was why it was popular with the superfit joggers they'd seen passing by. She'd somehow forgotten to mention that to Jake. The path sloped to the left, and a moment later all was revealed: an aggressively sharp incline, with a set of narrow stairs running alongside it.

Jake stopped immediately. "No."

"It's not that bad," she insisted.

"Let's go the other way."

"The other way was downhill when we got here; which means it'll be uphill going back."

"Uphill *both ways*?" he squawked. "What kind of *Twilight Zone* bullshit is this?"

"You'll be fine; you took your vitamins, remember?"

"Oh, so *that's* how it is," he said bitterly. "You pump me full of drugs like I'm a racehorse on demand?" He kicked the dirt. "I have a *mind*, too, you know. I have *dreams*."

Mira was doubled over, hands on her knees and laughing uncontrollably. She looked up at him through watery eyes. "I'm sorry!" she wheezed.

He crossed his arms. "It's not funny."

She managed to bring her body to an upright position. "Let me go first, to show you how easy it is."

"Fine," he muttered, finally absorbing the degree of the incline. "Are you going to do the stairs or just go up the hill?"

She considered the options. "I feel like the hill is deceiving. It seems gradual, but I think it'll end up feeling like an endless hellish trek. I choose stairs."

He gestured dramatically. "After you!"

Mira made it to the top of the stairs no worse for the wear, with only a little more sweat now coating her body.

Jake was struggling. She watched as he dragged his ass up the final half-dozen stairs.

He made it to the top and rested his hands on his knees. "Should've done the hill," he gasped between breaths.

✶

The rest of the stroll through the park had the semblance of a casual atmosphere, but Mira spent most of it calculating how many minutes it would take them to get to the final stop. If Jake was concerned about the time that remained, he didn't show it, but he also wasn't commenting on every tree or flower or lily pad. He kept his arm around her though, which was nice. Couldn't she just enjoy the nice?

Time.

Once they transitioned from the park to the pavement of the quiet streets, the seemingly comfortable silence remained.

Minutes later, as they veered toward a sign for the métro, Mira heard Jake release a long breath.

"Thank God," he said. "My legs are done."

"I figured."

Secretly, she didn't give a fuck about his tired manly legs. The only thing on Mira's mind was time, and if they didn't take a shortcut of six speedy métro stops, they would never have time for the final stop. For the only ending that could do them justice.

He squeezed her shoulder. "This kind of makes up for those stairs back there. I forgive you."

She chuckled at his dramatic declaration, not having the heart to tell him that the saga of Jake and the stairs wasn't over.

"See?" she said, enjoying his pale blue eyes before they turned into fireballs of hate. "Everything always works out; you just have to trust me."

He pulled her into a tight hug. "I do."

CHAPTER
twenty–five

J

Ten a.m.

When they stepped into the subway car, Jake could see it was already busier than their journey from earlier in the morning. Tourists seemed to be the biggest reason, with several families huddled together debating how they'd spend the day.

It was the sort of atmosphere that didn't really allow for Jake to pull Mira onto his lap, like he'd done on their previous métro trip. Or to kiss every inch of her neck, and feel her hot, gasping breaths against his ear.

This time, he sat beside her but stared straight ahead, safely keeping both hands to himself.

When they came back out to street level, the scene was vastly different from the quiet neighborhood they'd come from. It wasn't just the tourists, but the traffic, too, and Jake wasn't sure if he liked it.

"This way," Mira said, leading him up a narrow street heading north. He noticed they were leaving the heavy traffic behind, a change that came as a welcome relief. Underneath it, though, he didn't truly care where they were headed. What mattered more was his latest calculation.

Only two more hours until the airport.

As much as Mira tried to lighten the reality of leaving Paris by calling the airport Voldemort, it was very grim and very real. What was also real, was how much closer they'd gotten in the last few hours. His west coast secret was out in the open, and even though things had seemed hopeless at first, he felt closer to her than ever.

But he didn't want it to end.

With each passing minute his frustration grew, a frustration that was starting to distract him from the present moment.

The narrow street gave way to a wide square. He noticed that it sat at the foot of a grassy hill, which had endless stairs running alongside it. There was also a white-domed church at the summit.

Stairs.

"No," he said immediately. "Forget it."

"I know three sets of stairs seems bad . . ."

"Three?" he sputtered. "But it only looks like one!"

"It's three."

"Can't we chill somewhere?" He sighed. "I just don't have the energy to see another church." He eyed the white-domed structure with disdain.

Jake knew he sounded whiny, but two days without any sleep was really taking its toll.

Mira narrowed her eyes. "I never said our plan was to see the Sacré-Coeur Basilica, and I never said we weren't going to chill."

"I just don't get what's so important up there. Why can't we hang out here?" He turned and gestured to the carousel. "We can take a ride on the wooden horses." He could tell from her expression that she hated the idea. "Or how about some ice cream?"

"Those are really good ideas," she said, her bald-faced lie crystal clear. "But I thought you said you trusted me." She was literally batting her eyelashes now, an obvious attempt to get him on board.

"I trust you with food stuff but not with stairs," he declared. "*Never* with stairs."

Mira joined her hands in a prayer-like gesture. "What if I told you that at the top of all those stairs, was the highest hill in Paris, where you can lie on the grass and see the whole city below, the city we've been traipsing around in for the last twenty-two hours, and the city where we've made so many memories; what would you think about that?"

"I'm intrigued," Jake admitted, while imagining lying on the grass with Mira and staring deep into her eyes.

She grabbed his hand and pulled him toward the first step. "Then let's do it! It'll be worth it, I promise."

As he faced the stairs, his fantasy of lying close to her gave way to an image of his comfortable bed in New York. He thought about his plan of sleeping for sixteen hours once he made it back, which was the only way he'd find the energy to take another trip the day after. But now, as he shifted his gaze back to Mira, his pillow-top mattress with climate control suddenly didn't seem so important.

"Fine," he said. "But this is the *last* time."

"Totally, for sure, 100 percent the last time; now come on!"

Mira took the lead, and as he watched her freakish rubber legs bound up the stairs two at a time, he remembered their very first staircase from hell. He'd only been killing time that afternoon, and had assumed that after a couple of hours they would go their separate ways. He couldn't believe how much had changed.

With a sudden surge of strength, Jake followed Mira up the stairs at his fastest pace yet. Despite his newfound power, his speedy footsteps stalled when he was only halfway up. By the time he reached the top of the first staircase, he was spent.

As he took a moment to catch his breath, he could see that the hillside was split into three grassy sections, ideal for lying around and admiring the city view. They'd now reached the top of the first hill, with two torturous staircases to go.

As he glanced behind him, he realized he was already looking at a stellar view of Paris.

"Hey, Mira," he said.

She came over. "Need a break?"

"I was just thinking; the view is already amazing. Why don't we just admire it from here?"

"It'll be better up top, believe me."

"I'm not really sure you'll be able to notice the difference." He could see he was letting her down. He did a scan of the surroundings, feeling a bit better when he spotted a backup solution. "See that trolley thing?" He gestured to the funicular on the other side of the hill. "We can go back down and take a ride to the top."

Mira looked over at the area where the passengers were boarding. "There's a lineup, though." She glanced back at him with a look of worry. "If we take that ride, I'm afraid we'll run out of time."

Time.

"That's true."

"Actually, this is stupid."

"What is?" He was unsure if the stupid thing was him.

"Needing to go to the top; it's not really that big of a deal."

He wasn't remotely convinced by her performance. "Mira—"

"No, I'm serious," she insisted, the emotion building in her voice. "I've been dragging you around since yesterday, and you haven't asked for anything. You haven't made me compromise on a single thing." She managed a smile. "I really appreciate that, but it's not exactly fair." She stepped onto the grass. "Let's find a spot here and chill."

Jake still wasn't sure if she meant it, but he followed her anyway.

They found a spot on the grass and sat down, which gave his body some much-needed relief. He was tempted to lie down, but for now was content to stretch out his legs and put his arms around Mira. He pulled her toward him and squeezed tight. "Quite a view, huh?"

"Amazing."

Amazing?

He may have only known Mira for a short while, but a generic description like *amazing* seemed unlike her.

He craned his neck to catch a glimpse of the view behind him. There were a handful of people lounging at the very top of the highest hill, and even if he couldn't see their faces up close, he had a gnawing feeling they were the happiest loungers of all, with their VIP view and superiority complex.

Dammit.

He released Mira and rose to his feet. "Get up."

She shaded her eyes from the sun. "Excuse me?"

He crossed his arms, trying to seem in command. "I said get up, rubber legs. Take the rest of the stairs and I'll meet you at the top."

She smiled at him but wouldn't stand. "Jake, it's really okay."

He grabbed her by the arms and pulled her up, practically lifting her off the ground. He never missed arm day at the gym, after all; it was only his legs that needed some work. Not that he would ever admit that. "Go," he said firmly. "The longer you wait, the less time we'll have, and you're the one that said we shouldn't waste it."

She immediately bolted.

Jake watched her go but made no move of his own. He needed a few moments to gather his strength, and even though he knew he'd need an ice bath as soon as he returned to New York, he had a feeling it would be worth it.

✳

"Well?" Mira said, both of her arms wrapped around Jake. "What do you think?"

Jake's ego was reluctant to admit this was a better view, but it felt like he was looking at every rooftop in Paris all at once. There really wasn't anything like it. "It's all right."

"*All right?*"

"Okay, I'll be honest. I like how the sunlight reflects off some of the rooftops, and how it feels like we're in the clouds. And is that the domed shape of a cathedral down there?"

Mira laughed.

"It isn't quaint, but it's grand; extremely grand."

She squeezed him tight. "I love Jake's travel show!"

"Where should we go next?"

She looked into his eyes. "Didn't Eloise say her family has a villa in Italy?"

He nodded. "Done."

She smiled at him before shifting her gaze to the view. He could see a hint of sadness in that smile, so he didn't say anything further. Instead, he stroked her arm, ran his fingers through her hair, and pulled her closer. It felt good, but it also made him sad, which, in a way, seemed ridiculous, when only a day before, he'd been perfectly fine without ever knowing her at all. But had he really been fine with the meaningless flings and endless parties? He'd been filling up his life with empty things, as if emptiness could somehow fill a void.

"You weren't dragging me around," he said. "Just so you know."

"Hmm?"

"You said you'd been dragging me around since yesterday, making me do whatever you wanted."

"I mean, you *were* very accommodating."

"But it wasn't like that," he said, turning her to him and looking into her eyes.

"Okay, then I'm glad you liked killing time with me."

His stare intensified. "No, Mira, I wasn't just killing time. I was doing whatever I could so I wouldn't have to leave you. It wasn't something I understood or could even admit to myself at the time, but that's what I was doing."

She went quiet for a moment.

"Wow," she finally whispered, before taking a long breath. "Can I admit something too?"

He immediately pulled her onto his lap. "Please."

They were now face to face, everything on the line.

Mira slid both hands behind his neck, her brown eyes staring into his. "I'm obviously in a messed-up personal place, given the last few weeks."

"Which is totally understandable."

"*And yet*, it didn't take long at all to start feeling like a fucking schoolgirl around you." She narrowed her eyes. "If you want to say something funny, this is your last chance."

"No. Keep going."

"Okay. So here I am, thinking, *why are you acting like a schoolgirl, dummy? Is this really the smart thing, after the hell of the last few weeks?*" She scowled. "Just garbage timing."

He felt himself hanging on her every word. "Horrible timing."

"Then I think, it must be Paris, or it must be the brief suspension from reality, or it must be the wine, but the more I got to know you, it was literally the simplest thing: I just really, really like you."

He felt a surge of warmth in his entire body. "I really, really like you too."

"And I guess we already said that, but it fucking bears repeating."

"It fucking does."

"Anyway . . . if I'd met you at some other time, under some other circumstance, there wouldn't have even been a question; like date two, date three, date four . . . just give me everything you've got."

He was acutely aware of her choice of words.

If. Other time. Other circumstance.

The warmth he'd been feeling started losing out to sadness, but he wasn't yet ready to take the loss. "You could've had whatever you wanted, Mira."

Her eyes glistened with the threat of tears, but she carried on. "And then I find out you're moving thousands of miles away, and unbearably soon, no less. So now all the things that could've happened after going back to New York, they're just . . . gone. And I know you told me not to focus on the *after*, but I can't help it." She choked back a sob. "I'm going to miss you *so* much."

Jake could feel his eyes watering. "I'm going to miss you too."

She took a long breath and gathered her emotions, tucking them away in some secret place he couldn't see. "And honestly, if it didn't make you think I was a stage-five clinger, I might've even quit my job and followed you to LA."

His eyes brightened. "Cling away! You said Bloom bums you out anyway, right?" He nodded firmly. "Yes. You should do it."

She stroked the side of his face. "I appreciate you thinking it's not an absurd idea, but the only way I can make breaking off an engagement feel *right*, is if I take the time to really figure out what went wrong. And what my life is really supposed to be."

He knew she was right, and he probably wasn't ready to jump into anything either, but he'd still enjoyed living in a momentary fantasy.

"That makes a lot of sense," he finally said.

"It just sucks, when the right thing is the sad thing."

"People should only do wrong and happy things."

"Definitely."

Jake lowered himself onto the grass, bringing Mira right along with him. She immediately buried her face in his neck, a feeling he couldn't get enough of. He held her tight, knowing the time was passing, yet somehow feeling less aware of it than before.

It was the perfect escape, but eventually, reality came calling.

"Can you check your watch?" she murmured. "I can't see mine and I don't want to move."

He checked the time and frowned. "How long does it take to walk back to the hotel?"

"Twenty minutes or so?"

"Fuck. We should go."

"Nooo . . ." she whined.

He gently peeled her face away from his neck. "It's okay," he whispered, stroking her hair. "We can do this."

He kissed her softly, wanting more, but knowing the moment had passed.

*

As Mira and Jake rounded the corner of the white-domed basilica, hand in hand, he could sense a buzz of activity growing closer. Before long, a square emerged, with tourists looking on as artists painted scenery on the spot. The square was surrounded by café terraces and shops for buying souvenirs.

"This is where the good ones are," Mira noted.

"Huh?"

"Remember after Shakespeare and Company? When we passed by that street with the shitty restaurants and souvenirs?"

"Yeah."

"That was the *bad* souvenir section. The no-no zone. But here? You'll find the better *and* cheaper options, especially on that tiny little street." She gestured to her right before looking back at Jake with pleading eyes. "Just one souvenir to remember the trip? *Please*?"

He surveyed his surroundings, pretending to seem on the fence. "Hmm . . ." His serious expression broke into a smile when he had an idea. "How's this? Let's buy *each other* a souvenir, but it has to be a surprise."

She gasped. "Yes!"

"Ten-euro limit," he declared.

"And it can't be a beret or coasters or a calendar."

"Done. Meet me back here in five minutes."

Mira hurried off to the street with the best stuff, and while Jake followed, he made sure to go into a different shop.

Once inside, he was overwhelmed by the wall of postcards, the baskets of keychains, and the random chef hats on the wall. He started to worry he would wind up getting Mira a souvenir she didn't like. But how could she not like it if it came from the heart?

NOT the chef's hat, then.

Five minutes later, Jake returned to their meeting spot, and there she was, holding something mysterious behind her back. He was doing the same, and he felt pretty good about his choice.

"Ready?" she said.

"Yup."

He held out a small white paper bag. She did the same.

"Same size," she noted.

They swapped bags and when she opened hers, she immediately burst into laughter.

He opened his bag and couldn't believe it. "*How*?"

"Are you really surprised? This was the nicest option under ten euros."

"I thought about getting you the one with the view of the river at night, but I worried it might remind you of that time on the boat, when I was sort of on a date with someone else."

"Too soon, Jake, too soon."

He took a moment to study his gift, the small acrylic print of the basilica with the grassy hill just below it. The print was nailed to a wooden easel, making it perfect for displaying on a desk; maybe the desk that would be in his office in LA.

"Thank you," Mira said, clutching the identical print against her chest.

"And thank *you*. Now, we'll always remember."

CHAPTER
twenty-six

M

Eleven a.m.

As soon as Jake and Mira made the crossing from the idyllic cobblestoned streets of Montmartre to the surrounding area of the 18th arrondissement, she felt the distinctive shift.

Reality.

And as soon as she saw the sign for the shitty hotel up ahead, she felt her stomach drop in a dramatic fashion.

It's over.

Mira had no intention of filling up her head with hope. She wasn't going to comfort herself with the belief that it was only the beginning, nor would she start imagining how they'd talk and text and visit and love. Maybe there'd be more or maybe this was it, but all she knew for certain was that her feelings were raw, and far too vulnerable to deal with any dangling hope.

As for the old fallback of protecting her heart by reminding herself she'd only known him for a day? That downplaying game had ended on the top of the grassy hill, in that moment when they'd told each other everything.

He really, really likes me.

It was only five words, but somehow the memory could still make her smile. She held it close, gripping to the goodness as tightly as the white paper bag she was clutching in her hand.

Jake pulled open the hotel door, its filthy window mocking Mira's perfect little day.

"Hope it was worth it," said the window.

Actually, it was, you soiled window bitch.

Jake and Mira didn't say much on the way to the room. Everything that mattered had already been said.

She opened the door to the room and stepped into the ugly dwelling; the place where natural light went to die.

"Smells worse than yesterday," she said.

"I'm really glad we didn't stay here."

She spun around, suddenly distracted by his funny choice of words. "Technically, *you* weren't going to stay here at all, remember?"

He rubbed his forehead. "Please don't remind me that I almost ended up prostituting myself, all so you could get a boat ride."

Her jaw dropped. "Excuse me?"

Jake shook his head like he was playing back the whole fiasco in his mind. "Man, that was a close call."

As he awkwardly reminisced, Mira struggled to put the pieces together. "I thought Colette was fine with doing you a little favor."

"That doesn't mean there wasn't a price." He sighed. "We made a deal, of sorts."

"What kind of deal?"

"Let's just say that certain eggplant emoji assurances were made."

She finally started to understand. "So, if you hadn't needed Colette for the boat ride, and if you hadn't made that deal . . ."

"I would've canceled the date way earlier. One hundred percent."

Mira thought back to those earlier moments from the evening before, when she'd secretly hoped he would cancel—before convincing herself he never would. Or later, in the middle of the night, when she'd assumed that Jake was having the time of his horny life.

He would've canceled.

Only minutes before, Mira had assumed that everything that mattered had already been said.

She'd been wrong.

They locked eyes as she set down her paper bag. And then, with a single click, she unhooked the fanny pack affixed to her waist, letting it fall to the floor. It certainly wasn't a conventional move in the woman's art of seduction, but he definitely got the message.

Jake's body crashed into hers, lips searching and hands roving. All the while, with tongues intertwined, she could only breathe through her nose, which made the musty smell of the room even worse.

Don't. Think.

She did her best to follow her brain's final order, her hands getting started on the urgent task of pulling Jake's shirt over his head.

But alas, the smell got to be too much.

She broke free of his lips and gulped in the musty air. "Sorry!" she gasped.

"Is it the smell?" he said, catching his breath. "Because it's definitely gotten worse since we closed the door."

"I know." She was completely dejected. Until she thought up a possible solution. She unzipped her carry-on and rifled through the contents. "I don't have perfume, but this travel-size hairspray smells like coconut."

"Mira . . ."

"Just wait a sec." But she could already feel the moment slipping away.

"I don't want it to be like this."

"Like what?" she whispered, unsure if her unwashed body was causing the sexual impasse.

"This bed is disgusting. And the floor? Probably worse. I don't even want to touch the walls, to be honest."

Mira stood, turning toward him with a playful look. "Floor? *Walls*?"

He scratched his head. "I was just planning out the possible positions . . ."

"Of course," she said, inching toward him. "Due diligence and all."

"But it's still too gross." He blocked her from coming any closer. "We deserve more than this." His stare was profound. "Don't we?"

Mira was moved by Jake's desire to make things between them special. She just wasn't sure when that moment would happen, which made her increasingly desperate to find a solution.

"How about the bathroom?" It was a last-ditch attempt, but it was something.

Jake approached the plywood-like panel masquerading as a door. When he slid it back, she stood on her toes and peeked past his shoulder. The first thing she saw was the dust and dirt that had gathered in every corner. The rest of the space didn't add any peace of mind, with grime and mildew visible between the tiles.

"Fucking tragic," she muttered.

"Yeah."

He turned back and kissed her forehead, his eyes strangely hopeful. "When it's right, it'll be worth it."

While Mira appreciated his optimism, she took careful note of how he hadn't made any promises. It was of course the right thing, to not make promises he couldn't keep, but it was also the sad thing.

"I guess we should take quick turns in the shower," she said, wanting to take her mind off their failed experiment. "You can go first."

"You sure?"

She nodded.

"Okay. I'll be out in a flash."

As she searched through her carry-on for a change of clothes and whatever else she needed, she couldn't help but notice how serious Jake had been about being speedy. The water turned on and off within minutes; it was almost as if he was hyperaware that their final moments were dwindling.

She vowed to be speedy, too, grabbing only the essentials to save whatever time she could.

When Jake reappeared, he looked refreshed and sexy as hell, in a pair of khakis and a collared shirt, the sleeves folded halfway up his muscled forearms. "Ran out of casual clothes," he said sheepishly.

"That's okay," she said, taking a moment to study him from top to bottom. "I needed another chance to eye-fuck you anyway."

"Two more times and we'll be even." He stepped forward and kissed her cheek, his no-sex mandate in full effect. "I think I'll step out and get us some water. Can I have the key?"

She handed him the key and felt a sense of relief; they may have gotten closer, but that didn't mean they were close enough to have him overhear her on the toilet.

Too soon.

*

After scrubbing the last twenty-four hours off her body, and then brushing her teeth for what felt like fifteen minutes—but really only thirty seconds, in accordance with her vow to save time—Mira pulled her hair into a messy topknot.

The day before, Mira had wound up looking nice for the airport by accident, after getting herself dolled up for that fancy breakfast before the flight. But now? After Jake had already seen her at her all-nighter, makeup-smeared worst? It simply didn't matter.

Despite the absence of makeup on her freshly washed face, she managed to slather on some moisturizer—anticipating the dry-ass recycled airplane air—along with some lip balm in the hopes of one last kiss.

On the other side of the thin wooden panel, she heard Jake returning to the room. She hurriedly pulled her leggings up over her belly, not wanting to waste a minute of one-on-one time. She couldn't remember why she'd packed leggings for a business trip, but her expanding waistline was eternally grateful. On the downside, she'd run out of clean T-shirts. She settled for a light sweater instead.

"I'm readyyy," she called, before pulling back the plywood panel and stepping into the room.

And then, she froze.

Jake stood before her, fresh baguette in one hand, and a block of foil-wrapped butter in the other.

Her mouth couldn't formulate a single word.

Luckily, Jake did all the talking.

"Yesterday you said you'd be having a morning baguette slathered in butter." She remained unable to speak. "Then this morning, with things getting so intense and all, I can see how you would've forgotten." Though she still couldn't manage to say anything, she could feel the warmth pouring out of his eyes, brighter than the sun. He held out the fresh baguette and the butter. "I didn't want you to miss it."

Mira felt her eyes welling up with tears, a physical response she couldn't control. All she could do was accept the deep-down feeling that had broken through the surface.

"You found *butter*?" she croaked, tears streaming down her cheeks.

He struggled to control his smile. "Yeah, at the grocery store."

"You found a *grocery store*?" she squeaked.

"They didn't have any butter at the convenience store, so I Googled the closest supermarket."

"*I don't want you to go!*" she sobbed, the intense emotion making a goddamn scene. "*I should follow you like one of those groupies who follows the band on tour!*"

He placed the baguette under his arm and went over to her, stroking her cheek with his free hand. "You can follow me anytime," he said softly. "But I think right now you're just really tired."

"*I am SO tired!*"

He pulled her into a hug. "I know, and it's okay."

Once Mira's chest stopped heaving from the sobs, she pulled away and wiped the tears.

"Thank you," she whispered.

"No need."

"If we'd had more than one stupid day," she said, "I would've done something nice for you too. I just wanted you to know that."

"You've done more for me than you realize. Trust me."

"Okay," she said with a final whimper. "Can I have my baguette now?"

"Of course."

"Should we eat it on the bed?" As soon as she said it, she cringed. "Or maybe it's better to stand."

"No bed and no standing," he said, opening the hotel room door. "We still have a bit of time before checkout. C'mon."

She was halfway down the corridor when she remembered an essential item.

"My biodegradable butter knives!"

*

Mira followed Jake down a side street, ambiance nowhere in sight. "I don't think there's anywhere to sit around here."

He looked back. "Don't you trust me?"

She was charmed by the sudden role reversal. "I do."

He made a turn into another street, his eyes now glued to his phone. "Almost there."

She followed close. "You're the boss."

He glanced up from his phone. "I see it!" He spun around and showed her his phone screen. "See that little patch of green on my map?" He pointed up ahead. "It's there."

Mira had never seen anyone so excited about the basics of online maps, but like all the other moments she'd found so amusing or downright adorable since the beginning of their unexpected journey, she tucked it away in the safest part of her heart.

Once that was done, she took note of his discovery. It was only a grassy median with a single, backless bench, but in this neighborhood of little inspiration, it was everything.

"It's perfect," she said.

They sat down and didn't waste a moment, Mira unwrapping the butter, and Jake breaking the crusty baguette in two. She placed the butter between them, and he dutifully handed her one half of the baguette.

"Knife?" he asked.

She gave him one of the minibiodegradable knives she'd been clutching in her hand. And with that, they were off.

Spread. Bite. Chew. Repeat.

"So good," he mumbled between mouthfuls.

"And so simple," she mumbled back.

"I'm kind of glad we had that green juice now."

"Mmhmm. Total reset."

Time was of the essence, but they handled it well, downing the combo of carbs and fat in five minutes.

After wiping the crumbs off their respective laps, they stared ahead in silence.

"Five more minutes and then we have to head back," he said.

"Sounds good."

Head back? The mere idea of it made her want to vomit.

Five minutes was plenty of time for a final intense make-out, but Mira didn't have it in her. The dark cloud of inevitability had reached her. Jake must've felt the same because even though he took her hand and squeezed it tight, he didn't try for anything more.

"We probably should've gotten used to this by now," he said.

"I know. I've been bracing for it since the moment you told me."

"I've been bracing for it since last night."

She leaned into him. "How many more minutes?"

"Four."

"Dammit."

He cleared his throat. "Look, I know you don't want to talk about that thing we're not allowed to mention—"

"It's okay, Jake, you can say airport now; the jig is up."

He put his arm around her shoulders. "I was just wondering how we're getting there; to the airport, I mean. Is the strike over?"

"Even if it is, I don't trust that shit." She pulled up the ride app on her phone. "Look, no surge pricing."

He studied her screen and nodded. "Then I guess we have a plan." He didn't sound happy at all, a feeling they had in common. "Three minutes."

She suddenly felt stupid. Here she was, sitting on this bench and not even looking at this wonderful guy. Why was what had been so effortless before was nearly impossible now? She needed to be tougher than this. And sometimes being tough meant having the courage to kiss the wonderful guy like it was the last thing you'd ever do. There was just one thing she needed to know.

"Hey, Jake?"

"Yeah?"

"If we make out again but don't do anything else, will you be okay? It won't make your balls explode, will it?"

He covered his face with his hands and laughed. It was the first time she'd seen him truly embarrassed. And it was about damn time. "Ohhh man; did you really just say that?"

"I'm just being sensitive to the struggles of being a man. I don't even know how you guys overcome the adversity. It's inspiring, like those animal videos where the cat learns to pee in the toilet and flush."

His face contorted in confusion. "That just took a turn to a really weird place."

She sighed. "I guess that's where I'm at right now: a really weird place." The sarcasm drained from her eyes, as she studied every inch of his lovely face. "What do you think, then? Can I kiss you the way I want to?"

He stared back. "You can kiss me however you want."

And so, Mira did what was needed. She climbed onto his lap, gripped his neck, and devoured every inch of his warm lips, enveloping herself in his breath like it was keeping her alive.

Zero minutes.

*

The wheels of their carry-on luggage rolled against the cruddy carpet of the hotel corridor.

Mira promised herself that when all of this was over, she wouldn't allow this shitty hotel to hold her memory hostage. It would not be the setting of her final moments in Paris with Jake, no way.

Instead, their saga would be remembered as reaching its crescendo on the grassy hill at the foot of Sacré-Coeur. Or on the bench. The bench was okay too.

She returned the key to the shifty-eyed man at the sad excuse for a reception desk. Once that was done, she carried on with the perfunctory tasks required to complete the checkout. Her body and brain performed these tasks with precision, but her heart was caught between the recent past and a vision of the future too blurry to hang any hope on.

When the checkout was done, they stepped outside, waiting for the black sedan that was less than a minute away.

"It was a really good day," he said, watching as the car rolled toward them.

The threat of fresh tears swelled in Mira's eyes, but she managed to keep them at bay. "Yeah. A really good day."

CHAPTER
twenty–seven

<u>M</u>

The journey back...

The departures area of the airport was a fickle bitch.

Back in college, when Mira had been headed to Cancún with Sophie, each step in the departure process had been a downright delight. The excitement of officially checking in, the jokes exchanged with security when her belt had triggered the alarm, buying donuts for breakfast since the diet was officially on pause . . . these seemingly mundane activities had all added up to the purest joy.

But now, as Jake and Mira approached the check-in kiosks, it was almost like someone had stripped all the color from the atmosphere, forcing her to go through the motions in hues of gray. It was similar to how she'd felt earlier, during the lifeless hotel checkout. Only worse.

Jake spotted an empty kiosk and made his way over to the glowing screen.

"Wait," Mira said suddenly.

He turned back. "What's wrong?"

"Can we check in at the desk?"

"Why?"

"If we check in there, maybe they can shift things around and let us sit together."

It wasn't much, but even in the grayish fog, Mira still remembered how to grasp at straws.

"We can probably choose our seats on this," he said, gesturing to the touch screen.

"Remember how hard it was to even find two tickets? The only way we'll get two seats side by side is if we use our charm to convince them to switch things and screw over somebody else." She scanned the clerks at the check-in desk. They were all attractive women. She nudged Jake and gestured to the desk. "This is your time to shine."

He seemed uncertain. "I don't think it'll work."

She held him by the shoulders. "Jake, you're a *salesman*."

He smiled. "Oh yeah; I forgot about that." She didn't blame him, given how the last twenty-four hours had been a total suspension of reality. He practiced his best smoldering face. "Let's do this."

As he made his way to the lineup, Mira grabbed him by the forearm. "Wait." She rolled up his shirt sleeves a few more inches on each side. "That's better."

"If I weren't trying to sit next to you, I wouldn't let you pimp me out like this."

"Yes, yes, blah-blah-blah, you're more than just a piece of meat, got it."

He frowned. "*Blah-blah-blah*?"

"Just go."

Jake entered the line and she followed, keeping her distance so he'd have the best chance to showcase his wares. This was serious, airplane-seat-manipulating business, and if nothing else, it temporarily allowed Mira to focus on something besides all the doom and gloom.

The three passengers ahead of Mira and Jake had now all been called to the counter.

"You're next," Mira whispered. "*Don't fuck this up.*"

"Stop pressuring me!"

The three airline attendants varied in age, and one of them was giving off a bored-unsatisfied-wife-with-a-wandering-eye kind of vibe. She was the one.

It was like watching a game show, nervously waiting to see which passenger would finish their check-in first. In the end, it was the passenger who'd been helped by the bored-unsatisfied-wife-with-a-wandering-eye who ended up walking away first.

YES.

Mira pushed Jake forward. "Go!"

His mouth twisted in worry. "But she didn't summon me yet."

Mira's resulting eye roll was so intense it almost gave her a migraine. "*God.*" She stripped his carry-on from his hands and wheeled it behind her along with her own, refusing to miss out on this woman's potential thirst.

By the time Jake joined her at the check-in counter, the woman straightened her suit jacket and walked away, only to be replaced by the man from the day before.

"*What the fuck?*" Mira whispered.

The man who had sold them their tickets may not have been Mira's actual nemesis, but based on their previous interaction, she was all but certain he would simply shrug if she suddenly dropped dead in front of him.

"Hello again," Jake said, trying to salvage their plan with his salesman touch. "Remember us?"

The man studied them from overtop of his wire-rimmed glasses. "Ah. Yes. The last-minute passengers."

"But today we're here on time," Mira said, showcasing her best fake smile.

The man gave a slight nod. "Congratulations."

He took their passports and started typing. After too many seconds of silence, Mira elbowed Jake.

"We'll need to be seated together," Jake said, skipping right past the begging and going straight into authoritative mode. "You see I'm . . . responsible for helping her take her medication." He squeezed her shoulders supportively. "If she doesn't get her pills every two hours, there's no telling when her heart might stop."

The man surveyed Mira with mild contempt. "She seems more than capable of taking some pills with a glass of water."

"It's a suppository!" she blurted. The man's stare was hauntingly blank. "A butt pill," she clarified, as Jake held back a snort. "And the way it works is . . . it travels to my heart . . . from my butt."

The man narrowed his eyes at Mira. Without a word, he resumed the task of typing. The typing seemed more furious now, and Mira wondered if it was the sort of typing that was needed to change seats. Would the man finally take some pity on the pathetic American woman who wanted to be with her man so badly, she'd invented a heart condition requiring butt pills? She could only hope.

After tapping a final key, the man placed his hand under the printing slot. Seconds later, it spit out a couple of boarding passes. "Voilà," he said, slipping the first boarding pass into Jake's passport. "Row 22B for you, and . . ." Mira held her breath as he slid the other boarding pass into her passport. "Row 48J for you, mademoiselle."

Her heart sank. "Seriously?"

"Please, sir," Jake added, no longer above begging. "It would mean the world to us."

The man shooed them away. "Have a safe flight. And good luck with your . . . heart condition."

Mira stumbled away, shell-shocked.

Jake put his arm around her, guiding her toward the security checkpoint. "We gave it the good ol' college try," he said.

"Uh-huh."

"And hey," he added, kissing the top of her head. "There's still an hour and a half until boarding time."

"Great," she mumbled, barely hearing his words through the cloud of disappointment.

Row 48-fucking-J.

*

Customs and security had only taken fifteen minutes, so at least that was something, Mira thought, clinging to the final scraps of positivity.

Like all passengers, Jake and Mira were required to pass through the duty-free shop before reaching the various departure gates. As they did, it was hard not to slow down and ogle the wide selection of French merch; the tall display of plastic Eiffel Tower–shaped containers full of chocolate, the expensive teas, the biscuits in Paris-themed tins, all kinds of wine at 10 percent off, and of course, the oversize Toblerone—which had no real reason to be there, but somehow always ended up making an appearance.

It was all rather indulgent, and yet, meaningless. The only parting gift that mattered was tucked away in her carry-on.

"Hey look," Jake said, pointing to a poster in the fragrances section. "It's your Tom Ford model."

The point-of-purchase display was smaller, but there he was, in all his drenched, chiseled glory.

Mira hooked her arm with Jake's. "Who cares? I've got my Tom Ford model right here."

She led him away from the display, but to her surprise, he steered her back. Without a word, he grabbed the cologne tester and sprayed some onto her sleeve. "Since I won't be near you on the plane."

It was a seemingly silly gesture, but it almost brought her to tears. She bit her lip and forced herself to focus. "But what about you? They don't have that Dior one I tried at the department store."

"That's okay, I'll just admire that horrible selfie of you."

She gasped. And then scowled. "You said you deleted that!"

"I did," he confirmed. "In the same way that *you* deleted the photo with the Nutella on my face."

Touché.

They wandered out of the duty-free and passed by a series of shops ranging from Louis Vuitton to Starbucks.

"Need a final croissant?" he asked.

She scoffed. "This morning we took the métro to get the best butter croissant in Paris. It was *that* important. So do you really think I'm going to debase myself with an *airport mass-produced croissant*?"

"Fighting words," he said, smirking. "But you're right; I should've known that."

"Don't beat yourself up; you haven't slept in two days."

They found a place to sit at one of the less-crowded gates, the one for a flight to Chicago that wouldn't be boarding for two hours.

Too bad he isn't moving to Chicago.

To her surprise, Jake sat across from her.

"Why are you all the way over there?"

"I want to look at you."

She instinctively adjusted her messy topknot. "Okay, weirdo."

After five minutes of Mira looking away each time she noticed Jake staring, he hopped out of his chair and plopped into the one beside her.

She gave him a healthy dose of side-eye. "You done creeping now?"

"Yup." He put his arm around her and pulled her to his chest. And then he took out his phone. "I need a selfie with you."

"You've got to be kidding me."

He pressed his mouth into a firm line. "I'm as serious as a heart condition that can only be treated with suppositories."

Mira hid her face from the embarrassment. "I can't believe that was an actual conversation." She sighed. "Do you think the guy at the airport will tell that story at dinner parties?"

"I think he'll forget you ever existed by the end of the day." Jake smiled. "But *I* won't." He pulled her closer. "Now come on, let's take this photo."

Mira reluctantly assumed the selfie position, triggered by her complicated relationship with the art form. She could never get used to how one of her eyes always looked droopy in selfies, or how her hair looked wrong, or how sometimes her mouth looked crooked. By the end, she'd usually wind up with two-dozen selfies, and only one that she didn't hate.

But now she didn't have that option.

As she watched Jake take charge of the photo shoot, she was reminded of that moment on the boat, when Colette had pushed past her to get that precious selfie with him.

"Hey, Jake, how come you don't seem disgusted?"

"Hmm?"

"Last night on the boat with Colette, it seemed like you hated selfies."

He looked deep into Mira's eyes. "She wasn't you."

Even though she'd been hoping he'd say that, his words still struck her in a deep way. So deeply in fact, that she didn't have a chance to recover before he took the photo.

Miraculously, she didn't hate it. A few seconds later, she heard her phone vibrate from within her bag.

"Thought you might want the photo," he said.

You have no idea.

*

Mira had refused to board the plane when they called her zone, waiting instead until Jake could board too.

No one will ever tear us apart.

Once they got on the plane they were immediately separated.

Until they do.

In all the frustration of knowing she'd be in row 48 when Jake would be in row 22, she hadn't processed the fact that the letter *B* was on the opposite side of the plane to the letter *J*. She now realized she wouldn't even be able to talk to Jake on her way to the bathroom. If she tried to, her only options were to walk all the way to business class to get to the other side—which probably wouldn't go over very well—or to crowd-surf over the block of seats between them.

Despite the letdown, she arrived at row 48 with a clear focus: to get to her window seat as easily as possible. Unfortunately, it was a goal made difficult by the man relaxing in the aisle seat.

She coughed and raised her eyebrows, hoping he would get the memo. Instead, she was forced to stumble over him, as he sort of stood but not really, seemingly unable to bear the inconvenience of stepping into the aisle for two seconds.

Once Mira crammed her body into the window seat, she noticed her newfound nemesis settle into the man-spreading position, which, though not at all surprising, was nonetheless infuriating.

She took a long breath, hoping to avoid the sort of confrontation that would wind up going viral on Twitter. She distracted herself by trying to catch a glimpse of Jake, but between the woman violently shoving her carry-on into the overhead, the bathroom partition, and the twenty-six rows between them, she couldn't see a thing.

She fired off a text:

I miss you

He replied immediately:

Miss you too

He continued typing:

Sitting between a grandma and a teenage boy

She messaged back:

Eww middle seat?

He sent a sad face in reply, just as her eyes drifted over to the empty seat beside her.

She sent another text:

My middle seat is empty. If no one comes, sit here!

He responded two seconds later:

Definitely. Keep me posted.

As Mira's feeble heart began to fill up with hope, a round-bodied Indian woman shuffled her way to row 48.

She was similar in age to Mira's mother, which evoked an

uncomfortable feeling. When the woman checked her boarding pass against the seat labels, she nodded her head and smiled.

Dammit.

The man-spreading asshole tried to pull the same shit as before, but the woman wasn't having any of it.

"You cannot stay there," she chided in a strong Indian accent. "You must move to let the other passengers access their seats."

Mira nodded in approval.

Go girl.

The man obeyed, and once the woman was settled, he didn't even try to man-spread. It was almost as if he was afraid of the Indian woman's wrath. With this one small step for womankind, the Indian lady became a hero in Mira's eyes.

Despite her newfound admiration, she still had to break the news to Jake:

Sorry, middle seat taken now

The woman gave Mira an appraising look, like she'd just finished processing the racial aspects of her being. "Hello, *beta*," she said beaming, using the standard affectionate term for whichever generation came next.

"Hello, Auntie," Mira said, following the rule of calling every Indian elder an auntie or an uncle, regardless of whether they'd only just met.

"Are you returning from a trip to India?" the woman asked. "Were you visiting family?"

Mira realized that Auntie must've been on a connecting flight from Delhi. She shook her head. "No. I was in Paris."

"I see," Auntie said. "Were you in Paris *with* someone?" Mira could sense the woman trying to root out the scandalous presence of a boyfriend.

Nice try.

"Of course not," she lied, pretending to look shocked. "I was on a business trip." She felt more at ease about the last part, which was technically the truth.

Auntie's glimmering eyes clearly approved. "Having a good salary is very important." Mira didn't even flinch at the conversation switching to money. That was just how Indian Aunties rolled. She was, however, growing weary of Auntie, worried she'd try to talk her ear off during the flight. If Mira couldn't have Jake, she at least needed to sleep.

As casually as possible, Mira pulled her earbuds out of her bag and slipped them into each ear.

Auntie gave her a nudge. "It isn't good to listen to music during the flight. It will give you motion sickness."

Mira knew this was a total lie, but logic wasn't going to get her out of this. "It's not music," she said. "It's a podcast."

Auntie wasn't convinced. "*Podcast*?"

"It's a documentary series about business," she lied. "My boss says I have to learn from it to get promoted." She sighed. "But at least that will mean a higher salary," she added, hitting all the notes of the Indian Auntie love language.

Auntie clapped her hands. "This is wonderful!" She gestured to the earbuds. "You listen then. And pay attention to the teachings."

Mira let out a small sigh, relieved her web of lies had saved the day. She turned on her sad song playlist and pulled up her selfie with Jake, careful to keep the angle of the phone screen obscured from Auntie's view. She zoomed in on Jake's smile. It wasn't a big and bold grin, but it was clear that he was happy. *Me too.* She zoomed back out to examine the full picture of the two of them together. She liked how natural they seemed, but the more she stared at it, the more it made the future seem tragic.

To complete the masochistic cycle, Mira inhaled the edge of her sleeve. The scent of cologne transported her back to the riverbank of Île Saint-Louis.

Five a.m. and the warmth of your neck.

She turned to the window and closed her eyes, a move that kept the tears from streaming down her cheeks.

Within minutes, her breathing steadied and she fell asleep.

*

Somewhere between a dreamless sleep and reality, Mira had the foggy sensation of pressure being applied to her upper arm. As she squinted one eye open, she felt the urge to hiss at the harsh lighting that was pouring its way in. She quickly pulled down the window shade, and as she slowly opened her other eye, fully reentering the conscious world, she felt the repeated prodding of someone poking her arm.

Auntie.

Mira wiped the drool that had trickled down her chin and turned to face Auntie, or more accurately, the tray of airplane food she was shoving in Mira's face.

You woke me up for AIRPLANE FOOD, you bitch?

Mira's inner thought stayed buried deep inside, since her childhood had conditioned her to never speak to Indian elders in a disrespectful manner.

"No, thank you," Mira managed. "I don't want any."

Auntie glowered. "What do you mean you *don't want any*? They are offering you this, so you take it." She raised an eyebrow. "And it will give you more energy, so you don't keep falling asleep from your podcast teachings."

Mira lowered her head in shame and took the tray. "Thank you."

Earlier, when Auntie had dealt with the rude man sitting in the aisle, Mira had felt a glimmer of hope that maybe this woman was one of the cool ones—despite the fixation on money that was ingrained in the Indian Auntie DNA. But after the way Auntie had reacted to the possibility of a boyfriend, and now, with her pushy insistence that she eat this sludge simply because it had been offered, Mira could see that despite her good intentions, Auntie was stuck within the boundaries of her generation. Just like her parents.

Mira lowered her tray table and set down the food. She stared at the options in silence, not knowing which container of horror to open first.

"I got you a vegetarian one," Auntie said.

At least that's something positive, Mira thought, since whatever passed for "meat" on an airplane made her shudder.

She examined the tray to root out the least offensive item, ultimately landing on the bun. She attempted to cut the bun with her plastic knife, but the utensil quickly snapped in half.

"Shit," she whispered. Almost immediately, she felt Auntie's glare searing into the side of her head. "Sorry."

Mira then ripped the stale bun in half, trying her best to spread some half-frozen butter on each side.

Each chew of unpleasantness made her long for the crusty Parisian baguette and the creamy butter from the countryside of Normandy. But that was what happened when you deigned to do a thing like leave Paris. You suffered.

Mira set down the crappy bun and studied the touch screen affixed to the headrest in front of her. They were somewhere over the Atlantic Ocean.

Five more hours until New York.

CHAPTER
twenty-eight

M
New York

"We've got some rain on the way but the temperature's warm, and hey—it's New York. So, enjoy it." Some passengers chuckled and a few even applauded at the pilot's jovial spirit.

But not Mira.

She stared out the window as the aircraft taxied to its designated gate at JFK. The dark clouds threatened a downpour, a sight she welcomed with open arms. She crossed her fingers for crackling thunder and a sky streaked with lightning, the only fitting tribute to the dramatic undoing of Mira and Jake.

Mira stretched her neck and immediately winced. She was sore, miserable, and exhausted, after barely getting two hours of restless sleep on the plane.

When the seat belt sign went off, dozens of passengers immediately stood, despite having nowhere to move.

Idiots.

Mira hung back in her window seat, rubbing her neck and

watching as the man-spreader stood. He now stole space from the other humans by spreading out his arms, ensuring he'd be the first to access the overhead compartment.

Auntie leaned over and tapped him on the arm. "Can you please hand me my luggage? It is the blue one."

Man-spreader knew better than to ignore Auntie, and before long, he was swarmed with other carry-on-related requests.

Karma's a bitch.

Auntie then turned toward Mira. "Which one is yours? He will get it for you."

While Mira would've enjoyed subjecting the man-spreader to even more manual labor, she didn't want him anywhere near her carry-on. She gestured to the bag underneath the seat in front of her. "This is my only bag."

It was a necessary lie, because her carry-on had been in Paris, and the only other person besides herself who had touched it was Jake. Which made it sacred. Except not really. Mira was simply at the point of clinging to irrational things, anything to stop her from drifting even deeper into sadness. She hoped being aware of it would help her in her quest to get over it, but for now it was simply too soon to tell.

One of the things about sitting in the back was that it meant more time waiting on the plane, but for Mira that was fine, as making a break for the luggage carousel was the last thing on her mind. For one thing, she'd only packed a carry-on for this trip, and for another, she was too busy wondering if Jake had left the plane or if he was somewhere up ahead, waiting for her. She hadn't seen him for eight and a half hours, which for *them* was 33 percent of the entire time they'd spent together. Did he look different now? Had he aged? It was completely messed up how their deep connection had defied the concept of time. But that was the two of them, and this was the world they knew.

"Come, beta," Auntie said, as the passengers ahead of them finally cleared out.

Mira didn't want Auntie anywhere near her reunion with Jake. Not after decades of negative reinforcement when it came to the mere idea of being affectionate with a man who wasn't Indian. And even if Auntie was only a stranger, she might as well have been a software program of advanced AI, one that combined every blood-related Indian auntie and family friend she'd ever known.

And Mom.

"You go ahead," Mira said. "I have some questions for the flight attendant about booking my next business trip."

It was a dumb lie, but luckily Auntie nodded in approval; maybe it was because the trip reminded Auntie that Mira had a stable job and salary. "Okay," Auntie said. "I will see you at the baggage carousel."

Mira smiled as she shuffled away, wishing her well in her mind, but hoping to never lay eyes on her again.

As Mira moved through the plane, her stomach wound into a tighter knot with every row she passed; the forties, the thirties, and finally, the twenties, where Jake had been sitting and where he might still be waiting.

But he wasn't.

She told herself it made sense, as no sane human would spend more time on a plane than was required.

Even if it made sense, it only prolonged the uncertainty of wondering what it would be like to see him again.

Mira waved good-bye to the flight attendant and exited the plane.

When she rounded the corner, there was Jake, standing next to a stack of folded-up strollers.

"Hey," he said, hands in his pockets and looking casual as ever.

"Hey." She felt an instant rush, as she recalled and reabsorbed every detail from their day.

"How are you?"

"Tired. Are your legs as sore as mine?"

He winced, no longer looking casual at all. "I'm in total agony." They moved to the side so other passengers could pass. "How was the flight?"

Mira didn't give a fuck about the flight. She only wanted to know what was next.

Don't think about the after.

"It was annoying, drooly, and boring," she said, doing her best to steer clear of the burning question that was racing through her mind.

"Pretty similar for me. Except for the drool. That's disgusting."

She found herself smiling, her first real smile in nine hours. "I'm not ashamed by my salivary gland production."

"That's the first time I've ever heard that." He stepped forward and studied her chin up close. She hoped he was going to pull her in for a kiss. It had been so long, after all. Instead, he rubbed the side of her chin. "Looks like some of the drool dried up over here, forming a crusty film." When she swatted his hand away, he laughed. "Come on. Let's go."

Without another word Jake proceeded down the walkway, his gait slightly altered by the soreness from their staircase adventures. Mira was also feeling the burn, but there were no more pit stops or hangouts; it was time to go.

As Mira hobbled along, she fixated on his words *let's go*, which somehow seemed so intimate now, after everything they'd experienced. Those words represented a togetherness she desperately wanted to cling to, but how much longer would it even last?

The lack of knowing was a special kind of agony, but when Jake slowed down and put his arm around her shoulders, she started to feel a little bit better.

Time moved fast in the world of counting down to the dreaded good-bye, and by the time they'd passed by the baggage carousel, there were no more delays she could think of to avoid getting to the exit. But that didn't mean there wasn't any shame.

She felt it when she noticed Auntie's glaring eyes. The hot blood rushed to Mira's cheeks, bringing her back to that feeling of getting caught. It was something she'd experienced several times in her youth, when all she'd wanted was the chance to be a normal American teenager. Even as an adult, the shame would periodically reemerge, finally fading away when her parents met Dev. Until a few weeks ago, when everything had changed. Now the shame spiral was back in full force.

"Why is that lady glaring at you?" Jake asked, his arm never leaving Mira's shoulders.

"Long story," she said, not wanting their final minutes to be an expletive-filled rant about Indian elders.

As Auntie's stormy glare passed out of view, Mira promised herself that in the future she'd be louder and prouder about her choices. For now, though, her heart was too raw to spend any time on self-improvement.

The automatic doors slid open, welcoming Jake and Mira into the muggy New York air.

They stepped outside.

This is it.

"Where are you headed?" he asked, the intensity of his stare unexpected for such a run-of-the-mill question.

She had a feeling she would cry if she got too lost in his beautiful eyes. Luckily, she managed to look away before it happened. "I guess the area with the buses. There's one that goes to Manhattan with stops every twenty blocks or so."

"Okay. And what's your neighborhood?"

She tentatively looked in his direction. "It's almost Hudson Yards but technically it's Hell's Kitchen, and sometimes I lie and say it's Chelsea."

"That's a pretty wide berth of deception," he said, trying not to laugh.

She shrugged. "Depends on my mood and who I'm trying to impress."

"Hell's Kitchen isn't too far from the Upper West Side."

Mira made a mental note of the fact that he lived on the Upper West Side.

But only for the next two weeks, dummy. And for one of those weeks he'll be in LA, dipshit.

Jake pulled out his phone. "There's no point in taking the bus when we can share a ride. I'll just add a second stop." He looked up from his phone. "Address?"

Before Mira knew what was happening, she was rhyming off her address to Jake.

Two minutes later they climbed into a shiny black car.

She checked her map to get a read on the traffic. When she realized it would take almost an hour to get to her building, she felt the tiniest flicker of happiness.

One last hour with Jake.

*

"So aside from your leg pain . . ." she said.

"Because of the stairs you made me climb . . ."

"I know, *sorry*. But aside from that painful reminder, did you get any sleep on the plane?"

"In the middle seat? Nah."

"You must be exhausted," she said, as the car passed through an underground tunnel.

"Borderline delirious. I plan on sleeping for sixteen hours straight."

"And when's your flight to LA?" It was hard to ask these questions without the risk of stepping on emotional landmines. But she needed to know.

"Flight's tomorrow evening at six," he said, his state of mind impossible to detect. "It's as late as I could make it to get a good sleep in LA before the morning meetings."

"Makes sense," she said, hurriedly doing her own mental math.

It was already six thirty in the evening now, so once Jake got home, settled into bed, and slept for sixteen hours, he wouldn't have much time before getting himself ready for the airport.

This is really the end.

The conversation was sporadic as they emerged out of the tunnel and back into daylight, gray and gloomy as it was. Maybe she should've expected the silence, given that they'd already talked about everything.

She started to wonder if it might've been better to say good-bye at the airport, but there was nothing she could do about that now. She could only watch as the car drove along 37th Street, passing Park Avenue, Madison, and getting closer and closer to her building.

When the driver turned onto 10th Avenue and made the approach to West 41st Street, the pit in her stomach felt larger than ever.

And then the car slowed before finally rolling to a stop.

"Can you open the trunk, sir?" Jake said. "I'll be back in a minute."

One minute left.

Jake stepped outside along with Mira, pulling her carry-on out of the trunk and following her to her building.

The dramatic thunderstorm that Mira had been hoping for hadn't transpired in the slightest. Instead, the noncompliant clouds offered nothing more than a misty drizzle, a pathetic denouement to her emotionally charged adventure with Jake.

"So . . ." he said, hands behind his back.

"So . . ." she said, wanting to die.

"That was fun, huh?"

She nodded, already fighting back the tears.

Jake pulled her into a tight hug, and for the millionth time she felt the warmth of his breath against her neck. She would miss that.

"This isn't over," he whispered.

She held back a sob and gripped his neck. "Okay."

It nearly killed her when he let her go, but his expression seemed hopeful and determined. "I've got a whole week when I come back from LA. So, we'll see each other, okay?" He nodded like he was trying to convince himself of it. "We'll talk."

Mira managed to bury the remaining mountain of her feelings. "Yeah, for sure."

He caressed her face, his glassy eyes revealing his emotion. Just as she started to get lost in those eyes, he kissed her one last time. But hopefully not the final time forever.

He stepped away and headed for the car, turning and giving her a final wave before getting back inside.

As Mira watched the car roll away, she wondered how long it would take for their twenty-four hours in Paris to fade away. She hoped it wouldn't happen quickly, but a part of her worried it would already be awkward by the time he got back from LA.

Before she could fall too deep in imagining the worst-case scenario, the car abruptly stopped.

Her heart seemed to stop along with it.

Jake jumped out and ran toward her, looking more determined
than ever.

"Hey," he said, slightly out of breath.

"Hey." The stomach butterflies of hopefulness were now in a
full-on frenzy.

"I was just thinking; even if I slept for like . . . *twelve* hours instead
of sixteen, I'd still feel pretty rested."

She felt herself beaming. "Totally. I don't even think a sleep clinic
would let you stay unconscious for sixteen hours. You could die."

"It's incredibly risky." His eyes focused in on whatever was really
on his mind. "Are you busy tomorrow afternoon? Because if you're
not, maybe we could . . . go on a date or something."

Mira felt her heart exploding in her chest. Luckily, she was still
alive—feeling more alive than ever, really. She wanted to say yes
immediately, but the thing about Jake was that he never made her
feel like she had to be conventional with her answers.

"*Day date?*" She cringed. "Aren't day dates usually for the backup
prospects?"

He shrugged. "Well . . ."

She slugged him hard. "Don't push it."

"Pick you up at noon?" he said, his blue eyes twinkling.

"Sounds perfect."

"Cool. Then I'll see you tomorrow."

He started jogging back to the car but turned back around after
just a few steps. "I guess I could've just texted you that, instead of
making a dramatic scene."

Most endearing person on earth.

"For the record, I like a dramatic scene. In fact, I think people could stand to be a lot more dramatic."

"I agree."

"Like put down the phone and make a scene once in a while!" She waved her arms around like a frantic Muppet.

He laughed. "Live a little!"

"That's all I'm saying."

His laughter faded into a meaningful look. "See you tomorrow."

He returned to the car, and this time the driver really drove away.

Mira watched as the car disappeared around the corner. Her heart swelled at the thought of what came after. It wasn't a long-term view of the future, and she still had a lot to figure out, but it was nice to know that even though Paris was over, that didn't mean *they* were over.

Hey, you never know...

ACKNOWLEDGMENTS

Thank you so much for reading *24 Hours in Paris*. I wrote this all-new version of the book during the part of the pandemic when we couldn't travel to France, so believe me when I say this was a love letter to my favorite city in the world. I hope you felt that too.

I originally wrote *24 Hours in Paris* just for fun on Wattpad in 2015. Back then, Mira and Jake were just a couple of kids on a college trip to Paris. Much later though, in January 2021, Wattpad Books came along with an awesome idea: What if we brought to life an adult romantic-comedy version? What an opportunity!

Thank you to the editorial team for trusting me to dream up a whole new draft, and for the incredible editing support along the way.

And to the creator management team: you are amazing! I'm so grateful to have had your support throughout this whole new publishing journey—it's been a ride!

Finally, to the ones in my life who've supported me along the way, you know who you are, so I'll refrain from turning this section into a whole big thing.

Besides, the story of Mira and Jake isn't over, so . . . I should probably get on that.

ABOUT THE AUTHOR

Romi Moondi is a Canadian writer who primarily writes romantic comedies with the aim to make you laugh, activate your heartstrings, and maybe even make your eyes produce some salty discharge. When she's not writing novels, Romi can be found dreaming up screenplays, copywriting for clients, traveling, trying out new recipes, and loving *Seinfeld* forever.

Turn the page for a sneak peak of

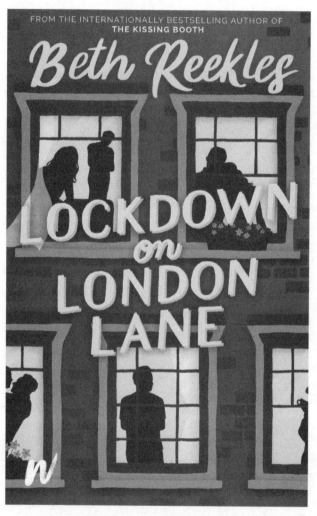

Available in print and ebook,
wherever books are sold

Sunday

<u>URGENT!!!!!!!</u>

<u>DO NOT IGNORE THIS MESSAGE</u>

<u>NOTICE TO ALL RESIDENTS OF LONDON LANE,
APARTMENT BUILDING C</u>

Dear Resident,

As you will be aware from our previous missives on the subject, due to the current situation in which we are potentially facing a global pandemic due to a highly contagious virus, building management has made the decision to impose a seven-day quarantine on any apartment building in London Lane where a resident is found to have the virus.*

Unfortunately, someone in BUILDING C has tested positive.

BUILDING C is now in a seven-day lockdown. Please remain calm, remain safe, and wash your hands regularly. We ask that you avoid use of the elevators except for emergencies and avoid contact with other residents. Most importantly, please remain in your apartment.

Have a good week!

With kind regards,

The London Lane Building Management Team

*PLEASE NOTE: If you think you have contracted the virus, you are to inform your building's caretaker immediately. If you do not follow instructions, management reserves the right to serve notice of eviction to any tenant or to impose significant fines for breach of contract. Your caretaker for BUILDING C is MR. ROWAN HARRIS.

Chapter One

It's starting to get light out; the venetian blinds are a pale-gray color that does nothing to keep the sunshine away. The entire window seems to glow, and pale shadows fall across the rest of the room, obscuring the organized cluster of hair products and cologne on the dresser, playing tricks on the hoodie hanging in front of the wardrobe doors. There's a knee digging into my thigh. I rub a hand over my face, feeling last night's mascara congealing around the edges of my eyes, and start to peel myself out of the bed, hissing when I discover an arm is pinning down my hair. I bunch it up into a ponytail, slowly, to ease it free inch by inch.

The mattress creaks when I sit up, but—Nigel? I want to say Nigel—snorts in his sleep, still totally out of it, oblivious to my being in his bed.

I glance over my shoulder at him.

Still cuter than his profile picture, even with a line of drool down his chin.

"This has been fun," I whisper, even though he's fast asleep. I blow him a kiss and creep across the bedroom to silently wriggle into my jeans. I look down at the T-shirt of his I borrowed to sleep in. It's a Ramones shirt, and it feels genuinely vintage, not just some ten-pound H&M version. Actually, it's really goddamn comfortable. And cute, I think, catching a glimpse of myself in the mirror leaning against the far wall. Oversized, but not in a way that makes me look like a little kid playing dress-up. I tuck it into the front of my jeans, admiring the effect.

Oh yeah, that's cute.

Sorry, Neil—Neil? Maybe that's it—this shirt is mine now.

My long brown hair, on the other hand, looks kind of scraggly and definitely not cute. Yesterday evening's curls have dropped out, leaving it limp, full of kinks, and looking pretty sorry for itself. I run my fingers through it, but give up. Hey, at least the smeared mascara is giving me some grunge vibes that totally match the Ramones shirt.

Collecting my own T-shirt and bra from the bedroom floor, I tip-toe into the open-plan living/dining room. Where'd I leave my bag? Wasn't it—a-ha, there it is! And my coat too. I stuff my clothes into my bag, then look around for my shoes.

Come on, Imogen, think, they've got to be around here some-where. I can't have lost them. I wasn't even drunk last night! Where did I leave my damn shoes?

Oh my God, no. I remember. He made me leave them outside, saying they looked muddy. Like it was my fault it rained last night and the pathway up to the apartment block was covered in mud from the flower beds. And I joked that they were Prada and if someone stole them this had better be worth it, even though I'd only bought them on sale from Zara.

I do a final sweep just to make sure I've got everything. Phone—check. House key—yep, in my bag.

I hesitate, then do a quick dash back to the tiny two-seater dining table near the living-room door to nab a slice of leftover pepperoni pizza from our delivery late yesterday evening.

Breakfast of champions.

I step over some junk mail as I sneak out of the front door. It can't be much later than seven o'clock. Who the hell delivers junk mail that early in the morning? Who is *that* dedicated?

My shoes are exactly where I left them.

And, all right, in fairness, they do look like I trekked through a farmyard. I really can't blame him for making me take them off outside the apartment. I'm going to have to clean them up when I get home.

I hold the slice of pizza between my teeth as I wriggle my feet into them—and *ew*, they're soggy—and then I slip my coat on.

Okay, good to go!

I skip down the stairs to the ground floor, munching on my pizza and already on the Uber app to get myself a car home. These shoes are cute, but not really made for a walk of shame.

"Excuse me, miss?"

Despite there being nobody else around, I don't realize the voice is directed at me until it says, "Hey you, Ramones!"

When I turn around, I find a tired, stressed-looking guy with a handful of leaflets. Mr. Junk Mail, I'm assuming. He's wearing a blue surgical mask over his mouth and ugly brown slippers.

"Thanks, mate, but I'm not interested," I tell him, and make for the door.

Except when I push it open, it . . . doesn't.

I grab the big steel handle and yank, and push, and rattle, but the door stays firmly locked.

What the fuck?

Oh my God, this is how I die. A one-night stand and a serial killer peddling leaflets. Please, please don't let anybody put that as cause of death on my gravestone.

"Miss, you can't leave," the man tells me wearily. "Didn't you get the note?"

"What note? What are you talking about?"

I turn to him, my phone clutched in my hand. Should I call the police? My mum? The Uber driver?

The man sighs, exasperated, stepping toward me, but still maintaining a good distance. Like me, there's a rumpled look about him, but he looks more like he rushed out of the house this morning, not like he's just heading home. There's a huge ring of keys hanging from his belt. Then I clock the white latex gloves he's wearing and get a sinking feeling in my stomach.

"We got a confirmed case from one of the residents. The whole building's on lockdown. That door doesn't open except for medical needs and food deliveries."

I stare at him, all too aware that my mouth is hanging open. After a while, he shrugs in that *What can you do?* kind of way.

It's a joke, I realize.

It's got to be a joke.

I let out an awkward laugh, my lips stretching into a smile. "Right. Right, yeah, good one. Look, um, totally get it, real serious, but can you just . . . you know, use one of those keys, let me out of here? Cross my heart, I'll be *super* careful. Look, hey, I'll even cancel my Uber and walk, how about that?"

The guy frowns at me. "Miss, do you realize how serious this is?"

"Absolutely," I reassure him, but instead of sounding sincere, it comes off as fake, like I'm trying too hard. Condescending, even. Shit. I try again. "I get it. I do, but look, the thing is, I was just visiting someone. So I shouldn't really be here right now. And I kind of have to get home?"

There's a flicker of sympathy on his face, and I let myself get excited at having won him over. But then the frown returns, and he tells me sternly, "You know you're not supposed to be traveling unnecessarily, don't you?"

Damn it.

"Well, I mean . . . couldn't you just . . . "

I look longingly over my shoulder at the door. At the muddy path on the other side of the glass, the washed-out flower beds with the droopy rosebushes and brightly colored petunias. Freedom—so close I can almost taste it, and yet . . .

And yet all I can taste is my own morning breath and pepperoni pizza.

Which is not as great now as it was two minutes ago.

What are the odds I can snatch his keys off his belt and unlock the door before he catches me? Hmm, pretty nonexistent. Or what if I just run really hard and really fast at the door? Maybe I could smash the window with one of my heels? Ooh! Could I hypnotize him into letting me out of here? I could definitely give it a go. I've seen a few clips of Derren Brown on YouTube.

"Seven-day quarantine," my jailer tells me. "I've got to deep clean all the communal spaces. Anyone could be infected, and unless you're going to tell me you've got fifty-odd tests for all the residents in that bag of yours, nobody's going anywhere. Believe me, this is no fun for me either. You think I want to be playing security guard all day long just so I don't get fired by management and end up evicted?"

Okay, *fine*, well done. Congrats, Mr. Junk Mail, I officially feel sorry for you.

"But—"

"Listen, all I can suggest is you go back to your friend"—I appreciate that he says *friend* as though we're talking about an actual friend here, when it's so obvious that's not the case—"and see if you can get a grocery delivery slot, and maybe one from Topshop or whatever, see you through the next week. But unless you need to go to a hospital, you're stuck here."

*

I trudge slowly, grudgingly, back up the stairs. My shoes are pinching my toes, so I take them off, slinging the straps over my index finger to carry them. Mr. Junk Mail stays downstairs to scrub down the door I just put my grubby hands all over, almost like he's warding me off, making sure I don't try to leave again.

What the hell am I supposed to do now?

Ugh.

I know exactly what I'm supposed to do now.

But still, I hope for the teeniest bit of luck as I jiggle the handle for Apartment 14.

Locked.

Obviously.

Weighing up my options, I finally sit down on the plain tan door-mat, my back against the door, and press my hands over my face.

This is what I get for ignoring all the advice.

Not so much the *stay home* stuff (although that, too) so much as the *You're not in university anymore, Immy, stop acting like it* advice—from my parents, my friends, my boss, hell, even my little brothers.

As I always say, who needs to grow up when you can have fun?

This, however, is decidedly *not* fun.

My only option is to do exactly what I would've done back in university: phone my bestie.

Despite the early hour, Lucy answers with a quiet but curt, "What have you done this time?"

"Heyyy, Luce . . . "

"How much do you need, Immy?"

"What makes you think I need money? What makes you think I've done *anything*?" I ask with mock offense, clutching a hand to my heart for dramatic effect, even though she can't see me. And even though I can't see her, I absolutely know she's rolling her eyes when she gives that long, low sigh. "Although, all right, I am in . . . the *littlest* spot of trouble."

"Did you forget to cancel a free trial?"

Lucy's so used to my shit by now that she knows how melodramatic I can be over something like that—melodramatic enough to warrant an early-morning phone call like this.

But, alas.

I open my mouth to tell her I'm stuck with Honeypot Guy, the guy

I've been messaging for the last week or so, whom she specifically told me not to go see because there's maybe a pandemic, and now I'm stuck quarantined in his building and I only have the one pair of underwear and I didn't even bring a toothbrush with me and . . .

And I *hate* admitting how right Lucy always is.

Even if, technically, this is all *her* fault, because she was too busy with some stupid wedding planning party last night to answer her phone and talk me out of going to see the guy in the first place. So I decided to go, and not tell her about it until I was safely back at home, just to prove a point about how she always makes a big deal out of nothing, how she worries too much.

"Oh Jesus Christ, you went to see him, didn't you? Honeypot?"

I *cannot* tell her the truth.

At least, not yet.

"No! No, no, of course I didn't," I blurt, even though I fully expect her to see right through me. "I, um, I'm just . . . well, look, so, the thing is . . . "

I don't like lying to my best friend—to anybody, really, if I can help it. If anything, I'm a total oversharer. But I decide this is for the greater good. I mean, really, I'm just doing her a favor, right? If she knew, she'd only spend the week worrying and stressing about me. I'm just sparing her that.

Lucy cuts me off with a sigh, understanding that whatever it is, it's a bit more than the usual mischief I get myself into, and she says, "Oh, you're properly fucked this time, aren't you?"

"Thanks, Luce."

Thankfully, she doesn't push me for answers. "How's your overdraft?"

"Not great."

"Did you run up your credit card again this month?"

"A little bit."

We both know that actually means "almost completely."

"Will a hundred quid cover it, Immy?"

"I love you."

"I'll add it to your tab," she tells me, and I know she's smiling. "Are you sure you're all right?"

"Oh, you know me!" I say, laughing. I'm weirdly relieved that being quarantined with a one-night stand isn't the craziest thing that's happened to me in the last month or so. It's definitely not as bad as the night out where I climbed onstage to challenge the headlining drag queen to a lip sync battle, is it? "I'll work it out. Just . . . yeah. Thanks again, Luce. I'll tell you everything when I see you next."

"Don't you always?"

Lucy has a way of ending conversations without having to say good-bye. I know her well enough to recognize that this is one of those moments. I say good-bye and thank her again for the money she'll send me, the way she always does, which I will repay in love and affection and memes until one day in the distant future, when I have miraculously gotten my life together enough to pay off my overdraft *and* have enough left to put a dent in my ever-growing tab at the Bank of Lucy.

Feeling at least a little better, I stand back up, dust myself off, and knock on the door.

It takes a few minutes to open.

He's disconcerted and groggy and wearing only his boxer shorts. The carefully coiffed blond hair I'd admired in his pictures is now matted, sticking up at all angles. The dried line of drool is still there on the side of his mouth.

I give him my biggest, bestest grin, cocking my head to one side and twirling some hair around a finger.

"Hey there, Niall. Um . . . "

He yawns loudly and holds up a finger to shush me before covering his mouth. He shakes his head, blinking a few times, then looks at me, confused and none too impressed.

"I hate to be an imposition, but your building is kind of . . . quarantined."

"It's what?"

I look for the piece of paper I stepped over earlier and bend down to pick it up. It's a printed notice that, at a quick glance, instructs residents to stay indoors for a seven-day period. I hold it out to him, staying silent and swaying side to side, hands clasped in front of me, while he reads it, rubbing his eyes. He has to squint, holding it up close to his face.

"Oh shit."

"There's a guy downstairs, and he won't let me leave," I say. "I'm *really* sorry, but unless you want to take it up with him . . . "

I step back inside the apartment, leaving my shoes outside once more. He's speechless as I put down my bag and coat.

"I'm just going to use your bathroom. You know, wash my hands." I waggle them at him, as if to prove what a responsible grown-up I am.

When I come out he's still standing by the door, still clutching the paper.

"So, Nico, listen—"

"It's Nate."

"What?"

"My name?" He raises his eyebrows at me, looking more pissed off than tired now. "Nate. Nathan, but . . . Nate."

I bite my lip, grimacing. I'd kind of hoped if I ran through enough names, I'd hit on the right one eventually. I'd also kind of hoped if I said them quickly enough, he wouldn't notice.

"Sorry. You're . . . you're saved in my phone contacts as the honey-pot emoji. You know, 'cause you . . . you said that if you were a fictional character, you'd be Winnie-the-Pooh, and you said your mum kept bees and . . . and that your favorite chocolate bar is Crunchie, which has honeycomb in it . . . I thought it was cute at the time, and funny, but then I realized I'd forgotten your name, and you deleted your profile off the dating app, so I couldn't check *that* . . . "

Nate's face has softened.

But then, as I take my coat off, he realizes what I'm wearing and lets out a loud, disbelieving laugh. "You're really something, aren't you? Talking your way over here when everyone's meant to be social distancing—"

"I didn't hear *you* complaining," I mutter, none too quietly.

"Sneaking out without so much as a good-bye, *and* you were planning to make off with my favorite shirt. Wow."

"Maybe it was just going to be a good excuse to see you again."

He laughs, rolling his eyes. "Imogen, believe me when I say I have *never* met anybody like you before."

I curtsy, even though it sounds like an insult, the way he says it. "Thank you."

That, at least, makes him laugh. Nate-Nathan-Nate runs a hand through his hair, taming it only slightly, then tells me, "There are spare towels in the bathroom cabinet if you want to take a shower. I'm going to see if I can get a food delivery slot online. Then, I guess we'll . . . I don't know. Figure this out."

I'm not exactly sure what there is to "figure out" besides maybe ordering some frozen lasagnas and a few pairs of underwear, but I nod. "Right. Totally. You got it, Nate."

So much for my swift exit.